The Memory Plague

and Other Stories

Other Books by D. Thomas Minton

The Calypto Cycle

Fire in the Snow
Shackles of Doubt
Threads Unravel
Messages from the Sand
Tiger Unbound (forthcoming)

The Memory Plague

and Other Stories

D. Thomas Minton

This book contains previously published material.
All stories copyright © D. Thomas Minton
All Story Notes © 2024 D. Thomas Minton
Cover by Paramita Bhattacharjee

This book is available in print and electronic formats and at most online retailers.

ISBN: 9780998304298

This one is for Martin

My Friend. My Brother.
I wish we could go back in time and
take the ride a second time.

Table of Contents

The Memory Plague

First published in *Lightspeed Magazine*, January 2021

IN THE BEGINNING, WE ARE ONE, and we are ignorance.

Our skin is chaffed tender from the womb-sac and the exit ring. Out, we writhe blindly in the grit that cuts our softness until the dryness of the air hardens us.

Slowly, receptors awaken.

Muted colors curve across the night, outlining the glistening ribs of the drop chamber arcing over us like planetary rings.

Instinctually, we grope through the hard stillness. Our tac-pads draw against lines of unmoving flesh, cold like a memory of interstellar vacuum. A dome of skin radiates faint warmth. Flesh peels away like the rind of a fruit, and a stone pops forth, slick with life fluid gone cold.

Comfort bleeds from it, easing our fear, but insufficiently to fill the void. We curl away from the shadows, afraid, sheltering the stone in our knobby appendages. There must be more, but in this darkness, alone, our primal yearning to feed is overwhelming, and the stone, smooth as starlight, slides effortlessly into us.

Its first sliver dissolves. From it, a memory seeps into our consciousness.

We are Audu.

We are the first.

#

Air moves through the breach in the side of the drop chamber. Our simple receptors detect shadows of movement, but we taste only bitter bio-lubricants and inorganic metal oxides. The shadows sway too regularly to be living, to be feed, but we shield our vitals with our hardened back skin and withdraw our tac-pads. As the first of our vorta, we hold the ancestral fears rooted deeply to when the Vortive were primeval and planet-bound.

Another sliver of memory dissolves into our being.

We are the hundred and sixth vorta in our lineage, and the stone contains our collective memories. We do not remember the homeworld—out of necessity, the Vortive went to the stars before we were birthed from the collective consciousness—but we remember traversing the void with our brethren in a living matrix of organo-crystalline structure, vagrants of the stellar winds.

We are on a feeding ground, but we sense no other vorta, and the comforting hum of the collective consciousness is absent. Perhaps, in those confusing, initial moments of the culling, our drop chamber was launched into the wrong sector, as once happened to the eighth vorta in our lineage. But even then, the thought-sphere buzzed with excitement, with hunger destined to be sated.

But here, now, silence.

Yet, they must be out there. They would not leave us because we are of the one and the many.

#

Omi is birthed from pain so intense it is a flash of white-hot light. Then, through the shadows and the muted shapes cut the hard-edged geometry of metal and glass, scattered across the floor like grains of stellar dust—alien debris come in through the jagged hole breached in the side of the drop chamber.

Coated in birthing fluid, Omi sits up on our segmented tarsi, thrusting eyestalks high. *What is this place?* Omi asks, always curious, as is Omi's purpose.

The feeding ground, we say.

Omi accepts our answer, as Omi is meant to, but it draws attention to the hollowness eating within us. For a vorta, harvesting feed is our contribution to the Vortive. Without us, the collective consciousness will cease to exist.

On the wall opposite the breach in the drop chamber, the plates have separated, exposing a crevice filled with a tangle of fluid vessels and fleshy organs that feed the drop chamber's womb-sac and connect Omi to us through the thought-sphere. The organs glow warmly under Omi's long-wave scrutiny, but otherwise reveal nothing.

Bored, Omi click-clicks across the floor, our eyestalks sweeping and spinning, taking in the carbon scoring that blackens the plating along the jagged edge of the breach. Omi thrusts our body out into the yellow light. From the ground far below, alien pillars of stone and metal thrust upward, twisted and broken, their outer walls torn away, their tops sheared off, their insides gutted black from fire and rot.

Omi scuttles out the hole, the nano-bristles on our tarsi holding us fast to the vertical surface. Far beneath us, visible only due to Omi's advanced photoreceptors, green stalks sway in the moving air. They sprout from deep cracks in the ground, between crushed metal and glass containers and blocks of fallen stone riddled with twisted metal bars, like bristles.

Omi, come back.

But Omi scuttles down the wall, intent on the movement below. We reach the ground, and Omi sniffs the fleshy green blades with our nasal-bulb.

Instinctively, we know they are not feed. In the universe, energy comes in many forms. These green blades lack the complexity of sentience. They offer nothing to sustain the collective consciousness.

Omi moves on, scuttling and stopping, our tarsi click-clicking on the hardened ground. Each time we stop, Omi thrusts our array of receptors upward to gather inputs. The ground reeks of long-chain hydrocarbons and oxidized metal. Small things scurry before us, twisting down into the cracks as we approach.

Without Omi, the drop chamber is muted again. We curl away, afraid, as shadows brush by us. They feel substantial in the solitude as if something tangible lurks within.

Come back, we say, our fear palpable.

Omi trains our eyestalks upward. Our drop chamber is embedded near the top of one of the alien towers. We detect nothing perched outside poised to attack, but that does not comfort us. We are not complete, so we are not yet equipped to hunt. Instead, we are vulnerable, and Omi should return.

Yet Omi's curiosity drives us across the rubble field, our bulb scenting the ground, while our eyestalks search for heat signals. We slither through dark holes and twisted spaces under metal beams and around decaying debris. Each turn carries Omi farther from us and increases our discomfort.

Through the thought-sphere, Omi senses our rising fear and reluctantly breaks off our search.

Only when Omi draws close does our fear retreat.

Soon, we will be three, we say, as Omi scuttles back into the drop chamber, and huddled together, we find comfort knowing that soon we will fulfill our purpose. Soon we will hunt.

#

Another sliver dissolves, and we remember the taste of our first feeding ground like it is today and not generations past. The sentients, our feed, had yet to achieve interplanetary travel and offered futile resistance. Our drop chambers rained down on their crude settlements like embers from a fire, and the vorta burned across their world, consuming everything. No refuge spared them from their purpose, and when the grounds were filled with their empty husks, the Vortive departed, following our advanced scouts across the void to the next culling. We have fed on countless grounds, scattered across the glitter of the dark. These worlds, holding sentient life fresh and ripe for our arrival, are our birthright.

#

Snarling, Rhu's lithe form shakes off the birthing fluid and undulates across the grit, circling the chamber like angry smoke. Rhu snuffles the air currents.

Where are they? Rhu growls.

Omi scuttles to the jagged hole, Rhu in our wake, and together we lean out. Even with night nearing, the urge to feed is strong.

Rhu growls again, deep and raspy with menace.

The scent of feed should be heavy on the air, but even Rhu's sensitive tri-lobed bulb detects only decay, sweet and sharp.

Already Omi is out the hole and down the face of the tower, eyestalks sweeping for signs of movement. Rhu follows, the sticky pads of our feeding strings giving purchase on the pockmarked wall.

We alight on the ground, spreading out. Rhu slips through webs of metal netting, squirts between chunks of concrete. Our nasal bulb close to the ground now, we catch scent, familiar but faint, that sends shivers through us. Excited, Omi scuttles over the top of the debris, seeking a better vantage from which to triangulate.

Rhu delves down through the rubble, slithering through the tight spaces to the bottom, where we clatter into a pile of bleached sticks. Rhu holds one close, its scent stirring memories. Our feeding strings encase the bone, but these husks are now devoid of sustenance.

We howl with rage, and the bone splinters in Rhu's grasp.

Omi's eyestalks droop.

Our hunger and disappointment threaten to consume us. Yet, before that can happen, a new memory dissolves from the stone.

We came from the dark side of their moon, from an angle undetectable by their primitive sensors. By the time the Vortive dropped into orbit and disgorged the drop chambers, it was too late. We covered their planet, their cities, their forests, their oceans, like cinders from a pyre.

They were creatures of carbon and oxygen and hydrogen—the stuff of stars. We recall then the taste of their energy, each rich and complex, each different, each shaped not by a collective consciousness, but by individual ripening, individual experiences, creating memories unique and sweet as our memories of the fruits of our homeworld.

Rhu purrs.

Omi shudders with pleasure, our tarsi click-clicking on the rusted metal in the planet's dying light.

This memory, while pleasurable, fails to comfort.

We shuffle around the small drop chamber. Pushed up against the wall is the lump of tissue that was our progenitor, now partially recycled by the chamber's regenerators. The body is cold and lifeless, the flesh peeled open where our stone once burned. We have no memories of this vorta, but as the holder of our lineage's collective memories, they were a first, like us.

They, too, were Audu.

Our tac-pads slide across the dome of skin on our torso. The stone, hard and smooth, pulses warmly beneath the thin tissue.

"You are not the first."

The simple truth had been within us all along, but we do not possess the deductive abilities to reduce the evidence to such a simple statement of fact. Yet phrased succinctly, it is evident; we are not the first vorta of our lineage to be birthed on this feeding ground.

Then, quickly, we realize that statement arrived not from the collective memories of our lineage, but through our tac-pads.

We lift our attention from the body of our progenitor. Except for the motes spinning in the dying light streaming in through the breach, the drop chamber is still and warm. Again we feel soft vibrations in the air, and we shift our tac-pads to gather the sensations.

"Ring-a-ring o' roses ..."

We rotate our tac-pads, trying to triangulate the direction of the sound, but the source eludes us. It moves behind the walls, first next to us, then across from us, then back at our side.

"... A pocket full of posies ..."

How does it move so quickly and effortlessly when the space behind the metal plates, packed tightly with organs, is accessible only to the chamber's regenerators?

"... Hush-hush, hush-hush ..." The sound continues, growing quieter as if imploring us to silence.

Who are there? we ask.

Omi rises up on our rear tarsi. *Where?* Our eyestalks scan across the rubble field. Nearby, Rhu slithers from a hole, our sleek body bristled with feeding strings, all waving excitedly.

Where are you? we ask. Our fear rises quick and hard, radiating danger signals into the thought-sphere. Instantly, Omi drops onto all tarsi, and scuttles over the slabs of crumbling stone toward the alien tower in which our drop chamber is embedded. Rhu follows, driven by the urgency of our fear.

"... Or we all tumble down."

We retreat first one way, then the other. Whenever we move away from the sound, the vibrations shift so that we are moving toward them again. We consider fleeing out the breach, but our stocky form is slow and clumsy. We would never make it down the vertical surface of the alien tower. But our skin is thick and tough, and we can curl up so that our vitals and our receptors are safely tucked away. In that way, surely, we would survive long enough for Omi and Rhu to return.

We see something then. In the crevice where the metal wall plates have separated, barely visible among the tangle of vessels and organs, glistening white orbs darken for a half second as membranes slide over them and retract. They are set in indentations on a soft globe of lumpy flesh, which, as it seems to move forward, coalesces into what we instinctively know is a face.

We tremble at the memory of its taste.

Feed.

Omi rushes forward, our tarsi click-clicking as we scale the vertical surface toward the drop chamber. Rhu is ahead, nearing the breach.

Vibrations emanate from the hinged orifice along the bottom of the face and dance across the air to our tac-pads. The sound resonates through our consciousness, forming images that, beyond reason, carry meaning: "Not feed. Human."

The membranes slide over the white orbs, and the globe of flesh withdraws deeper into the crevice, fading away like dissipating smoke.

Rhu bursts through the opening, feeding strings whipping with enough vigor to emit a low frequency hum. We dart across the room and plunge into the crevice, squeezing in among the tightly packed vessels and soft organs, but our nasal bulb detects only bio-lubricants and us.

Rhu trembles with pent up aggression. *Where are they?* It is an affront to our superiority that this feed eludes us. Rhu turns to delve deeper inside, but our actions are injuring the delicate bio-machinery of our drop chamber. Gently, we urge Rhu to come out.

We must feed, Rhu says, refusing to listen. Rhu knows only the hunt, cares only to feed, and our primal hunger drives us deeper into the cavity. The microbarbs on the tips of our feeding strings lacerate the chamber's organs. Fluid oozes out, puddling on the floor. The chamber's regenerators buzz to life behind the walls and move to stem the damage.

We call to Rhu a second time with no effect.

Omi arrives and searches the chamber for other cracks in the wall plating through which to peer. Finding none, Omi scuttles outside and searches the exterior of the drop chamber for other entries. Omi slips through a space between the external heat skin and the alien tower and drops into a shadowy interior. Wires and cables dangle from the ceiling tiles. Where our chamber has not destroyed the internal structures, the space is sectioned into a grid of cells by mold-covered walls that are only slightly taller than us. Omi click-clicks along an exposed metal beam, our eyestalks sweeping back and forth.

Finally, Rhu stops our thrashing and collapses, flaccid, among the oozing organs. The damage is significant, but fortunately, repairable.

Where are they? Rhu asks, despondent.

We saw them? Skepticism colors Omi's tone.

Certain, we say.

Then where are they? Rhu demands.

We have no answer.

Omi breaks off the search and scuttles into one of the grid cells. On a table-like platform, covered in a skin of dust and residue, is a thin rectangle of metal and electronics and a discolored board with punch-keys. A wooden frame, face up on the platform, encases a two-dimensional image behind a dusty pane of transparent silicate.

Our eyestalks swivel closer.

What are these? Omi asks, in reference to the four fleshy globes that comprise the image.

Human, we say without hesitation.

Hoomon? Omi savors the name like the sweet essence of feed. Omi likes the sound of something different, and it piques our curiosity. We scuttle into the adjacent cell and find another image tacked onto the soft, moldy wall. The paper is curled and blackened, but the image is another pair of faces.

What are these? Omi asks.

Human, we say again.

They are first? Omi asks.

They have no second, we say.

How can they all be hoomon, then? They are all the same but different. Not like the vorta.

They are feed, Rhu says. *Nothing more.*

All lifeforms are less than the Vortive. We are the pinnacle of sentient design, our superiority ensured by the unified knowledge of our existence shared through the collective consciousness.

Hoomon ... how do we know this construct? Omi asks.

We are afraid to explain to Omi and Rhu because we do not understand how we could communicate with feed. How did they access our thought-sphere and understand us? These are questions we are not yet capable of addressing.

Fortunately, Omi's attention shifts, and we scuttle down the aisle between the cells, poking our eyestalks into cubicle after empty cubicle.

Rhu angrily stalks the drop chamber. *Not even a*

scent.

They were there, we assure. As real as Rhu or Omi, the human was there. They had nowhere to flee, yet they are gone like a wisp of ozone. Not ozone, for even that leaves a trace.

Another memory bleeds from the stone. A memory of this feeding ground, rich and sweet under its unremarkable yellow star. Humans everywhere, but after the shock of the initial culling, they realized they could not resist us, and they fled into the tunnels and dark spaces under the rubble of their primitive civilization. Our progenitor hunted those narrow dark spaces, passing through conduits where our feeding strings were compressed by the tightness of the walls. In dark corners, behind barricades of metal, quietly trembling in the sputtering light of flaming sticks, we found them. These humans were crafty, good at hiding, but for all their wile, they could not escape us. We found them in pairs and triplets, small and large, each one different and succulent, each one strong and determined to escape, but failing. Human faces flash by, each in their final moments as our feeding strings pulled their energy from their organic vessels. Their eyes grew wide as they embraced their fate, and the shadow of their fleeing existence descended over those gleaming orbs.

In one of these faces, we recognize the landscape of their features. We must be mistaken, confused by the superficial resemblances among the individuals, but as we study the face, our certainty rises. Rhu had found this human in the tunnels long after we had first landed. Unlike their brethren, this one and their companion had survived for many days. Curiously, they had not tried to escape while Rhu drained their companion, and like all the other feed, ceased to exist, the gleam slowly, inexorably draining from their eyes as they were culled. We know this because it is in the collective memory of our lineage. Yet, with certainty now, we are sure the face in this memory is the same that confronted us today.

#

Night on this feeding ground is darker than the vacuum of space. Its atmosphere dampens our vision in many wavelengths, and the background glow of the universe, beautiful and bright, is muted.

Driven by hunger, Rhu slithers through dark spaces, nasal bulb snuffling, but detecting only the reek of dust and decayed metal, and the faint, persistent odor of ancient bones. It is as if these grounds are empty.

Elsewhere, Omi clicks across stone floors stained sticky with organic residue. Human faces hang on the walls, and Omi stops to study each of them in turn, cooing, hoomon softly, absent-mindedly.

We shuffle our stubby torso over to the breach in our drop chamber and turn our gaze up to the quiet, star-filled night. What has happened to the Vortive that this world is so quiet. Our collective memory tells us the feed were culled efficiently, yet they still exist, whereas the Vortive seems to not.

Our torso vibrates to comfort us, but our fears do not subside. Only the hum of the collective consciousness will bring us peace, but instead of the collective consciousness, we hear again the human sounds, "Ring-a-ring o' roses, a pocket full of posies, hush-hush hush-hush, or we all tumble down." A strange feeling that is more than the hollowness of our hunger turns uncomfortably within us.

Fearing the human may have returned, we turn our insufficient receptors to the crevice, but in the darkness, they are not up to the task. We wish Omi and Rhu were here to show us nothing lurks within, but we are afraid to call to them through the thought-sphere.

"Why did you kill her?"

In the shadows to our left, the human stands over a fallen companion. The scene matches our memory of their culling, and scanning to our right, we sense Rhu, as in that memory, circling in towards the small human. Yet unlike our memory, Rhu slows as we grow closer to the human, until finally, Rhu's sleek form becomes still and shadowy.

Is this a collective memory? We know Rhu has not returned to the drop chamber; we sense Rhu below us, among the ruins. Yet, we also know this human no longer exists, except in the collective memory of our lineage.

"Why did you kill her?" the human asks again.

We do not understand our compulsion to respond, nor care that we lack the mechanisms necessary to produce the human's sound. *They are feed*, we say.

Omi pauses from our inspection of the human images. *Audu?*

I realize then that Omi and Rhu do not share this experience; this human is for Audu alone. As the first, we are the keeper of the collective memories of our lineage, to share them, to augment them, and when our vorta's time is complete, to pass them on to the collective consciousness.

Slender appendages hide the human's face, and their body shudders. Human communication is crude and primitive, limited to a narrow bandwidth of sound, imperfect visual cues, and reeking chemical emissions that lack subtlety, but we do not understand this reaction.

What is this? we ask.

The human looks up, their eyes glistening in the moonlight. "I'm sad because she is dead, and everything she was is now gone forever."

We do not understand. At the end of every culling, the organic form of the vorta are re-absorbed by their drop chamber, and we cease to exist in this form. The energy we extracted during the culling is uploaded to the Vortive, and the collective memories of our lineage are processed into the collective consciousness. Vorta are destined to exist, not exist, and exist again, but there is never loss.

The click-click of Omi's tarsi coming in through the hole draws our attention. Rhu follows, feeding stalks waving rapidly in agitation, but Rhu does not charge into the corner and attack the human. When we turn back, the human and their companion are gone. So too is the unmoving Rhu, and we are left shaken, afraid, and unable to understand what is happening to us.

Audu? Omi asks again, and we choose to remain silent.

#

Ba's bulbous and wrinkled body lies motionless on the metal plating beneath the womb-sac, and for a moment we fear stillborn. Then stumpy appendages sprout from our dorsum and the turgid, fleshy mass rises. Instinctively, Ba tries to wriggle into a narrow recess in the machinery beneath the dripping womb-sac, but the machinery has been damaged, and we no longer fit.

Ba emits a quivering noise that grates across our tac-pads, causing consternation. Ba needs to be sheltered to function, to attain our purpose as the fourth. Turning, Ba searches for another place and notices the crevice between the damaged wall plates.

We do not want Ba to go in there, but Ba's despondence is nearly crippling, and we do not block them. The human, if they ever existed, is gone now, and the crevice is safe. Once pressed in among the chamber's vessels and organs, Ba coos serenely, drawing the tension from us like a toxin.

After a time, Ba says, *The thought-sphere is quiet.*

Memories flash as Ba extracts them from us for processing. They reach back to the feeding ground where the first vorta in our lineage tasted the succulent sweetness of a successful culling. Then the second feeding ground, equally ripe, the third where the resistance was strong but ultimately futile, the fourth, fifth, sixth—each memory speeding past our consciousness faster than those before it. The memories stop abruptly on this world, with the human face that has haunted us.

Sensing Ba's activity, Rhu and Omi halt, raise their nasal bulbs and eyestalks into the air.

Awash in the memories of feed, we purr and shake with pleasure. When the memories finally end, the hollowness of our hunger is greater. Left unsatiated, our flesh will soon begin to die once the last of the memories have dissolved from the stone left by our progenitor.

We are eager to resume the culling, but we await Ba's wisdom.

Finally, Ba speaks. *The feed are depleted. The Vortive have departed. Our purpose is ended.*

Rhu's feeding strings weave agitated patterns through the air. *This ground is not empty. Audu sensed one, but it escaped.* We hear the disgust in Rhu's tone. *Tell us how to find it*, Rhu says gruffly.

The thought-sphere is quiet; therefore, the Vortive have migrated, Ba says, carefully articulating our logical argument. *The Vortive migrate only once the feed are gone. Therefore, the feed are depleted.*

The Vortive does not abandon vorta, we say.

Ba rustles dismissively. *This assumption is unsupported by the collective memory. When vorta are defective, they are excised to ensure the integrity of the Vortive. The collective memories contain four instances of vorta abandoned on feeding grounds.*

How can vorta be a threat to the collective consciousness if they are part of that consciousness?

Ba emits displeasure at our temerity. *They are a threat if they introduce memories inconsistent with the identity of the Vortive*, Ba says. *The one and the many are the same.*

Ba's statement disturbs us. We should not challenge Ba's analytical capabilities—it is not the place of the first to do such—but Ba must be wrong. We possess no defects in ourselves or our progenitors, and we pose no threat to the collective consciousness. The one and the many are the same, so we do not understand why we have been left.

When we do not respond, Ba turns inward to ruminate, leaving us alone in our drop chamber.

Our tac-pads detect faint vibrations. "If the one and the many are the same, are they not just the one?"

Eyes materialize from the darkness near the breach. They are followed by the faint outline of the human's face and the grey silhouette of their spindly, frail body.

Collectively, we are more. We are the Vortive.

The one and the many, Omi says, far below us.

Again, the vibrations are faint, as if the human noise is intended to be soft. "That doesn't make sense," they say.

What is this creature that seems to both exist and be a memory?

"I am Tru," they say. "I was named after my grandmother, Gertrude, because my mom says my dad lacked imagination."

The communication between us is not clear, but we discern that Tru is a name designating this entity of feed, like Audu-Omi-Rhu-Ba designates our specific vorta within the collective consciousness of the Vortive.

Yet, this was not what we wanted to know.

As if they can penetrate our mind, the human responds again, "All that I am will be gone forever. You fed on me." The face fades back into the darkness, and the eyes wink out of existence, like light into a blackhole.

Our crude receptors sense only metal and air and darkness.

Afraid, now, we curl about ourselves protectively. We have no memory of feed possessing the ability to come and go like smoke. If Tru is only a figment of our mind drawn from a collective memory, then the feeding ground is empty, as Ba deduced. It is another realization that scares us more. Collective memories are not capable of interacting with the existing. Yet this memory seems to be not of the collective memory, but an intrusion of the human's energy, an infection capable of appearing at will and communicating with Audu, an independent sentient entity capable of challenging the core tenants of our collective consciousness. To which we are drawn to one conclusion.

Ba is correct; we are defective.

#

We are not capable of fully processing this information, and it cripples us into inactivity.

Ba, however, wriggles from the crevice and stands next to our curled torso. Ba's cooing, along with the sense that Ba knows what needs to be done, provides comfort.

We must cease to exist, Ba says, after a time.

Sensing something has gone wrong, Omi and Rhu pause their hunt. Rhu howls in denial and turns back to chasing spectres. We try to comfort Omi by vibrating.

Ba shuffles over to the machinery under the womb-sac and pushes up against the interface plate. Ba intends to disable the chamber's regenerators, shutting down the womb-sac so no new vorta will be birthed, and our collective memories will dissipate into the ether. Our lineage will cease to exist.

We are numb to Ba's effort because the enormity of … death is beyond our experience. Feed die; vorta do not.

"No one wants to die." Tru watches us from where they squat against the wall next to the breach that opens out onto the star-filled sky.

You do not exist, we say, willing the human to leave us, but they do not disappear.

Ba pauses, emitting scents of confusion. Ba cannot

detect the human because it resides within us, among, but not of, our collective memories.

Our loathing transforms into anger. All that we are will end forever, and our primal instincts, which reach back to our time planet-bound and primitive, struggle to accept this.

Tru's head shakes from side-to-side, and the act seems to diffuse our emotion. "You don't have to die, you chose to."

The one and the many are no longer the same. The words sound hollow as we watch the human before us. We have never considered the sentient design of feed—they are inferior to the Vortive and irrelevant—but all humans are the same and also different, each its own lineage with only one generation. Yet, looking at the gentle curves of Tru's starlit face, we find it hard to accept that this difference makes them truly inferior.

"Different is just different," Tru says.

Alone, we contemplate this concept.

Ba circles the drop chamber, sweeping the space with our crude receptors. Finding nothing, Ba stops near the breach, next to the squatting, yet unseen, human.

What is wrong, Audu? Ba asks.

Why must the one and the many be the same?

Ba is silent, our confusion obvious. Ba's logic is bound by the evidence of the collective memories, and we realize Ba is incapable of reaching any other conclusion. As the first, our primordial instincts do not bind us to such limitations.

We are defective, Ba says. *We must cease to exist.*

We do not want to die. As we tell this to Ba, Tru echoes our words within our consciousness, and we understand then, that if we die, then all human lineages will die with us. The Vortive has always culled feed to extinction. We have always known it to be our birthright, yet we have never questioned this assumption.

The stone dissolves a final time, and the last of our lineage's collective memories flood our consciousness. We have been trapped on this world for fifty-seven generations, repeating this cycle of existing and not existing, passing on the memories of our lineage as we were made to do. Every generation of our vorta has struggled to understand what has happened, and every generation has ultimately reached the same conclusion: the one and the many being different has a beauty to its design, and we are arrogant to believe the Vortive is superior to all other sentients.

This is wrong, we say.

This is the only way, Ba says.

When Ba moves back toward the womb-sac, we shuffle forward to block them. Ba tries to evade us, but we bump them back. Ba does not stop, however, so we bump them again, this time harder, and Ba, being awkward in physical form, tumbles backward and out of the breach.

Ba's terror—our terror—is sharp and painful as the ground rushes upward. The force of the impact knocks us over, and for a moment, we believe we have ceased to exist, but our receptors slowly recover from the shock, and we lay prone on the floor of our drop chamber, alone and no longer four.

We had not intended for this to happen, but we also know that this generation will not be the last. Ba has ceased to exist, but Ba is not dead.

Above us, the womb-sac clicks to life. The

regenerators hum behind the walls.

The drop chamber is empty, although, with satisfaction, I sense Tru is still with us.

The stone, now empty, can no longer sustain. Omi settles down before one of the images of the humans, our tarsi now silent, our eyestalks settling into the sticky organic residue that coats the floor of our tomb. Rhu's lithe form slows and comes to a final rest in the tunnels deep beneath the rubble, in among the spaces where the humans of this dead world once tried to evade their extinction. We were an agent of that destruction, but we now have a chance to redeem our arrogance. Humans are not yet extinct, and they survive now as long as we survive.

We grow tired and can no longer right our torso. We sense our organic energy dissipating. The stone burns now, recording our final moments for the next generation, appending it to the legacy of our lineage's collective memories.

The end and the beginning are the same but not the same.

In the end, we are one, and we are regret.

STORY NOTES
THE MEMORY PLAGUE

Sometimes writing a story can be easy. An idea comes to me, and the words flow out like a river. Editing goes quickly, and if I'm fortunate, I sell it on my first try.

I've had that happen a few times, but usually, short story writing is more of a process. My stories often need time to gel. First drafts often meander, and the editing process is agonizingly slow (but still my favorite part). Selling a story can take months or years.

"The Memory Plague" is likely my most extreme example of this. It had its origins back around 2016, when the title jumped into my head one day. I had no story to go with the title, but something about the juxtaposition of those two words—memory and plague—made it stick in my head, and I knew I wanted to write a story that would fit it.

Around this same time, I learned that my mom had Alzheimer's. This disease affected her memory, and over the next few years, I watched my mom slip away, piece by piece, as her memories were consumed. She became an entirely different person— she even took on a different appearance—and I realized that our memories make us who we are. If those memories are lost or changed, we become different people. This became the core of what would eventually become "The Memory Plague."

Several months later, the first pieces of "The Memory Plague" started to coalesce. I decided I wanted it tell a first-contact story, and that I wanted to tell that story from the alien's perspective. I often find the portrayal of aliens in science fiction to be a disappointment because the aliens simply aren't that "alien," so I wanted to challenge myself and this convention. I wanted to present an alien perspective that was as strange as possible, while still allowing a very human story to be told. The alien Vortive were born from this desire.

The first draft of "The Memory Plague" was completed near the end 2016 and was not very good. The story was long and unfocused, and simply put, had no heart.

So, I put it away, and a short time later I stopped writing short stories to focus on my book series, *The Calypto Cycle*. I didn't forget about "The Memory Plague." It stuck in my mind, like a musical earworm, and over the next several years I dusted it off several times and tried to re-work it. I must have failed a half dozen times, and after each failure, I would put it back in the trunk, only to be drawn back to it a few months later. In 2019, I again pulled the story out, determined to finish it this time, and after many days of hard work, I knew I had something special. I finally had it right.

"The Memory Plague" is very personal to me. It's the hardest story I've ever written, and thus one of which I am very proud. I am saddened that my mom never got to see this one. She passed away from Alzheimer's several years before it was finished and published, but she still lives on in my collective memories. I guess I could say, "We are Audu."

Observations on a Clock

First published in *Asimov's Science Fiction Magazine*, February 2012

THE CLOCK SITS IN THE DARK, counting down time. Alone.

Except for Chevalier.

"It is ridiculous to kneel before it," says Maria Tessauda.

Chevalier senses her presence in the blackness. He has never met the real Tessauda. She died three hundred years before he was born. She lives, however, as a MEM in his head, put there—reluctantly he is now sure—to share her knowledge of the Clock.

"It does not count down to your Revelation." She takes every opportunity to tell him this. She is not a believer; it offends her academic sensibilities.

"Leave me in peace." Chevalier knows she will not. Three years ago, she tricked him into altering her MEM programming. Now she comes and goes at her will. His need for companionship, especially from a woman, drove him to such foolish action.

"Your Testament is illogical."

Unable to contain himself, Chevalier says, "The Testament is Truth."

He cannot see her smile, but he feels it. She has fifty different smiles. Most are unpleasant to witness.

"If your Testament is true, you have nothing to fear by looking. The digger is ready, it only needs a command. If you allow, I can—"

"No." He will not be tricked again into giving more autonomy. "If I do this, will you leave me alone?"

"That is the only reason you will do it?"

Chevalier sighs. His breath crackles as it crystallizes in the eternal night. He fights her only because giving in emboldens her.

"You should do this because you need to know."

What more is there to know? The Testament has proven itself by saving humanity from self-annihilation. It has prepared them for the coming Revelation, which will arrive when the Clock runs its course. Chevalier cannot doubt. As Don Cristobol has counseled, without doubt, there is no fear.

"I am not afraid," he says aloud. Yet he is uncertain he believes his own words.

Chevalier's implant tells him the digger still sits at the edge of the platform where he found it a decade ago. Without word or motion, he orders it to life. "Show me where to dig."

#

Chevalier finishes his log entry, but does not light-beam it to Earth. It contains his first mention of the digging, even though the machine has been at work for several days.

The fusion lamp sputters as if it is a real flame. He closes his eyes and remembers the way the candles used to flicker shadows across the walls of his seminary chamber. The beeswax smelled faintly of honey, and the gentle echo of prayer off the ancient stone vaults comforted him like his mother's arms.

Chevalier inhales deeply, but the fusion lamp is odorless.

When he opens his eyes, there is only the lozenge-shaped ship that carried him across fifteen light-years of time and space. The halo of light feels cold and insubstantial.

Chevalier light-beams his log back to Earth. Its contents won't matter, he decides. In fifteen years, when someone reads it, his mission will be long over.

Immediately Chevalier senses a presence. At the edge of the shadows stands Don Cristobol in his holy sash. His face is round and plump with a generous grey beard. Upon his forehead is the mark of the sacred third eye.

Chevalier bows clumsily, nearly knocking over the lamp. "Your holiness," he says, lowering his eyes.

Like Maria Tessauda, Don Cristobol is a MEM in Chevalier's head. Unlike her, he knew Don Cristobol, the flesh. It is because of Don Cristobol that Chevalier is here, alone.

Chevalier senses Don Cristobol's disappointment, which is worse than any reproach. "The woman … she …" Nothing he says can explain, but he cannot help himself. "I am sorry, I only thought—"

"Do not think, Chevalier. Do what you are here to do."

"I only wish to affirm the Clock's divine creation."

"Affirmation comes from faith, not digging. Nothing can be learned by digging because there is nothing here but the Clock."

Chevalier wants to look up, but does not. "Nothing is what I intend to find. That will prove—"

"Nothing proves only that you have found nothing. However, the act of looking proves that you doubt."

Chevalier's chest constricts. "You are right,

Holiness. The Testament saved us all. I do not doubt it." He feels the need to prove the veracity of his words. He locates the digger where it works dutifully in the darkness excavating regolith from a hole at the edge of the platform. At his command, it retreats.

"It is finished," Chevalier says, but already Don Cristobol has left.

#

Soon after he stops the digger, Tessauda arrives unannounced.

Standing in a wide basin, Chevalier washes with a tattered rag. His skin smokes in the cold air.

Tessauda grins as she ogles his nakedness. "You used to be happy to see me, Chevalier."

His face flushes hot. Chevalier has no reason to be embarrassed, yet he is. Tessauda is not what he considers a physically beautiful woman. Her features are hard and angular, like splinters of flint. But she is still a woman.

Chevalier continues to wash himself, unwilling to be goaded by her. His green skin used to disconcert him, but after ten years he finds comfort in it. The chlorophyll is one of his many genetic modifications so he can complete his mission.

Apparently bored with taunting him, Tessauda asks, "Why have you stopped the digger?" Shadow eclipses her face as she stops between him and the fusion lamp.

Chevalier does not answer, hoping she will leave. He finishes washing himself and wraps a towel around his waist. The light from the lamp appears unusually pale.

"Order the digger back," she says.

"I can't do that."

A knowing look flares across her face. "Why do you listen to Don Cristobol?"

Her dismissiveness piques his anger. "If I do not listen to him, then all I have is you."

She places a wide, flat palm against his chest. Her skin is warm, unlike her smile. "Am I no longer enough, Chevalier?" Her hand slides downward.

He catches it at his navel. "Go away and do not come back."

Tessauda steps away. Light waxes across her wide eyes and round mouth. After a second, her surprise is gone. "You are a fool, Chevalier. Idiot, imbecile, bastard. You take my precious life work and then dismiss me like a whore."

Chevalier tries not to wince. He knows her words are meant to manipulate. Even so, his guilt burns. Unable to look at her, he lowers his eyes. When he looks up to apologize, she is gone.

#

Tessauda does not visit for weeks. At first, Chevalier is relieved to be free of her fifty smiles. He spends half his waking hours searching the heavens for the seven signs described in the Testament. For the other half, he kneels before the Clock, praying for enlightenment. He finds neither.

When he turns out the fusion lamp, he sometimes hears voices in the darkness. When he turns up the light, the halo is always empty.

"Don Cristobol, where are you?" he asks once as he floats in blackness viscous as the sea.

Silence.

He wonders if he has always been alone.

Unable to sleep, Chevalier passes time by walking from the platform edge to the Clock and back again. He times his passage—there and back and there and back—by the minutes falling into the night. He has been here for nearly eleven years, because his ship traveled a fraction of cee faster than anticipated. The end is now only weeks away—but he is no longer sure he can make it.

Is he the idiot Tessauda branded him? He finds it troubling how her words still burn. He still believes, because he must, but what if Tessauda is right, and the Clock does not mark the Revelation?

Doubt begets the bastard child named fear.

Chevalier goes to the digger.

A few meters from the platform, the squat machine has excavated a trench just long and wide enough that Chevalier could lie in it like a coffin. The beam from the fusion lamp plays off the crisp edge, but illuminates nothing within.

He is angry at himself for doubting.

Eventually, Don Cristobol comes. He stands at the edge of the halo of light. His sash looks grey, but Chevalier is too tired to determine if it is only an illusion of the light. Chevalier has begun to believe that the lamp is fading, but when he has paced out the diameter of the halo, it always seems to be the same.

"You look troubled," says Don Cristobol.

"I am weary of the dark. I cannot find the signs. I …"

"I am here, Chevalier."

If that were true, then where have you been all this time, Chevalier thinks.

Don Cristobol's face is round and gentle, how Chevalier's father would have looked if he had not been killed in the violence before the Order had given humanity its hope. For some reason, Chevalier is not comforted.

"I am not strong enough," Chevalier says.

"You were chosen by divine right," Don Cristobol says. "You are the only one who could undertake this mission."

Chevalier does not believe him. The mission has been difficult, certainly, but many could have done it better than him.

"We must dig within to find our strength. It allows us to overcome our doubt. Without doubt, we conquer our fear. Without fear, we can embrace the Revelation when it comes."

Chevalier knows the teachings of the Testament. Doubt begets fear begets darkness. Humanity has been to that brink before. Chevalier has stood there, too, before he embraced the teachings of the Order. Only the Testament averted destruction. "I need to be stronger."

"Do not doubt your strength, Chevalier. You have the power to stay humanity's course."

Chevalier can feel the pressure of the dark against the halo of light. Humanity awaits the Revelation, and Chevalier, as witness, is to be their conduit to understand the future. His mission is more than just bearing witness to the greatest event in human history. It is to save humanity from doubting its place in the universe. "I am strong enough to do what must be done."

#

In forty-two hours the last of the micro black holes that power the Clock's core will evaporate. Its energy spent, the Clock will reach its end.

Chevalier runs a systems check on the light-beam transmitter. It has been weeks since he has sent or received anything from Earth, but the equipment is working properly.

As he finishes, he senses Tessauda's presence and nearly drops the transmitter's casing on his foot.

She looks different. Her smile is gone and the lines at the corner of her eyes look like fissures.

Chevalier wonders if her absence has changed her.

"What do you fear you will find?" she asks.

Chevalier is not put off by her lack of pleasantries. They are not her. "There is nothing to find," he says. "The Clock is divine."

Tessauda's predatory grin returns. It is different from her other forty-nine smiles because it shows her teeth. "Come with me, then. I have something you should see."

She has not changed.

Already Chevalier is annoyed by her return, but at the same time, he draws comfort from it. He allows her to lead him to the edge of the platform. There, he steps down onto the hard-packed regolith. Before him is the trench excavated by the digger. Tessauda lurks behind, a tiger in the shadow of the underbrush.

"I had hoped that in my absence you would come to see."

Chevalier's lips are icy with crystallized breath. "I see nothing."

Tessauda's shoulder brushes against his, startling him. "You see nothing because you do not try even to look." She kneels at the edge and reaches into the hole. "The light!" Her voice is sharp, as if meant for an insolent child.

He shines the lamp down where she points. The trench is only twenty centimeters deep. The bottom is hard and smooth.

Tessauda's hand sweeps at the fine grit covering the bottom of the hole, but she cannot move it. "You must do it," she says.

Chevalier is momentarily shocked by this reminder that she is a MEM. "There is nothing—"

"Just do it, and do not crow your ignorance a third time."

Chevalier scowls but brushes the grit aside. As he does so, his fingertips catch a groove. He traces a rectangular stone, then a second one abutting the first.

Tessauda's smile slides across her face. "Now you see," she says. "Something was here before your divine Clock."

#

The fusion lamp pushes the dark aside as Chevalier flees across the platform. Tessauda's mocking smile cuts at his shoulder blades, and he curses his foolishness for ever wishing her back.

He tries to forget the foundation that she has shown him, but he cannot flee the implications. Someone built the Clock atop a foundation of cut stone that differs from everything he associates with the Clock.

As he nears the Clock, he stops to extinguish the lamp, as he always does before approaching its Divine presence.

"Why do you hide it in darkness?" Tessauda circles from behind and stands between him and the Clock.

"It is divine." Chevalier regrets speaking the

moment the words thoughtlessly tumble across his lips.

"I don't pretend to know what this device foretells, if anything at all, but I see no proof it is your Revelation."

"It will come," says Don Cristobol.

Chevalier turns toward Don Cristobol, standing behind him.

"It must come for the sake of humanity," Don Cristobol says.

"Tell me, Chevalier, what happens if you are wrong?" says Tessauda.

He turns to look at her, and is struck by how similar her eyes are to Don Cristobol's. He has never seen the two together at the same time before, but by their eyes, they could be father and daughter.

"What happens if the Clock reaches its end and the Revelation does not come?"

"It will come," says Don Cristobol. "It is divine."

"Divine." Tessauda spits the word as if it is bitter alum. "To our ancestors with stone tools, you are divine, Chevalier."

"The Testament of Celestial Unity foretells the coming Revelation. Humanity is ready to embrace it as at no other time in its history. Through Chevalier, we will experience it and understand our higher fate."

"Something is coming," says Tessauda, "and it will be a revelation, but will it be the one you seek? That is the question."

Chevalier glares at her. "There is nothing to fear as long as I have faith."

"Fear is a good thing, Chevalier. Fear is what drives us towards excellence. Without fear—fear of failure, fear of death—we are nothing."

"Fear nearly destroyed us," says Chevalier. He remembers when his family was killed by Tensari soldiers during the war, and he was afraid to live. He recalls the first time he held a disruptor in battle and was afraid to die. He had been afraid to love, to succeed, to fail, to … The Order showed him how to conquer his fear. He never wants to be that person again.

"Stupidity nearly destroyed us," says Tessauda.

"It was doubt about our place in the cosmos," says Don Cristobol. "The Revelation will affirm our place."

"What will happen if the Clock strikes zero and there is nothing but the dark?"

A hole opens in Chevalier's gut. He is ashamed to admit that more than once the thought has occurred to him.

"That will not happen," says Don Cristobol.

Chevalier spins, first looking towards Don Cristobol, then Tessauda. When he stops spinning, his head is so light it feels like it can float free of his neck.

He drops the fusion lamp. As it hits the platform, Chevalier's universe goes dark and quiet.

Don Cristobol is right; Chevalier holds humanity in his hands. To light-beam a document back to Earth showing the Revelation to be nothing would destroy the Order. Without the Order humanity would regress into what it once was. It would be better to send nothing and let them think he had failed.

"I am sorry, Don Cristobol. I am not strong enough." Chevalier drops to his knees, alone in the dark, as he has always been.

Except for the Clock.

STORY NOTES
OBSERVATIONS ON A CLOCK

Often no single thing, place, or event inspires a complete story. Stories rise up from a tangle of inspirations, but sometimes a significant story element can be traced to a specific thing.

"Observations on a Clock" has its root inspiration in a call for submissions for a themed anthology. In the summer of 2010, a publisher issued a call for stories about "alien" archeology. My writing group, Hopefull Monsters (yes the extra "l" was intentional—that's our story, at least), decided to use that theme as a writing prompt, and we brainstormed ideas. I was interested in exploring alien artifacts that weren't weapons or miracle devices that would save or benefit humanity. I wanted to explore the idea that alien devices were just that: *alien*. As such, any attempt of humans to interpret those artifacts would suffer from the "human element." How could humans understand something that was truly alien?

Two ideas came out of that brainstorming session. One developed into my story "Hoodoo"(which also appears in this volume), and the second developed into "Observations on a Clock," which I finished after the anthology's submission deadline.

The Negotiation

First published in *Daily Science Fiction*, July 2013

ALEXANDRE FOUND SAMSON exactly where the card said. The card hadn't mentioned the gun or the explosives or the twenty-seven ashen-faced hostages, but he could work with that.

"I'm just here to talk," Alexandre said when Samson's gun swung in his direction. Since the police had arrived and cordoned off the block around the bank, Samson's already accelerated heart rate had tripled. Alexandre felt it like a subwoofer beat pulsing at the core of his body.

"I didn't ask for no negotiator."

"But you did, the second you walked through that door."

Samson's face contorted grotesquely. Alexandre thought it a look of confusion, but Samson's face was a knot of gristle and bone and incapable of looking anything other than grotesque. A shame, Alexandre thought, his brow crinkling, because Samson didn't have the aura of a bad man. Since the divorce, Samson's life had been a downhill toboggan run on a sheet of black ice. Alexandre had seen it before: personal hardship leading to depression to hard drugs to a career spiraling down the proverbial toilet to a poor life choice. (In Alexandre's opinion, strapping C4 to your chest and holding twenty-seven hostages in a failed bank robbery qualified as a poor life choice.)

Alexandre hoisted himself up onto the counter that held the bank's withdrawal slips. "Is this the best you have?" he asked loudly, addressing the room.

The hostages, in a neat line on the floor along the front of the teller's counter, drew away from him as if he were something contemptible.

"How did you get in here, man?" Samson clutched a dead man's switch to his chest. He jabbed his pistol in the air like he was poking at Alexandre with a sharpened stick.

"You knew this was going to end badly." Out of habit, Alexandre used his calming voice, the one that had never averted bad endings in the past. Those bad endings haunted Alexandre, draining the color from the world. But today would be different.

"Wha'chu mean?" Samson asked.

Alexandre pointed at the brick of C4. "You don't wire yourself to blow if you expect to walk away." Alexandre threw his hands up and gazed into the air. "Really, how will this demonstrate anything?" he asked.

One of the hostages whimpered. Alexandre tried not to look at him—a middle-aged man, plump from sitting behind a desk and probably caught in the wrong place during his thirty-minute lunch break— but his aura shimmered with the love of a dowdy wife and three kids in Catholic school.

Alexandre's stomach soured. Maybe this wasn't going to be so easy.

He exhaled loudly. If this was how it had to play out, then so be it. "We all get dealt a shitty hand of fucked-up," he said, turning back to Samson. "Some of us deserve it."

"I didn't deserve nothing," Samson said.

"Sure you did. What was his name? Pepe?" Alexandre knew he had it right because Samson's whole body clenched. "He got in with your wife because she didn't want you. You were lousy at your job, worthless as a son, and a horrible friend. Even I don't like you, and I'm predisposed to like everyone."

"What kind of negotiator are you?" asked the whimpering hostage.

Alexandre flashed a smile, and was momentarily surprised when the man recoiled away. His smile once had the power to calm—not that it ever helped—but no more. He focused his attention on Samson so he wouldn't think about the hostages.

Samson's left eye twitched.

"Just do it," Alexandre said, his voice surprisingly calm. "You've got nothing—"

In a flash of prescience, Alexandre dropped to the floor as bullets flew. The staccato chatter of Samson's weapon punctuated splintering marble. The screams—thankfully, they didn't last long. Then a final gunshot, and the bank was quiet.

Alexandre's muscles thrummed with adrenaline. Standing, he brushed chips of marble from his shirt. The smell of blood made his nose itch more than the lingering gun smoke. Twenty-eight, he thought. If Samson had wired the explosives right, he might have gotten some people in the street, too, but twenty-eight should be enough.

His assessment sat better than he would have expected.

"So? How'd I do?"

Alexandre reached into his pocket and felt another card, cool and crisp like a razor blade. He could cut himself on it, he thought.

"Ouch."

He put his finger to his lips. Something about the metallic taste of blood now pleased him.

As he removed the card, a whiff of sulfur calmed his itchy nose. YOU'RE HIRED, said the words next to his bloody fingerprint. One corner of Alexandre's mouth rose slightly. He could not remember the last time he had successfully negotiated a "good" outcome, but maybe, just maybe, he had been working for the wrong side. Good outcomes, after all, were a matter of perspective.

He flipped the card over. On the back was a new name and address.

As an Angel of Mercy, Alexandre had been a failure and a joke among his peers. As an Angel of Death?

He could be a good Angel of Death.

STORY NOTES
THE NEGOTIATION

Sometimes a story's inspiration is clear and strong, and I can pinpoint it with ease. Other times it's not so easy.

The inspiration for "The Negotiation" is easy to identify. This story was inspired by a writing prompt through the Codex writing group. Each year the group did a series of "weekend writing prompts," where a prompt was given on Friday, and participants submitted a finished story (anonymously) on Monday. The submitted stories were then read and ranked by Codex members, and a weekly "winner" was crowned (but really everyone who finished a story was a winner). Unfortunately, I don't write stories that quickly, so I never managed to submit a weekend story, let alone "win" the event.

"The Negotiation" was inspired by one weekend writing prompt: *write about someone who failed in a previous profession, but now has some success in a new one.* I brainstormed possible jobs, starting much too mundane and getting progressively more interesting until I finally hit one I liked. From there, the pieces of "The Negotiation" began to fall into place—a failed bank robbery, a whimpering hostage, a tense negotiation—and the story was born. I wrote this one in a single sitting, with a wordy first draft that came in at nearly twice the finished story's length. Two revisions later, I had the final story, clocking in at a tight and respectable 850 words.

Strand in the Web

First published in *Goldfish Grimm's Spicy Fiction Sushi*, June 2012

BY THE TIME SANDOVAL CAUGHT up with the poachers, the slaughter was nearly over. As he approached under cover of an Andrussan feather fern, two poachers wielding mono-wire saws finished cutting off the last of the aerodon's nine, man-sized tusks. With a sickening snap of connective tissue, it dropped to the spongy moss. A mountain of pink flesh convulsed, and ripples ran across the aerodon's bulbous lift-sac like waves snapped across a collapsing canvas tent. It emitted a plaintive whine that turned Sandoval's stomach. The poachers hadn't even bothered to kill the great beast before butchering it.

Sandoval eased his neural tangler from its holster. It felt flimsy in his hand. He wanted something to bludgeon these men with, not the Reserve Authority's standard-issue, non-lethal pacifier.

A third poacher unloaded an industrial bulkhead cutter from a nearby skimmer. "Get 'em loaded while I finish up." The cutter slung over his shoulder, he disappeared behind the quivering mass.

Sandoval adjusted the nasal cannula that supplied O_2-enriched air. He wiped away the droplets of cloud mist clinging to his goggle lenses. It was now or never, while the poachers were distracted and separated.

He crept from his hiding place toward the two men muscling a tusk into the skimmer's cargo bed.

His tangler discharged crackling arcs. He left the poachers twitching on the ground, their nervous systems overloaded, and edged around the aerodon. A few meters to Sandoval's left, the island's slick granite ended abruptly, plunging precipitously through the cloud mist to Andrussa's surface, four thousand meters below.

Helium hissed from a harpoon puncture in the animal's float bladder. Otherwise it was quiet.

Cautiously he leaned out. Where Sandoval had expected to find the poacher, he saw only the cutter lying in the waterlogged moss.

He mouthed a curse, but before he could do anything, the skimmer's engines roared to life, and the craft lumbered over the top of the aerodon. Its heat wash blew droplets from Sandoval's hair and beard as it passed overhead and disappeared into the mist.

Sandoval's energy drained away, leaving his body trembling. He sat down on a rock to collect himself.

He recognized this aerodon from the distinctive markings on its mantle tissue. He had frequently sighted it drifting through the mist near his station. An older male; its ring of tusks beneath its lift-sac was one of the largest Sandoval had ever seen.

The aerodon whined again, a high pitched sound that constricted Sandoval's throat.

He wished he had a way to end its suffering.

Sandoval holstered his tangler. Maybe its death didn't have to be needless.

One of the stunned poachers was already dead. His cannula had been ripped free when he had fallen. Sandoval pulled the other poacher's cannula from his nostrils. Within seconds the man started to wheeze.

"Can't …breathe …" The poacher tried to reinsert the tubes, but his overloaded nervous system would not respond.

"If I get answers, you get air. Where's your ship?" In the three weeks he had been pursuing the poachers, Sandoval had been unable to locate their rendering ship in the Cloud Island Reserve's three-dimensional maze of rock pillars and dense, scanner-blocking fog.

The poacher wheezed loudly as his skin began to tinge blue.

"Suit yourself." Sandoval ripped the man's cannula free and threw it into the nearby vegetation.

The poacher clawed at his boot, but Sandoval shook him off and went back around the still quivering aerodon. His nose crinkled at the metallic smell of blood pooling at the base of a deep incision in the aerodon's mantle. He pushed aside ragged folds of tissue until he located a glistening green mass an arm's length inside the body cavity. With his fingers, he ripped the connective sheath and removed the fist-sized organ.

Sandoval weighed it in his hand. He could extract over a year's worth of HeepA.

Carefully he slipped the green mass into an airtight pouch; then he sat quietly in the mist until the aerodon stopped moving. With nothing more to do, he left the carcasses and headed back to the station.

\#

For the next three hours, Sandoval's skimmer slipped through the mist. Periodically islands of rock and olive green vegetation materialized like specters, and disappeared as quickly. The C.I. had over a quarter million islands, although most were nothing more than slender granite spires.

Sandoval's right hand started to tingle. He flexed the fingers, but he knew it wouldn't help. Only a dose of HeepA would alleviate the pins-and-needles. Thankfully, he was nearly at the station.

As he made his final approach, he saw another skimmer already on the roof-top landing circle. Nearby, a man in a crisp, brown Reserve slicker wiped at his goggles as he looked upward.

Sandoval cursed and pulled up. In his nine years in the C.I., he had never had a visitor, so why was a ranger on his roof now?

Sandoval circled around for another approach. As he did, he carefully tucked the aerodon organ under his seat.

"Stay calm," he told himself.

He settled the skimmer onto the edge of the landing circle. Air hissed as the canopy unsealed and slid back.

The ranger in the slicker met him as he clambered out of the skimmer's cab. "I'm Ivan Boerstein from District H.Q.," he said. "I'm here to help with your poaching problem."

Sandoval knew the name, but not the man. Boerstein was head ranger in charge of enforcement for the seven reserves scattered across the District's five planetary systems.

Sandoval kept himself between Boerstein and the skimmer. "I've got it under control."

Boerstein arched an eyebrow. "Seventeen butchered aerodons isn't exactly under control."

Sandoval's face flushed hot. He fought the urge to look away; people with things to hide shied away from eye contact. Stay calm, he thought again. "Fair enough," he said. "How can I help you, Mr. Boerstein?"

#

Once inside, Boerstein went directly to the desk in which Sandoval kept his syringes and vials of HeepA. Sandoval reached for his tangler, but relaxed when all Boerstein did was study the map of the C.I. projected on the wall above it.

Boerstein slid the map view around with his hand, stopping to read Sandoval's many annotations. "Your observations are detailed."

"I really wish you wouldn't." Sandoval reached around and turned off the projection.

Boerstein's brow crinkled.

"I've been in the field for several days; let's talk while we eat."

In the kitchen alcove, Sandoval activated the map projection on the small table. His muscles relaxed when Boerstein sat down and began to study it.

"Lots of places to hide in two hundred thousand square kilometers …" Boerstein said absently.

Sandoval heated a box of broth and poured it over a tangle of rice noodles and nori strips. He moved deliberately because now his left hand tingled. It wasn't serious yet, but he didn't want to attract Boerstein's attention by spilling anything.

He set a bowl at Boerstein's elbow and then leaned against the counter, hoping he didn't look as nervous as he felt.

"Show me where you found the latest carcass," Boerstein said. "We'll start our search there."

Sandoval paused in stuffing noodles into his mouth. "*We'll* start our search there?"

"You know the C.I. better than anyone, Mr. Sandoval."

Sandoval couldn't argue the point. For the last nine years, he had patrolled the C.I. and protected its unique wildlife. He knew the reserve better than any man alive, but that hadn't enabled him to stop the killings. He knew he needed help, but joining Boerstein in the field could prove … awkward.

"Is there a problem?"

Sandoval swallowed the lump in his throat. He needed to pull it together before Boerstein began to suspect something. "There's no problem," Sandoval said.

#

On the map, Sandoval showed Boerstein where he had found all of the poached animals and patiently answered his questions. Eventually Boerstein fell quiet.

"While you process all this, I'm going to get cleaned up." Sandoval locked himself in the bathroom and turned on the shower. From the cabinet, he retrieved a syringe and filled the cylinder with a dose of HeepA. It glittered emerald green as he held it up and tapped out the air bubbles.

Sandoval's mouth was dry. More out of habit than need, he wiped the steam off the mirror so he could see what he was doing.

Every day for the last twenty years he had injected a half cc of HeepA into his spinal column. He had tried synthetic drugs, including numerous HeepA analogs, but none of them had proven effective in mitigating the neurodegenerative symptoms associated with his late on-set Bennington's disorder.

Unfortunately, when appropriately hydroxylated and diluted, HeepA produced a potent euphoric. Ecko had become the illicit recreational drug of choice fifteen years ago, and, as the population of Andrussan aerodons had declined, HeepA in its pure form had become nearly impossible to obtain.

Without it, Sandoval's condition was fatal.

Gradually the tingling in his fingertips faded and the warmth returned.

For the last nine years Sandoval had carefully harvested enough HeepA to keep his condition in check. He had personally killed only two animals, and both of those early in his tenure in the Reserve. Since then, he had managed to collect glands from aerodon carcasses. Regardless, if the Reserve Authority ever learned about his activities or his condition, they would terminate him, figuratively and literally. Yet, at the rate the poachers were slaughtering the last flotilla, aerodons would soon be extinct, and he would follow soon after.

Sandoval pinched the bridge of his nose, hoping to ease his blossoming headache. The survival of the aerodon—his survival—was at stake. All his efforts to stop the poaching had yielded only more butchered carcasses. He needed help, but at what cost?

#

They arrived at the aerodon carcass at first light. Boerstein dictated notes into a button logger on his collar while he meticulously photographed the dead poachers, the severed tusks, the bulkhead cutter, and the aerodon. At first Sandoval tried to explain what had happened, but Boerstein seemed not to notice him. Eventually Sandoval gave up, and followed a few steps behind, uncertain what else to do. He began to wonder why he was there.

When Boerstein finally began to examine the incision in the aerodon's mantle tissue, Sandoval's mouth went dry. Surely he couldn't be connected to the missing gland.

"The third poacher got away with the green gland?"

Sandoval jumped at the sound of Boerstein's voice. "I couldn't stop him," he said quickly.

Boerstein grunted and turned back to photographing the incision.

Sandoval wondered what the grunt meant. Did Boerstein believe him? He tried to recall the exact question, wondering if he had missed something, but failed.

"Are you ready to hunt the hunters, Mr. Sandoval?" From the skimmer, Boerstein retrieved a half-meter long metal wand. "Every vehicle leaves behind a distinctive mixture of volatile compounds and trace metals," he said. "This chem-sniffer can detect trace concentrations." He dragged the wand across the broad leaves of an Andrussan fanplant that had been flattened beneath the poacher's skimmer. "Let the hunt begin," he said, grinning.

They flew east to the next island. While Boerstein searched for a signal, Sandoval wandered among a stand of slender-stalked aobabs. Their three-meter tall trunks glistened in the morning light as symbiotic ciliated lifeforms captured droplets and extracted trace metals and nitrates, which were shared via thread-like hyphae that penetrated the aobab's fibrous dermal layer. The C.I.'s unique aeolian montane ecosystem seemed built upon an intricate web of symbiotic relationships. Without them, Sandoval was convinced everything would collapse.

After about twenty minutes, Boerstein called him back to the skimmer. "We're on the right trail," he said, climbing in.

They continued on from island to island. Boerstein would spend twenty minutes wanding vegetation, and if he found a signature, Sandoval would plot it on their map. By noon, they had acquired a consistent easterly trajectory and increased their pace by skipping islands.

As the day wore on, Sandoval's body began to ache. It was too early for the HeepA to be wearing off, so he assumed it was stress-induced. Sandoval's tightly wound muscles simply would not relax. He had seen no obvious indication that Boerstein suspected anything, but Boerstein had earned distinction as the district's top ranger the last two years. He had to be good at what he did, which was capture people like Sandoval.

Boerstein stowed his equipment and surveyed the darkening mist. "We should stop here for the night."

They pitched a pressure tent and activated the O_2 enricher. After a few minutes, the oxygen partial pressure had risen enough that the two men shed their cannulas.

Boerstein heated a box of soup and poured it into two mugs. He handed one to Sandoval. "What made you volunteer for the C.I.? This is a long way from Besel."

Sandoval wasn't in the mood to swap life stories. As tired as he was, he feared he might let something slip. He hoped a non-committal shrug would be enough to restore the silence.

Boerstein continued to watch him. "This isn't exactly a prime stop on the career path," he said.

"I like the quiet." Sandoval hoped he didn't sound evasive.

Prior to joining the Reserve, Sandoval had worked in an illegal lab on Besel synthesizing Ecko. That had allowed him to skim enough HeepA to stay alive, at least until the syndicate boss learned of his activities. It had taken every favor he had accumulated to get off Besel alive, but with his small stash of HeepA, he wouldn't have stayed that way for long. Fortunately the Reserve had been hiring, and the remote C.I. was an unpopular duty assignment. An application that omitted mention of his condition and a review process that lacked rigor had resulted in a job offer.

Boerstein cradled his mug in his hands and breathed the steam. "I need something more than mist and more mist."

Sandoval remembered thinking the same thing when he had first arrived. His first years had been difficult, and he had thought more than once that death would have been a better choice. Over the years, the C.I. had gradually revealed its beauty.

It was too easy to misjudge the place.

Sandoval frowned. If only Boerstein could see …

He watched Boerstein finish his mug of soup. The man's face still glowered red from the bite of the cold mist. His shoulders slumped with fatigue.

If anyone could appreciate this place, it was Boerstein.

Sandoval lowered his mug. "I want to show you something," he said.

#

They hopped by skimmer to the next island. From there, Sandoval led Boerstein through the cold moonglow to the island's edge. There, a wall of cloud tumbled upward, sparkling like glitter.

"A thermal vent on the planet surface creates this upwelling," Sandoval said. "The shimmers are crystallized carbon, nitrates, and trace minerals from a lower altitude."

To their left, a wide slab of granite projected into the mist. Without hesitation, Sandoval climbed out to the end. The up-draft blew droplets from his hair and snapped past his ears.

Boerstein inched out behind him but stayed away from the edge.

Sandoval pointed into the bluish mist.

Boerstein's eyebrows pinched together. "What is it?"

A dark form shifted and flowed through the currents like a conjuror's handkerchief. The shadow grew darker as it coalesced into something substantial. The aerodon was easily twenty-five meters across, with a skirt of shimmering tusks ringing the base of an enormous balloon-like sac. Beneath it, a half-a-dozen frilled appendages danced in the sparkling mist.

Boerstein's eyes widened. He dropped to the rock as the behemoth sailed a few meters overhead and vanished into the mist.

Sandoval laughed. This was the first place he had ever seen a living aerodon. Even after nine years, the exhilaration of seeing one hadn't faded.

"They feed on the detritus blown up from below, like Earth whales on krill. I've found dozens of these upwellings in the reserve, and on any given evening, aerodon ride the thermals."

"I've not heard of this behavior."

"Few have." Sandoval intended to keep it that way.

A second aerodon grew larger as it rose from below. It spun slowly like a top, its frilled appendages weaving intricate patterns in the mist.

As it crested the granite outcropping and floated overhead, something angular and square caught Sandoval's eye. Attached to a tusk was a metal box, but before Sandoval could get a good look at it, the aerodon turned back into the mist.

Sandoval blinked, not sure what he had seen. "Did you—"

Boerstein nodded. "That looked like a transmitter."

Sandoval's gut tightened. "A Judas goat."

"That only works with social animals. Aerodon aren't social."

"For the most part, they aren't." In his time in the C.I., Sandoval had learned much about aerodon ecology. At first, his interest had been fueled only by his need for a steady supply of HeepA. Eventually it developed into biophilia.

"They come together the night after the full moon," Sandoval said. "If I had to guess, I'd say it's a lekking behavior."

"You've seen this?"

"Several times. Always at the same place." Sandoval's mouth was dry. "The full moon is tonight."

"We need to be there," Boerstein said. "How far is this gathering place?"

"If we leave at first light, we'll be there tomorrow afternoon."

#

Sandoval lay awake in the pressure tent. Upon returning, his body had warmed up, but the tingling in his right hand had not subsided. He needed another dose of HeepA.

The syringe in his cold suit pocket pressed against his thigh as he lay in the moon-glow, but Boerstein dozed fitfully only a half meter away.

Sandoval tucked his fingers into his armpits. He couldn't risk it. Not yet.

#

Over the course of the day, the tingling spread to Sandoval's left hand and foot, and handling the skimmer became challenging. To make matters worse, Boerstein had been energized by the encounter last night and wanted to learn more about the C.I. and the aerodons. Sandoval found it increasingly difficult to respond, and gradually his answers grew shorter and, he suspected, less coherent.

"I'm just on edge," Sandoval said after one of his responses drew a questionable look.

The gathering place was a kilometer wide area ringed by granite columns and scrub-topped islands. The columns funneled an easterly wind into a vortex that drew down cold air, flash freezing the mist into fine snow.

The skimmer shuddered in the buffeting wind as they circled one of the perimeter islands. Sandoval's landing sent a painful blow up his spine. He exhaled heavily.

Boerstein's grip on the edge of his seat eased and his fingers turned pink again as blood flowed back into the tips.

"The aerodon will enter over us," Sandoval said as

he powered down the skimmer's systems.

Boerstein squinted through the ice storm at the stunted vegetation. "At least this will provide cover," he said.

"Are you always this optimistic? Every day you see the worst of humanity."

Boerstein started to reply, but stopped. He licked cold-chapped lips. "I also see its best," he said. "The people who care, but, for whatever reason, can't get it done. I do more than just catch criminals; I help those who need it."

Ordinarily Sandoval would have mocked such an over-inflated hero-ego, but something in the way Boerstein's brow pinched together suggested his personal conviction had come with a price. His sincerity was genuine.

"Are you okay?" Boerstein watched Sandoval rubbing his hands together.

Sandoval tucked his fingers into his armpits. "Just cold," he said, turning away and pretending to look out the skimmer window. "So, do you have a plan?"

"When they realize they've hit the mother lode, I expect they'll bring in their rendering ship to facilitate harvesting. I've got a shoulder EMP cannon in the back capable of damaging a moderate-size ship at five hundred meters. Unfortunately its fuel cell is only good for three shots, so they need to count."

Sandoval shook his head, not sure if he'd heard Boerstein correctly.

Boerstein began checking his cold suit and O_2 enricher. "We just need to stay quiet until the ship comes in. Then a few well-placed shots ... Nothing but cleanup after that."

"Are you sure about this?"

"We don't exactly have time to call in reinforcements." Boerstein inserted his nasal cannula and took an experimental breath.

Sandoval's stomach hurt. This idea was crazy. Before he could protest, Boerstein cracked the canopy and stumbled out of the skimmer. The wind-driven sleet stung Sandoval's cheeks, and his exposed face went numb.

From the rear storage compartment, Boerstein unloaded the EMP cannon, a bulky cylinder tipped with a parabolic reflector and fitted with a curved shoulder stock. He handed a holstered pistol to Sandoval. "In case they're out of tangler range," he yelled above the wind. "We're only going to get one chance."

They hunkered down behind a granite boulder, out of the wind and sleet. Warmth seeped back into Sandoval's body, but the numbness in his limbs remained. In the dying light, the amber snow swirled around his head. Everything seemed surreal.

How many poachers were they facing? Certainly more than the two of them could handle, even with surprise on their side. Were they armed? So many unknowns ... too many things could go wrong.

As it darkened, the pit in Sandoval's stomach deepened. This was a stupid idea, he thought. They were going to get killed.

Gradually the mist began to glow blue as the unseen moon rose. Boerstein's breathing had settled into a deep rhythm.

At such close range, it would be easy for Sandoval to shoot him. A story about Boerstein's valiant death and his tumble into the abyss would satisfy headquarters. The thought surprised him, but it was a simple solution.

Slowly he drew his tangler, but the weapon turned in his numb hand and dropped to the ground. He cursed the pins-and-needles stabbing his elbow.

"Did you hear that?" Boerstein rolled to his knees and peered over the boulder.

Two skimmers shot overhead, barely visible in the driving snow. Startled, Sandoval ducked.

"They're down," Boerstein said. "Two skimmers, six men." In the faint moon-glow, his face was shadowy and grim. "They need you," he said, extending his hand toward Sandoval.

At that moment, the first aerodon arrived, a dark shape in the grey mist. Three skimmers darted across the sky, circling and spotlighting it, herding it toward the island.

Sandoval reached for Boerstein's hand and with the man's help scrambled to his feet. He braced his weapon on the boulder, but Boerstein covered the end with his glove. The move nearly knocked the weapon from Sandoval's hand.

"Not yet."

A harpoon gun cracked. Sandoval flinched.

The circling aerodon tried to turn away, but was struck in its float bladder by the harpoon.

The poachers cheered.

"They'll kill it."

"If they get away, more than that one will die."

Another harpoon gun cracked. The aerodon squealed. Its tentacles whipped the air.

The poachers attached the line to a skimmer-mounted winch and began to reel the aerodon in like a bloated fish.

A second aerodon floated through the spotlights.

Then a third. Skimmers darted overhead, ensuring the animals stayed close while the poachers scrambled to reload the harpoons.

The cannons cracked over the howl of the wind.

"They're going to slaughter them."

Boerstein's brow crinkled. He scanned the mist. "Where are you?"

The harpoon cannon fired again, striking flesh and drawing forth another cheer from the poachers.

Sandoval had a clear shot at the poacher manning one of the harpoon cannons, but his hands trembled violently. He tried to tighten his grip, but the weapon would not sit steady. He felt helpless and betrayed. "Do something."

The sky lit up as if the sun had gone nova, overloading Sandoval's retinas. It seemed to take forever for his vision to clear, but when it did, a wide disc, rimmed with lights, hung in the mist like a phosphorescent sea creature. Two massive engine cones mounted on opposite edges of the disc held the ship in position just off the cloud island.

Sandoval heard a high-pitched whine and a delicate pop as Boerstein discharged the EMP cannon. As the weapon recharged, he adjusted his aim. He pulled the trigger again.

"I need to get closer." Boerstein darted forward in a crouching run. About twenty meters from the boulder, he dropped to a knee and steadied the cannon on his shoulder.

Sandoval heard nothing, but the ship's spotlights went out and one of the engine cones went dark. The ship listed to the side. Hot exhaust from the other engine blasted through the poachers on the ground and knocked Boerstein from his feet. Sandoval's goggles flew off his face. The hot wash burned his cheeks and eyelids.

The ship's disc caught the wind, driving its edge downward. The engine wash lifted away from the island as the ship dropped suddenly. As it fell, it struck the granite edge of the island, shearing metal in a shower of sparks. The ground shook, and Sandoval thought the entire island might crumble.

Caught in the down-drafting vortex, the ship buckled, its hull whining as it folded and tore. It tumbled into the abyss, venting gases and flame that lit the mist sunset-gold.

Sandoval pulled himself back up onto the boulder. The heat from the engine wash had melted the ice, which was quickly refreezing into a glassy skin. He blinked at the ice crystals in his eyes.

In front of him nothing moved. One of the skimmers lay on its canopy. Its spotlight now cut a harsh white line across the landscape. For the moment, the C.I. was quiet.

Sandoval saw movement out of the corner of his eye. Dragging his left leg behind him, Boerstein pulled himself toward the upside-down skimmer. One of the poachers, who must have been shielded from the fiery explosion by the other skimmer, popped up and surveyed the area. When he saw Boerstein, he dropped down, out of sight.

Boerstein arrived at the skimmer and propped himself against it. He rubbed his injured leg.

The poacher crept across the open space between the skimmers. He held a pistol.

Boerstein appeared unaware of the approaching danger.

His tangler gone, Sandoval drew the pistol

Boerstein had given him. He had a clear shot at the poacher, provided he could steady the weapon. He tightened his grip, but the muzzle trembled. His back ached as if someone had kicked him in the kidneys.

He looked at the fingers he could no longer feel. Even if he made it through this, he realized it was all over. He would not be able to hide his condition from Boerstein, and the Reserve Authority would remove him from the C.I. He wondered how long he would live using the inferior HeepA analogs.

Sandoval eased his finger off the trigger. If he did nothing, the poacher would solve his problem. He could then inject his HeepA and escape in the skimmer. The remaining poacher was not a significant threat.

Overhead, an aerodon floated through the spotlight. Still tethered by its harpoon, it traced a gentle arc back into the darkness.

Sandoval wondered what he would do the next time poachers came to the C.I. He had not been able to stop them. Boerstein had saved the aerodons. Would his replacement be willing to fight for those who could not fight for themselves?

Sandoval bore down on the weapon and, propped against the rock, managed to steady the barrel. Sandoval grimaced against the stab of pins-and-needles in his arms and legs. It was now or never. He squeezed the trigger and the weapon jerked against his hand, but he held it steady.

The poacher spun and dropped.

Sandoval's legs buckled and he fell onto his back. He lay stunned. With each breath, his ribs ached. He fumbled at his cold-suit pocket, but his fingers could not work the zipper. He collapsed back and lay still.

An aerodon floated across his vision, its body ringed by rainbow halos from the ice in Sandoval's eyelashes. Sandoval smiled.

His view of the sky was eclipsed by Boerstein's face. Blood flowed from a cut that vanished into the hairline above his right eye. The right shoulder of his cold-suit hung in tatters. "Your syringe, where is it?"

Sandoval blinked at the ice. Had he heard Boerstein correctly over the wind? "How ..."

"It all adds up," Boerstein said. "The muscle twitches, the aerodons, Besel. Yet I wasn't sure until just now. Your syringe, Mr. Sandoval."

Sandoval looked in the direction of his cold-suit pocket. Boerstein removed the syringe. Backlit by the spotlights, the cylinder of HeepA glowed like an emerald.

Boerstein rolled Sandoval onto his side and gently pushed his head forward to separate the cervical vertebrae.

A pinch at the base of Sandoval's neck was followed by warmth washing across his shoulders and up into his head. Then he was on his back again, looking up into Boerstein's face.

"You are a rare species, Mr. Sandoval. To live, they must die, yet you are willing to give your life for them. What you were willing to do, and not do, to protect these animals speaks volumes. You are an important part of this place. It needs you as much as you need it. I can't think of a better person to do this job."

Sandoval flexed his tingling fingers. The nerves burned as feeling returned. He grimaced.
Overhead the harpooned aerodons continued to trace graceful circles through the snow. As soon as he could, Sandoval would set them free.

Story Notes
Strand in the Web

Way back in 2010, my writing group, Hopefull Monsters, decided to do a writing challenge in which we each supplied a writing prompt, and then selected one from the collection, and wrote a story. We had a collection of four or five fantastic prompts, and I selected the one from fellow writer, Annette Bowman: *My, but it is lovely tonight. The pink elephants are dancing spectacularly.*

Something about the idea of pink elephants, and all it suggested, appealed to me. I started brainstorming ideas about elephants, which are endangered animals often poached for illegal trade (*e.g.*, bladders, tusks, etc.). I decided early on to set the story in an extraterrestrial nature reserve, where illegal poaching was a problem. After that, the other pieces for "Strand in the Web" quickly fell into place: a main character who was morally grey, yet sympathetic; an entire ecosystem, not just the "pink elephants," that could be explored; and an environmental theme, linked closely to the main character's internal and external conflict.

I wrote the first draft of "Strand in the Web" in less than a week, and received fantastic feedback from the group. Revisions took another nine months— actually eight months of it sitting untouched, followed by a few weeks of intense rewriting. It made the rounds to a few places, until *Goldfish Grimm's* picked it up.

Portraits from the Shadow

First published in *InterGalactic Medicine Show*, August 2013

WHEN TRUNG DISEMBARKED AT LAX, the dead began whispering to him. In the underground tunnel connecting the international terminal to the domestic one, the spirit of a young woman whimpered from the murky shadows. He tried to console her, but only managed to attract the attention of a uniformed man who told him to move along. In Denver, the ghost of an angry teen hissed at him as he stepped off the rental car shuttle. All along the lonely road twisting up through the forest of snow-capped pines, lost spirits glared at him from the edge of the blacktop. America, like Vietnam, had a problem with ghosts.

Trung was thankful when he arrived at Hampton McElvy's cabin and found no spirits haunting it. His fingers ached as he released the steering wheel and sat quietly, trying to collect himself. He had traveled halfway around the world to speak with McElvy. What if the man couldn't help him? Trung wasn't sure he could handle another disappointment.

He touched the pocket of his jacket. The crinkle of the paper within reassured him. Trung dismissed thoughts of failure.

After several deep breaths, he climbed onto the porch and rapped quietly on the plank door. The hinges creaked; an eye squinted out through the narrow crack.

"I don't give interviews anymore," McElvy said,

his drawl sounding like John Wayne. To Trung, every American sounded like John Wayne.

The door started to close.

"No interview," Trung said, putting his hand against the wood. He removed the yellowed rectangle of newsprint from his pocket and held it up for McElvy to see.

"I don't talk about that anymore," McElvy said.

"Please, I came from Vietnam to speak to you."

The eye blinked at him.

"I am hopeful you can tell me about this man," Trung said. "He is my father."

#

Trung set the clipping on the table between them. Three weeks ago, he had found it among his mother's things after her funeral. Trung had never seen a picture of his father before, but his uncle had confirmed the identity of the man in the newspaper photo.

McElvy studied his knuckles as his knobby fingers worked them over. Life had taken a knife to his face and carved fissures around his eyes and across his forehead. "Ask what you need to ask," he said.

Even with the wood fire in the stove, a chill clung to the room.

"My name is Nguyễn Hiếu Trung. I am from Vietnam. For twenty years I have searched for my father's spirit so I can bring it home, but I cannot find him. Do you remember this man?"

The way McElvy's mouth twitched, it looked to Trung like he was having a conversation with himself.

Trung shifted in the wooden chair. He thought about the money he had spent to get there and was starting to regret his decision. Impulsive and wasteful, he chided himself. Maybe his uncle had been right after all. Why would an American remember a single North Vietnamese soldier he had photographed over forty years ago?

"I remember 'em all," McElvy said, his voice barely audible. "They don't let me forget …"

#

In January of '68, I volunteered to go to Vietnam as a stringer for the Associated Press. If you wanted to make a name for yourself, that's what you did. I was fresh off the tarmac when the North launched the Tet Offensive. They took the ancient city of Huế, about fifteen miles north of where I was housed with the 5th Marines.

Huế was crawling with NVA. Bullets and bombs. Booby traps everywhere, and not the kind that killed you fast, but the kind that took off a foot or a hand or cut you deep enough that you'd bleed to death 'cause they couldn't get choppers in with all the heat.

I spent two weeks thinking I'd never see another day. I slept next to bodies, with their stink for a blanket. When I ate my rations, I ate death. At night, we'd hole-up in some dark building, and we'd hear screaming and groaning outside. Sometimes in English, sometimes not. Nothing we could do. We learned that lesson quick, when a marine tried to help a little boy burned by napalm. He took a bullet in the neck and screamed until he finally died. Seemed like it took an hour, but couldn't have been more than a minute. We couldn't get to him; all we could do was watch and listen, listen to him gurgling and weeping, as he bled into his lungs.

Lance Corporal Stillman. Nineteen. He had a girl back in Omaha and a baby on the way who would never see his daddy.

#

McElvy's Adam's apple slid up and down his long throat like a yoyo on a string. "You can't learn to survive something like Huế," he said. "It was sheer dumb-ass luck who came home and who didn't."

Outside, the day darkened as snow began to fall. The yellow light from the overhead bulb huddled around the two men, as if it was afraid to venture into the room's darkening corners.

"We lost a lot of good people over there, but then, so did you."

Every person Trung knew had lost family members in the war: fathers, mothers, brothers, sisters, millions of Vietnamese people. Many of them had never been found or properly buried, leaving their ghosts trapped in the shadow between the pain of the living and the peace of the afterlife. As long as their loved ones were lost, the living had failed their ancestors and would not prosper.

Trung had devoted his life to using his gift to reunite families with their lost dead, or just as often, the dead with their lost families. Yet, after years of searching, he had never been able to find the one ghost he truly needed to.

McElvy's bloodless-white knuckles gripped the edge of the table. "In Huế, I was sure death was looking for me," he said. "I couldn't have been more right and more wrong."

#

The day after Stillman died, we got lit up by the NVA. In that craziness, I got separated, which is not a good place to be with nothing but a Nikon F. Not knowing what else to do, I ran. No care for how or where.

I ran until I got my wits back enough to realize running like that would do nothing but get me killed. I ducked into a building that at least had walls and a roof. I found a dark corner and sat there and shook and shook. Couldn't stop myself.

About that time is when I saw him. He came in through a doorway from another room. A marine, young, face smeared with dirt and paint, all quiet like. He squatted next to me, leaned on his rifle like it was a walking stick, and that's when I recognized him.

I thought I was hallucinating or maybe it was his brother. I didn't know. I said, "Is that you Stillman? You okay?"

He had this look on his face, serene, like the world no longer mattered to him, like he was beyond it all, aloof. Yet I could see a sadness in the tilt of his eyes and the way he looked past me, like watching something faraway, something wonderful that he could never get to.

I touched his arm to get his attention. It was cold, unnaturally cold, and my stomach dropped out of me like I fell out of an airplane.

I did then what I was trained to do. I took his picture. I shot his face wide open at a thousandth, because of the light. Soft on the edges, but the eyes were sharp enough to see right into his soul. Right in, like lookin' down a well. Then he stood up.

I hissed at him to stay down or Charlie might see him, but he didn't need to worry about that anymore.

He paused at the doorway he'd come out of, and motioned for me to come with him. Then he was gone.

#

McElvy's mouth worked like he was chewing a piece of gristle. "I saw Stillman die, but there he was."

Realizing he hadn't been breathing, Trung drew a sharp breath. He couldn't decide if McElvy was telling the truth or if the stress of combat had caused him to see things. Vietnam was full of spirit mediums who claimed to have the gift to commune with the dead, but in Trung's experience, few people had the true gift to do that. Most were charlatans taking advantage of people's need for closure. "In Vietnam, we believe the dead can haunt the living. They can be helpful or they can hurt you. Vietnam is a land of ghosts, many from the War with America, and we cannot forget the lost ones. To do so dishonors them and dishonors us."

McElvy looked up from his hands with weary eyes.

The room seemed cold enough to crystallize the old man's breath, but only words came out of his mouth.

#

After Stillman went through that door, I sat there for a long time trying to figure out if I was hallucinating. It crossed my mind that maybe I was already dead, and to be honest, to this day I don't know if I am or not.

But I was a photographer, a journalist, and my curiosity wouldn't let me be.

As I neared the doorway, I heard a droning sound.

Some light came in through a hole on that side of the building, so I could see into the other room. It was filled with flies, everywhere, like a cloud of black pebbles. The biggest flies I've ever seen, but then, with all them bodies, what did I expect?

Must have been two, three hundred of 'em, laying on the ground like they were knocked over bowling pins. Women still clutching little kids, old men with their hands tied behind their backs. Many of them gaped up at me appalled, like I'd crashed some private party. They was all shot in the back of the head, execution style.

I just stood there, looking, 'cause I didn't know what else to do, and that's when I saw her. A young woman, movie-star beautiful. Sitting there with no expression I could read on her face, sort of as if she had no opinion one way or the other about what had happened. She looked through me, with eyes like Stillman's—faraway. The pupils big, so I could see right into them. I could see flashes of who she was, her life, like little vignettes played out with shadow puppets.

My hands were shaking so much, I could barely lift my camera, but when I got it up to my eye, everything just changed. My hands went rock-steady. Without thought, they worked my Nikon's settings: f/16 at a thirtieth, because I wanted to see every strand of dark hair as it framed her face. I shot only one picture; then she got up and left. As she did, an old man sat down in her place. I shot him from slightly above, f/4 at one-five-hundredth, so his face would rise up out of the bodies beneath him.

More came. Kids with their mothers, men not fit to fight, more women, some beautiful, some not. I never changed film; it never occurred to me. I just kept shooting and shooting and shooting, picture after picture, and then they'd get up and leave and go someplace I-don't-know-where because someone else always sat down. I took pictures until it got too dark.

Then everything got quiet. No flies, no explosions, no screams. Just quiet.

For the first time since entering Huế, I felt at peace.

I sat in that room all night, so dark I could see nothing. The stink must have been incredible, but the whole damn city stank, so I didn't notice.

I saw him with the first light. Where he came from, I don't know. He sat among the bodies, like a heron in a rice paddy. Sat there, perfectly still. He wore a NVA uniform, and scared me so much I nearly pissed myself. But then I saw his face, and I knew I had nothing to fear. I saw what looked like regret, maybe for things done, or maybe not done.

We sat like that until the dawn moved across the floor and put light on him. Then I took his picture. It was the last one I remember taking.

#

McElvy held the yellowed newsprint in his trembling hands. "I photographed your daddy wide open at a thirtieth. It never should have come out," he said, "but he wouldn't be denied."

Trung's body thrummed. If he could find the building, maybe he could find his father's spirit, not to mention the hundreds of others that likely still haunted that killing ground. "Where was this place?"

McElvy shrugged.

Trung's face flushed hot. How could McElvy

72

dismiss his question? Trung restrained himself from raising his voice. He was in McElvy's home, and as an American, McElvy could not understand the importance of bringing lost spirits home. Trung lowered his eyes as he tried to balance his challenge with a show of respect. "You must help me find that building."

"It wasn't far from the place they call the Citadel, but I can't say more. Getting there was crazy. Getting out, *I* was crazy. A group from the 5th Marines found me seven days later, still sittin' there. They heard my camera clicking, and pried it out of my hands, so I was told some days later. I don't remember any of it after that first night. Finding that building doesn't matter, though, because he ain't there. None of them are there anymore."

Trung exhaled a sharp breath. He closed his eyes and concentrated on slowing his pulse. What did this American know? It didn't matter that the bodies were no longer there; the bodies were not important.

McElvy grabbed Trung's wrist; his cold fingers sucked away any warmth remaining in Trung's arm. "He ain't there." McElvy's eyes had a wild gleam to them.

Trung pulled his arm away. His chair scraped back several inches with the sudden motion. He had seen that same glint in the eyes of some of the Vietnamese veterans, the ones who hadn't been able to leave the war behind.

"There ain't no rhyme or reason," McElvy said. "Why does one man die when his buddy next to him lives? What makes good men do bad things?" McElvy rose. In the sepia halo of light, he seemed much taller than Trung remembered. "You came all this way to find your daddy, didn't you?" He retreated into the shadows lingering at the room's perimeter. He stopped at a door that Trung had not noticed before.

McElvy tugged at the bolt with his knobby fingers until it gave.

Trung rose and backed away. "What's in there?"

McElvy pulled the door aside. The opening was a black rectangle etched on the darkness. Without answering, McElvy stepped through the doorway and was gone.

Silence settled on the room like a snowfall. Trung hugged his arms and shivered. Out the window, snow collected on the windshield of his rental car. At the rate it was sticking, the road would soon be impassable, and he would be trapped here. Trung became uncomfortably aware of how little he knew about McElvy or his prejudices.

Trung picked up the newspaper clipping and stuffed it into his pocket. McElvy had admitted that he had nothing else he could tell him about the whereabouts of his father. If he left now, he could at least get back to a road that might still be clear of snow. Yet, Trung had crossed the world to learn everything he could about his father. Was there anything else McElvy could tell him? If there was anything more, no matter how small, he could not leave.

Trung stopped at the doorway through which McElvy had disappeared. Cold air, like that from a meat locker, blew out the opening and sent a violent shiver through his entire body. After several long seconds, his eyes adjusted to the dimness of the narrow room, its windows covered with thick oil cloths to block out the light.

McElvy stood before a bank of file cabinets. The mist from his breath swirled around his head as he spoke.

#

I spent a month in a hospital in Saigon; then I left Vietnam. I gave my film to the AP, and told them I was done. When I got home, I put my camera in a box and tried to go about my life, but you don't just go back to life after that. You don't just shower away that kind of filth.

I started hearing voices, soldiers, women, crying babies, English and Vietnamese and God knows what else. I thought I was going crazy. They were coming from my closet. When I opened the door, I would hear them like they were hiding in the pockets of my shirts. I pulled my closet apart, looking everywhere for them. My shoes. The pockets of my pants. The boxes of junk. Then I found my Nikon. The voices were coming out of it. I opened the back and inside was a roll of film.

I'm sure I gave the AP all my film, every last bloody roll of it. Yet there it was, and as I held it in my hands, I could hear the voices so loud in my head, all talking at me so I couldn't separate any single one, like I was in a huge crowd, and all of them were clamoring for my attention.

I cleared off my dark room and developed the roll, but the film was blank, until I started making prints. Then I saw the faces. The first one was Lance Corporal Stillman. When I touched his print, I heard his voice in my head, clear as if he was standing next me and speaking into my ear. He told me about how much he missed his wife, and how sorry he was that he would never see his baby grow up. He begged me to find them and tell them that he loved them. He begged me to take him home.

I promised him I would.

I printed photo after photo, hundreds of 'em, all from that blank roll of film. Each portrait spoke to me as I printed it and hung it to dry. There were more faces than I remembered from that room, there were soldiers, both American and Vietnamese, more civilians, more children, more women and men. Hundreds upon hundreds like everyone who died at Huế had lined up for their portrait.

Sometimes they asked me to find their parents or husbands or wives. Sometimes they begged me to tell their story. Sometimes they just cried, and I couldn't understand what they wanted. Most I couldn't understand, 'cause I don't speak Vietnamese.

I kept my promise to Stillman. It took me months to find his widow. When I told her why I was there, she slapped me across the face and slammed the door on me. I slipped the portrait underneath. As I let it go, I felt Stillman's presence leave in peace. He was home, and he seemed to know it.

As I walked away, the door opened, and she stood there, tears on her face, holding my picture in one hand, Stillman's baby in the other. She didn't say anything to me, but I could see everything I needed to see in her eyes.

#

McElvy pulled open a drawer of the file cabinet. Stuffed inside were old manila envelopes.

Trung came forward, as if reeled into the dark room by a string. He felt an energy emanating from the drawer. At first it rose up from the tattered envelopes like a murmur, but as he drew nearer, it grew louder, like a crowd awakening from a long sleep. In the noise, Trung heard voices, jumbled together like noodles.

"I tried to find them all," McElvy said, "but I didn't even know where to start. In '76, I went back to Saigon—Hồ Chí Mihn City—not an easy thing to do at that time. With the help of a Vietnamese art dealer, I hung pictures in some galleries, hoping someone would recognize them, hoping someone would hear something and believe me. Your daddy's picture was one of them. But I got nothing."

Trung's hand hovered over the envelopes. Goosebumps rose on the back. Without thought, he reached into the drawer and pulled out an envelope. It took both hands to work it free.

"I took good care of them," McElvy said, "as well as I could, but they want to go home. They need to go home."

Trung's fingers shook so much he had difficulty unwinding the thread that held the flap closed. He slid a glossy print halfway out. His father's eyes, stared at him. He looked younger than he ever imagined.

"I—" Trung's voice cracked in his throat. He pressed the photograph against his cheek, unable to speak. The picture smelled of mildew and age, but it was warm against his skin, like a parent's comforting hand. Trung closed his eyes and imagined what his life would have been like with his father. His uncle had done as well as he could, but sometimes a boy simply needed his father.

"It's me; it's Trung," he whispered in Vietnamese.

"I'm sorry," his father said gently into his ear.

Trung held the picture out and looked again into the eyes. They were crisp and clear, the edges pulled with sadness.

"If only I had obeyed, I would have been there for you," his father said.

In his father's eyes, Trung saw the room in Huế, the hundreds of unarmed people kneeling with their backs to a line of Vietnamese soldiers. Over the crying children and women, a Vietnamese officer screamed at the soldiers to rid Vietnam of the imperialist sympathizers. When the soldiers hesitated, the officer drew his pistol and shot the soldier nearest him who had lowered his rifle. As the bullet ripped through his father's head, the line of rifles popped and rattled.

Trung screamed out, the picture crumpling in his hand. He pressed it to his forehead and wept.

#

The photo in Trung's shirt pocket warmed his chest as he loaded the last of the sealed boxes into the back of the rental car. As he let go of it, the voices faded but did not go away.

Trung turned to McElvy standing in the snow to the side. He bowed to the old man. "I owe you—"

McElvy took his hand. "No," he said, and pressed a wad of green bills into Trung's palm. "To help."

Trung looked at the money. He had done nothing to deserve it, but to give it back would be an insult. He would earn the money then, he decided. "I will find their families," Trung said, knowing it was what McElvy needed to hear.

The lines around the old man's eyes softened.

As Trung pulled out onto the snowy road, the murmuring in the back of the car grew animated. The dead knew their journey home had finally begun.

Inspiration is an odd thing. Sometimes I know what inspired a story; other times I don't. While I don't know exactly what inspired "Portraits from the Shadow," I can think of three things that were at the front of my mind as I wrote it and certainly affected the final story.

Some time ago, a member of my writing group Hopefull Monsters posted a story for critique about a woman whose paintings became the reality for her world. It was a wonderful story and an even more wonderful idea. That story didn't inspire "Portraits from the Shadow," but I believe it played a role in the process.

Many years ago, I spent six weeks traveling in Papua-New Guinea. I spent two of those weeks in the highlands, among some of the most diverse cultures I've ever experienced. Before going, I was advised to refrain from photographing the indigenous people for a couple of reason: (1) it's rude to just take someone's picture without asking, and (2) some of the cultures believed creating an image of them would steal their soul. This experience also didn't inspire "Portraits from the Shadow," but I thought about it a lot while I was writing.

Finally, my father fought in the Korean and Vietnam wars. He never talked about his experiences in either, and I never asked. I figured these were likely not the best years of his life, and based on the stories I've heard from soldiers who fought in Vietnam, these were likely memories best left unvisited. My father passed away many years ago, and as part of his memorial, my siblings and I assembled a slide show of his life, including pictures from his time in Korea and Vietnam. Those pictures really moved me; he was so young (much younger than I am now), and he had already seen things I could never imagine, and that I hope to never see. Those events shaped who he was, even if he never spoke of them, and for the first time, I thought I understood my father better than ever before. I knew then that the Vietnam War had to be an important event in "Portraits from the Shadow."

While none of these things directly inspired "Portraits from the Shadow," they all helped shape it after I had started writing it. Regardless of where this story came from, this one is among my favorites for very personal reasons. It's a story about sacrifice, love, and family.

Mementoes from My Lives (Un)Lived

First published in *Nature: Futures*, June 2021

"WHAT ABOUT THIS ONE?" my granddaughter Sky asks, pointing her tiny hand at a length of rubbery hose, coiled neatly on the shelf. Her wide eyes hang like twin moons in the night.

"That's the leash from the surfboard I rode to the big wave world championship," I say. "I was fifty-seven."

"That must have been a long time ago," she says with the innocence only a six-year-old can bring to such a statement. "Was it scary?"

"I suppose so." In this universe, I've never surfed a wave, but Sky has already moved on to the next item on my shelf of mementoes, a petite, ceramic spoon nestled atop a velvet pillow. "That's from when I served as the royal ice cream taster for King Olaf of Norway." The spoon, crafted to fit the curves of my hand, is keenly balanced and insulated so the handle never gets cold, even left submerged in a double scoop of chocolate decadence.

My daughter Dakota, Sky's mother, looks up from her crossword puzzle. "Dad …" She sits down the hall, in the wingback chair near the fireplace in the cabin's "great" room.

"It's true," I insist. "The multiverse makes it so."

Dakota rolls her eyes. "You're filling her head with

fantasies."

"Since when are fantasies a bad thing, right Sky?"

The little girl squeals, jumping up and down. "Fantasies are awesome!"

"And this," I say, picking up a small silver bell, "was from my time serving as the Bell Summoner in the court of our Tardak overlords."

Sky's lips roll into an "oh" shape.

I show her the bottom of the bell. "Notice it's stuffed with cotton. If I were to ring it, the Tardak would appear from a transdimensional rift and enslave our planet."

"Did you hear that, Mommy? They come on a transdimental raft if papa rings the bell."

Dakota shakes her head and turns her attention back to her crossword with an exasperated, "Daaaaad."

"How did you do all these things?" Sky asks waving her hands at the dozens of mementoes we have yet to explore.

I have spent years collecting the items. I palmed the queen of diamonds from a casino in Monte Carlo while I was swindling the house as a card shark. The ostrich feather had been plucked from a large fan in the middle of my head-turning dance as a female impersonator in a vaudevillian revival. And the spiked collar? I removed it from the neck of a convicted man brought to justice when I served as an Enforcer of the Seventh Seal of the Proterean Assembly. Every memento came from a life I lived, even if it wasn't my life.

Sky stares up at me, still awaiting my answer.

"The universe is limitless," I say, tussling her hair. "We all have the potential within us to be anything and everything."

"Even me?"

"Especially you."

"I want to be a unicorn brusher."

"A unicorn brusher? Now, that is a very important job." I retrieve a small purple brush with a sparkly handle from the top shelf. "I used this on fairy horses when I worked as a groom for the Lady of the Mushroom Circle, but I don't see why it wouldn't work on unicorns."

Sky looks at her mom in the adjacent room.

Dakota sighs and nods, knowing that she'll be taking home another cheap, plastic toy. But what Dakota doesn't realize, is the brush is not a cheap, plastic toy, but a memento that her daughter will now cherish.

Sky takes the brush and dashes away to try it out on one of her stuffed animals.

Dakota joins me at the hutch in the hallway. "Where did you really get all this stuff, Dad?" She picks up a sleek, metal spyglass and holds it up to her eye. The brass cylinder is engraved with unintelligible runes. "You never had these things when I was little."

"Where do you think I went when I was attending those conferences." I tap finger quotes around the word "conferences." Motioning to the spyglass in her hand, I say, "That's from my time as navigator aboard Slick Silver's sky corsair."

Dakota returns the spyglass to its spot on the shelf. "You know unicorns don't exist, right, Dad?"

"I believe they exist somewhere, and in that universe, they'll have unicorn groomers."

"Your multiverse and wave whatchamacallit stuff."

"Wave functions and probability densities," I say

with a nod. "In an infinite multiverse, anything is possible; some outcomes are just more probable than others. In truth, dear daughter, all possibilities will exist because—"

With a shake of her head, Dakota finishes what I was going to say "—because in an infinite multiverse, every event with a non-zero probability is a certainty."

"Truly, you are my daughter," I say with a touch of pride.

Dakota smirks. "In this universe, yes."

One of my mementoes catches her eye, and she picks up a pair of small, leather shoes, only slightly scuffed. Her left eyebrow arches in my direction.

My throat tightens. Frowning, I say, "Life is precious and to be cherished because a long life is not necessarily our most probable outcome."

Sometimes the kernel of an idea just seems to come to me, like it was spontaneously generated from the aether. However, this isn't the case for "Mementos from My Lives (Un)Lived." The origins of this story are fitting for the publication in which it originally appeared. *Nature* is one of the top scientific journals in the world—for biologists, it's the equivalent of an *Asimov's* or *Magazine of Fantasy and Science Fiction* to speculative fiction writers—so I guess it's fitting that this story arose from an analytical approach to story writing.

Sitting around one day during the COVID lockdown, I decided to build a random prompt generator. I use writing prompts on occasion to force myself to think outside of my usual creative box. I spent about an hour compiling hundreds of prompts from dozens of internet sites and feeding them into a simple randomizer built in Microsoft Excel that would output a new prompt every day. On the second day using this prompt generator, I drew: *You get to go to any museum in the world. Which one do you choose?*

Inspired, I immediately began brainstorming the most unusual types of museums I could imagine, and quickly hit upon a museum of artefacts from different dimensions, all of which would tell the potential life story of a single person. From there, it was a short jump to the personal story of a grandfather (who very much reminds me of my father-in-law, a theoretical physicist) and his granddaughter, Sky, all tied together by one of my favorite sayings about probability: given enough time, the improbable is certain to happen.

This story essentially wrote itself, taking about an hour and appearing pretty much as it was published. I am particularly proud of the range of emotion captured in this story, going from light and whimsical to darkly serious in the span of about 850 words.

Carbon Zero

First published in *Lightspeed Magazine*, December 2023

"Is there a problem, officer?"

"We're not the police." My partner, Enrico, places his palm against the door, ready to test the old man's resolve.

I tap my finger against my thumb and SNAPbeam the warrant to the old man's synaptic cache. "We're EPF."

"Oh," the old man whispers, as if his voice has been snatched away.

No one likes the police showing up on their porch, but they would rather the police come knocking than the EPF. Years of aggressive action against climate violators has given the Environmental Protection Force its well-earned reputation.

We give him a moment to review the warrant, signed, sealed, and legally enforceable in any jurisdiction on Earth.

"Give me a second to tidy—"

Enrico doesn't let the door close. "We don't care if you haven't dusted, Mr. Costa."

Being no match for two young, modded investigators, Costa retreats. "Close the door," he says. "You're letting in the smoke."

Spurred by the early arrival of the annual heatdome and the decades-long drought, the Agalhor Creek fire has been raging for weeks and recently combined with three smaller blazes to produce the season's first mega-inferno event.

It's going to be a bad fire year, and the UNEP has already issued warnings that our suppression systems might not protect key population centers. Indeed, Agalhor Creek is spitting off dozens of fire whirls, and the turbulence was so bad, our hydro-cell skimmer nearly diverted during our final approach to the drop zone at the end of the old man's driveway.

Costa stands thin-lipped, arms crossed in defiance. My IR lenses clearly register depressed skin temperatures due to heavy sweating.

With the windows' thermal screens in place, the modest living room is cool and dim. A threadbare couch. A small dining table. One of those plug-in atomizers gently hisses, contributing to the room's oddly-cloying odor intended, one would assume, to mask the smell of the fire.

"Check his spongees," Enrico says, unclipping his analyzer from the belt ring next to his holster.

Costa raises his hands. "You have no right to touch me."

"International bylaw seven-seven-three gives me the authority." I SNAPbeam the relevant regulation to him, and without waiting, press my thumb to Costa's forehead. In a blink, I download his BIO-log to a secure evidence partition on my synaptic cache.

"I think you'll find everything in order," Costa says.

"I'm sure we will," Enrico mumbles as he follows his analyzer around the room's perimeter.

A day ago, Enrico had arrived from the Barcelona Office to assist our unit, which had been hard hit by the recent Lygma-13 outbreak among the rank-and-file investigators. Even I had been called back to the field. For the last eighteen months, I've been jockeying paperwork in the processing office because it afforded me the flexibility to be with my wife, Elena, during her chemo treatments.

I scan through Costa's data. His metallo-organic corpuscles and chloroplast implants are functioning within operational ranges. Costa's CO_2 emissions are below detectable levels as the bio-engineered MOCs in his lungs capture the carbon dioxide from his exhalations and shunt it to the photosynthetic nodules on the back of his hands for metabolic processing.

"What are you looking for?" Costa asks. His thermal signature tells me he's scared, although anyone hearing the tightness in the voice would already know that.

"It's in the warrant," Enrico says.

"I'm a historian, not a lawyer."

I almost hear the disdain in Enrico's eyebrow rise.

"Well, well. What have we here?" Enrico pushes open what should have been a bedroom door. He tosses the light switch, and several spots come alive. According to my lenses, they aren't standard LEDs, but full-spectrum lamps more typical of a greenhouse than a residence.

"That's just a hobby," Costa says.

Enrico extends his arm to stop the old man from entering the room.

"Let me guess," I say, coming over to the doorway. "Six vats?"

Enrico hands me his analyzer. "Close. I count seven."

The small room has been converted into an algae-growing facility. Seven one-hundred-litre containers have been hastily plumbed with water circulators and temperature modulators. Tucked among the vats is a portable air pump whose intake hose snakes over to the door. All but one of the tanks has murky, blackish water in them. If not for the air freshener in the other room, the whole house might have smelled sweetly of decay.

Enrico dips his finger into the one tank that has a skin of green algae on its surface. He holds it up in front of his left eye, and his lens magnifiers click as they cycle into place. "*Chlorella*," he says.

"I—I'm growing my own protein supplement," Costa says, again trying to enter the doorway.

"Stay over there." I point across the room, and reluctantly, Costa retreats.

"What was it?" Enrico asks, stepping out of the grow room. "A sudden bloom and then a die-off? *Chlorella* can be tricky that way, especially if you don't harvest it regularly. It takes a lot of know-how to get the growing medium balanced just right."

Costa is sweating heavily again, his eyes fixed on me as I raise the analyzer and resume the search pattern Enrico had started.

"But tell me," Enrico continues, "why seven vats for just the two of you? That's a lot of protein—"

Costa's eyes flick in Enrico's direction.

"Oh, yeah; there's supposed to be two of you here. You and your wife. What's her name? Susan or ..."

"Suzanna," Her name barely squeezes through the constriction in Costa's throat.

"That's right," Enrico says, as if he didn't already know the answer. "She out in the garden?"

Costa winces at Enrico's question.

I don't like where this is going, so I clear my

throat, hoping to divert my partner. We know Costa's wife has been ill, even if her sealed medical records deny us any specifics. Costa is more than likely up to something illegal, but that doesn't give us license to be cruel.

I turn my attention back to the climbing CO_2 numbers on the analyzer. They peak near the bookcase, and then fall off as I move past it.

"Those analyzers are top of the line," Enrico says conversationally. "Sensitive to carbon dioxide down to micromolar concentrations. It can detect a single exhale from a person without spongees."

I'm not sure Costa heard him; his gaze is focused intently on what I am doing.

"Seven vats," Enrico says again. "Did you know that's almost exactly the amount of *Chlorella* that would be needed to scrub the carbon dioxide from the exhaled air of one person?"

I push against the bookcase and feel it wiggle.

"Please ..." Costa says. His eyes shine wetly in the yellow light streaming in from the vat room.

My stomach tightens. I have an inkling of what I'm about to find, and I pray I am wrong. I push harder on the edge of the bookcase. Something clicks. The bookcase shifts and swings open on a set of concealed hinges.

My helmet lamp flickers on.

A scuffle breaks out as Enrico wrestles Costa against the wall and clips a neural restraint onto his forearm. The device saps the strength from Costa's muscles, and he slumps to the floor, barely able to even sit upright.

The old man wails like a wounded animal. "Don't hurt her! It's not her fault!"

A woman sits on the floor pressed into the corner of what must have been a coat closet before the bookcase had been installed. Her legs, little more than skin and bones, splay awkwardly beneath her like twigs strewn onto the ground. The backs of her hands are covered with black pustules where her chloroplast nodules should have been. Her head slowly rises, and she fixes me with pitiful eyes too large for her face.

"The cancer," Costa says. "Her body rejected the MOCs because of the cancer."

I grip the edge of the bookcase; my head feels like it will float away. What cancer has done this? Is this a preview of Elena's fate?

Enrico comes up next to me, his expression grim as he stares down at the husk cowering on the closet floor. "Seven-seven-three violation."

Decades of inaction have driven atmospheric carbon dioxide concentrations above five hundred parts per million. The world burns around us, caught in a positive feedback loop that threatens to run away. Net zero is no longer an option, and the direct air capture facilities cannot scrub fast enough. The Seven-seven-three mandate requires all humans to be modded to carbon zero because we have no wiggle room left between our survival and our extinction.

"Well?" Enrico asks.

I do not need to check the analyzer, but I do anyways. The readout flashes; CO_2 levels in the hidden room are above the acceptable range. Clearly Enrico's determination is correct, and yet, I hesitate, something I've never done before. For the first time in my career, I see, crumpled on the floor of that hidden room, something other than just a Seven-seven-three violation.

"I need your concurrence, Investigator Munich."

The analyzer beeps as it finishes logging its evidence with Geneva.

Costa sobs against the wall behind me. Surely, he knows what my concurrence means. The mandate exists for a reason and leaves no room for compassion or exception. I can do nothing except what is required by my oath and the law.

"Yes, a Seven-seven-three."

Before I have even finished speaking, Enrico draws his pistol.

I grab his arm and start to say something, but what case can I make?

My partner's eyes narrow. "She's dead anyways, and every breath she exhales is only killing the rest of us."

"Can we just—"

Enrico fires.

My knees buckle. I stumble against the bookcase for support.

Enrico turns. "Caesar Costa, you are an accessory to the violation of International Mandate Seven-seven-three. Do you have any defense?"

Costa has stopped crying and stares blankly up at us. "I loved her."

In my years as a field investigator, I have heard accessories offer many excuses, but none have risen to the level of a defense. I wonder now if this one should. Yet, I know it cannot. Not for Costa. Not for anyone, not even me.

I flinch as Enrico fires.

He holsters his pistol. "Our ride's incoming."

Enrico leaves the door open, allowing the reddish glow from the Agalhor fire to filter in through the smoke collecting in the room. The fire is only a few kilometers away, with the suppression walls the only thing left standing between this house's survival and extinction. Even if it doesn't burn down, will anyone want to live here after what we have done?

CARBON ZERO

For a while, I had wanted to write a story about climate change, but I hadn't been able to find a compelling story idea. As a biologist who is constantly confronted with the realities of the changing climate in my work, it was important to me that any story I wrote not sugar-coat the trajectory humanity is on. A few years ago, British Columbia, Canada (where I live) experienced one of the worst climate-driven, forest-fire seasons in its history. The smoke from the fires filled my home town and transformed the usually idyllic summer days into an apocalyptic landscape. It was so suffocating, I considered moving away from my home. During those days, it became clear that if we are to have any chance at averting a climate disaster, we must do more than just reduce our carbon output—we need to get to carbon zero or better.

In 2022, I saw a call for a small-press anthology that wanted science fiction stories about law enforcement. This call proved the catalyst for "Carbon Zero." Surprisingly, this story came very fast after I settled on the basic idea and had the main character and his conflict sorted out. This doesn't happen often, so it's notable when it does. I wrote the first draft of "Carbon Zero" in about an hour. I then did some additional research to nail down the details. I had the final story completed within a few days of when I started. "Carbon Zero" explores the human cost of what may become humanity's last chance to avert its own downfall. (As for that anthology prompt, "Carbon Zero" ended up being too long to submit to the anthology, but I guess things still worked out in my favor as it found a wonderful home at *Lightspeed Magazine*).

Forget the Rain

First published in *Kasma SF*, January 2014

WITH OUR SCOUTS COMMITTED to the defense of the northern front, it took me twelve days to find the Tembowatu. The first sign was a cloud of red dust smeared across the horizon like a smudge of blood.

A bad omen, I thought, washing the heat from my tongue with a sip from my canteen.

I set off across the ochre and beige scree on my cycle, which was old and ill-suited for the terrain. After a day, grit and heat crippled its engine. I nearly turned back, but I knew the Oluchi army stood poised to overrun my tribal lands and beat my people back into the dust and obscurity from which we had risen—those they did not slaughter, that is. So I continued on foot, stopping only to dig for water when my canteen grew dusty. I was rewarded late on the second day when I struggled to the crest of a ridge and found the Tembowatu watering their olophants at a muddy puddle.

I leaned on my rifle, panting heavily. Seeing the dark mud, I realized how thirsty I was, but I knew better than to approach the milling herd of giant beasts and their guardians.

Presently, a Tembowatu warrior hiked up to me. He wore only a pair of shorts, stained red from the mud he had smeared across his bare chest and into the dreadlocks of his hair. The dreads he had looped atop his head like a turban and affixed in place with two sticks of polished, blond wood.

"I am Masika," I said, when he stopped before me.

He balanced a long barreled rifle in his hand.

I tipped a finger of water into my canteen's dusty metal cap and extended it to him. "I bring water from the Land of the Sun and his eminence Isoba Chimola."

He eyed my offering warily. Eventually he took it from my hand. "This land is wide," he said, after he had returned the empty cup. "Surely your wives miss you."

"I hope to return to them soon," I said, "but to do that, I must first speak with Taonga." I watched his face, but saw no sign that my directness had offended him.

"These words must be important," he said.

"I bring an offer of prosperity."

For a moment I thought he would turn me away. Like most tribes, the Tembowatu and my people, the Masata, had a history of unpleasantness between us. Our war with the Oluchi went poorly, however, necessitating the need for allies.

He grunted and pointed at my rifle. Reluctantly I handed it to him; then I followed him down the slope, trying hard not to stumble.

\#

As I approached the waterhole, my neck craned back farther and farther to take in the great beasts. The olophants towered four stories over the red muck, siphoning muddy water into their mouths with thick trunks. The mud on the edge of the nearly drained hole cracked in the afternoon sun.

"Wait here," the warrior said. He trotted off, his

long-barreled rifle slung over his shoulder.

Descendants of elephants, the Tembowatu olophants were all that remained of the lineage. Generations of selective breeding had resulted in their great size, and the mutualistic relationship between the olophants and their guardians had led to the development of other peculiar physical traits.

I had never believed the stories until I saw the great howdahs upon their backs. Running along their sides, from the shoulders to the flanks, were platforms of spindly camelthorn branches. Yet it was the ivory ring glinting on the olophant's side that drew my eye. It framed an opening into the side of the great beast, leading to an internal chamber in which the Tembowatu lived. The arrangement was akin to the savannah trees that provided home-chambers and nectar for ants in exchange for protection from hungry grazers.

I shielded my eyes and watched the warrior shimmy up a rope to one of the platforms and disappear through the ivory ring.

The muck squished around my ankles. The earthy stench of mud and dung crinkled my nose.

Around me, in the shadow of the olophants, Tembowatu children scooped skittering lungfish with woven grass nets. Several stopped chasing fish and cautiously eyed me from a distance. How many of them knew what my people had done to their parents and grandparents?

The ground trembled as an olophant stomped the mud, startling me.

The children laughed and went back to their fishing.

Eventually the warrior returned. "Taonga will see

you."

#

Without the knots at knee-length intervals along the rope, I would not have managed to reach the platform twenty feet above me. The warrior motioned me toward the ivory-lined hole.

I peered into the darkness and forced myself not to turn away from the musky scent within. I stepped over the ivory frame into the gloom. The light from outside cast an oval on the floor, but did not penetrate deeply into the chamber. I stood just inside the opening, waiting for my eyes to adjust. Slowly features crawled out of the darkness.

The narrow chamber ran forward toward the olophant's head. It was inside the beast's ribs; thick bones rippled along the outer wall, curling into the floor, which was covered with soft hide mats.

A light flared at the far end of the chamber before dying back into a sputtering flame. A lamp swayed from a long cord, illuminating an old man sitting cross-legged on the floor. The dim light played off his wrinkles, making his face look like someone had drawn black lines on it with a charred twig. Two ivory sticks held his turban of woven hair in place.

I pressed my hands together and touched the tips to my forehead, bowing forward. "May you always have water and shade," I said.

Taonga motioned to a worn cloth pillow, and I sat.

He poured a white liquid into a small cup and handed it to me. The cup was hand-pounded metal, the hammer blows still visible along its surface. The liquid smelled strongly of sour musk. Fermented milk. I grimaced as it coated my tongue and the back of my throat. I handed back the cup.

Taonga poured a second measure and drank it.

"You are not of the Nyika?" he said.

Nyika was what the Tembowatu called this wasteland. "I have traveled far," I said.

Taonga nodded and let forth a soft *hmmm*, as if he expected such an answer. We sat for a moment without speaking. Through the chamber I could hear the soft sound of the great beast breathing and a rhythmic thump, deep in tone so that it shook my guts.

"Is there rain in Ogliwa?" he asked.

"No," I said. Several days ago I had passed through the small town on the eastern edge of the wastes.

"What about Nnamdi. Is there rain in Nnamdi?"

"I saw no rain in Nnamdi," I said. Taonga was narrowing in on Baraka, the center of the Land of the Sun and where my journey had started. "We had rain in Baraka many days ago. It wet the dust, but did not fill the aquifer."

"Are your wives well in Baraka?"

"My wives are well. They have shade and water."

"Good, good," said Taonga.

"Your shade is cool and wide," I said.

"We are blessed," said Taonga. "The rains stay away, but the waterholes are still wet."

For several years the rains had failed. To feed our crops, his eminence had diverted the river that watered the Nyika and those that flowed north into the lands of our enemies. In the last year, the rivers had brought less water, and I did not know how much longer the springs would fill the waterholes.

We talked in this manner for a while longer, slowly

extracting information about each other without ever asking. I knew I had satisfied Taonga's curiosity when he finally asked, "Will you continue on to Chilagos today?"

"I do not travel to Chilagos," I said. "I bring words to the Tembowatu from his eminence, Chimola."

Taonga poured another measure of fermented milk and passed it to me. I accepted it with a bow of my head and drank it in a single gulp.

"Your milk is life," I said.

Taonga grinned strong and white teeth, which surprised me.

"His eminence praises the strength of the Tembowatu," I said. "He has sent me to negotiate an alliance."

In the flickering light, I tried to read Taonga's face, but the lay of his eyes was foreign to me.

"Our enemies threaten to overrun us" I continued. "We hold them in the mountain passes, but they will soon use their numbers to flow into the Land of the Sun. The Tembowatu can stop this from happening. In exchange his eminence will give you water that is your own."

"We have water."

"But it is not your water." The Tembowatu were nomadic, and existed only because Chimola allowed.

Taonga grunted softly, understanding my meaning. "It is our way to follow the rain," he said. "There is no water here when the rain walks north, so we walk north. Can Chimola make it rain?"

"His eminence can promise more than water. Money. Land to farm."

"We cannot drink metal. Our herd cannot eat dust. Chimola has nothing to offer."

I shifted uncomfortably on the cloth pillow. The chamber was warm enough to coax the sweat from my body. It ran down the side of my face, filled the furrow of my spine, and dripped down my sides.

"His eminence has let you live in peace—"

Taonga harrumphed loudly.

I tried to ignore him, but my train of thought faltered. It took a moment to find it again. "It is your way that friendship moves to and from." I extended my hand from my chest toward his, and back again.

Taonga leaned forward so that the light from the hanging lamp penetrated into the hollows of his face. His dark eyes narrowed. "Chimola did not bring peace. We are the buzzing fly, and he has more important wasps to fight." Taonga tapped his temple with a slender finger. "I remember the first rains that darkened the sand. I remember the blood."

My stomach tightened. Taonga's tone put a shiver through me.

I jumped when the chamber began to shake. I dodged the lamp as it swung toward me on its cord. Outside, olophant trumpets blared.

Taonga rose to his feet, riding the shifting floor with ease. "It is time for us to move."

"I wish to talk more."

"The next water is two days from here. Our shade is yours until then."

Two days would bring us to the mountains that formed the border with our enemies. There the Tembowatu would lead their herd through a narrow pass to their northern forage grounds—beyond our influence, but within that of our enemies.

I could not allow that to happen.

#

I pulled myself up the rope to the howdah and watched quietly as the Tembowatu climbed aboard their olophants. The beasts milled through the rapidly drying mud, anxious to be underway. Once everyone was aboard, the herd set off, Taonga's olophant leading the way. From beneath the shade of the howdah canopy, I watched two Tembowatu boys perched between the beast's massive ears guide the animal north with gentle taps from a slender switch. The herd spread out behind us, twenty-six adult olophants and a dozen juveniles, lined trunk to tail. The dust rose in a fan, smearing the sky ochre red.

I stayed in the howdah, alone and ignored, until the sun dropped and the stars pricked through the purpling sky. There would be no rain tonight.

I climbed down to the platform where children sat around a bowl of stones playing kudoda. Inside the chamber, I shared a meal of flat bread and spicy meat stewed in olophant milk. They served more fermented milk and finished the meal with salted water beetles, a delicacy based on the eager eyes that watched as I ate one.

The food and the warmth and the gentle rocking of the chamber made me drowsy. My eyelids were heavy from my days of pursuit. Most of the Tembowatu did not speak my language, so I watched them silently from one end of the chamber. Occasionally I made simple gestures that I believed they did not understand. Mostly, they left me alone and went about their business of living.

Taonga stayed at the other end of the chamber, in council with a ring of serious-faced Tembowatu. To his left sat the warrior with the blond sticks in his woven hair, the one with whom I had shared water earlier that day. Several times I caught his eyes with mine, and under their predatory gaze I looked away.

I leaned against the chamber wall. The olophant's hide was warm, and I felt the thumping of its heart against my cheek. Gradually, my breathing slowed to match its rhythm, and soon I slipped into the land of sleep.

#

Sharp pops rattled me from a dreamless sleep. The floor rolled beneath me, and I splayed my limbs to stop from being thrown in the darkness and injured. Olophant trumpets filled the night, a terrifying cacophony that set my heart racing. The pops echoed over top the cries, and I realized they were the crack of rifles.

I crawled toward the opening, barely able to stay on my hands and knees as the chamber tossed beneath me. Outside, the Tembowatu lined the platform's railing, their rifles flashing. Beyond them, the moonlit landscape reeled as the olophant charged in staccato bursts of movement. I gripped the ivory frame and pulled myself up so I could see the ground.

In the cold moonlight, dark forms scattered like ants among circular mud huts. A migrant Tabo hunting village, I realized. With each crack of the Tembowatu rifles, one of the shadows stiffened awkwardly before tumbling to the ground. Huts and several jeepnees were flattened under the olophants' massive feet. Goats bounded away into the darkness after their camelthorn palisades were splintered like kindling.

I wanted to draw away, but I could not let go of the frame without being tossed onto the floor, so I clung desperately to it, trying to hide my eyes, but unable to tear them away from the massacre.

I understood now why I had been sent to enlist the Tembowatu to our cause. They would make a terrifying ally, but an even more terrible enemy.

Within minutes the killing was over and the gunfire fell away as the olophants thundered back into the wastes.

I doubted anything remained alive in the Tabo village.

The genocide at the hands of the Tabo had happened long before any of these Tembowatu had been born, but as Taonga had said, the Tembowatu remembered the first rain that had darkened the sand. Among the tribes, old wrongs were never settled; the cycle of retribution just seemed to go round and around.

#

I could not sleep, I think the result of the stuffy air in the chamber and the unsettling quiet with which the Tembowatu returned to their sleep. I had never seen such cold efficiency before, not even among his eminence's most hardened warriors.

I climbed to the howdah, hoping the fresh air would clear my head, and curled up in the back. My mind continued to hear the cracking rifles and the trumpeting roar of olophants as they smeared Tabo woman and children into the dust.

Silhouetted against the setting moon, the two young Tembowatu boys danced atop the olophant's head as they guided it into the darkness. From their excited voices, they still reveled in the slaughter. My stomach felt hollow; they did not realize they had sealed the future of their children in violence.

At some point, in the warmth of the night and under the roll of the howdah, I dozed off. I was awakened at dawn by a Tembowatu leaning on the railing next to me. I recognized the blond sticks holding his weave of hair in place.

"You seek help with your war," he said, just loud enough for me to hear.

The directness of his statement caught me unaware and for several seconds I wasn't sure if I had heard him correctly. I thought perhaps my mind played tricks on me.

We were alone on the howdah, except for the two boys on the olophant's head, but that did not lessen my caution.

"I can help you," he said.

I pulled myself to my feet and leaned against the rail. I was fully alert now. "Who are you?"

"I am Dabuko."

I waited for him to say more, but he did not, as if his name was enough. I studied his profile: the height of his forehead, the prominence of his cheeks bones, his dark, sharp eyes. All, along with his flat nose, were reminiscent of Taonga.

"You are Taonga's son?"

Dabuko's face turned to me, the eyebrows up as if surprised by my deduction. "I am."

The coming conversation fell into place in my mind; it told the story of nearly every tribe. Dabuko was next in the patrilineal line, provided he had support among the other family clans. He wanted to bring a new way to the Tembowatu, and he was tired of waiting for his father to step aside or die. If I could help, he would be in my debt.

Of course, Dabuko said none of this, but as he watched me, I knew the same conversation had already played out in his head.

"I propose nothing," Dabuko said, anticipating my question. "I simply observe that we will reach the mountains before tomorrow's dawn. If something were to happen to my father before then, I would hear Chimola's offer with gentle ears. I understand that friendship must pass to and from." He swept his hand from his chest toward mine, and back again.

Dabuko left me to watch the mountains bounce along the horizon. They seemed far away, but I knew Dabuko was right; we would reach them sometime during the night. Much too quickly, I feared, leaving me little time to decide what I needed to do.

#

My attempts to meet with Taonga were rebuffed throughout the day. He was resting, or in council, or eating, and constantly I was turned away. During meals, I watched him from the rear of the chamber as he talked with his wives or Dabuko. Never did he make eye contact with me. By late afternoon, I was convinced he was ignoring me.

I resigned myself to staring at the desolate landscape as it rolled under the pounding feet of the herd. With each passing kilometer, the mountains crept closer. Even if I had wanted to help Dabuko, how could I do anything if I couldn't even get close enough to Taonga to talk?

The sun dropped, but the air did not cool. Unblemished by clouds, the horizon was a deep purple, fading to star-filled black overhead. The olophants continued on.

I grew weary of their motion.

Alone on the howdah, I contemplated what I would tell his eminence to explain my failure. I tried in vain to find the words I would say to my wives and sons. Lost, I did not immediately notice the dark shadow join me along the howdah railing until it spoke, startling me.

"There will be no rain tomorrow." Taonga said.

"It will rain soon," I said. "It has to."

"The world is changing. The rain has walked far to the north and does not want to come back. It has taken with it the balance among our tribes."

Over the last decade the rains had become less frequent as the clouds had moved away from the Land of the Sun. The Nyika had always been dry, but never this dry. I wondered how much longer the Tembowatu would find forage for their herd in the Nyika. If things did not change, they would need new lands to browse.

"Did you see rain last year?" I asked.

"I saw no rain last year."

"Did you see rain before that?"

"Yes, but not in the Nyika. This is our third trip to the Nyika without rain."

It was my turn to *hmmm* and nod.

"Sometimes I think the rain will never return, because the world is different today. I do not understand a world where it never rains."

Taonga sounded as though he might be open to discussing an alliance; then, he might not. The nuances of the Tembowatu way were difficult for an outsider. Feeling I had to say something, I said, "I do not understand it either."

Taonga grunted softly. "I remember when it would

rain three or four times in the Nyika. The water would turn the ground red like blood. Water is the blood of the land. Water is the blood of our herd and the blood of the Tembowatu. We cannot survive without blood."

"His eminence can undam the rivers and return water to the Nyika," I said.

"Without the rain, there is not enough water for us all. Our herd would starve. Only the rain can bring enough grass to the Nyika. Can Chimola call the rain?"

"No."

"Then nothing else matters." In the darkness, Taonga's shadow slumped against the rail. The howdah rocked gently. The two boys guiding the olophant were barely visible against the darkening sky. Surely they would barely see us, were they even to look in our direction. If timed with the sway of the howdah, I could flip the old man over the railing.

Blood pounded in my ears. Through the night and the dust I could just see a lamp on one of the olophants behind us. The olophants were impressive war machines, capable of bringing victory to his eminence and the Land of the Sun. All that stood in the way was this frail old man, longing for a world gone into the dust.

"So you will go north?" I asked.

"We will follow the rain, as is our way."

As the howdah rocked in our direction, I moved quickly across the blackness between us and grabbed Taonga's arm. I yanked him toward the railing, intending to use the momentum of the rolling beast to hoist him over it, but Taonga spun from my grip. His hands struck me across the head with surprising strength. Off balance, I crashed against the railing. My feet came off the floor. I clawed at the air as I turned upside down, and got a hand on the railing as my feet came over. My shoulder wrenched painfully as my full weight stopped suddenly.

My body bounced against the side of the olophant. I tried to get traction, but my sandals slid off the olophant's dusty hide. I swung my left arm up to grab the railing, but Taonga slapped it aside.

My fingers ached as my grip started to fail.

"In these dry times, I worry about our future. I nearly forgot Chimola's deceit, but Dabuko said you would show your true self if tested."

If I hadn't been struggling to hold the howdah's railing, I would have raged against Dabuko's trickery. Even as I squeezed the rail with all my strength, my fingers continued to slip.

"Friendship must flow to and from," Taonga said. "Tell Chimola we will never forget." He pried my fingers free.

Taonga's face flew up into the night as I slid down the side of the great beast and fell into the darkness.

#

Miraculously, my fall broke no bones. For a long time, I lay in the dust listening to the fading thunder of the herd. When dawn came, I saw no dust against the horizon; the Tembowatu had passed from the Nyika into the mountains. They were gone and would not return until the grass in the north had turned brittle and the promise of rain drew them south again.

If fortune was with us, that was when we would see the Tembowatu again. Yet, with growing trepidation, I feared I would see them sooner, storming down out the mountains, their olophants trumpeting and rifles cracking, to settle the score for what we—for what I—had done.

STORY NOTES
FORGET THE RAIN

I wrote "Forget the Rain" shortly after joining the Codex writing group early in 2011. Codex is a large online community of predominantly new speculative fiction writers who share information about the publishing business and encourage its members to write. Shortly after joining, they held a writing "contest" in which a series of prompts were given, and anyone who wanted to take part could write a story and submit it for comment. I wrote "Forget the Rain" based on one of the provided prompts, in this case an image. I don't know if the image is copyrighted, so I've not reproduced it here, but it's a fascinating picture of a real mechanical elephant with a howdah on top and chambers in the side. The image really appealed to my sense of the bizarre and exotic.

For my story, I decided to make the mechanical elephant a real one, and then brainstormed from there: *What were the chambers for?—Who would live with such creatures?—Where would they live?—How would they live?*

Eventually a story of genocide and war and one man's desperate effort to save his tribe and his family emerged, and I wrote a decent first draft of "Forget the Rain" in a single weekend.

The Beauty of Wynona

First published in *Lacuna*, October 2012

I. Arrival at Penketh

OUR CARRIAGE JERKED TO A STOP before wide stairs leading up to the pillared entrance of Penketh Manor, the country estate of Mr. Prufit and his new wife. The end of our long journey north from London should have been a joyous occasion, but Master Hurlock, the world's foremost portraitist, frowned as he squinted out into the afternoon sunlight.

"I am not up for this, Stevens." Master Hurlock drew back from the carriage window, letting the curtain drop and casting us back into shadow. A man of modest build and swarthy complexion, he looked unusually small in the darkness of the carriage, as if he had been reduced under the weight of his concerns.

I had initially attributed my master's recent melancholy to an imbalance of humors, but of late, I had begun to suspect that he had taken recent allegations, always spoken under breath, to heart. Unlike lesser portraitists, Master Hurlock did not simply paint people; he painted beauty. I have seen it with my own eyes, and I do not understand it, but he would spread his paint on canvas, and it would become more than just strokes of pigment in the likeness of his subject. Some men have said that Master Hurlock's paintings were so beautiful that they diminished their subject. Others have implied that he drained the beauty of those he painted with dark magik and encased it in a prison of ochre and lime for posterity. I knew these claims to be false slander by small men.

"Without this commission, sir, I fear they will put you in debtor's prison."

For many months we had lain idle, our last commission, Mrs. Giddings of Lexington Cross, having been completed before the ice broke on the Thames. During this time, Master Hurlock, pleading ennui, had turned down three commissions, all of them promising lucrative remunerations. By the time Mrs. Prufit's man arrived with her generous offer, I had already limited our visits to the butcher and turned away the woman who came round fortnightly to tidy the windows and thrash the carpets.

Master Hurlock sighed. "As always you are right, Stevens. What would I do without you?"

I followed Master Hurlock from the carriage. As I directed the footmen in the careful removal of our luggage, the door to the manor swung open and a portly man of advancing years strode out to the top of the stairs. He wore a starched shirt with a rounded collar, riding pants, and high boots stained with mud. In the crook of his right elbow, he balanced a rifle. His prodigious mustache was waxed into fashionable points and his ample sideburns blended into a fringe of salt and pepper hair that ringed his balding pate like a laurel wreath. He handed his rifle to one of the servants and gazed down over us, unencumbered.

"Mr. Prufit," I whispered to my master. "He is an avid hunter and clay pigeon shooter. A man of considerable emotion." One of my primary duties was to advise my master on people. While Master Hurlock had no peer with oils and canvas, he was a novice with flesh and blood.

Apparently satisfied with the impression made upon us, Mr. Prufit came down the steps. Even at his age and with his slight but noticeable limp, he was an imposing figure, but Mr. Prufit was more than a physical presence. He carried about him an aura of command, much like a decorated general's coat. This did not surprise me given his military experiences during the Russian War.

"So you are Mr. Hurlock," said Mr. Prufit, his mustachio vibrating. His eyes appraised my master, as if weighing him for market

"I am." Master Hurlock extended his hand.

Mr. Prufit shook it gently, as if concerned he might break it if he were to seize it with his usual force. "Baines will show your man to your room and then where he will stay." Mr. Prufit's intonation in reference to me made clear my status. I would be staying in the attic with the servants, not a side room near my master, an arrangement to which I had grown accustomed over the years.

"Once you have had time to refresh, you will join me in the parlor. My wife is eager to make your acquaintance. Now, if you will excuse me." With that, Mr. Prufit climbed the stairs, retrieved his rifle, and disappeared inside.

II. Meeting Lady Prufit

Mr. Baines, a wiry man with a pinched face and fastidiously manicured hair, showed us to a small but comfortable guest room on the second floor. While the furniture was of the highest refinement, the walls were covered with portraits of inferior quality by men of name, but little talent. My master studied them politely while I unpacked his shirts and trousers and arranged them in the bureau.

After Master Hurlock had washed away the road's dust and changed into a clean shirt, we joined Mr. Prufit in the parlor. Master Hurlock accepted the offer of gin, although I knew it to be a drink he did not favor, his taste running more towards refined scotch.

While Mr. Prufit poured the drinks along the side board, my master examined a daguerreotype of a young man in military regalia. The youth, no more than a tender seventeen years, bore a resemblance to the elder Prufit, but was obviously not the same man.

"John Henry, my son," said Mr. Prufit, his face gone pale. "He was killed at Sevastopol."

"My condolences," Master Hurlock said.

Mr. Prufit interposed himself between Master Hurlock and the daguerreotype. He motioned to a floral wing chair on the opposite side of the room. "Sit. I wish to talk before my wife arrives."

My master sat in the indicated chair. I stood against the wall, unnoticed.

"I must be frank with you, Mr. Hurlock. This portrait was not my idea. If I had known of this commission earlier, you would not be here."

My master squirmed in his chair.

"If anything happens to my wife, I will kill you."

Master Hurlock's drink stopped halfway to his mouth. His face blanched white as a boiled potato. The glass rattled on the table top as he set it down. "I assure you, sir, that threats are unnecessary."

Mr. Prufit smiled, his grin wide and predatory. "I

wanted to make sure we understood each other."

At that moment, the sliding door opposite Master Hurlock opened, flooding the parlor with light. But it was more than just the afternoon light that chased away the shadows. Mrs. Wynona Prufit, who was not even half her husband's age, radiated a golden light all her own, and it was her radiance, not the afternoon sun, that lit the room.

She had more than physical beauty, which for her was, without doubt, considerable in itself. She had an inner beauty that glowed beneath her perfectly unblemished skin and lit her eyes like sapphire lamps. Everything about her was grace, from the gentle spiral curls of her blond hair and the delicate curve of her neck as it tapered into slender shoulders to the way she floated through the light like a naiad in honey.

If I could soak up her essence, I was certain it would sustain me for an eternity. Yet standing in her presence, I felt base and ugly, a creature unworthy of even looking upon her.

She dropped into a graceful curtsy and extended a delicate hand. "Master Hurlock," she said, "you do me great honor to come here."

Master Hurlock stumbled to his feet. "I-I—" His ears flushed pink. "You honor me, Mrs. Prufit," he finally said. Bending, he pressed his forehead to her fingers.

As my master spoke, Mr. Prufit's smile flattened into a sinister line. Had he a knife, I feared he would have gutted and splayed my master upon the floral divan.

To my considerable surprise, Mrs. Prufit then curtsied before me. "You must be Mr. Stevens," she said upon straightening. "Penketh Manor welcomes you."

I was rendered slack-jawed. Never in my years of service have the genteel approached me with such genuine warmth. More often, their eyes have passed over me like I were an uninvited but innocuous spectral emanation: I was either unseen or unworthy of their acknowledgment.

How I managed to recover before Mrs. Prufit turned away, I am not certain, but I bowed deeply and said, "The honor is mine."

"What time tomorrow shall we begin?" Mrs. Prufit asked.

"I will need to see the sitting room first," said Master Hurlock. "The light will dictate the time."

Mr. Prufit stepped between his wife and my master. "How long will this portrait take?" he asked gruffly.

"Putting a time on art is difficult, Mr. Prufit, but most commissions are finished in a few weeks—"

"A few weeks? I will pay you double to be finished by the end of this week."

"Titus, don't be a boor," said Mrs. Prufit. Even her frown could not mar her beauty.

Mr. Prufit smiled weakly at his young wife. "We are here to spend time together, Wynona. It is best to finish this business quickly."

"It may be possible to paint Mrs. Prufit and then finish the portrait's background in London," my master said.

Mrs. Prufit's frown deepened, as did my dislike for her husband. I had heard that Mr. Prufit, in his jealousy, had sequestered his new bride at Penketh to keep her away from the eyes of other men. She was, most certainly, a sought-after prize by the fashionable young gentlemen of London.

Mr. Prufit turned Master Hurlock away from his wife and walked him toward the door. "Baines will show you the room selected for the sitting. I expect you have many things to prepare."

My master gazed back at Mrs. Prufit. He shook his head, as if to clear it of too much intoxication. "Yes, quite correct, Mr. Prufit. Stevens, fetch the etui and easel."

III. An Unexpected Dinner Party

The location selected by Mrs. Prufit had large windows that flooded the room with warm light. A set of French doors opened onto a flagstone patio overlooking a lush yet manicured garden of trellised roses, forsythia bushes, and beds of creeping myrtle, red and yellow zinnias, and vibrant dahlias. Ordinarily the focal center of a garden, the Prufit's gazebo stood off to one side like a forgotten child in the shade of a copse of beech trees. Instead, a large sun dial stood center, surrounded by rich beds of aster.

I arranged the divan and end table that my master had selected for the work and then laid his brushes as he liked: the horse hair brushes ordered by size and shape to the right of his easel, the sable ones similarly aligned on the left.

As I worked, my master selected his paints, gently setting a rainbow of jars in his easel tray. I never touched his paints. Master Hurlock mixed his own oils from mortared cadmium, titanium, and cobalt, eschewing the mass-produced tubes that had become fashionable of late among lesser portraitists. Master Hurlock often said that not even all God's skill could overcome inferior pigment.

Finally, I set his canvas in place. It would be the last time I touched it until I framed the finished portrait prior to delivering it to its owner.

As we finished our preparatory work, Mr. Baines arrived to announce dinner. He led us to the parlor adjacent to the dining room. As we approached, I heard unfamiliar voices within.

"Will there be other guests, Mr. Baines?" I asked.

"Mr. Prufit has taken the liberty to invite a few friends."

"I wish we had been informed."

"There is no need for concern. The guests are few and friendly. Your master should have no difficulties." Mr. Baines swept opened the parlor doors and the small crowd within fell silent.

Master Hurlock took a step back. I gently nudged him forward with a hand in the small of his back.

Mrs. Prufit took my master's arm, while I stepped off to the side.

I immediately recognized Mr. Blackstone and his wife. They were well-known around London for their charitable works, and I knew them to be good friends of Mr. Prufit. Mr. Blackstone, a short man with copious facial hair and a war wound that had crippled his left arm, had served with Mr. Prufit during the Russian conflict at Balaklava. His wife, a slender woman with silver hair and a penchant for flashy jewels, clung to his good arm.

Also present was a young priest, who I assumed was the local clergy. Mrs. Prufit introduced him as Reverend Cooper. He said little and his eyes darted about like a nervous lamb. By the way he fingered his collar, I assumed he was new to the Parish and likely to the cloth.

Presently, Mr. Baines announced that dinner was ready, so everyone retired to the dining room. Mrs. Prufit, who sat at one end of the table, led my master to his seat directly on her left. Reverend Cooper sat on my master's left. The Blackstones lined the opposite side, and at the table's head sat Mr. Prufit.

I took my usual position along the wall behind my master.

The first course was set and served, and the staff fell back to their stations along the perimeter or into the kitchen. Presently, the conversation turned to Master Hurlock.

"I understand you have been commissioned to paint Mrs. Prufit," said Mrs. Blackstone. "While your reputation precedes you, of course, have you painted anyone I might know?"

My master set his spoon aside and took up his fish fork. The smell of stewed trout was strong. "Perhaps you know Mrs. Sanders? I finished her portrait last year. Or Mr. Thomas. I was quite pleased with his result."

"You recently finished a commission for Mrs. Giddings, did you not?" asked Mr. Prufit.

His question made me straighten. He asked as if he already knew the answer, even though he tried to speak with an innocuous intonation.

"Indeed," my master said, not seeming to notice. "I finished it several months ago."

"I did not realize Mrs. Giddings had sat for you recently," said Mrs. Blackstone quietly. "A pity, is it not?"

"I do not understand," my master said.

Mrs. Blackstone placed her hand over her breast.

She appeared flustered, as if suffering an attack of the vapors.

"Mrs. Giddings's health has not been good," Mr. Blackstone said.

"I had not heard," said Master Hurlock. "She was an exceptional study." While I knew my master did not intend it, his statement sounded aloof, almost clinical and cold.

"I have heard that her illness is unusual," said Mr. Prufit.

"Mr. Giddings remarked to me several weeks ago that his wife's condition has the medical community baffled," said Mr. Blackstone. "It's as if her life force has been drained out of her."

"It is not the consumption?" Mrs. Prufit asked.

"No, no," said Mr. Blackstone. He dabbed a piece of trout out of his copious beard with his linen napkin. "I have heard that it is not a condition of the body at all, but of the soul."

Mrs. Prufit gasped. "The soul!"

Everyone stopped eating. Mrs. Blackstone dropped her fork.

"Perhaps this is not appropriate conversation for dinner," Reverend Cooper said.

"I agree," said Mr. Blackstone. "This is better conversation for dessert." He chuckled, but when no one else responded, his laughter trailed away.

The first course ended and the servants removed the dishes. The guests talked quietly and drank sherry while they awaited the entrées. Presently, lamb cutlets with peas, braised veal, and larded sweetbread arrived. While the guests were served, Mrs. Prufit said, "Reverend, you would be considered an expert on matters of the soul. Have you any observations regarding poor Mrs. Giddings?"

Reverend Cooper squirmed under the attention of the table. He set his fork aside and took a deep breath. "A matter of the soul," he said absently, as if considering the phrase for the first time. "That is, of course, the providence of God and His will is mysterious. But you mentioned, Mr. Blackstone, that the doctors can find no physical ailment to explain her condition. I would venture that they have not looked hard enough. The soul is a powerful force; for it to simply drain away is unlikely. Unless—but, no."

"Unless what, Reverend?" asked Mrs. Prufit.

"I must apologize, but I would rather not discuss such topics."

"Come now, Reverend, we are all adults here," Mr. Blackstone said. "You suspect foul play of a spiritual nature."

"I did not say that."

"But you do not deny it," said Mr. Prufit without looking up from sawing off a chunk of veal.

"Are you suggesting that Mrs. Giddings has been cursed?" Mrs. Prufit asked. "But who could do such a thing?"

Mr. Blackstone waved his fork around, his eyes sparkling. "The real question, Mrs. Prufit, is not who, but what?"

Everyone at the table began to talk at once, except for my master. He had stopped eating his veal and put his fork down on the edge of his plate.

Gradually the clamor subsided.

"You speak as if you know something of this topic," said Reverend Cooper to Mr. Blackstone.

"Only what I have read," said Mr. Blackstone with a false modesty.

"My Henry reads many books." Mrs. Blackstone's voice trilled with pride.

Mr. Blackstone ignored his wife's adulations. "It is true I have read numerous books on spiritualism. The topic may be fashionable and peopled with charlatans, but I believe there is some truth to it."

Again the table broke out into murmurs.

Mr. Blackstone waited for the conversation to subside again. The sparkle in his eyes had not faded. When all attention had turned back toward him, he said, "The spirit world is rife with things we are just beginning to understand. I recently read a translation of a text by a little known Russian spiritualist called Bogdanov. He surmises that because both the spiritual and the mortal worlds were made by God, that both must have similarities."

"An appropriate supposition," said Reverend Cooper.

"So by extension, Bogdanov postulates that within each world the structure of nature must be the same. In our world we have animals that prey on others. It is the natural order that lions eat zebras and zebras eat grass—"

"And that we shoot lions," said Mr. Prufit with a chuckle. His guests joined in.

Mr. Blackstone smiled, but I could tell he was perturbed by the interruption. "Yes, yes, we humans sit above it all in our rightful place in God's image—"

"Unless you believe that Darwin chap, then we are devolved from apes." Mr. Prufit's comment triggered a lengthy side discussion of Charles Darwin and his theories. While this transpired, the staff cleared the remnants of the entrées and brought the second course, a haunch of venison, boiled capon, a braised ham, and a saddle of lamb.

Savory aromas filling the room left my mouth watering. I had not eaten since a wholly inadequate meal at a small tavern in Guildford. I did my best to focus on the discussion as it turned away from Mr. Darwin and returned to the Russian spiritualist.

"If Bogdanov is correct," said Mr. Blackstone, "then it would follow that the spiritual world is also structured with a hierarchy of forms and natural roles."

Mrs. Prufit leaned forward. "So you believe in spiritual predators and prey?"

"Precisely."

The table fell silent for a moment while they ruminated on Mr. Blackstone's theory.

"What has this to do with Mrs. Giddings?" asked Mrs. Blackstone.

"Obviously something has attacked her spiritually," said Mr. Blackstone matter-of-factly.

I fought the urge to loosen my collar, which seemed suddenly to constrict my breathing.

Reverend Cooper began to speak, but stopped. His face crinkled in contemplation. "We all know the spirit world exists," he said finally. "If we believe the self-professed spiritualists, we can even communicate across that barrier between the living and the dead— and no, Mrs. Prufit, I do not believe we mortals can do that because that is the providence of God, but that is another matter entirely. But how can a … predator, as you describe it Mr. Blackstone, attack a spirit that has not crossed over and is still contained within a mortal vessel."

"A good question." Mrs. Blackstone stared expectantly at her husband.

Mr. Blackstone rubbed at his jowls. "I don't know."

"Perhaps," said Mr. Prufit, "this predator does not reside in the spiritual world, but has assumed a mortal body." As he said this last, he stared at Master Hurlock.

The room went quiet. The guest looked from one to the other.

As if the air had been drained away, I found it difficult to breathe. I wiped at a sheen of sweat on my brow.

Mrs. Blackstone coughed awkwardly. The spell broken, the diners resumed eating.

"How do you suppose such a creature would come to exist?" asked Mrs. Prufit.

"It would need to be summoned, of course," said Mr. Prufit, "or perhaps a pact with evil has caused some corruption of a mortal soul." The ominous tone of his voice put a pall over the dinner table.

The diners said nothing more through the remainder of the second course. They began to speak again in guarded tones as the third course was laid. Even at my close proximity, I could barely hear their words over the clink of silver on porcelain. Once the final course had been consumed and several pastries had been sampled, Mr. Prufit invited the men to share brandy in the parlor. My master, never one for flawless etiquette, declined.

"The long ride up from London has taken its toll," he said. "I wish to be rested for Mrs. Prufit's first sitting tomorrow morning. I hope you will excuse me." With those words, he retired for the night.

IV. A Conversation Overheard

The dinner conversation had unsettled my master more than I had realized. To calm his nerves, I urged him to drink a draft of laudanum. Once he had downed the tonic, his body eased noticeably, and before I had finished brushing and hanging his coat and trousers he was asleep. I doused the lamps and left him.

Still unsettled myself, I decided to forgo sleep and take a walk in the garden. I descended the main stair, and passed the parlor where we had first met Mrs. Prufit. As I turned into the corridor leading to the sitting room, I jerked to a halt.

A narrow rectangle of light, cast through a cracked door, was splashed across the floor and up the wall. I could hear voices, but they were sufficiently muted that I could not make out the words.

I nearly turned away, but hesitated when I heard Mr. Prufit say, "He is responsible. I have no proof as yet, but I am certain. Did you notice how quiet he became during dinner?"

"Keep your voice down," said Mr. Blackstone.

I crept closer to the door. Cigar smoke tickled my nose, and I pinched back a sneeze.

"I did not like this Hurlock fellow from the beginning," said Mr. Prufit.

"I have viewed Mrs. Giddings. Indeed, I believe she has been fed upon by some spirit predator, but I am not convinced yet, Titus."

"Who else could it be, Henry?"

I found I was holding my breath.

"I don't know," said Mr. Blackstone. "I personally viewed many of Hurlock's other patrons from the past two years, and none of them displayed any adverse symptoms. Mrs. Giddings's condition may be unrelated."

I exhaled through clenched teeth.

"We've worked too hard on this, Henry. Wynona is perfect, and needs to stay that way for six more days. If anything were to blemish her spirit, it would ruin everything. Had I known earlier she had contacted this Hurlock, I would have interceded and put an end to it."

Mr. Blackstone harrumphed. "You still had a chance to cancel this commission, but that's what happens when you put old Nebuchadnezzar out to grass, Titus."

Mr. Prufit sniffed loudly. "No need to be coarse."

"What is done is done," said Mr. Blackstone with finality. "So what do we do from here?"

A moment of silence passed, and I feared that they had somehow detected my presence. I exhaled quietly when Mr. Prufit spoke again.

"I know someone who can prove Hurlock is our man—or whatever. Shall I make arrangements?"

"And if he is, then what? We can't just get rid of him. Someone would notice."

A wave of fear flooded over me, and I put a hand to the wall for support.

"True, Henry," said Mr. Prufit, "but we can't risk this going awry. We will need to deal with—what was that?"

I too had heard it, a loud clatter from the kitchen, like a clumsy oaf had knocked metal pans onto the floor. While not loud enough to wake those upstairs, it was surprisingly loud in the hallway. Wanting to remain undetected, I retreated to my room in the attic.

As I sat in the dark unable to sleep, I considered departing Penketh Manor immediately, but, after considerable struggle, I dismissed the idea. I did not believe Mr. Prufit and Mr. Blackstone were sufficiently desperate to commit murder … at least, not yet. This did not ease my worry, however, because I was unsure if I had actually reached this conclusion logically or if I had convinced myself of its truth because of the circumstances.

While my master's safety was foremost in my mind, I also could not let Mrs. Prufit come to harm. I could not accept that she would knowingly be involved in any nefarious plot. I did not know the danger that threatened her, but she was too important to both my master and me.

After hours ruminating on these matters, exhaustion overtook me, and I drifted into a restless slumber.

V. Discoveries

We had arranged with Mrs. Prufit to begin promptly at ten o'clock the next morning. Master Hurlock and I arrived in the studio an hour before to finalize the placement of the furniture with respect to the morning light and arrange fresh-cut asters in their urn. As the hour neared, my master loaded his palette with his oils.

Precisely as the mantel clocked chimed the hour, the doors to the studio swept opened and Mrs. Prufit arrived.

Her dress of blue silk, trimmed with pearls and lace, accented the color of her eyes. Her hair was worn up in a neat bundle atop her head, except for two golden ringlets that cascaded down the sides of her face. Her radiance straightened my shoulders, and, for the moment, lifted my fatigue and worry. She was the morning sun burning off the night's mist.

This euphoria, however, did not last, for close upon her heels entered Mr. Prufit.

Master Hurlock frowned and fumbled his palette, but managed to keep his hold.

Mrs. Prufit threw a disapproving glance toward her husband but said nothing. I sensed this was an addendum to an ongoing disagreement. She sat on the divan with her legs folded up under her, and I helped to arrange her dress to accentuate the way the light played off its folds.

Mr. Prufit stood off to the side, his arms folded across his waistcoat, his face pinched into a scowl. Even his mustachio seemed to glare hostilely.

"Mr. Prufit," my master said diplomatically. "The act of painting is stimulating for the artist, but, I must confess, is frightfully boring for the observer."

"Do not concern yourself, Mr. Hurlock. I am interested in the craft and will not be a nuisance."

I wanted to say that his very presence was a nuisance. But then, perhaps that was his intention. This impudence rankled me. He would succeed only in compromising the integrity of the portrait. I wondered how long my master would allow such conditions to exist before he became more direct. Master Hurlock disliked conflict, but he disliked an inferior portrait even more.

My master took up a slender stick of charcoal and drew in fits—entirely different from his typical sure strokes—glancing frequently over his shoulder at Mr.

Prufit. After redrawing several times the oval that would become Mrs. Prufit's angelic face, Master Hurlock put down his charcoal.

"Mr. Prufit, I would be distressed if my presence kept you from important business."

Mr. Prufit casually checked his gold pocket watch. "I have nothing to attend to at the moment."

Master Hurlock frowned. He took up the charcoal again and continued to work, but the longer he labored, the more his hand began to shake. Once he could no longer draw a flat line, he stepped back in embarrassment and dropped his charcoal into the easel tray.

"Sir, perhaps a tincture of chamomile would help?"

He looked at me as if hearing my voice for the first time that morning. "I think that might be a good idea," he said. "Mrs. Prufit, you may step out to refresh for a few minutes, if it pleases."

I went to retrieve the tincture. As I walked down the corridor, I approached the door to the room where I had overheard Mr. Prufit and Mr. Blackstone talking the previous night. Unlike earlier that morning, the door now stood ajar, perhaps left open by one of the maids. My curiosity piqued, I nudged the door farther open.

Along the opposite wall, a mantel and fireplace of luminescent Sienna marble formed the focal center of Penketh Manor's library. To either side and covering the remainder the of the opposite wall, rosewood bookcases stretched from the parquet floor to the open timbered ceiling. The shelves burst with gilt-bound tomes of all sizes and styles. Several wing chairs, an ornate desk of darkly lacquered mahogany, and a solid wooden table sat on islands of rich

Moroccan carpet. The odor of varnish and fine tobacco filled the chamber.

My eyes, however, swept over these fineries with little interest. I had seen many gentlemen's libraries and most were primarily show for boorish men who would as soon wear a ladies frock as crack the leather binding of a book.

What drew my eye in Mr. Prufit's athenaeum, was a single shelf sealed behind frosted glass doors. More specifically, the frosted glass doors were sealed with a prominent brass lock.

Seeing no one around, I entered and went directly to them. Behind the swirls of opaque glass were books, but I could discern no details other than the fact they did not look like the cheaply bound volumes of a more lascivious nature that were popular with some gentlemen. I tried the doors, but they were locked and sturdy.

I turned to leave, but four daguerreotypes on the desk caught my interest. While I appreciate the miracles of science, I have always found the daguerreotype to be a poor substitute for a portrait by a master. These specific images, however, caught my eye not for what they were, but for what they were not. All four images were of Mr. Prufit's son, John Henry. It is not unusual for a father to have images of his son, but as I now thought back, I had seen no evidence at Penketh of Mr. Prufit's daughter. I knew that he had a daughter who resided in London with her maternal aunt, an arrangement enacted by Mr. Prufit following his second wife's death when the girl was a toddler. I have no children of my own—my life is not one such that children are feasible—but I wondered what would bring a man to surround himself by specters of his lost son, while ignoring his living daughter.

"May I help you, Mr. Stevens?"

I jumped at the sound of Mr. Baines's voice. "I was simply admiring your master's daguerreotypes," I said. "I have noticed that all are of his son. Are there any of his daughter?"

Mr. Baines said nothing, so I let the question hang, hoping the silence would encourage him to speak when he otherwise might not. However, he remained unrattled and said nothing, as any good man would.

"Forgive me if I seem to pry," I said. "I am simply interested in images such as these."

The corners of Mr. Baines's mouth rose slightly. "I am aware of no other images, Mr. Stevens."

"He must have been very fond of the lad."

"Aren't all fathers fond of their sons?"

My throat tightened, which, after all these years, surprised me. I looked away. "If only that were true, Mr. Baines."

"Mr. Prufit was devastated by his son's death. Only recently does he seem to have reconciled his grief."

"Mrs. Prufit is an exceptional woman."

Mr. Baines arched an eyebrow but said nothing more. The silence now made me uncomfortable.

"Forgive me, Mr. Baines, but I need to tend to a matter for Master Hurlock." His gaze prickled the back of my neck as I hastily retreated to my master's room.

While I procured the tincture of chamomile from the kit of remedies and tonics, movement out the window caught my attention. Mr. Blackstone stepped from behind the gazebo, wearing his red riding coat and carrying a burlap sack. He checked his pocket watch and glanced back toward the house. After a moment, Mr. Prufit joined him, and the two disappeared into the copse.

Intrigued, I slipped the bottle of tincture into my coat pocket and went out the kitchen door. The morning sun had burned off the dew, but the heat of the day had not yet settled in. After acquiring my bearings, I cut through the manor's vegetable garden, passed through an ivied gate and approached the gazebo across an expanse of freshly-mown lawn.

Across the garden, the French doors into the studio stood open, and within I saw Master Hurlock at his easel. With Mr. Prufit no longer a distraction, I anticipated my master had calmed sufficiently to make progress on the portrait and that my absence would go unnoticed.

I reached the edge of the copse of trees and saw no easy path. In the shade, the dew had not burned off, and I noticed a trail on the lawn leading into a recently disturbed cleft in the undergrowth. I pushed through the small dogwoods, and found myself on a trail that wound through the beech trunks and a scattering of buckthorn and elderberry.

My shoes, wholly unsuited for a cross land excursion, clicked as I stepped forward. Moss had overgrown the edges of a flat stone, nearly obscuring it. Much like a garden trail, a line of such stones wound deeper into the copse, its regularity marred periodically by tree roots.

I moved slowly along this trail, trying not to make a sound, but the hard soles of my shoes were incapable of stealth. I thought for certain that Mr. Prufit and Mr. Blackstone would hear me, no matter how far ahead they might be.

After some distance I lost the trail. It must have turned, while I had proceeded straight. I backtracked, hoping to reacquire it, but I succeeded only in turning myself about and getting thoroughly lost.

I chided my carelessness. While I was certain I could find my way back if I simply chose a direction and held the course, I had no knowledge of the size of the copse, and I did not welcome spending my entire day getting back to Penketh. I pulled my coat a little snugger about me and turned a slow revolution trying to acquire my bearings.

I heard the faint sound of Mr. Prufit's voice off to my left. I was certain he would view my presence unkindly, but I also knew he would return to the manor house at some point, and following him was a better prospect than striking out on my own. Besides, had I not followed him and Mr. Blackstone to learn their purpose?

I slowly picked my way through a tangle of ferns and low creeping cover, placing each step with care so I did not snap any twigs. The undergrowth, which had been relatively sparse, grew denser, obscuring my vision.

Mr. Prufit's voice grew in volume. I could hear him clearly, but oddly, I could not discern what he was saying. With a suddenness that nearly staggered me, I realized I could hear him perfectly, only his words were not in the Queen's English. I listened intently, but he spoke no language that I recognized.

I continued to edge forward into the trees. I paused when Mr. Blackstone joined Mr. Prufit in a haunting chant sung in a minor key. The deep resonance of their voices set my nerves vibrating.

Sensing they were very near, but unable to see

them through the dense shrubs, I crouched down and crawled forward on my knees. I stopped suddenly when I noticed Mr. Blackstone's red riding jacket. Uncertain if I had been detected, I remained still, moving only my eyes within their sockets as I searched for Mr. Prufit.

After a moment, I realized that Mr. Blackstone's coat was not upon his shoulders, but had been removed and hung across a shrub.

Out of the corner of my eye, I saw a flash of movement to my left. In a small clearing, Mr. Prufit and Mr. Blackstone stood several feet apart, facing each other. Between them was a solid block of dark stone, ornately carved along its edges, but intervening vegetation obscured the pattern so I could see no motif.

The scent of burning incense reached my nose.

I realized with a rush of fear that they were performing some type of arcane ritual, perhaps consecrating an altar.

I almost emitted a yelp, but managed to hold my tongue. All of this talk of spirit predators acquired a sinister relevance. Mr. Prufit and Mr. Blackstone were more than curious amateurs; it appeared that they had moved beyond that into practitioners.

My gut had the hollow feeling I sometimes get at the end of a winter night, when I have not eaten since the evening meal and my room is damp and cold and black as the depths of a grave. I thought it wise to immediately depart Penketh, but again I dismissed the idea. The danger to Mrs. Prufit had now become tangible and sinister. That I might avert her harm made me stay.

VI. Messages from the Beyond

An hour later, I slipped back into Penketh the same way I had left, but now the kitchen buzzed with cooks seasoning racks of meats and kneading mountains of spongy dough, while maids clattered dishes in a large sink and polished silverware.

I learned from a scullery maid that another guest was expected that evening: Madame Borevsky, a noted medium from Liverpool who had family in the area.

Later, when I informed Master Hurlock of the new guest, he reacted with an unexpected smile. "Some light entertainment will be better than all that talk of spirit predators," he said.

I was not as certain as my master, however. While I knew that mediums were frauds peddling a good show, I also knew a charlatan willing to say anything to make a quid was as dangerous as a true practitioner of dark magik. Try as I might to dismiss this Madame Borevsky, I simply could not shake free the tendrils of dread in which I found myself entangled.

At precisely the appointed hour, I helped my master into his coat and we descended to the parlor. We arrived to find the room a flurry of activity. Mr. Baines directed the footmen in positioning a circular table in the center of the room. This required considerable rearrangement of the furniture. The table placed, a maid spread a lace cloth on it while the footmen unfolded six wooden chairs. The guests, gathered around the perimeter, watched the activity with interest while sipping drinks.

Mrs. Prufit met us at the entry with Madame Borevsky in tow. The spiritualist was a diminutive woman with a thick braid of rich black hair pulled over her left shoulder so it hung down to her waist. She wore what I had come to consider the medium's uniform: a lacy dress that seemed more confection than cloth, jangly oversized bracelets and earrings, and thick face paint that did little to draw attention from her cleaver-like blade of a nose.

My master hesitantly shook Madame Borevsky's hand, almost as if he expected her to shout out his imminent doom.

Mr. Prufit cleared his throat and the polite conversation died down. "Madame Borevsky has kindly agreed to conduct a seance."

A grin split Madame Borevsky's face. She directed my master to sit to her right. Mr. Prufit took the chair to her left, and the others took seats around the table.

Mrs. Blackstone clapped her hands excitedly and giggled like a child. "I do love a good seance," she said. She placed her hands flat on the table, and the rest of the guests followed suit.

Mr. Baines pulled the heavy drapes and dimmed the lamps. He retreated to the dining room, pulling the doors shut and leaving me alone in the darkened room with the six shapes at the table.

"Reach out to the spirit world." Madame Borevsky's voice had deepened and she now spoke with a distinctly foreign accent. It seemed that all mediums these days were from exotic places on the continent. Whatever happened to good home-grown mediums?

"Reach out to a loved one who has passed over that boundary. Call someone you trust to this room."

For a moment, nothing happened. I could hear everyone in the room breathing, and the air grew stuffy with the dining room doors closed.

"Everyone must try," said Madame Borevsky, her tone almost chiding. "Negative energy will bar the spirits. Believe, and they will come."

At least a minute passed in which nothing happened. By now pearls of perspiration beaded my hairline. A trickle of sweat inched its way down the channel of my spine.

The table began to rattle on its legs. The noise made me jump.

"There is a spirit among us," said Madame Borevsky. "A woman wearing a pale blue dress and holding … I can't quite make it out, but maybe a flower?"

Mrs. Blackstone gasped. "That's my mother. I miss you, mother."

"She is trying to tell me something …"

I saw no evidence of Mrs. Blackstone's mother among us. The table continued to rattle, a noise I now found disconcerting. I could not shake the feeling that Madame Borevsky was more than she appeared.

"She is pointing to something around her neck," continued Madame Borevsky. "It looks like a locket."

"My mourning locket! I've lost it. I am sorry, mother; do you know where it is?"

"She says that it is not lost and that it will find you soon."

Mrs. Blackstone heaved a sigh of relief and nearly burst into tears.

The rattling of the table increased. Instead of just turning on the floor, it began to bounce about.

The action startled me sufficiently that I bumped back into the wall. I had seen such vigorous tilting on one other occasion. The medium involved had later been exposed as a fraud, who by use of intricate parlor tricks, had made tables levitate and dance. But I could not see how such a feat could have been done here. I had watched the table assembled. No wires or other gimmicks could have been installed.

Madame Borevsky began to chant an incantation that was in no language that I recognized.

My throat tightened. I stared wide-eyed as the table bounced like a hound beneath a treed fox.

"What's happening?" Mrs. Prufit exclaimed.

"Madame Borevsky, what is it? What do you see?" Mr. Prufit asked in a rush.

A sharp pain shot through my stomach, like a hunger pain, but much stronger. It ricocheted through my body like a ball of black lead shot. Doubling over, I sucked air through my clenched teeth and pushed back against it. I managed not to scream.

Madame Borevsky did, however. At the same time she flew back out of her chair.

The table caromed wildly, striking Mr. Prufit and toppling him onto the floor. Mr. Blackstone grabbed Mrs. Prufit from her chair and shielded her as the table swung around. The edge of it crashed into his back. He grunted and stumbled to the ground, scattering chairs, but taking Mrs. Prufit with him, safely in his arms.

Mrs. Blackstone raised her hands to protect her face and exclaimed a loud plea to God to protect her.

The table flipped up on edge and flew into the wall no more than an arm's length from where I stood. A large framed mirror shattered as it hit the floor. The table fell still, its energy spent. For a long moment, silence shrouded the room.

Light flood the parlor as Mr. Baines opened the dining room doors.

I squinted in the brightness.

Master Hurlock sat on the floor looking shaken but otherwise unharmed. I went to his side, but he brushed off my attempts to help him. "Let me sit for a moment."

"Madame Borevsky!" Mr. Prufit pushed himself to his knees and crawled over to Madame Borevsky who lay in a heap of petticoats.

I looked away from her exposed undergarments and legs.

"Is anyone hurt?" Mr. Blackstone had left Mrs. Prufit sitting on the floor and gone to his wife who clutched her crucifix. The color had drained from her face.

Mrs. Prufit, with Mr. Baine's assistance, got to her feet. She clung to his arm unsteadily.

Mr. Prufit had righted Madame Borevsky. The medium breathed loudly and tried to speak, but the words got caught in her throat. Finally she managed to force them out. "A spirit ... A dark spirit ... In this room ... Ripped from the other side ..." She swooned, then, into Mr. Prufit's arms.

In the commotion, I do not think anyone had heard her except Mr. Prufit and me. Mr. Prufit glared disapprovingly in my master's direction.

Needless to say, the evening was in greater shambles than the parlor. Madame Borevsky recovered, but still felt faint. Mr. Prufit insisted on personally escorting her home. Mrs. Prufit and the Blackstones retired to their rooms, no longer feeling social.

My master, shaken by the evening's events, also

decided to retire.

VII. Decisions

Creases furrowed Master Hurlock's brow as I helped him undress. I turned down his bed, and he sat on the edge, watching me fold and lay his trousers over a chair back. He did not move while I brushed his coat and hung it in the armoire.

"Tell me, Stevens," he said at length. "Am I a good man?"

His question stupefied me, and in the moment I could not respond. Before he turned his face away, I saw pain wash over his features.

"Forgive me, sir. My hesitation was not a condemnation, but the result of my surprise at your doubt. You are a good man." While any gentlemen would have responded thusly to his master regardless of the truth, I spoke with genuine sincerity. Master Hurlock had lifted me from the gutters and opium dens of the East End and given me the opportunity to see that I could be more than a parasite feeding on the cankerous underbelly of society. What he saw in me on that day that I had tagged him as my next mark, I do not know, but his kindness then and through twenty-five years of service had allowed me to regain some thread of my lost humanity.

Master Hurlock forced a wan smile, but I could see he found no comfort in my assurance. "Do you think it possible that a man can unknowingly weave evil?"

I knew now what this was about: the allegations of dark magik that had occupied the lips of the London gossipmongers. "I think men are capable only of what is in their hearts. A man with only good in his heart will do what is good."

"But this matter with Mrs. Giddings…"

"Coincidence, sir, nothing more." I turned away, unable to meet his eyes for fear that he would not believe me. I went to the sideboard and mixed a draught of laudanum to ease his nerves.

"This commission …" Master Hurlock shook his head. "I have never painted one such as Mrs. Prufit. If I were twice the artist I am, I do not think I could paint her justly, but even the poor shadow that I put on my canvas will be worthy to hang in the Royal Academy."

I helped him under the covers and handed him the glass.

"There are many reasons to stay, Stevens," my master continued, "and equally many to leave."

I pushed the glass toward his lips. His uncertainty tore at my conscience, and I wanted to ease his turmoil, as much for him as for me. "It has been a hard day, sir. Make no decisions tonight."

He drank the laudanum, and I took the glass and set it on the bureau.

Master Hurlock lay back on his pillow. Already his eyes grew heavy. "I must finish this portrait …"

I extinguished the lamp.

"… it will be my *pièce de résistance*."

I stood in the dark unsure what to do. Master Hurlock was in danger, a danger that was not of his doing, but to leave now carried its own risks. I owed it to Master Hurlock to sacrifice any needs I may have for him. My shoulders slumped as I realized that the instinct for self-preservation was stronger than any bond I had to him. If any hope remained that we could both achieve our needs, then I could not bring myself to leave. I needed to learn what lengths Mr. Prufit and Mr. Blackstone would go to insure their plot. I knew of only one place to learn more.

VIII. The Secrets Under Glass

With the rest of the household indisposed and Mr. Prufit not yet returned, I crept down unobserved to the library. I left the door cracked wide enough to allow in sufficient light from the corridor so I could maneuver without incident and went directly to the frosted glass doors.

As a gentleman, I am embarrassed to admit that I possess certain skills that would be common place among ruffians and the uncouth. I pulled a pick from my coat pocket, and confident that no one was within hearing range, proceeded to rake the tumblers of the brass lock holding the glass doors shut. Being a lock of more than common craftsmanship, it took several attempts to open it.

Behind the glass doors were a dozen or so worn tomes. The writing on the spines was either non-existent or faded beyond legibility, but otherwise the books appeared in good condition considering their apparent age. I unshelved a volume and was surprised to find it in Latin with English translation. It was handwritten with neatly drawn letters that were easy to read. Upon reviewing the frontispiece, I nearly dropped the book. The image of a winged demonic creature carrying a sword surrounded by candles and arcane symbols disturbed me. But its title is what sent a shiver through me: "Key to the Gate of Hell."

Resisting my desire to drop the book, I opened to a random page to find the text was written backwards.

I understand this to be a common practice for magical incantations, where the transcriber of the book fears that the mere act of writing the words would cause the spell to be enacted. Afraid, I returned the volume to the shelf and closed the glass doors. With my jacket sleeve I buffed away any smudges I may have left. With only more questions, I retired, troubled, to my room.

IX. News From London

I can understand a man, desperate and destitute and loveless, seeking dangerous knowledge in hopes of improving his lot, but Mr. Prufit seemed none of these. He had wealth and comfort and the graces of the Queen and, most significantly, the companionship of a radiant woman. What more could he want that would drive him to risk all these bounties? How did Mrs. Prufit fit into his plot? These questions churned my gut like one of those Indian dishes from a London streethawker.

I eventually drifted off with no decisions made, only to awaken with a start sometime later. My lingering fatigue suggested that I had slept only minutes, but grey morning light leaked beneath the shade on my room's small window. I glanced at the clock on my bedside table. Seeing the lateness of the hour, I sprang from my sweat-damp sheets. I dressed and, still straightening my tie, rushed from my room, hoping that my master, too, had overslept.

My stomach tightened when I found his room empty. My initial fear—that Mr. Prufit had disposed of Master Hurlock—was allayed when I noticed my master's shaving brush still held a trace of fresh lather, his armoire door hung open, and several coats and pairs of trousers were strewn around the room.

I found my master at his easel. Skillfully he attacked the canvas with precise strokes of his brush, much like an accomplished fencer might wield his epee. The portrait had begun to coalesce, and I could see that this painting, would indeed, be his master work.

I was startled to find Mr. Prufit propped in a corner like a forgotten trinket. He did not scowl or jeer; in truth, I do not think he even noticed me enter, his gaze was so locked upon the strokes of my master's brush.

I stepped off to the side, unwilling to disrupt with a word or sound.

Not long thereafter, however, Mr. Blackstone burst into the room. "Titus, urgent news from London," he said. "Mrs. Giddings is dead."

Mrs. Prufit gasped and covered her mouth with a gloved hand. For the first time, my master's hand faltered.

A hollowness filled me.

"There is more." Mr. Blackstone gazed at my master. "Perhaps we should retire to somewhere private."

Mr. Prufit nodded and the two men departed.

Master Hurlock set his brush aside. His jaw hung slack, and he had the quizzical look of a man whose previous night's binge had left him in a strange room.

Mrs. Prufit's face had gone pale. I feared she might swoon. "Perhaps some water, Mrs. Prufit?"

She smiled weakly at me and seemed to regain some of her color. "That would be wonderful, Mr. Stevens."

While I was indeed concerned about Mrs. Prufit's condition, I had an ulterior motive for my offer. Seeing no one in the hallway, I paused at the library door. I heard Mr. Blackstone speaking within.

"Prior to coming to Penketh, I commissioned Lucius Santonelli to investigate. He is exceedingly gifted and knowledgeable in spiritual matters, but not one of those overly public figures who attracts a great deal of attention."

"I know of Santonelli," said Mr. Prufit. "His reputation is good."

I heard a clinking noise as a drink was poured.

"I received word from him this morning," Mr. Blackstone said. "As we suspected, he detected extensive damage to Mrs. Giddings spiritual force. He described her as tattered."

"Tattered?" Mr. Prufit said with surprise.

"It sounds like it was worse than we suspected," said Mr. Blackstone.

"And what about Hurlock?" asked Mr. Prufit.

"Santonelli had a chance to examine Hurlock's painting. It had—how did he put it—an unusual odor to it."

"Odor?"

"Yes, odor," said Mr. Blackstone.

"What does that mean?"

"Spirits leave a trace of their presence where ever they pass. You and I can't sense it, but people like Santonelli are attuned to such things. He described it as akin to a lady's perfume, although much less alluring. Apparently, Mrs. Giddings had a distinct odor on her, and it matched the one on the painting."

"First Madame Borevsky's finding of a dark spirit in the vicinity and now this. It can be no one else,

Henry. Are you now convinced?"

"I am," Mr. Blackstone said without hesitation.

I should have retreated then, retrieved my master, and made a fast departure from Penketh Manor, but my legs did not respond to my mind's desperate urgings.

"We need to get Wynona away from Hurlock," Mr. Prufit said.

"Yes, and we must not allow this creature to escape," said Mr. Blackstone. "It will surely attack again."

"An exorcism then."

My stomach tightened at the word.

"Assuming he, or should I say *it* can be detained." Mr. Prufit's voice moved away from the door as he spoke. I heard the sound of a drawer opening. "I think we should be prepared for whatever needs to be done." A series of metallic clicks stood the hairs on the back of my neck on end. I recognized the sound of a revolver cylinder being opened, examined, and snapped back into place.

My legs began to move, almost of their own accord, carrying me quickly back to the studio.

X. A Gentleman No More

Master Hurlock lowered his brush as I entered. He had been working on the portrait's background. "Stevens, you look unhinged."

On the patio, Mrs. Prufit gazed over the garden, her blue dress shimmering in the mid-morning sun.

"We need to depart, sir."

"Depart?" He dabbed his brush into a dollop of cadmium blue.

"There isn't time to explain, sir." I crossed the studio to retrieve his etui from near the French doors. There would be no time to pack anything, but at least all would not be lost.

"Explain you must. I cannot leave now."

Before I could insist further, Mr. Prufit burst into the studio followed by Mr. Blackstone. "Mr. Hurlock, I must ask you to come with me," Mr. Prufit said.

"Mr. Prufit, can this not wait? The light—"

Having seemingly escaped notice for the moment, I slipped behind the drapery next to the French doors and peered from between the panels.

Mrs. Prufit brushed past my hiding spot as she came in from the patio and stopped an arm's length in front of me. "Titus, what is this?"

"Wynona, dear," Mr. Prufit said, "this business does not concern you."

"Sir," said Master Hurlock, "There is no need for that tone with the lady."

Mr. Prufit's glare swung over to my master. "And you will remember whose house you are in."

Master Hurlock stumbled back as if Mr. Prufit's gaze had been a blunt object.

"Titus!" Mrs. Prufit made his name a reprimand. "This is outrageous."

"This is for your own safety, Wynona. For the last time Hurlock, come with me."

"I don't like your tone, sir." Master Hurlock set aside his palette. "I think I am finished here."

"You leave me no recourse." Mr. Prufit drew his pistol from the waistbelt beneath his jacket.

My master made an audible noise, neither word nor scream. He immediately raised his hands.

Mr. Prufit brandished the pistol in the direction he

wanted my master to move.

"Titus, what has gotten into you?" Mrs. Prufit asked after she had recovered her wits.

"Now is not the time, Wynona." Mr. Prufit's military training had asserted itself; his voice was calm and even. The pistol, an old military-issue Webley Bentley revolver, was steady in his hand.

"Now is not the time?" Mrs. Prufit's voice rose an octave as she spoke.

Mr. Prufit ignored his wife. "Henry, find his man. He was here a moment ago."

I pulled behind a satin panel. It would take only moments for Mr. Blackstone to find me, yet my thoughts, much like my body, were paralyzed.

I heard a commotion and a loud crash that sounded like a piece of furniture splintering. Mrs. Prufit screamed, and I felt her back into the curtain that hid me.

I grabbed her by the wrist. "I'm a friend," I whispered and pulled her through the French doors onto the patio. She came without struggle. I could see by her glazed look that she had been rendered witless by the events.

I drew up at the edge of the patio and turned back toward the French doors. I have never been a courageous man, and, being no match for two armed men, I ordinarily would have left without hesitation, but I owed Master Hurlock a great debt for all he had done. My hesitation was but a brief moment, but it was enough.

A loud crack startled me. At the same time it shattered Mrs. Prufit's trance. She screamed and ran down the steps into the garden.

I looked back toward the studio. To go back would

surely have been my end. A second shot rang out, and I realized with regret that I could do nothing more for my master.

I managed to catch Mrs. Prufit as she entered the copse of trees behind the gazebo. I seized her wrist and pulled her to a stop. Her pulse throbbing against my finger tips made me aware of how alive she was.

"What is happening?" Mrs. Prufit asked, wide-eyed.

Through the trees, I saw Mr. Prufit and Mr. Blackstone descend the patio steps and start across the garden in our direction.

With my master gone, nothing held me to Penketh. There was only Mrs. Prufit. "I will show you," I said. Gently I pulled her deeper into the copse, and she came without resistance. I located the stone path and followed it as carefully as I could. I got turned around more than once, but eventually found what I sought.

"Oh my." Mrs. Prufit covered her mouth with her hand.

We approached the stone block, and for the first time I realized that it was not simply an altar, but a tomb. Inscribed on it were ancient Talmudic glyphs and symbols, most of which I only recognized from the popular press. Atop the sarcophagus lay a shallow dish filled with ashes surrounded by stubs of numerous candles. Near these items, the name of John Henry Prufit was carved into the lid followed by the dates 1838-1856.

The tomb, the book, and a living spirit filled with enough purity and power to—

"I can't allow this happen," I said.

"What is this?"

"Your husband must not be allowed to violate the

laws that divide this world from the next."

"I do not understand."

"Mr. Prufit wishes to pry open the portal between the land of the living and the world of spirit, to put flesh anew on his son's long dead bones, and rip him back to the mortal world. To do this, a living spirit must be traded, a vibrant and good spirit." In her eyes I saw disbelief and wondered if I could convince her.

"I am to be sacrificed?" she asked hesitantly. Her eyes darted from the candles to my face to the name of her husband's dead son. As she continued to speak, her voice gained strength, rising almost to the point of anger. "My husband is going to kill me to raise his dead son?"

I heard the sound of voices in the woods. Mr. Prufit and Mr. Blackstone had fanned out and were coordinating their search. We were now trapped between them.

"What are we to do?" she asked.

I smelled fear underneath her sweet perfume. I felt the heat of her body across the cool air. In my years as gentleman to Master Hurlock, I have basked in the radiance of more power and beauty than most mortal men have seen in life and dream combined. Mrs. Prufit made them all look like sullied rags discarded into a ditch.

"You must go back to them," I said. She began to protests, but I silenced her with upraised hands. "If they find you here with me, things will not end well for either of us. Tell them I took you and that you managed to escape. At your first opportunity, flee Penketh and never return." I could see the doubt in her face, and I wondered if this plan would succeed. I had already failed Master Hurlock. I could not fail again. "There is something more I must do," I said. I considered just doing what I needed without a word, but for some reason, I could not do it without her consent. "I can make it so that you are no good for their ritual."

"How?"

I shrugged my shoulders, not sure how much to say for fear of scaring her into the woods. "It won't hurt."

Her breathing had stopped even though her mouth hung open. She looked ready to break and run, but then her jaw clenched firmly shut and she raised her chin defiantly.

Slowly I encircled her with my arms and pulled her close to me. I could feel her life force, throbbing and plentiful. I had not realized the depth of my need. I drank deeply of her golden essence, sweet as divine honey. With each draught my hunger grew. It had been so long since I had last been sated, and it had cost Mrs. Giddings her life. I would not let that happen to Mrs. Prufit.

Mrs. Prufit gasped, although I am certain she felt nothing. She put her arms around me and buried her face into my neck. I could feel her breath on my reawakening skin.

It was an effort to stop myself from taking too much, but I fought the urge and pushed her away when I was confident she would no longer be any good to Mr. Prufit. I would find what more I needed elsewhere.

She stumbled back against the grave. I sensed she was diminished, her soul wounded and tattered. While her beauty was still considerable and, unlike poor Mrs. Giddings, she would live a long, fruitful life, I could sense the damage I had done. I was a vandal who had taken a knife to the Mona Lisa.

Mrs. Prufit put a hand on my cheek. Her delicate fingers burned warmly against my skin. Her expression of confusion slowly softened. With her gaining enlightenment, I expected horror or pity to surface in her eyes, but instead I saw compassion. "You were one like John Henry."

I was not accustomed to admitting who, or what I was, but she deserved to know. "My father brought me back, even knowing I would become this. Normal sustenance cannot sustain my body, because my flesh was, and still is, dead. If he had loved me, he would have let me go instead of making me this ... monster."

"You are no monster, Mr. Stevens." She looked toward the sound of Mr. Prufit's voice. It had grown close. "I will lead them away from here, so you can escape."

Escape to where, I wondered. Back to the streets of the East End to prey on the sordid souls that lurked in the darkness? Master Hurlock had shown me that humanity still lived within this monstrous being. I could not return to that life, but what options would I have when the need returned?

"God speed to you, Mr. Stevens," Mrs. Prufit said. She fled into the forest.

I turned toward the sound of Mr. Prufit's voice. He was very near. I would take no more innocent souls, I decided, as I moved quickly into the shadows.

STORY NOTES
THE BEAUTY OF WYNONA

"The Beauty of Wynona" is the longest story I've ever published, and it was one of the most fun to write, even though it has dark overtones.

This story had its roots in a variety of inspirations which all seemed to simply come together. These included: (1) an article on an obscure portraitist in The New York Review of Books, (2) the BBC show "Jeeves and Wooster" (with Stephen Fry and Hugh Laurie) based on the stories of P.G. Wodehouse, and (3) Connie Willis's delightful novel *To Say Nothing of the Dog*.

As I look at these inspirations, what strikes me as interesting is that two of them are comedies (and very funny ones at that), whereas my story, while it has some light moments, is fairly dark. Things like this make me wonder how the mind works.

I would be remiss to note that the title of this story came from a song (and album) by the incredibly-talented Daniel Lanois. This album lived in my playlist while I wrote this story. It would be foolish to think it had no effect on the resulting tale.

My Mask, Humanity

First published in *Daily Science Fiction*, September 2012

MY MISTRESS CALLS ME HER MIMIC. It's as good a
name as any, and I have had more names than I can
clearly remember. Each has left a trace in my genetic
structure, and, in a sense, I am all of those names and
none. I am, however, whatever name I need to be at a
given time, and today I need to be Cillian Truffant.

Unfortunately, this name is already owned by
another man. Not unfortunate for me, mind you, but
unfortunate for *him*.

From my position above the wide arcade in Titan's
Huygens City, I study Truffant as he moves through
the crowd below. The bob of his head when he
apologizes for bumping an old woman carrying a
large bag. The way he angles his body to slip through
a gaggle of youths who dropped unexpectedly to the
tiles around him from the second level. His smile as
he passes through the steam wafting from an open air
noodle shop. Truffant has a lopsided grin, boyish
almost, even though his hair is tinged with gray, and
he has witnessed more violence and hardship than
anyone, even in these difficult times.

I move along the railing, from support to support,
watching from behind the face-shroud I wear to
cover my primed skin. The crowd on the upper level
parts before me, because I look like a diseased man
on Hajj. I bow meekly to acknowledge their pitying
faces, but also to hide what I am and what I am not.

As quickly as the crowd passes me, I am forgotten.

Truffant stops to look at a new shirt. As he rubs the fabric between his thumb and index finger, my fingers do the same motion. He is meticulous in his inspection; his eyebrows rise when he finds a loose thread.

My brows arch in the same way. Once. Twice. A third time, when I finally get it right.

He leaves the shirt and moves on.

For a man who survives by seeing, Truffant is oblivious. Like the others, he shops for trinkets while my mistress burns the domes of Ganymede. It is as if through the mundane, they cope with the horrific inevitable.

I come to a marked drop area and step off the edge. As I float downward in Titan's low gee, Truffant stops to buy fried dough from a pretty woman in a skintight dress. I lose sight of him as I land within the arcade's shifting crowd. Moving quickly, I locate Truffant again. He takes the fried dough, and in three bites it is gone. One finger at a time, he licks the powdered sugar from the tips, his eyes closed as he savors the sweet. His mannerisms are distinct but simple.

It will be easy to be Cillian Truffant.

I slip through the crowd and bump him, making it look an accident. As I do so, the needle in my right hand removes a micro-plug of tissue from his thigh.

"Your pardon," I say, bowing so he cannot see my face. The needle is sharp, and in his distraction he did not feel it take a sample of his cells. I am gone into the crowd before he even notices he has been jostled.

#

I inject Truffant's DNA into multiple places on my face and body. The engineered lentiviruses placed within me by my mistress will attack it and absorb it, incorporating it into their RNA structure. Then it will be carried into my primed cells and reverse-transcribed into my own genome. My cells will translate the information that is Truffant and restructure my flesh to match his. The process will take several painful days. I embrace the pain. It is a small reminder that some part of me may still be human.

My mistress plucks the neurons that control my vision and my hearing, and she appears in the small room with me. Her skin is smooth as milk; her hair, inky lines scratched by an artist's repidograph. She has black eyes, iridescent as the wings of midnight beetles. She is not human, but I do not know what she is. With slender fingers she touches my cheek, a cold caress that shocks me like static electricity.

A smile slices open her face, and in her mouth I see the web of souls she controls. Like me, humanity serves her, willing or not, except out here, among Saturn's moons, where the remnants resist.

"Do not underestimate Marcus," she says. Her fingers rake furrows through my skin, but only in my mind. She plucks the neurons for pain as delicately as a harpist. "Once he dies, the resistance will collapse." The pain becomes pleasure, and although I wish I could remain standing, I fall to my knees.

Marcus hides somewhere among the rings of Saturn or its inner moonlets, a million possible places from which he coordinates the final resistance. Her web of spies, both flesh and nanite, have learned that Truffant will secretly meet and interview him, but I will see that it does not go as planned. When I find Timothy Marcus, I am to kill him and deliver humanity to my mistress. Souls in her mouth like grains of sugar.

#

Each morning I look in the mirror and my face has changed. My nose grows longer and wider. The hue of my eyes lightens to that of Neptune, blue and bottomless. My skin loses its newborn pink; it toughens and darkens. I have had so many faces I no longer remember my own.

In the mirror, I practice the boyish grin. "I am Cillian Truffant," I say in mock greeting. Once my vocal cords settle into their proper shape and position, the timbre of my voice is perfect.

From his dossier, I know Truffant's history better than my own. Orphaned at a young age, he did not weep at his mother's funeral. He slipped free of Europa, before my mistress could secure its orbital space, but his reports tight-beamed to the outer moons established his credentials as a field journalist of considerable acumen. His marriage to Susee, a reporter of equal skill, was a casualty of morality; she needed to do more than talk about the resistance. He still loves her. I know this because her picture is the only one on his stylus pad.

#

My mistress comes to me as I lay naked on my bed, fantasizing about Susee. Her nails, cold and sharp, press into my ribs.

"It is time," she coos to me, like my fantasy lover. She strums my nerves. My eyes roll back into my head, and I ejaculate in a spasm of pleasure.

Ashamed, I pull on pants and shirt and look in the mirror. My face is still flushed.

My mistress stands behind me, glowing like a specter in the shadow of my room. In her eyes I see the reflection of what I will be if I succeed. In her smile I see what will befall me if I fail. Both are terrible to behold.

"I am Cillian Truffant," I say, but when I blink, I am alone again.

Today Truffant is meeting Mitchell, who will take him to Marcus. I get to Truffant's favorite café, early and slip into the toilet. Truffant will visit here before he orders, because he always does.

Within a few minutes, Truffant enters. For a moment he is confused as he stares into his own eyes. "Who—"

In that moment, I break his neck.

I drag his still twitching body into the stall, prop him on the toilet, and latch the door. I inject him with a tissue lysing microbe. While I wait, I hastily strip off his shirt and slit his pants up both sides. By the time I finish removing his clothes, his body has begun to bloat. With my knife, I puncture one of his buttocks and a slurry of organics runs into the toilet. The body sags as the digested organs and bone drain. I fold the loose skin into the bowl and wait until the microbes partially digest it before flushing the whole mess down into Titan's sewer system.

Now I am the only Cillian Truffant.

Mitchell is late. While I wait, I retrieve Susee's picture from the dossier in my neural cache. She is tall with cafe-au-lait skin and her head shaved to fine stubble that on most women would make their face bulbous and bug-eyed, but makes her look like a new age Zulu warrioress. I close my eyes and imagine how her powerful hands would feel on my back. My breathing deepens. Somewhere in my past life, I had someone like Susee.

"It's good to see you, Cillian."

"I've missed you," I whisper back to her.

"Beg pardon?"

I snap my eyes open, but Susee does not disappear. She sits in the chair across from me.

"Marcus sent me," she says.

I blink several times, but she still does not vanish. She is as striking as her picture.

"You look good," she says. She touches the graying hair near my left temple. Her wrist smells faintly of musk.

"And you," I say. We sit in awkward silence. She studies her fingers. I stare at the curve of her cheeks.

As if an alarm has gone off, her head snaps up. She looks around seemingly expecting an attack, but only a fool would do so. Susee has killed more people than even me. She would do anything for the resistance, and I suspect she has. "We should go."

"Where?" I ask. I do not expect her to answer, certainly not in such a public place, but I must ask anyways.

Susee levels her gaze. "Even if I knew, I couldn't tell you."

I cock my head to one side and arch my left eyebrow. "You don't know?"

She graces me with her little half-smile. "Marcus doesn't tell me everything. It's safer that way. In case I am captured." She grabs my hand and pulls me from my chair. "It's now or never, Cillian."

#

The elevator shoots us up through Titan's dense orange clouds to the orbital docking hub. There we squirm through a boarding umbilicus to a cramped, windowless cabin that smells of sweat and oxides. Loose dandruff and other biological flock swirl around us as we strap into the two acceleration chairs.

The gel-pad cools my damp shirt. I shiver.

In other incarnations, I vaguely recall liking the tug of zero gee on my stomach. That was lives away, however—splinters of lost memory slipped under neural skin. Now I only really know Truffant's unease, born from several close calls in space and reported stories of freeze-dried bodies vented into vacuum.

Susee finishes entering her fragment of the coordinates to Marcus's location into the ship's navigation. Someone has already entered the other piece, she explains. "Here we go," she says.

A loud clang vibrates through the hull as docking booms disengage. Susee's hand dangles next to mine, but before I can take it, my organs slide back against my spinal column as our engines flare, and we accelerate away from the docking hub.

I grit my teeth.

Susee squeezes my hand. Hers is warm, unlike mine, which is clammy cold. I squeeze her fingers. Gradually the pressure eases as we settle into a one-gee acceleration. Susee releases her shoulder straps and lets her head lull easily against its pad. She takes a deep breath and exhales it loudly. "I never should have left," she says.

I look at my hands and realize that at one time they had explored the arc of her breasts, the folds of her body. For a moment I am jarred out of being Cillian Truffant because I realize that these are not real memories, only information extrapolated from the dossier I have studied. Or perhaps they are real, but lost to me, except as a mask for my mistress's masquerade.

Jealousy for what Cillian Truffant had stabs at me.

I struggle to be Truffant again. "I wish—"

"It wasn't you—"

We speak at the same time and fall silent together.

She left me to follow Marcus into this futile fight against my mistress. She had been covering Marcus's emerging movement for the Jovian news bureau and had allowed her objectivity to be compromised. Instead of reporting the news, she became part of it. After Callisto fell, she joined Marcus in his struggle. Appalled, I did not follow her, something I have always regretted.

The ship shudders as secondary jets fire. In my stomach I feel the ship change trajectory. I wonder how long it will take to get to our destination. Instead, I ask, "Why?"

"I couldn't just watch it, anymore. This is a fight for our lives, Cillian. It's a fight for the human race. I won't be enslaved."

A hollowness opens in my gut like a black hole. All her efforts, yet Titan will still fall. If only …

When I say nothing, she kneels beside my chair and leans in close. Her lips are soft and warm. Her fingers are gentle against my skin. I am breathless.

I pull away. "I—" My thoughts spin. I can barely think.

She frowns at me. "I'm sorry. I thought—" She covers her face with her hands and mumbles something. I realize she is cursing herself. "I thought there might be a chance …"

I realize that I do not know how to react. I did not expect her to be here, so I am unprepared. I wonder what we have shared in the past, those intimate moments that aren't captured on video. While I can feel them around me like golden eggs, I can never open them.

I see the lingering residual of those moments in the sadness that pulls at the corner of her eyes. I hear it in the tone of her voice. The memories are heavy, but I sense she would never give them away for anything.

I want them. Yet I know I can never have them or anything like them. My mistress would never allow it, and while I was once human, I am no longer certain if I still am. Oh, but to be human again.

"It doesn't matter, Cillian. Not anymore. Did you know Marcus asked for you, specifically? He thinks you are the only one who can save us."

#

Marcus's hideout is claustrophobic. I don't remember being claustrophobic. For some reason I cannot recall if Truffant is, but then I realize that if I feel claustrophobic, then Truffant is.

Susee leads me quietly through an underbelly of dimly lit accessways lined with exposed conduits, wiring, switches, and ragged insulation. The cold shadows smell of ozone.

This is the resistance.

When I finally set eyes on Marcus, I think that I have been tricked. The hunched, husk of a man before me looks nothing like the man in my dossier or in the subversive videos that urge his followers into action. His skin has lost its luster, like old leather, and I wonder what sort of radiation damage he has sustained. Clumps of hair float around the small room like ejecta from a collapsing star.

Yet, when Marcus looks up from tapping on his stylus pad, the fire in his eyes is unmistakably that of the man who has held my mistress at bay. He motions me toward the only other seat.

I wrap my feet around the stool legs and settle against the padding. It is odd to sit in near zero gee, but planet-bound conventions die hard. I reach to activate the recording device on my shirt collar, but Marcus raises a hand consumed with open ulcers.

"Okay, no video." I am mesmerized by the shell of humanity sitting opposite me. If my mistress had known Marcus's condition, she would not have sent me. I should feel cheated, I think, but I feel sadness instead.

"I am not what you expected," Marcus says without preamble. A smile, ugly and twisted, cuts his face in two like it is a piece of dehydrated meat. "I have worked hard to keep a good public image, but there are limits to how many times I can recycle images into something new."

As he speaks his voice grows weaker until it is barely audible when he stops.

"You're dying." It is as if my words are necessary to make what I see real.

"I will die soon, but the resistance must not. That is why you are here."

Yet, Marcus is the resistance. Without him the moons of Saturn, the last vestige of humanity, will fall into my mistress's dominion.

"Will it matter?" I wonder whose question that is.

"Probably not. We cannot fight against it. I watched Europa crumble, and nothing I could do stopped Callisto from following. I know it is only a matter of time before it takes Titan. You look surprised, but you know as well as me that this is true. How do we fight an enemy that we only know through the information that it allows us to have? We do not understand it because it is not human."

"And what is human?" I am startled at the sound of my voice.

"Surely, you can remember."

I draw back suddenly and hit the wall behind me.

Marcus's eyes lock with mine, and in them I see what it is to be human again, to be free to love something with a power that transcends flesh, and that can sustain even in death and beyond.

Marcus pushes his stylus pad across the space between us. It spins slowly as it traces a gentle arc into my hands. The pad is filled with video feeds, recently recorded personal interviews I have never seen before, documents he has written, contact names. Everything I would need to be Timothy Marcus.

"Who do you think leaked the information to your mistress to bring you here? A gamble, yes, but what do we have to lose? I am dead, one way or the other. Susee was against this idea, but she will help you disable your neural cache and free you from it."

Susee floats, wedged in the narrow hatchway. She does not look at me, and that sadness I saw earlier is still there. I wonder whom she mourns. I know it is not me, but I wish it was.

"It is useless to resist," I whisper.

"Climbing from the primordial seas was useless.

Riding into the vacuum of space was useless. We do what is useless because we are human."

Because we are human …

I study the way Marcus sits, his shoulders back. Even hunched and twisted, they suggest strength and conviction. His rheumy eyes are steady and his gaze penetrating. He absently rubs at his left index finger, and my hand begins to do the same.

It will be easy to be Timothy Marcus, but if humanity is to survive, I know I need to be more than what I currently am. I want to be more. I can be more.

STORY NOTES
MY MASK, HUMANITY

While often no single thing inspires a complete story, I can usually pinpoint one or two things that were important inspirations. I don't know what inspired "My Mask, Humanity." One day, the idea of a guy who could mimic other people popped into my head, along with a first line, "My mistress calls me her mimic." The rest of the story simply came together after that, and I wrote the first draft in just two sittings.

While I don't know the inspiration for the story itself, I can say that this story was influenced by the writings of fellow Hopefull Monster, Colum Paget. Colum wrote a lot of dark, high-tech stories, and "My Mask, Humanity" follows in a similar vein. I'm not sure why it went that way—at the time, I wrote very few stories quite like it—but I'm happy with the results. This story also happens to contain one of my favorite scenes that I've ever written involving a restroom on Titan.

Last Night at the Café Renaissance

First published in *InterGalactic Medicine Show*, July 2015

THE SECOND TIME I MET LUCIC, he was a chef.

He looked down at me, snowy flakes of ash from the persistent smoke settling on his shoulders. "What else do you have to do with your life?" he asked.

I pulled the tatters of my military jacket around my neck. The hollow pipes that are my legs burned against the flesh of my hips.

"I want you to run my floor," Lucic said, "be my maitre d'." He kept his hands in his pockets—good thing. The sight of them, pink and soft, might have driven me to violence.

"Why should I help you?" I asked.

"Because you have skills I need," he said.

Machine gun fire rattled briefly in the distance. Lucic and I craned our heads into the following silence, wondering when the battle would again resume in earnest.

After a time, Lucic cleared his throat. I could not tell if it was because of the smoke or just to jar me back to the present. "I need people like you—"

"Half-men, you mean." I tapped my metal fingers on my threadbare trousers. The metal beneath rang hollowly.

Lucic's jaw twitched. He hated the name half-men, but I found it fitting, considering how people like me were treated.

"You're a leader, Bolduc, or at least you were. The others will respect you."

I looked at anything but his face—the concrete rubble, the trees like driftwood, the grey, grey sky. The old timers talked about a world with color, but the only color I'd ever seen was red.

Lucic squatted next to me. His presence demanded my attention. "And I know you haven't given up on being human."

#

Before we open, Lucic reminds us all of our place. "You are restaurateurs, now," he says to the gathered half-men. "Whatever your thoughts about the Governor, put them aside."

One of the half-men, Paget, grumbles, but quickly falls silent when no one else joins him.

The Governor has grown fat on the blood of men like us. He sends us off to fight for his authority in exchange for the illusion of prosperity for the families we leave behind. When we come home broken, we are tossed aside like last year's toys.

That is all Lucic says. He expects it to be enough, and I trust his instincts. The staff breaks apart then, scattering into the kitchen and up into the rafters to make preparations.

#

Lucic opened his restaurant in the husk of a cathedral whose roof had been burned off long ago by incendiaries, leaving only the charred bones of thick timber crossbeams. On any given night, an observer—perhaps a forgotten military man—spying through a hole in the wall of the Café would have seen a half-dozen tables, clothed in white like marbles of moonlight, and the crimson sky reflected in the curves of spoons and the flats of knives. Around each table, dressed in their finest suits and gowns, men and women would sit savoring an aromatic daube with roots or the cef ravioli painstakingly crimped by kitchen hands. Occasionally, their eyes would turn upward toward the night sky, reddish-hued from the fires, but it's not the stars they sought.

The magic of the Café Renaissance wasn't in the arrangement of the tables, or the shine of the silver or crystal. It was in the food and the service. If our observer—perhaps an orphan girl, her face disfigured by burn scars—kept her eyes on the ground, she might draw the erroneous conclusion that Lucic had no serving staff. But his staff worked the floor without ever touching it. They worked it suspended from wires and pulleys and runners that allowed them to glide above the tables, trays in hand, as they dove like dirigibles on bombing runs, to deliver sweet carrot consommé or caramelized passerine yolks.

All of Lucic's staff were half-men, for whole-men were unavailable for something as frivolous as a restaurant. Even with this reality, I suspected Lucic always wanted people like me to work his Café. We were, after all and in a sense, his children, cursed and inadequate, with clumsy limbs that were inferior to those of flesh. Yet on the wires and unencumbered by our legs, we possessed the grace of hummingbirds. As we soared above them, the men and women below did not see half-men, but unexpected beauty.

\#

The Governor arrives with his wife on his arm and an entourage of sycophants in his wake. I am polite, as much as it pains me. I seat them at a table in the center of the room.

"How can he sit and drink and eat," I say to Lucic later, "while boys die in the mud outside the City." I think, but do not say: he is a ghoul, feeding on the dead.

An explosion rattles the hanging pots. That incendiary was closer than the others. An errant bomb or a shift in the attack, I wonder. I can see in Lucic's face that he wonders the same.

"Appearances," Lucic says. "Leadership is about appearances, especially when leadership is tenuous."

From my time on the front, I know this is true, but I refuse to concede. The Governor is the one who stopped the veteran ration for half-men. He is the one who turned us out of the infirmaries. He is the one who took the other half of our humanity.

Lucic holds up a flaccid strip of grey flesh capped with a white almond-shaped shell. With the help of the other staff, and at Lucic's request, I had fished the gooseneck barnacles from debris in the harbor several days ago. "No one thinks to eat a barnacle," Lucic says. "It grows in the filth and slime. It looks wholly inedible, but tonight it will be a delicacy to be worshipped."

Lucic returns to his labor, his point made.

On the counter next to him is a bucket. Inside several discarded barnacles cling to bits of refuse. Sometimes a barnacle is simply a barnacle, and no amount of culinary magic can make it anything more.

I bounce my body lightly and the rapeller in the rafters spins, launching me up into the night. Tilting my weight to the right, the pulley system shifts, and the kitchen falls away as I slide out into the dining area. Paget pivots to avoid me, shooting past in the near dark. The harness bolts tug at my hips as I loop to the left to avoid Marc-Andre. He slides by, silent as a ghost, a laden tray in his left hand.

Explosions flash across the sky in rapid succession. The building shakes.

For a moment, the diners pause. Each table is encased in its own droplet of candlelight. In the upturned faces, I see concern, but also resignation. No place is safe in the City. They think: if I am to die, then why not here, with a good meal in my belly.

I sweep downward toward the Governor's table. They have finished their course and sit conversing as they await the next. I pull the wires and slow to a stop above them, where they do not see me.

"The half-men are a danger," says one of the Governor's sycophants. They all look the same to me: plump and clueless. "The metal affects their brains and corrupts their moral capacity. That is what happened in Avignon, when the half-men rose up."

"They were no match for Avignon's army," says a second.

The first snorts. "Of course not. They are not men any longer."

"Where is your compassion?" asks the Governor. "They do not have metal hearts, unlike you perhaps." This draws snickers from the others.

"Now is not the time to grow soft," says a third sycophant.

The Governor's brow crinkles. "What have we become when compassion for our fellow man is weakness?"

"The world has no room for compassion," says the first sycophant. "Do you think our enemies will show us compassion? Send the half-men to the front, all of them, and let them prove—"

The Governor raises a hand, and the conversation halts.

I had not noticed the bombs going quiet. Now my gut constricts.

The Governor's wife turns her face up to the sky. She does not seem to see me, although she looks straight at me.

The sycophants look from one to the other, confused by the sudden quiet.

I drop down and pull to a stop at the Governor's side.

The Governor's face has blanched pale as a parsnip, and I realize he knows.

Before I can speak the door to the dining hall bursts open and soldiers flood across the floor, leveling bayonets and rifle muzzles at diners as they go. A man stands and reaches inside his coat. Pop! Pop! He falls, two holes neatly pushed through his forehead.

A woman screams. It takes me a moment to realize it is the Governor's wife.

Before I can bounce my wire, a ring of guns surrounds us.

The Governor raises his hands to show they are empty and places them, palms up, on the table in front of him. The sycophants do the same.

I could have pulled my wires. The rapeller is strong and quick. If the night had been darker, I might have, but the sky's red tint would have silhouetted me and these soldier-boys have the eyes of hardened veterans.

The ring of soldiers parts. Into the candlelight steps a mustached face I prayed I'd never see again.

Unable to stop it, a curse slips through my lips.

"Looks like we have our prize," says the General.

#

My only encounter with the General happened three years ago, when I was a whole man. We had been taken by surprise, among the rubble and bodies, beneath a sky black with smoke and red with fire. They killed Petr in the ambush's opening salvo; a bullet through the cheek will do that.

We were lined up, and the General himself walked our ranks, his right hand resting on the butt of his pistol like he fancied himself an old time gunslinger.

He stopped in front of me and eyed the bars on the shoulder of my uniform. From the crinkle of his nose, he didn't like the smell of me, but the General didn't like the smell of anyone wearing our colors.

Without a movement or a word, he somehow instructed his attaché to draw his pistol. The soldier-boy, who couldn't have been more than half my age, drew his weapon and pointed it at my nose.

At least a bullet in the face is quick, I thought. Assuming the angle is right.

But the bullet wasn't for me. The soldier-boy swung the pistol toward the man on my left and fired. Michel dropped, a hole in his stomach. He writhed on the ground, trying to be silent, but his grunting and whimpering wrenched my gut more than any scream.

"A bullet in the stomach," the General said. "A grisly way to die." His accent was from the east, but none of us knew from where he actually came. "The acid leaks from the stomach. Eats into the muscles and the intestines."

I would have told the General everything if it would have bought us all bullets in the head, but I knew nothing of value.

The General removed a cigarette and a wooden match from a silver case. On the lid was engraved "With Love D.A.S." To this day, I still wonder if those initials belonged to someone dear to the General or if they embossed a spoil looted from another man's life.

He lit the cigarette. Its sweet smoke reminded me of my father who sold me to the military when I was twelve.

"Nothing to say?" asked the General around the smoke.

Michel begged them to shoot him again.

"When that man dies, shoot another, and then another. When this one is ready to say something, bring him to me."

When Michel went still, the attaché moved to the next man, but before he could shoot, a bomb exploded in our midst. I remember little: a geyser of dirt, screams, a flash that burned a hole in my retinas, but not before I saw the attaché's head cut from his body by a piece of shrapnel the size of a dinner plate. Mostly I remember the pain in my hips where my legs used to be. As I bled out, a platoon of our boys funneled down out of the rubble shooting and bayonetting the last of the General's men. A medic knelt over me and slipped a tourniquet around my stumps.

"No, no," I pleaded, but in my shock I couldn't manage the words I really wanted.

#

The General's new attaché waves his pistol and the soldiers in the ring grab everyone from the table but the Governor and his wife and push them into the dark.

I wait for the gunshots, but silence continues to rest on us like a noose on my shoulders.

The Governor squeezes his wife's hand, but it does not still her trembling.

Alone, next to the Governor, I feel naked. I cover my metal fingers with my flesh ones, but I can do nothing to hide my missing legs.

The attaché leans in from the darkness. "Twenty-six prisoners, one dead, and fourteen mechs," he says.

I hastily tally the numbers in my head. They have everyone.

The General removes his gloves by meticulously pulling the tip of each finger before sliding his hand out. He stacks the gloves together and hands them to his attaché, who tucks them neatly into his shirt pocket.

The General smooths his mustache by running his thumb and index finger around the sharp edges of his lips. He has a hateful mouth, like a jagged line cut with a serrated knife.

"Bring me the one in charge," the General says. The attaché slips back into the darkness, as if he were a piece of it.

"I am in charge here," says the Governor. His words sound strained.

The General grins. His silence says more than any words: You are in charge of nothing anymore.

The General's gaze slides from the Governor to me. He gives no indication that he recognizes who I am. Why should he? Surely I was one of thousands he had interrogated. I am not an individual to him; no, I am far below that. What he sees are no legs and a metal hand.

At that moment, Lucic is brought to the table. He gives no outward indication that anything is wrong; his composure is startling. I do not think Lucic ever spent time on the front, but he would have made an exceptional officer. "Welcome to the Café Renaissance," he says.

I flinch. While Lucic's voice holds no hint of mockery, how can anyone interpret it differently?

"I do not know how you do it," the General says. "Your guests dine while the City falls. Is the food that good?"

"It is humble fare for difficult times," says Lucic.

"Food for the end of the world," says the General.

"Catastrophe cuisine, yes."

"This I must try."

The attaché glances sidelong at the General, but says nothing.

The General sits opposite the Governor and his wife. He points at me. "Mech, where is my napkin?"

I do not move until Lucic nudges me. I pick up an unused linen and snap the ash from it. The crisp white cloth glows in the citron light. Reluctantly, I spread it across the General's lap.

He grabs my hand and holds it up. The metal glints in the candlelight. "To tolerate such abominations," he says to the Governor. "No wonder your City burns. You lack the balls to cull the weak, and it weakens you all." He releases my hand.

"You are the cook?" the General asks Lucic.

"I am the chef," Lucic admits.

"Bring the food then. The Governor and I have

much to discuss."

\#

The General allows Lucic and the other cooks to return to the kitchen.

Before he departs, I grab Lucic's arm with metal fingers. "I will serve the General," I say.

Lucic considers my statement and delivers a curt nod.

Once in the kitchen, Lucic insists we prepare enough for the entire room. Several of the cooks look hesitantly in my direction. I do not share Lucic's optimism that this will be anything other than a last meal, but I nod at the cooks, and they set about finishing the next course.

A soldier-boy stands guard at the end of the counter. Based on the scars puckering his face and neck, he is a grizzled veteran. The attaché circulates through the kitchen, poking his grimy face beneath rattling pot lids.

I pretend to help Lucic by clumsily chopping carrots at his side. "The General will kill us in the end," I whisper. The sound of my knife on the wooden board is loud enough so that no one else can hear me.

Lucic's hands deftly debone a small bird—a pigeon or something like it that Paget had captured that morning from nests in the cathedral's rafters.

Pausing in my chopping, I watch his skillful hands extract each bone with little damage to the surrounding flesh. Those hands served him equally well on the battlefield; I imagined them cutting through the skin on my hand to remove the shattered bones so that metal ones could be grafted into their place.

"I know a place nearby to pick monks hood," I say. "A little in the sauce and that will be that."

Lucic's hands stop.

My brow furrows; I cannot look at him. To Lucic, the meal is sacred.

"Bolduc," he says. His voice is gentle, but tinged with disappointment. The way it stings me is confusing. "We must move beyond the killing," he says.

I bite my tongue.

The soldier ogles a turnip on the counter and sees nothing else.

"The payment for your morality will be a bayonet in the stomach," I say. "The General is a butcher and deserves to die."

"That is what some have said of me." Lucic gives me a knowing look.

"That was different," I say, averting my eyes.

"We are better than that."

Am I truly better than that? Right now I don't want to be.

My chopping knife sounds like a lazy machine gun staccato. Chunks of carrots roll across my board onto the stone countertop like little orange heads. I set the knife aside. My wrist hurts where the metal and flesh meet. The pain is always there, a constant reminder of what I am. I rub my hand, feeling where the metal phalanges meet the metacarpals under the skin of my palm. I have often thought that if I cut my hand off at the wrist no one would know what I am.

The grizzled veteran is still hypnotized by the turnip. I could bounce my wires and rocket up into the dark. Among the rafters and broken walls are many hiding places where those with legs could never reach. Then I look at my brethren scattered around the small kitchen, busily preparing the last meal, and I realize I cannot abandon them. I would rather be the first under the General's bayonet than to come down from the rafters at first light and alight among the human rubble.

Blood pounds in my ears, music that sings: you are still human.

#

The first time I met Lucic, he was a mechineer. In many ways, that's the same as a chef in that he took exotic ingredients that seemed ill-suited to be paired, mixed them in the right proportions, and produced something unexpected. For me it was copper pipe, lengths of filed steel—probably cut from a bumper because of the camo paint still on them—assorted brass gears, elastic bands, and bits of plastic and foam.

The day after I awoke in the infirmary, Lucic visited me. He brought with him a warm smile.

If I had been able to control the metal fingers he had given me, I would have stabbed them into his eyes, plucked them out and worn them like rings.

"You are alive," he said, "but you must eat and drink, or you will not stay that way."

Overhead, dirigible props thrummed the air, as they headed toward the front. I did not think it possible, but the stench of gangrenous flesh was stronger in the infirmary than in the trenches.

Lucic delicately probed the tender skin on my hip and made a note on a chart.

In the bed next to me, another soldier wheezed.

His left lung had been replaced with a bellow that protruded from his back, to the side of a segmented metal spine, like a centipede. My stomach threatened to revolt with every dry rasp of his breath.

"You should have let me die," I said.

"Death is not the answer."

"Except when the question is do I want death or to live like this?"

"You are the same man you were yesterday and the day before that."

I didn't want to be that man either.

I looked away from him, thinking that maybe he would leave if I ignored him, but all around me were half-men and glassy stares. I squeezed my eyes shut. I was surrounded by abominations.

"Your legs do not make you human," he said. "I have seen many with legs whose humanity I would question."

The words did nothing to soothe me.

Lucic visited every day, but I did not speak to him again. The night I was cleared to return to the front, I slipped in among the bodies piled in the dead-wagon and was dumped with them into an open, mass grave. The flies and squirming maggots nearly drove me mad, but I finally managed to free myself from the tangle of bodies, crawl over the lip of the hole, and escape into the night.

#

"Perhaps Paget should serve," Lucic says.

I shake my head. I cannot ask anyone else to serve the General—two-to-one the server doesn't survive the course.

My tray loaded, I take a moment to calm my

breathing. The attaché raises his pistol like a trophy. "Nothing funny, half-man," he warns.

I bounce my wires and ratchet up into the dark, tray in hand. Once among the rafters, I hear gunfire and bombs in a nearby quadrant of the city. I wonder if anyone will try to rescue the Governor.

I drop through the dark toward the tables below, picking up speed as I go. The wires thrum.

"—only to restore order to the chaos," the General is saying as I come in over the top of the table and stop several meters from him.

The Governor's frown looks like it has hardened onto his face.

"If I need to do it with a gun," says the General, "then so be it."

Balancing the tray with my metal hand, I place the General's plate on the table with my other. I lift the cover.

The steam makes my mouth water.

I have never seen a work of art, but the presentation on the plate is how I imagine it would look.

"Escabèche de colombe with bone marrow croquette and fairy ring mushrooms," I say.

The General eyes the food arrayed across the plate. I doubt he has ever seen such a fine meal. He snaps his fingers.

Two soldiers seize the Governor's wife and drag her chair around next to the General's. The Governor starts to rise, but a soldier-boy thrusts the muzzle of his rifle into his face until he sits again.

"There is no reason to hurt anyone," the Governor says. "You have me. Let the others go."

His wife's face is the color of a hardboiled egg.

The Governor should know this isn't about killing, right here right now. This is about the General asserting his power.

"I trust no one," the General says, "especially my enemies." He cuts a piece of meat and dredges it through the sauce. He holds it up to the Governor's wife's lips.

She clamps her mouth closed. Her smudged lipstick and eyeliner give her the aura of a soldier-boy, and for a moment I flash back to the General strutting before me while Michel writhes on the ground with a hole in his stomach.

The General smears the food across her lips. The sauce runs down her chin.

The Governor tries to rise and gets his temple opened with a rifle butt.

"This isn't necessary," he says. His red blood streams from under his hand, down the side of his face and onto his grey shirt. "If you do not trust yours, then take mine."

"What makes you think your life is worth any more than mine?"

The General grabs the woman's ear and tugs it. When she opens her mouth, he shoves the food in. "Swallow it or I'll kill you where you sit," he says, pushing the fork tines against her throat until the skin dimples inward from the pressure.

I want to tell her the food is safe, but I am afraid. For now, I have been forgotten.

The Governor's wife sobs as she chews and swallows the escabèche.

Satisfied, the General pulls the plate closer and begins to shovel the food into his mouth. He eats like he fights, gouging away ragged chunks of meat. He spears a mushroom onto the fork tines and appraises it like a head on a pike before grinding it between his teeth. All the while he grunts around each mouthful.

I find it difficult to watch. If Lucic ever were to ask, I would never tell him about the General's assault on the meal. Lucic deserves better.

#

I am not stopped from bouncing my wire and rising into the night. As I drop toward the kitchen, I see a flash of orange in the darkness near the back of the cathedral, and, for the briefest moment, the faces of the attaché and another soldier-boy shine. I alter my course and stop several meters above them, still wrapped in night.

"—outflanked us and are moving this way," says the soldier-boy.

The attaché makes a guttural sound. A cigarette tip flares orange, then is passed from one to the other. The sweet smoke makes my mouth water— chamomile, because tobacco disappeared long ago.

"We can't get enough on them. They'll be here soon."

"How soon?"

The soldier-boy drags on the cigarette. Its glow outlines his gaunt face. "Twenty minutes, maybe less," he says.

"Slow their advance—"

"We can't—"

"Find a way. I'll inform the General that it's time to leave."

The soldier-boy offers the cigarette back to the attaché who waves it away. He puts it back between his lips as the attaché slips into the night.

I do not even think about it; my military training takes over, and I drop behind the soldier-boy. He notices me at the last moment, but not before I am able to cover his mouth with my flesh hand and twist his head violently with the other. His neck pops. I bounce my wire, and we rise up toward the rafters.

I tie the body into the rigging and hang there for a moment collecting my breath.

My flesh hand shakes. I have killed dozens of men, with bullets and bayonet and once with a rock. Why is this one any different?

Tracers incise the night sky and leave afterimages on my retinas. Lost in the smoke, dirigibles thrum, a constant symphony to the unfolding battle. Not far away, muzzles flash like fireflies. The fighting is close.

If we can keep the General occupied, then maybe our soldiers can get here. Maybe there is—I shake my head. Hope is something that died long before my humanity. I will not come out of this alive, but if I can take the General with me … That is my goal.

My hands have settled, so I drop into the kitchen to find Lucic.

#

Lucic is busy plating the dessert, and I cannot bring myself to interrupt him while he skillfully shapes the custard. Once he has finished, I open my mouth to speak, but before I can say anything, the attaché orders us to the dining area. Lucic protests, but a pistol leveled at his face silences him.

"Help me," I say, extending my arm.

Lucic gives me a quizzical look, but takes my arm. Without my legs, I am a slave to the wires, which makes movement along the ground difficult. Lucic takes my arm and pulls me alongside him as the kitchen staff is herded toward the dining area.

"Tell me, Lucic," I whisper. "When you found me, how did you know?"

"That you had not given up?"

"Yes. How did you know?"

"A man who had given up would have gone back to the front." Or up into the rafters. He doesn't say this, but I see it in his eyes when they glance upwards into the night.

"Help is near," I say. "If we can delay …"

Lucic arches an eyebrow.

The General's men have lined up everyone, face to the wall and are prepared to shoot them in the back. A woman sobs and one of the Governor's sycophants mutters about his worth to the General as a prisoner of war.

"You." The attaché points at Lucic with his pistol. "Come with me."

Lucic does not release my arm as he follows the attaché. The Governor's wife is led past us, toward the execution line. I look back at her, as she fades into the night like it is smoke, and I wonder if she knows.

At the table, the Governor struggles against two soldier-boys, until a rifle muzzle to his gut bends him over.

The General snaps a round into the chamber of his pistol. He fixes us with cold eyes. "My compliments to the chef," he says. The way his eyes narrow, the compliment signifies no favor from what is about to happen.

"The meal is not over, General. You cannot judge—"

The attaché cracks Lucic's skull with his pistol.

Lucic crumples to the ground, clutching at the bloody gash above his right eye. Without thinking, I reach toward the attaché, but I stop when he swings the pistol barrel around to me. I see in his eyes that my life means nothing. I raise my hands, uncertain if it will matter.

I jump at the rattle of machine guns. Only after I realize they are distant can I draw a breath to speak. "How can we save humanity if we act like animals?" Instinctively I flinch, expecting a bullet. When it doesn't come I open my eyes.

The General fills my vision. If I could have, I would have stepped back.

"We are no threat to you," I say. My words are barely audible. "You can leave here with the Governor and probably put an end to the killing, for now. Why kill everyone?"

"To wipe away the ugly," the General says.

My hands shake. Somehow I do not piss myself.

"This is no way to make the world less ugly," I say.

"And this little restaurant is?"

Lucic groans from a spot on the floor that should have been next to my feet.

The Governor stares up at me from his knees. His head moves a fraction to either side, as if imploring me not to risk any more.

"The Café Renaissance," I say, "is a place where even the ugly in the world is capable of becoming something unexpected and beautiful, if given the chance. The Café Renaissance is hope."

"All that from a meal?" The General laughs. It is an awful sound like the barking of a mangy animal echoing through a culvert. "Perhaps the cook is right."

Out of the corner of my eye, the attaché's mouth opens to protest.

"The final course is prepared," I say before the attaché can speak. "It will take only a moment to retrieve it."

"Bring it to me, then. And quickly; my patience is small."

I do not hesitate.

I bounce my wires and rocket to the kitchen. I barely slow as I drop to the counter where Lucic had been working; the wires tug at the bolts fixed into my metal hip as I rapidly decelerate.

The custard has been plated, but the dessert is unfinished. My eyes scour the counter: a small bowl of crystallized honey, a few springs of glittery mint, a bottle of sauce, remnants of previous courses, utensils.

I may be a product of Lucic's magic, but I do not possess his talent to finish this work. Then my eyes land on the bone shears, and I grin with inspiration.

#

The General sits on the edge of the table, casually cradling his pistol in his crossed arms. If I did not know better, I would never have suspected he was about to order the deaths of nearly fifty people. I put the plate on the table next to him.

Lucic looks up from the ground, one eye wide, the other bloodied and swollen shut.

"Get on with it, half-man," says the General. He doesn't even look at me.

"Egg custard surprise with sweet honey globes and sugared mint," I say. I lift the lid.

The attaché gasps, but I force my eyes to stay on

the General's face. Everything else around me disappears. The world goes quiet as if the sound has fallen between the stretching seconds.

The General looks down. His brow crinkles. The plate is a jumble of custard and sauce adorned with golden spheres of honey. In the middle of it all stands a neatly snipped metal finger. The General's eyes widen.

Time snaps forward in a rush of sound and motion.

Machine guns erupt in the darkness.

The General's head snaps up.

I throw the metal plate cover at the attaché who stands transfixed by the dessert. I lunge forward, seizing the General in a bear hug that pins his arms between our bodies. The rapeller spins and yanks us up into the darkness.

Bullets whistle by. In the strobe of muzzle flashes, people scramble for cover. Lucic is on his feet, wrestling with the attaché for control of his pistol. Paget, and several other waiters lined up against the wall, bounce their wires and fly upward. Soldier-boys wearing the City's colors storm in over the rubble of the north wall, exchanging fire with the General's men.

With the General's added weight, the rapeller cannot hold us aloft. We slow, high above the tables, pivot in the harness, and begin to drop.

As we start back toward the ground, I try to release the General, but he grabs me around my neck, and it's all I can do to stop him from crushing my windpipe. Paget whizzes by, nearly colliding with us as we tumble groundward. We reach the end of the wires. With a snap, the bolts in my hips rip free, and I crash atop the General.

For a second, we lie stunned; then the General rolls to his knees and raises his pistol, which by some miracle he has not dropped. Marc-Andre swings out of the dark, but the General puts a bullet into his head, and his limp body continues on, leaking an arc of red blood.

I roll across the floor and under a table. My metal hand is mangled to the point of uselessness; I can't bend the twisted fingers.

The General empties his pistol cartridge, replaces it in a single smooth motion, and continues to kill. In the confusion, he has lost track of me, and he does not notice me on the ground near his feet.

The Governor moves in a crouch toward the General. A table knife gleams in his hand. His bravery is admirable but stupid.

The General turns, but before his pistol can come around, I slash at his ankles with my ragged fingers. The sharp metal cuts easily through his skin and underlying tendons. The wound causes the General's shot to miss the Governor's heart; instead the bullet clips the Governor's shoulder. I slash a second time, cutting deeply into his calves.

The General tumbles to the ground, clutching at his legs.

I grab a handful of his shirt in my flesh hand and pull myself onto his chest. He tries to roll away, but the weight of my body is enough to pin him. I push the sharp points of my fingers against his neck.

"Call them off," I say.

The General grimaces, and I realized it is his best attempt at a smile.

"Call them off or they'll all die."

"They are soldiers," he says. "They are parts of the machine, interchangeable and disposable." He closes his eyes when my fingers draw droplets of blood. What do I care about the General or his men? Their deaths would be a blessing.

Yet, I cannot drive my metal fingers into his neck.

The killing has to stop somewhere. Someone needs to be brave enough to make it stop.

"You took my legs, but I won't let you take my humanity."

#

That night, the City's army turned back the General's forces. Without their leader, they retreated to the east.

The City's military leaders pushed to pursue and destroy them, but the Governor, deciding there had been enough killing, called them back.

While not everyone who had been in the Café Renaissance that night lived to see it, the City survived.

#

Dawn comes, cutting the smoke and ash with shafts of yellow light. I sit with Lucic in the wreckage of the Café.

The dead, half-man and whole men, have been borne away together. For a time, the survivors had lingered, exchanging comfort. With help from the Governor's wife, Paget extracted a bullet from the arm of one of the sycophants while the others watched. Eventually, they trickle away in groups of two or three. The Governor is the last to leave, and only after extracting a promise from me that I would come later that day to discuss a proposition. "It is time for things to change," he says, as he carefully shakes the remnants of my metal hand.

I sit in the silence for a while, and I realize then just how quiet it is. Until that moment, I had not noticed that the war, for now at least, is over. I pinch my arm. The pain surprises me.

Lucic has finally located my legs in all the mess, and together we carefully slot them into my pelvis. "Now what?" I ask.

"I can fix your hand," Lucic says. "If you want."

"That's not what I mean," I say, "but I would like that."

Lucic finishes attaching the bands on my legs before looking up at me. "I think it is time for me to move on," he says. "I hear Avignon needs a restaurant."

"But the café—"

"It is yours, Bolduc."

I cannot find the right words, so I shake my head and say, "No. The Café Renaissance cannot survive without you."

"That is as well," Lucic says. "I don't think you need it anymore."

"Last Night at the Café Renaissance" is one of my all-time favorite stories. It's also one of my most unusual stories, described by Jason McGregor in his *Tangent* review as "... one weird story ... a blend of 'imaginary land' and 'alternate WWII Paris' ..."

I can trace the inspiration for this story to a conversation I had with two co-workers at my day job. We were on a business trip, and as we were driving back to the hotel from dinner, we started talking about what it was like to work as a waiter. It turns out one of my co-workers had spent a time in the restaurant business. He described at length how tired his feet would get working tables on a busy night. One thing led to another, and we started riffing off each other about ways to make waiting tables easier on the feet. One of those ideas was to suspend the waiters from trapeze wires and let them fly around the restaurant.

A restaurant like that would need to be *avant garde*, so I figured it would be a place specializing in something like molecular gastronomy. Waiters on wires, artistic experimental food—what a great image!

And so was born the Café Renaissance, its staff, and a delightful multi-course meal dubbed "catastrophe cuisine." Add a war-torn setting, and a very human story about loss, vengeance, and redemption, and I found a story that made *Tangent*'s recommended reading list for 2015.

Hoodoo

First published in *Specutopia*, July/August 2012

SAM GONDO HAS NEVER THOUGHT Luke Estes was a bright man, and this confirmed it. Only an idiot would gawk at a Bindi weapon. Not that the other xeno-geologists, statisticians and data techs were much better. They lingered in a small knot at what they must have thought was a safe distance, obviously unaware that a Bindi anti-personnel device had a kill radius of half a kilometer.

No accounting for advanced degrees.

Gondo adjusted his nasal cannula, improving the flow of oxygen. He wondered if his concentrator unit was working properly. Since dropping from the orbiter to Paralon's surface four-standard days ago, he had constantly felt like he was suffocating.

Estes noticed him and waved him over. "What took you so long?"

"I was setting a shot three points back," Gondo said. "Couldn't leave it unfinished." He climbed out of the two-man runner and could now see the object Estes had summoned him to examine. A slender cylinder of rust colored metal a half-meter in length stuck out of the corn-kernel regolith. Four razor-straight tail fins projected from its end.

It wasn't any Bindi-tech he had ever seen. That didn't give Gondo any comfort, however.

"What is it?" Estes asked.

"Damned if I know what it is," Gondo said. When

had he become the expert in unknown shit? Gondo realized then that he was the only member of the nine-person survey team that had served on the lines during the Bindi war. He doubted anyone else had ever seen alien-tech except in news-streams. "But it isn't Bindi."

Gondo cautiously approached across the loose regolith and knelt down on the opposite side of the object from Estes. Up close, he confirmed the red color was a skin of iron-oxide dust. Everything on Paralon—equipment, rocks, people—took on that color given time.

"Is it dangerous?"

Gondo ignored what he considered a stupid question. Of course it was dangerous. He had never encountered a piece of alien hardware that wasn't.

Gondo winced as Sandra Kaneal crunched across the regolith to where Estes knelt. Her heavy stride would have triggered a Bindi-weapon at twenty meters.

"Look at the angle," she said. The cylinder leaned slightly to the east, forming about an eighty degree angle with the ground. She stepped around Estes and reached toward the object.

Gondo seized her wrist with a speed that made her gasp.

"I was just going to wipe off the dust to look for re-entry burns."

"Don't touch anything." The only marks Gondo saw on the object were micro-pitting on the upper surface. "I don't see any evidence of re-entry."

"So it didn't come from orbit ..." She looked up into reddish sky, her eyes tracing an arc toward the east. Gondo could see she was already lost in mental calculations. Kaneal was the expedition's data jockey and thought more in numbers than in words. She took concussion wave return rates and angles of refraction generated from shot charges and thumper truck vibrations and transformed them into three-dimensional maps of subterranean features.

"Whatever it is, it's dangerous," Gondo said.

"So it's a bomb?" asked Estes.

Gondo shrugged. "I'm assuming our grid needs to run through here, so I recommend we set a Tovex charge, vacate the area, and blow it up."

"Blow it up?" Kaneal said. "You just said you didn't know what it was. We can't blow it up."

"We can, and we should."

"Look at the pitting on this thing. It's got to be centuries old, and it isn't Bindi. An archaeological find like this is incredibly important."

Gondo's annoyance with the woman was rapidly growing. In the four days he had been planetside, Gondo had never had a conversation of more than five words with her, or any of the other scientists for that matter. He hadn't come to Paralon to socialize.

"This thing jeopardizes everyone's safety," he said.

"Based on what?" Kaneal planted her fists on her hips.

"Five years of seeing people blown into pink mist by things we had never seen before—alien-tech like this." Gondo spoke directly to Estes, knowing mission decisions were his.

Estes began to speak, but Kaneal cut him off. "This is a science issue, Luke. You don't have the authority to make this decision without consulting the senior scientists."

Estes looked sympathetically at Gondo. "She's

right." He rose and dusted the red dirt from the knees of his thermal pants. "This will take only a moment." He and Kaneal went to talk with the watching scientists.

Gondo cursed. Estes was stupid enough to listen to them. He needed to find something to convince Estes of the danger.

The object had no seams, as if it were a solid piece of metal, and no obvious propulsion system. He blew at the dust, exposing some of the underlying metal. Even with the micro-pitting, it had a strange opalescence to it, like nacre. As he watched, the pitted surface smoothed.

Gondo rubbed his eyes with a gloved hand. Had he actually seen what he thought just happened? The patch he had blown now looked smooth and shiny, yet the surrounding area still looked pitted. Perhaps it was some kind of optical illusion from the sheen of the material. He removed the tips of his pressure glove and cautiously touched the surface with his fingertips.

The material was as smooth as it looked and warmer than he expected. His fingertips tingled as they swept the surface, leaving behind what appeared to be small furrows in the material. Gondo pulled his hand back.

He squinted at the spot he had touched. In the furrows, his reflection stared back at him, but as he watched, it twisted and became more alien looking. Watching the reflection made his head hurt, and he squeezed his eyes shut. The pain spiked like a migraine behind his right eye. Gondo pinched the bridge of his nose. He felt awash in emotions, all jumbled together so that he could not pull them apart or make sense of them. They left him feeling helpless and filled with despair.

Gondo opened his eyes and stared up absently at Estes and Kaneal. He had not seen them return. He pulled away from Kaneal's hand on his shoulder

"Is it a bomb?" Estes asked.

Gondo exhaled heavily, trying to clear his head. The ice crystals hung in the air for a moment before subliming. "I don't think it's a bomb." He wanted to say more, but for some reason he couldn't think what.

"That settles it. Sandra, figure out where it might have come from and we'll take it from there."

#

Kaneal explained that calculating the trajectory was easy. Estimating the needed parameters was harder, especially because Gondo had insisted they not touch the object and Estes had agreed. Kaneal had to guess its weight, its total length, and the resistance of the regolith. She used these to estimate the height from which the object had fallen.

"After that, calculating the parabolic arc was simple," she explained to Estes as they gathered around the small conference table in the crew's pressurized habitat module.

Gondo sat at the end of the table, thankful to be rid of the O_2 concentrator and pressure skin. His head still hurt, although the migraine had faded. He would rather have been setting shot in the next grid, alone, but Estes had insisted he be there. Like it or not, Estes now considered Gondo his alien-tech expert.

"How far?" Estes asked.

"It's not perfect," she said, "but it looks like it was

fired from three hundred kilometers to the east, more or less. Unfortunately we have no 3-d projections for that area. It's just outside our survey grid. We do have a high resolution image from the orbiter." She projected the 2-d image onto the table top and added a yellow dot on the spot she had calculated as the object's likely origin.

"What are these?" Gondo pointed to black speckles that covered most of the image.

"Most likely shadows from rock formations called hoodoos," said Estes. His training was in geology, with a specialty in subterranean mapping. "They're aeolian erosional remnants from when Paralon had a thicker atmosphere." He leaned closer to the project image. "Look at this." He pointed to a blackened area that extended from near Kaneal's yellow dot towards the northeast.

"Some sort of rift zone?" suggested Kaneal.

"Maybe, but some of these hoodoos look odd." Estes magnified the image and leaned closer.

"Those aren't rock formations," Gondo said, a coldness gripping his gut. He had seen similar things on reconnaissance images from Bindi bombed planets. "That's wreckage."

#

That Gondo had trouble sleeping that night, wasn't unusual. He hadn't slept well since Mariposa. But tonight, he felt muddled, like he had been concussed. It wasn't painful; something was just … off.

Frustrated, he got up and paced the narrow corridor of the habitat module. The rhythm of the crew's breathing was discordant in his ears. The module felt claustrophobic. After years of close-quarters fighting, Gondo hated tight spaces. People got killed in tight spaces.

Gondo pulled on his pressure skin and coat, inserted his nasal cannula and went outside.

In the cold night air, the inside of his mouth frosted over.

The sky was surprisingly clear of dust and very black. The stars were solid points in the thin atmosphere. Enough of them filled the sky to see by. Beyond the scatter of trucks and modules, Paralon's desolate landscape extended into the darkness.

Since Mariposa, the universe had felt like it was collapsing on him, with too many people telling him his life would right itself, when the only person he really needed was gone. Paralon had been his solution to escape the platitudes and—Gondo shook his head. He had come here because it was easier than facing a life suddenly empty. Yet the pressure of his loss had not eased, and the claustrophobia had only gotten worse since …

Gondo could feel the pull of the alien object. It lay out there, in the darkness.

He climbed into the two-man runner and drove to where the object stuck up out of the regolith. Covered in a skin of red dust, it was difficult to see, but it was as if Gondo could feel its presence.

He knelt next to it, his knees crunching down into the corn-kernel. His breath crackled in the cold.

The object had done something to him when he had touched it earlier, but he couldn't figure out what. He blew the red dust off another spot and pulled the tips off his pressure glove. The cold bit into his fingers as they hovered above the glittering surface. He felt compelled to touch it. Again the object felt smooth and warm. In the starlight it was hard to make out anything, but dark shadows seemed to flow across the surface where his fingers had touched it. He squeezed his eyes shut. His head hurt, a migraine stabbing into the sinuses around his right eye.

Emotions flooded into him again, but this time he recognized them. Fear …the memory of being in the drop ship with his squad hurtling toward the surface of Laguna, where his entire crew but him, a new recruit, were killed by a Bindi gravity bomb. Despair … his wife Liera, burned to the edge of death in the Bindi assault on Mariposa, but pleading to die so the pain would go away. Hopelessness … as Gondo looked across Paralon's starlit landscape, empty of all life, and knowing that he belonged here. He opened his eyes, disjointed, and the pain quickly receded.

He scrambled back away from the object, suddenly afraid. It had gone into his head and summoned those memories, but for what reason? Gondo scrambled to his feet and jumped into the two-man runner. He put it into gear and accelerated directly at the object. It made a satisfying thump as the runner ground it into the regolith.

#

Kaneal wriggled through the hatch connecting the thumper truck's operator cab to the pressurized crew space in the rear. She retrieved a water bag from the shelf and sat on the bench next to Gondo. He slid around to the opposite side of the table.

Six hours had passed since Gondo, Estes, and Kaneal had set off across the regolith to find Kaneal's yellow dot. Thankfully Gondo had been left to himself in the rear of the thumper truck, until now.

"That the latest news?" Kaneal nodded at the smart-paper near Gondo's elbow.

Without looking at it, Gondo slid it across the table.

When Kaneal picked it up, words and pictures materialized on both sides of the sheet. Every twenty-four hours they received a data burst from the orbiter containing the latest news-streams, which could be weeks or months old depending upon where the story had originated.

"Shit," Kaneal said. "The Bindi blew up our diplomatic team."

Gondo watched her emotions slide across her face as she read the article. People's naivety about the Bindi still amazed him. "It's what they do."

"What do you mean? Why kill a diplomatic envoy and risk the ceasefire? It makes no sense."

"They're aliens," said Gondo. "Our best psych and military minds haven't been able to understand them. They don't make sense because they aren't human. We can either tiptoe around them or wipe them out."

"Don't you think that's extreme?"

Gondo didn't. Every alien life form encountered by humans had had only one goal: the cold-blooded extermination of any human they encountered. The only reason the Drogs and the Tifen hadn't succeeded in making humans extinct was that they seemed to have no interest in conquest. When humans started avoiding Drog and Tifen space, the fighting effectively ended. The Bindi were different, however. They were aggressive, even if it made no sense. They had turned Gondo's home world, a planet far from Bindi space, into an uninhabitable cinder. Gondo had no idea how he and a few hundred others had managed to survive the attack. His wife Liera had not.

"Look, Gondo. I know you've got history," Kaneal said, "but we just haven't found a common ground yet."

Gondo pressed his hands flat against the table to stop them from shaking. "You haven't seen what they're capable of," he said. "Talking and making nice—" Gondo shook his head. "You're an idiot."

Kaneal's mouth dropped open. It took her a second to recover. "You're a bastard." She threw the smart-paper onto the table and folded her arms across her breast. "If you're anything like those in charge, no wonder they want to kill us."

The intercom crackled. Estes sounded like he was kilometers away. "We've got debris. Suit up, and let's take a look."

#

The debris ranged from fist-size to larger than the truck.

"You recognize anything, Gondo?" Estes asked.

Gondo shook his head. None of the pieces were sufficiently large to give him an impression of how the ship might have looked.

Before Gondo could stop her, Kaneal picked up a piece of the debris. She wiped off the red dust to reveal a blobby lump of blackened material. "It's light." She tossed it to Estes, who dropped it.

He picked it up and studied it. "We'll take it back and see if we can figure out what it is."

Gondo realized he was holding his breath and exhaled. The metal had not affected either of them. Could it be their gloves, or maybe the debris was different from the object he had touched? Gondo wondered if he had imagined it all.

He knelt next to an oblong chunk of debris about a meter long. He reached out with his gloved hand but didn't touch it. If nothing happened, he would still not know if he had imagined it.

He pulled off the tips from his pressure glove. Leaning closer, he blew the red dust away. The blackened metal underneath was dull. His fingertips tingled with cold as he had second thoughts about touching it.

Gondo swallowed hard. This was the only way to know.

Like the surface of the other object, the debris felt warm. Where he dragged his fingertips across it, he left lines of gleaming nacre, as if the black had been soot that he had rubbed away. Gondo jerked his hand back as if he'd been burned.

Pain stabbed through the right side of his face, nearly causing him to black out. He squeezed his eyes shut so tightly he saw explosions of light. They coalesced into a drop ship hurtling through atmosphere, but this time the ship was empty except for shadows, long and thin, like those cast by the hoodoos. Then he was holding Liera's lifeless hand, but it wasn't her, only another hoodoo shadow. He wanted to scream for his loss, but he knew it would do no good. He would never get her back, no matter how many Bindi he killed, or how hard he made his heart, or how far across space he ran.

Gondo opened his eyes. He sat on the ground, gasping for oxygen. His fingers burned in the cold air.

Kaneal stood over him, concerned eyes looking down at him.

"I'm okay," Gondo said, pulling away from her as she reached to help him up.

"I think we've seen enough," Estes said, turning back toward the truck. "We better get moving again."

#

The debris field grew denser as they continued east. They approached the heart of the wreckage spread over an area peppered with slender rock hoodoos. Gondo had never seen anything like hoodoos before; they rose up like eerie alien silhouettes.

After another hour of driving, a large piece of wreckage came into view. The force of the impact had left a five-hundred-meter scar in the ground and toppled hoodoos. A skirt of scree had been pushed along the leading edge. Fine red dust coated everything.

Kaneal leaned forward to get a better view through the windscreen. Her jaw hung open. "It's huge."

"Let's take a look," Estes said.

They suited up and headed out.

The wreckage towered at least thirty meters over top of them and Gondo got the feeling that this was only a small piece of the original ship. He swallowed hard, fighting to damp his sense of awe. Estes, however, had already approached the wreckage with outstretched hands. Nothing happened when he touched it.

"This is unbelievable," Kaneal said breathlessly.

Without any particular plan, they dispersed as things caught their attention.

Gondo saw a concentration of debris tucked up beneath an overhanging hoodoo and went to investigate. As he neared, he got a familiar, tingly feeling that made him stop short. The ship debris hadn't been thrown against the hoodoo on impact. He couldn't exactly say what the order was, but it certainly wasn't random. In his time in the military, Gondo had gotten good at detecting patterns. Order got people killed more often than random.

"What is it, Gondo?" Estes asked.

"That debris wasn't thrown there."

"Are you sure?" Estes approached slowly from Gondo's left. He reached the debris and pulled up suddenly. "Oh, shit."

Gondo rushed forward.

Just to the other side of a crate-like piece of metal was a flattened, leathery mass laid out on the ground. It was elongate and at least twice Gondo's size, with numerous leathery projections splayed off in different directions. Small curved hooks of some black material covered it.

Gondo's stomach clenched. It looked vaguely like the hoodoo shadows he had seen in his memories when he had touched the debris.

Kaneal joined them. "What is that?"

"I don't know," Estes said, "but it looks organic."

"Looks like it's been dead a long time."

"Hoodoo," Gondo said, not realizing he had spoken aloud until the others looked at him quizzically. "It's shaped like a hoodoo."

Estes nodded in agreement.

Gondo surveyed the other items in what he now thought of as a camp. In addition to crate-like pieces, spherical bulbs, abstract polygons with projecting flexible cords, smooth plates, and cylinders with ridges were stacked in no order he could discern.

Gondo couldn't begin to guess what any of it was. "I wouldn't touch anything."

"I don't see more of your Hoodoos," Estes said after he and Gondo reached the back of the camp near the rock wall.

"Luke, look at this." Kaneal stood next to a cylinder several meters away from the camp. At first Gondo thought it was an object like the one they had discovered in the survey grid, but as he approached, he saw it was actually a hollow tube held upright by regolith packed around the base. It leaned slightly to the west. Around its base was a halo of grey ash and cinder.

"That's where our object came from?" Estes asked.

"He must have been trying to launch it into space." Kaneal shaded her eyes as she stared up into the reddish sky.

Gondo tried to parse everything into something intelligible, but it made no sense. Anyone—anything with this level of technology would have known it was impossible to put a projectile into space without some type of onboard propulsion. The escape velocity necessary was too great on a planet the size of Paralon.

"An S.O.S., maybe?" Kaneal said.

"Look at the ash pattern. I see three—four separate residues." Estes traced their outlines with a gloved finger.

"That makes no sense," Gondo said. "It must have known it couldn't succeed."

"He was desperate," Kaneal said. "Maybe he had a mate back home."

Gondo bristled at Kaneal's use of the pronoun

reserved for people. This thing was an it. It didn't feel desperation. It didn't miss mates. Not the way a human did. Not the way Gondo did.

Gondo looked back toward the corpse. He couldn't shake the fact that it resembled the shadows from his memories the last time he had touched a piece of the alien debris. Was it possible the object they had found had implanted a message—a final, desperate message home from a lonely castaway—into Gondo's brain? Gondo dismissed the notion as ridiculous; he was projecting his own experiences and emotions onto a cold-blooded alien.

Yet as he looked at the evidence around him, he found it hard to deny the possibility.

"That's an odd S.O.S.," Estes said. "Where's the message?"

Unless the strange nacreous material itself contained the message and it only needed someone to touch it to release it. Memory metal, imprinted with the experiences of the Hoodoo. A crazy idea, Gondo thought; it was absurdly … alien.

"We should x-ray the object," Kaneal said. Neither she nor Estes seemed to have noticed Gondo's silence. "Maybe it's hollow."

Each successive time he had touched a piece of the alien metal, the emotions and memories had gotten clearer, as if it were learning how to communicate with him by using his own experiences and memories to tell a story in a way to which he could relate. It was finding a common ground. Gondo and the alien, he thought. It just couldn't be.

Gondo pulled off the tips of his pressure glove. Before Kaneal and Estes could say anything, he ran his fingers down the side of the cylinder and watched the opalescent furrows shimmer and lengthen. He closed his eyes, anticipating a pain that never came. He was among a dozen Hoodoos as their shimmering ship, damaged in an attack, bucked and rocked and came apart in Paralon's atmosphere. Their fear was palpable as the hull glowed white hot and began to melt. Then he was alone with memories of Liera, but not Liera. Something different, a Hoodoo far away but important to the one survivor of the crash. The longing was as strong and real and desperate as Gondo's. Like Gondo, the Hoodoo knew it would die with that longing, but it had never given up trying to get its message home, no matter how remote the chance of success. The Hoodoo had died here, alone, but struggling to the end.

Like a human would.

Gondo opened his eyes. Ice crystals crackled on his cheeks. Faced with a lonely death, the Hoodoo had never given up.

"You okay, Gondo?" Kaneal put a hand on his shoulder.

This time, Gondo did not pull away. He looked into Kaneal's eyes and saw sympathy, not pity. He took a deep, satisfying breath. "Let's get to work," he said. "We have a lot to learn here."

"Hoodoo" had its genesis in a brainstorming session with my writing group, Hopefull Monsters. Around 2010, Colum Paget, a big idea man and excellent writer, suggested we all submit a story to an archeologically-themed anthology. The idea for the central artifact in "Hoodoo" came to me during our group brainstorming exercise and evolved out of an initial idea that the artifact was a "message in a bottle."

The setting and title were inspired from a trip to Goblin Valley in the southwest United States (oh so long ago). Ever since that trip, I've wanted to set a story in a place like Goblin Valley, and I finally found the right tale.

The Illusory Truth of Magical Mike's Page Six

First published in *Etherea Magazine*, January 2023

LANCE LEANS HIS BUTT against my desk, trying to look like someone with whom I could relate. "So, Babych calls you 'Magical Mike.'"

My fingers pause, hovering above their home keys. I wish Lance, the Daily Telegraph's new columns editor, would spend less time "interfacing with his reports" and "delegating for success," and more time on something—anything—practical.

I smile, hoping my silent acknowledgment will convince him to move his pointless banter along to someone else's desk. I have a 3:20 deadline, and regardless of what Lance might think, Page Six doesn't write itself.

"Are you really a magician?" Lance eyes me over the top of his oversized coffee mug.

I stifle a sigh. Just as my column isn't a gossip piece, I am not a magician. Magicians work tawdry children's parties and suburban bar mitzvahs. I write Page Six, and every word I write about the elite, the high society, the well-to-do is meticulously sourced and painstakingly crafted. What I write is the truth or will inevitably become such. If anyone wishes to attribute that to some arcane power, then call me a thaumaturgist. At least that has gravitas.

While I manage to remain silent, Audrey, Lance's

assistant, cannot corral her own despondent sigh. She is half my age, twice as attractive, and from my few interactions with her, whip smart. That she is underappreciated enough to wind up the assistant to Lance shows this world has a misogynistic sense of humor. As her reward, she gets to marinade in Lance's stew of inane corporate jargon and nonsensical management philosophies.

"Everything you write turns out to be true," Lance continues, obviously not ready to move along. "That's an impressive record. Some might even say an impossible one."

I shrug off his implications. "Good sources."

I have worked the high society circuit for over three decades, and I know every doorman, dog walker, and nanny in the city. On occasion I even rub elbows with the powerful themselves—they know who can make or break their summer soiree or their portfolios with a few generous words.

"Yes, yes," Lance says with a sly nod. "Sources." He punctuates the word with finger quotes, which proves awkward considering the mug in his right hand.

Reflexively, I shield my laptop.

Audrey rolls her eyes.

"Is there something you need, Lance?" I refuse to call him Mr. Langston or sir.

Lance leans closer to me. Other than Audrey, I am likely the only one who can hear him now. "Babych said you'd deny everything, but he's told me the truth."

John Babych is Editor-in-Chief of the Daily Telegraph, and a man who metaphorically bleeds ink. We started together as copy boys with the Times before forging off on different publishing paths. Even though we have reached different zeniths, neither of us is uncomfortable sharing a Friday afternoon beer or the occasional professional prank. I have on good authority that he was overruled by Mr. Vincent Mayock, the owner and publisher of the Telegraph, in regard to the hiring of Lance Langston.

My chair squeaks as I lean back and fold my arms against my chest. "And what might that truth be?"

Lance is caught off guard by my question. Perhaps he expected me to crack like a street thug in a low budget police procedural and admit to practicing the arcane secrets of divination.

"Not important," he says, sloshing his mug dismissively. "However, might I share a tip with you? I've heard from a reliable source that Serge Ricardo, the multi-billionaire tech entrepreneur, has decided to invest a sizable sum in a start-up called L. L. Financial. That's L. L. Financial." Lance nods knowingly at me.

This is not the first time someone has tried to plant a rumor in my column with the hope that it will become true or at least spur some auxiliary benefit, generally of a financial persuasion. Most commonly it has been an estranged spouse hoping to smoke out an affair to facilitate a lucrative settlement, but second to that, is the investing tip designed to make a company look more desirable to the market, thus lining the pockets of those involved.

Not only are these tips false, but they are blatant attempts to manipulate the journalistic integrity of my column for personal gain. While I may handle my share of scandalous assertions, I have standards. Even if I do possess arcane powers to bring what I write to pass, I do not believe in the untruthful manipulation of reality for personal gain.

Grinning, I wink at Audrey and wave Lance closer. "I'm not sure if Mr. Babych explained the nuances of my power," I whisper. "It doesn't work if the tip is given solely for the benefit of the person sharing it."

"Well … right."

An awkward moment passes with neither of us speaking.

Audrey breaks the impasse by clearing her throat.

"Well, keep up the good work, Magical Mike. You're a real asset to the Telegraph." He fashions a finger gun from his left hand and points it at me. I must not have responded as hoped because Lance moves along without another word.

"Mr. DiMarco," Audrey says politely once Lance is out of earshot. "Is what you said true?"

I shrug, unwilling to confirm or deny.

Audrey's eyes narrow as Lance calls for her to keep up if she wants to learn anything. She leans closer to me, a devilish grin sliding across her lips. "You might be interested to know that I have on good account that Mr. Mayock has grown disillusioned with recent changes made in his publishing empire, and that he is looking to take some corrective actions, whatever those may be."

I have no idea where some stories come from. "The Illusory Truth of Magical Mike's Page Six" is one of those. The idea seemed to sprout almost whole from the aether. It's absurd, a little funny (I hope), and Lance has obviously been influenced by a character from the movie *Office Space*, one of the funniest workplace comedies ever produced.

I wrote Magical Mike's story in a single sitting, and it needed only the lightest of edits. I love it when a story comes together that easily because it doesn't happen often.

Now and Forever

First published in *What the #@&% Is That?*, November 2016

ELISE SITS ENDLESS VIGIL over our daughter, and my boy is nowhere to be found.

"I heard the door a while ago," Elise says, cool rag in hand. "I thought it was you."

I know immediately where Owen has gone. If I don't get there in time, he'll be dead. Like the others.

I grab the nail gun and my O_2 breather, but there's no time to don my skin-suit. The ribbon of nails bounces against my thigh as I sprint between dark rows of soybean and quinoa. The garden's grow-lights have yet to cycle on. Through the dome overhead, the Milky Way wraps across the great dark like a diamond-studded noose.

Fool boy! Thinks he can kill the Fiend, when forty-six others failed.

I reach the edge of the garden, and stumble onto the metal decking. I barely hear the thud of my feet on the metal plates over the rasp of my breath. The first door, welded shut and barricaded with a field cart, emerges from the darkness, bathed in red light from the night lamp above it. I've guessed wrong.

I fly past, on to the other door.

The cool air burns my lungs. The heat exchangers are failing; every day it gets a fraction colder in the dome, but those who could repair it died long ago.

Ahead, in the next ruddy halo, Owen takes a pry bar to the door. He's already broken the welds on the lower half and works feverishly to snap those across the top. Air hisses out where his efforts have warped the metal.

As I near, Owen must hear my breathing; he puts his weight behind the bar and the last weld pops. The door swings open, but a pressure differential sucks it shut.

The pry bar clatters to the deck as Owen stumbles back.

The door cracks open. Fingers pale as lice wrap the edge. They have nails like needles, hollow and filled with toxin. The Fiend can project them like darts. That's what put Daphne to bed and Elise into her vigil.

The nail gun is hard to steady as I run harder. Whump. Whump. Nails ping against the metal door, the frame, and finally the stream of metal zings through the crack. I throw my shoulder against the door.

The Fiend's fingers crunch and are sheared off by the sharp metal. They plop to the deck still wiggling like a half-dozen severed lizard tails.

"Dammit, boy! You want to die?"

Through the pounding of blood in my neck, I hear the clicking of the Fiend's mandibles.

"Give me the pry bar." I kick at the fingers inching across the deck toward my foot. They'll keep crawling toward anything with warm blood.

Owen's face is ashen, his eyes locked on the wriggling fingers.

The door bounces out of the frame, but my weight is enough to slam it back into place.

"Owen, the bar!"

The boy is frozen and worthless, his stupid

courage drained away by reality.

My toes hook the curl of the pry bar, and I drag it to me. I wedge it under the door—it barely fits—then drive it fast with the heel of my boot.

The trencher that had blocked the door sits to the side. I clamber behind the controls and press my thumb against the ignition scanner, and it whirs to life. I slam its backend against the door, and drop the cutter against the deck for added leverage.

From a bottle I keep under the seat, I squirt accelerant on the fingers and scrape sparks from a lighter on them until they flare into blue flame.

Owen hugs his knees to his face and hides his eyes behind them. His knuckles are white.

I'm too afraid and relieved at the same time to have room for anger. If I had been five seconds later … What's gotten into him, thinking he can take the Fiend by himself? This isn't the first time, either. I've always stopped him, but each time he gets a little closer. I don't know what to do with him. I can't lock him up, and I can't talk sense into him.

The Fiend's scratching grates my nerves. Even with the metal door, it's too close, too dangerous. I think it can sense us, even through the pressure door. Like it can smell our blood, or maybe our fear.

I pick up my boy, frail in my hands. His shaking doesn't stop.

"Please, please, don't ever do that again. I can't protect you out there."

Owen nods his understanding into my shoulder.

#

We were four years out, not even to the halfway point of our transit to Echelon Colony, when the first body turned up riddled with pin-prick holes and strung up like an animal being bled. We thought we had a murderer on board, but the doctor assured us that no one on the ship was capable of that level of savagery.

But people are capable of a lot.

Then the sightings started. A pale creature lurking the corridors of the engineering module. Scrapings on hatches. Clicking sounds from air ducts. How it got aboard, we didn't know. You'd think something like the Fiend couldn't hide on a ship so small, but it was like a splinter of nightmare driven into the flesh of our reality.

After that, the bodies began to collect like regrets. Smart and deadly, the Fiend was a relentless killer.

Attempts to hunt it failed, so we launched the SOS beacons, and retreated to the garden because it was two acres of open ground with limited entry points. We sealed everything up, but still it found ways in and picked us off one by one. Iulian … Traci … Michal.

We decided to kill it by disabling the environmental systems in the rest of the ship. Four of us shut them down, but the Fiend found us in the dark corridors, and I was the only one to make it back.

Now it's just me and my family. And the Fiend.

Nothing can kill it. Like the evil in men's hearts.

#

I make sure Owen is secure in his room. He's scared and unharmed, his courage drained away. Elise is where she always is: sitting at Daphne's bedside. I lean against the door frame, exhausted after the adrenaline rush has faded.

Elise sings gently to our daughter, a lullaby we used to sing when nightmares ripped her from peaceful dreams.

I can't remember how long ago Daphne was attacked; the days run together. She had been harvesting peas in the far field when I heard her scream. By the time I got to her the Fiend had pulled her halfway into a duct. The pop of nails from my gun made it drop her and retreat.

Elise arrived, crying, and scooped our daughter into her arms.

I stared at the open vent, the unbroken grate on the deck. How could I have missed sealing it?

Daphne's arms twined weakly around Elise's neck. Her voice, a whisper I could barely hear, pierced my heart like a needle. "It hurts … I'm cold … ."

By the time we got her back to the house, Daphne had slipped into unconsciousness.

As her father, it was my job to keep her safe. I failed.

Elise startles when she notices me in the doorway. Her face is all shadows, and where her eyes are supposed to be are dark pits, like holes in a skull. She never sleeps, best I can tell, and it's pulled her essence into something insubstantial like spun sugar.

"I didn't mean to scare you," I say.

"She's burning up and we're out of medicine."

I check the cabinet.

Elise stands in the doorway to Daphne's room like she's unable to cross its threshold. "She needs medicine."

My stomach curdles. The only medicine is in the infirmary.

I check the cabinet again, and all the other drawers

in our small house.

Elise watches me, arms crossed.

Nothing. My knees weak, I collapse into a chair. How can we be out?

Elise turns her back on me and retreats to Daphne's side.

I wring my hands. The fingers are cold and numb. It's my fault. That's hard enough to live with, but every day I see the accusation in Elise's face.

Saying nothing, I pull on a skin-suit and slide the hood over my head. It'll keep me warm in the habitat module, and its compression bands will keep the blood from pooling in my extremities in the low pressure.

I pick up the nail gun and decide against taking a second belt of nails. If I get into a fight with the Fiend, I won't survive long enough to use it, so why lug the extra weight?

"I want to come."

Owen's voice startles me, and I nearly drop the nail gun.

Sepia light leaks from his room, casting his face into a jigsaw of black and grey.

"I need you to protect your mother and sister in case ... ." I work my mouth, but find no moisture. "You need to take care of things until I get back."

He digs his trembling hands deeper into his pockets. I can't tell if he's relieved or not.

I want to hug him, but I can't do it. I'm not ready to say good-bye to any of them.

"You better come back," he says, his voice chopped off as I pull the door closed behind me.

I jog along the decking on the edge of the soybean field. Overhead, stars spin in the great dark. I arrive at the door and need to sit for a moment. My mind is a jumble of regrets. My inadequacies threaten to paralyze me.

The first of the grow lights come on, simulating dawn. The garden, once quiet and beautiful, is our prison.

I visualize my route to the infirmary and back. In my head it takes me only seconds, but I know if all goes smoothly … . "Five minutes," I whisper to myself.

I clip the O_2 cannula against my nostrils and concentrate on slowing my breathing.

I press my ear to the door.

All quiet.

I move the trencher just enough to allow me to squeeze through without damaging my suit, and prop the pry bar near the door.

My body trembles, and I will my hands to stop shaking. I leave the garden.

The door shuts behind me, pushed by the outflow of warm air.

My breath crackles as it crystalizes. I breathe through my nose, drawing warm oxygenated air through the cannula.

The circle of light from my headlamp plays down the walls and across the floor. Ice rimes the conduits snaking along the ceiling and the metal support struts that rib the corridor. On the floor a black line smears off into the darkness. Dried blood.

I move quickly from intersection to intersection, picking my way through the dark toward the infirmary. Even with my light, it's black as a grave, and the cold bites hard into my fingers and nose.

A clang shivers through the metal floor, and I

freeze. Metal groans.

Quiet settles again.

I'm breathing so hard now, the O_2 enricher labors to compensate.

I hustle on; several turns, and I'm there. With the power out, my thumb chip won't cycle the door. The manual release is frozen fast with condensation.

I flash my light down the corridor in both directions. Shadows scatter away, but otherwise it's empty.

I slam the butt of the nail gun against the release. A dull thud rings out. I hammer the lever a second time, and the ice gives with a loud crack.

I listen into the dark, but it's hard to hear over the pounding in my chest. I swing the hatch aside, and pull it closed behind me, but there's no lock to secure it.

The infirmary is a jumble of overturned furniture and medical supplies spilled onto the floor from rifled cabinets. Glass and metal crunch under foot, a carpet of broken surgical tools, syringes, and vials. I can't remember which cabinet held the medicine, so I search haphazardly. Nothing.

The front room, the clinic, has been thoroughly ransacked. The door to the surgical theater doesn't open, but a blow to the handle with the end of the nail gun gets me inside. The cabinets here have been ripped open, too. I search the debris on the shelves, the countertop, and the sink, finding sutures and bandages, broken glass, gauze, tubing, but no vials.

I throw my hands up, spinning, but see nothing except my failure.

A small bottle glints in my light as it skitters across the floor and under the surgical table. I drop to my hands and knees and peer underneath.

"Where are you?" I mutter, maybe out loud, maybe in my head. Either way, it's loud in my ears.

I move my head lamp around so I can see between the cables and struts of the table's hydraulics. I see it! I can't read the label, but it's the only medicine I've seen, and anything is better than nothing at this point.

I work my hand into the narrow space. My fingertips touch the curve of the bottle, but I can't get enough purchase on it to roll it toward me.

"Dammit. Dammit."

The sound of crunching glass freezes me. I don't move, not even my eyes, as I strain to hear. Maybe my mind is playing tricks, but I still can't bring myself to take a breath.

Crunch.

Louder this time, coming closer, slowly.

Crunch.

I can't move, paralyzed by my fear.

Crunch.

At the door to the surgical theater. It'll be on me in seconds.

My bones compress as I force my hand into the tight space until I can get my fingertips around the backside of the bottle's curve and tap it so it rolls closer to me. Extracting my hand, I gash my thumb. Blood drips onto the floor and steams, but fortunately my hand is numb enough I don't feel it. I scoop the bottle into my pocket without looking at the label.

The glass crunches on the other side of the surgical table.

I scramble away tearing a hole in the thigh of my suit on the debris. The gun thunks as nails blur through my headlamp beam, clattering off the table edge and flying into the blackness.

A high-pitched scream. Slender arms flash through my lamp beam as a small person rolls away from the stream of nails. Glass crunches as Owen scrambles back into the clinic.

"Owen!" I leap over the surgical table. In the front room the door to the corridor hangs open like a black maw. I sweep my light around, whispering my boy's name and praying he hasn't run into the corridor.

I find him curled up in an open cabinet, shaking, but unhurt. I kneel next to him. Set the nail gun on the floor. He tries to squirm away, but I get him into my arms. "It's okay," I whisper. Eventually he turns into my shoulder and hugs me. His warmth spreads into my limbs.

"I wanted to help you. I wanted to help Daphne."

"I know," I say, then shush him. I should be angry, but all that matters is he's safe, and that I keep him that way. "Let's get out of here."

I pick up the nail gun as Owen climbs out of the cabinet. At the door, we pause while I peer down the corridor. "You know the way?" I ask.

He nods, and we head off.

I keep Owen behind me, but within arm's reach. We stop at the first intersection. I hold my breath as I peek around the corner. A series of metallic clangs echo in the distance.

Owen's eyes are large and glow white in the blackness. "What was that?"

My finger shakes as I hold it up to my lips.

The noise stops. As we dash through the intersection, I look down the corridor, but my headlamp doesn't cut the darkness deep enough to see anything. The Fiend is close. I sense it, as clearly as I sense my boy laboring a step behind me.

At the next intersection, we don't stop—nor the one after that—but fly through like panicked dogs.

The garden is near.

The gash on my thigh aches and my muscles burn.

I run harder. Owen's ragged breaths fall behind me. I slow as I approach the last intersection and turn to find my boy. He materializes at the edge of my lamp beam, his skin pale and translucent as a specter. His eyes widen; his mouth stretches open to scream, but only a terrified rattle comes out.

I spin. My light glares off the Fiend's milky skin and the smooth dome of its head, shiny like the carapace of a beetle.

"Run!" Nails spark off the ceiling and walls. The gun echoes in the tight space. We must have surprised it as much as it surprised us because it falls back into the dark.

I run without looking back, my head lamp wiggling such I can't see where I'm going, so I run on instinct.

I catch up with Owen as he's slipping through the crack in the door.

"Go, go, go!"

Behind me, the Fiend comes clicking up the corridor. I fire the nail gun, hoping to hold it off long enough for Owen to get through. The nail belt is almost empty. Firing one-handed, I dig the medicine bottle from my pocket and push it into Owen's hand. "Get this to your mother."

My last nail zings into the darkness.

I push Owen's shoulder, and he squirts into the garden. The door slams shut with the finality of a coffin lid.

Behind me the Fiend squeals angrily. I don't look back; I don't want to see it.

Warm piss runs down my leg.

I throw my weight against the door. It opens wide enough for me to get a shoulder and arm through. I topple over, half into the garden. The empty nail gun pops from my hands and clatters out of reach.

Fingers wrap around my ankle.

I kick at the claws with my free foot, but the hard blows don't weaken its grip. Any second it will rip my leg off and feast on the bloody muscle.

I grab the pry bar from next to the door and stab through the opening, hoping to hit the Fiend's arm. I strike my own leg. Pain burns up into my gut, but I don't stop, swinging again and again until finally the Fiend's claw releases me.

I drag the rest of my body inside.

The door snaps shut.

I lie there, drawing labored breaths. Out of the corner of my eye I see the medicine bottle on the deck. In his panic, Owen has forgotten it. I roll over and grab it. Pain shoots up into my hip and across my groin.

I see now my leg is in a bad way. The Fiend's claws have peeled the flesh down on the front of my ankle. Blood soaks my shoe and the tattered pieces of my skin-suit.

My stomach betrays me, but there's nothing in it, so it only convulses painfully.

The door clangs into the back of the cart. The Fiend chitters and clicks in frustration. I nearly black out scrambling away.

How I get back to the house, I'm not certain, but I stumble inside, weak and lightheaded. I leave a trail of blood smeared across the tiles.

I've no feeling in my foot. From the floor where I have fallen, I drag a rag off the table, and wrap it around my ankle. The blood soaks through before I can tie the knot.

"Elise." My voice is just above a whisper.

I know she's in Daphne's room straining to hear the smallest rustles of our daughter.

My vision blurs. I won't die in my house like this. "Owen."

The boy comes out of Daphne's room. His eyes widen, and I know now it's as bad as I thought. He covers his mouth and steps back.

The look of terror on his face bites into my heart.

"The medical kit," I say.

Owen backs down the hallway, dissolving into the shadow.

Don't leave me, boy. I need you.

Outside something rustles near the door. Claws scrape over the lever.

With a cold lump in my belly, I realize the nail gun isn't with me. There's nothing in the small room—no club, no knife, nothing I can wield against it. I curse my stupidity.

I struggle onto my good foot. The adrenaline masks the pain.

The door latch lifts with a click loud enough to shatter my eardrums. I charge, but my foot cannot hold my weight, and I crash to the floor. The Fiend descends on me like the hunter it is.

I scream, driving strength into my limbs, and thrash around trying to buck it off me, but it's too heavy. It claws at my arms and head, chittering and squealing.

"Run, Elise! Run, Owen!"

A needle drives into my leg. Weakness spreads through me as the toxin works its evil.

"Elise … Owen … run." The words come hard and quiet across my lips. I hope they escaped out the back and find a place to hide until it drags me away.

But how long will they last without me? Owen is not ready to protect even himself. Elise is wrapped in a shroud of grief, and Daphne—I've already failed Daphne.

A click and a hiss of air.

With effort I turn my head.

A woman in an environment suit shakes out her short hair. She sets her helmet on the table and touches a small boom hugging her cheek. "Request medical assistance on my location." She does not take her eyes off me, and all I can do is stare into them.

"My name is Nadia," she says, kneeling next to me. "We found your S.O.S. beacon." She has strong bones in her face, but a soft nose and lips. "I've given you a sedative, but you need to lay still. I don't want you to hurt your leg more than it already is." She takes my thumb and presses it to a scanner pad on the wide wristband ringing her left forearm. She reads the information that scrolls up the band's display.

I try to move, but my body is slow, like I've spent an hour in the sauna making jelly of my muscles. "It killed everyone. Have to—" My head spins and threatens to float away.

"You need to stay still, Paul."

I don't immediately recognize my name; I haven't heard it in a long time.

Two more environment suits arrive. They crack off their helmets and set the domes on the table next to

Nadia's. One of them kneels over my injured ankle.

"Delman's going to fix you up," Nadia says. "You're safe now."

I reach out toward her. She takes my hand, and finds the medicine bottle wrapped in my fingers.

"My daughter," I say. "She's sick."

Nadia looks at the bottle. Her brow pinches into a vertical line. "What happened here, Paul?"

"My daughter … the Fiend … ." Why can't they understand me? "First door on the left."

"Try to relax." She pats my shoulder, then goes to confer with the standing man. Snippets of their hushed conversation reach my ears, but I can't piece them together because my attention is absorbed by the outer door, which they've left unlatched.

Elise peeks out from Daphne's room. I call out loudly, attracting everyone's attention. When that happens, Elise quietly backs into the shadow.

Nadia returns to my side. She repeats my name several times, gradually drawing my attention back to her. "Timmons will check on your daughter." She continues to talk at me while the man goes into Daphne's room. I strain to hear anything, but Nadia is speaking too loudly.

"—ship records say your daughter was injured in an equipment accident—"

No, no. The Fiend hurt her.

"—and put into a medically induced coma—"

I crane my head, trying to see around the kneeling woman. Down the hallway, Owen's door is ajar. Through the narrow crack, his eyes glitter with fear.

A soft chittering outside the window drives a spike of fear into me. My breath leaves with a force that spins my head. "It's coming," I say, the words

239

insubstantial as fog.

"Just a minute more," says Delman, tearing a strip of tape from a roll.

But there isn't a minute. It's coming.

Timmons returns from Daphne's room, his face grim. He pulls Nadia to the side.

A shadow darkens the crack under the unlatched door. My breaths come shallow and rapid, but no one seems to notice.

"Two of them," Timmons says softly. "One in a chair; a child in the bed. From the looks of them, they've been dead for years."

Nails like needles scrape the lever.

"I found these lodged in the skull of the one in the chair." Timmons hands Nadia grey slivers of metal.

"What the hell are those? Nails?"

The latch moves.

"It's here! Oh, god it's here!" I kick away from Delman, surprising the medic and knocking him over. Nadia lunges at me, but I scramble under her hands. Behind me, the door bursts open, and the Fiend rushes in, chittering insanely. I don't look back, but claw my way across the floor to Daphne's room. Furniture tumbles behind me. Nadia and Timmons scream, but their words are swallowed by the staccato of the Fiend's clicking mandibles.

I slam the door, and fumble the lock into place.

The Fiend continues to scream.

Fists pound on the door, but I push my back against it, even though I know the lock is strong.

"Paul! Let us in. Paul!"

Elise cowers in the chair at Daphne's bedside. Owen stands in the corner, his back to me. In the darkness he looks like a standing lamp covered with a black sheet, but I am relieved that he's here and that he's safe.

"Paul!"

I shove my fingers into my ears. The noise outside is horrific and it echoes painfully inside my head.

Elise's lips move silently in the shadow of her face.

"I will protect you," I say. The dull thuds of fists on the door slow. Everyone in the room is still and quiet like shadows in the night, as we wait for the Fiend to finish its grisly work and leave. Then we will go on, like we always have. Now and forever.

STORY NOTES
NOW AND FOREVER

I'm very interested in the craft of storytelling. How does a writer use words to create tone? How do they reveal information to make you care about the protagonist? How do they build tension to pull you through the story? To get you so invested emotionally in the main character, that you're devastated when the story's climax brings something bad for them?

"Now and Forever" grew out of my interest in telling a story in which the narrator—someone the reader generally trusts—turns out to be unreliable and to have committed horrific deeds.

Dreams in Dust

First published in *Lightspeed Magazine*, December 2012

THE ARRIVAL OF THE DUST-COVERED girl caught
Keraf by surprise. The girl's slender face, sun-beaten
to a deep brown, blended seamlessly into the cloth
wrapped around her head. She couldn't have been
more than seventeen, but she wielded her rifle with
ease.

Keraf didn't even try for his own rifle, slung over
his shoulder. Shooting her would be a waste of his
last bullet because she didn't appear to have a
canteen.

"My sand sled got demasted four days ago," he
said in response to her unspoken question. His
tongue, dry and dusty, made it difficult to speak. "I
have things I can trade for water."

Her eyes roved over Keraf's gauzy robes, his
keffiyeh wrapped around the lower half of his face,
his rifle, the narrow metal cylinder at his waist, and
the empty water bag slung over his back.

"I could just shoot you," she said.

With roles reversed, Keraf might have said the
same. In the wastes of the Atlantic Basin, bandits
outnumbered honest men. He didn't think she would
believe him, but told her what he thought was the
truth. "I'm carrying something that could save the
Earth."

"Nothing can save the Earth," the girl said.

"Water can."

Keraf thought he saw the tip of her rifle dip, but the sun was strong and the shadows stark.

The girl's eyes narrowed. "Start walking, and don't try anything. I've deaded better liars than you."

#

The girl led him across the dunes to an earthen embankment. Keraf hadn't realized it was there until he was upon it; the mound of earth blended with the beige and umber monotony of the rippled dunescape. They were met by a boy covered more in sand than clothing. After a whispered exchange with the girl, the boy set off running up and over the hill.

Keraf waited with the girl, collecting a thicker skin of dust.

After a few minutes, the boy returned with a bundle of cloth-wrapped poles slung over his shoulder. A stoneware bottle bounced from a cord against his left thigh. He gave the girl the bottle, then set about erecting a canopy from the poles.

The girl's lips glistened when she lowered the bottle.

Keraf watched the water evaporate. He licked cracked lips with a sandpaper tongue. Six swallows, he had counted, more than a day's ration in the lamasery.

He unslung his water bag and dropped it in the sand at the edge of the canopy. It wasn't any cooler in the shade, but at least he was out of the sun.

The girl eyed him, but said nothing. She shared the same fine bones and gold-flecked eyes as the boy. A family compound, then, Keraf thought, hidden somewhere over the embankment. They couldn't have had more than a condenser or two, but maybe a trade was still possible.

After a few minutes, an older man and woman came over the embankment and down the sand face. The woman carried a naked toddler on her hip. When the girl saw them, she ran to meet them and exchanged her rifle for the little boy.

As they came into the shade, Keraf pushed his shoulders back and rose up to his full height. The man peeled his checkered keffiyeh aside to reveal cheeks covered with coarse gray stubble and skin pitted from where the cancers had been cut away.

In his hands he carried another stoneware bottle capped with a small metal cup. He wiped the dust from the inside of the cup with the sleeve of his robe and poured a finger of water. He extended it to Keraf.

Keraf pressed his palms together and touched his fingertips to his forehead. "Your water is life," he murmured. When he reached for the cup, the old man pulled it back.

"Your face," he said. "I want to see who drinks our water."

Keraf unclipped his keffiyeh, exposing his face. Even though the air was hot, it felt cool on his black skin.

"The mark of the Mechanists," the man said, nodding at the metal ankh hanging at Keraf's throat. "We don't see many of your kind here." He extended the cup a second time. "I am called Faruk," he said. "You have met Imani, my grandniece." He motioned to the girl with the toddler in her arms.

The child's top lip was split from his mouth to his nose, a defect of birth. Keraf had seen such deformities in small enclaves before. It gave him hope that the one thing he could trade had value.

Keraf stared down into the water, and forced

himself to sip. It cooled his burning tongue. He licked every drop of moisture from his lips before tipping the last of the water into his mouth. He handed the cup back to Faruk.

"I am Keraf," he said, now that his throat was lubricated. "Your water is life; I owe you my life."

Faruk handed the cup to the little boy in Imani's arms. The boy's slender red tongue snapped in and out through the cleft in his lip, licking dry the beads of water that clung to the metal.

Keraf found it difficult not to stare. "I am on a mission to Costa de Santo," he said, pulling his eyes from the toddler. "Four days ago, my sled capsized crossing the mid-Atlantic mountains. What water I had was lost. I seek water so I can complete my mission."

Faruk's eyes narrowed. "We have no water to spare."

Keraf did not expect anyone to give him water. A single condenser could produce a gallon a day from the basin's arid atmosphere, enough for only a handful of people and a few plants.

"I can trade," he said. "I carry a fully-functional uric acid modification, enhanced melanin, and high-efficiency sweat glands." The genetic modifications had become fixed in the Earth's human population prior to the final dewatering by the Orbitals, but small enclaves could regress through inbreeding. "My semen is worth a few days of water."

"It's worth nothing if we dry out."

From Faruk's expression, Keraf could not tell if the man was simply negotiating. The Atlantic Basin was isolated, and opportunities to maintain his clan's genetic viability could not have presented themselves often. Pressing the issue this early in a negotiation could offend.

"You have the advantage," Keraf said. "My rifle is worth something, as is my water bag. I'm willing to work for a ration."

Faruk looked unimpressed.

"I beg your compassion. My mission is important."

"He says he carries something that could save us," Imani said. The toddler squirmed in her arms, and she set him down. The boy hid behind her robes and poked his tongue out at Keraf through his cleft.

"The Earth is dead," Faruk said. "Those who believe otherwise are chasing fantasies in the dust."

"What if he speaks the truth? We can spare—"

Faruk hissed and the girl fell silent. The toddler started to cry. The tears on his cheek made Keraf's mouth water.

Imani knelt and pulled the boy into her arms, quieting him. She collected his tears on her fingertips and put them in her mouth.

Keraf pretended to ignore the exchange, even as his mind tried to construct what Imani had intended to say. Could they spare water? No one could spare water, for there was none to spare.

"Let me show you." Keraf slowly unclipped the metal cylinder from his belt and unscrewed the cap on one end. "These are copies of a document discovered by my Order." Keraf removed a tube of handmade paper and carefully unrolled it. It was covered with intricate lines and neat blocks of hand-printed text. "It is a plan for a deep drilling machine, but my lamasery lacks the resources to construct it. The Mechanist Court at Costa de Santo can build it, and if they do, they can bring water to the surface."

Faruk studied the document for a moment, but Keraf suspected the man could not decipher it. Without water, industrialization and the skills associated with it had collapsed. Other than condensers, little remained from the wet-Earth.

Faruk's lips pulled downward into a frown. He waved the paper aside. "The deep ocean? A myth. I won't spend time looking at what I don't have, only to lose sight of what I do. My grandniece should do the same, for her son. We cannot help you. We have no water to spare."

"Please, I am at your mercy." Keraf reached for Faruk, but the man stepped back.

Faruk pushed aside a fold of his robe to reveal a revolver in his belt. "It's best you be on your way."

Imani grabbed her great uncle's arm. "You talk of the future, but my son has no—"

Faruk pulled his arm free. "Enough!"

Imani lowered her face.

"How long will your condensers last?" Keraf tried to keep the desperation out of his voice. "Ours run on sweat and prayer. Out here, it must be—" An odd sound drew Keraf's eyes to the toddler. The boy was peeing on the sand.

Keraf dropped the paper. His eyes grew wide. "You have found water," he whispered, as he fell to his knees.

Faruk drew the pistol from his belt. In a single fluid motion, he leveled it at Keraf's chest.

Keraf could not take his eyes off the arc of lemon-yellow water. The toddler did not have the genetic modification to produce uric acid instead of urine. He would need over a gallon of water a day to survive; yet he lived.

The toddler finished peeing, and Imani scooped him into her arms. Keraf watched the puddle sink into the dust. He ached to hold the wet sand in his hands.

Faruk pulled back the hammer on his revolver.

"Don't, Uncle," Imani said.

"He will bring others. They will take what we have."

"But the drilling machine …"

"Those drawings are probably not even real," Faruk said. "A ruse to steal water from our mouths."

"Already the seep gives less than it once did. If the paper he carries can bring back the water …" Imani squeezed the toddler in her arms. The boy squirmed but could not slip free.

Keraf stared, no longer seeing the toddler's cleft lip. "Your child is the future," he said, "one where we have enough water to wet the ground with our urine." He looked up the revolver's barrel, past the three bullets arrayed in the chambers. "I have dedicated my life to bringing water back to the world," he said. "I have heard it used to fall from the sky. I have never seen such a thing, but I dream that our children will. If you shoot me, at least deliver these plans to Costa de Santo. I believe they can save us."

Faruk's eyebrows pinched together. "Why do you believe?"

"If I do not, then everything is just dust." Keraf waited for the bullet. He imagined a heaven with cool rain.

The pistol wavered. "The last time I saw the rain, I was a small boy," Faruk said. "We ran outside with pots and plates and cloths—anything that could hold water. It rained for less than a minute—only a fine mist really—but enough to dampen my face." He touched his cheeks, as if wiping moisture from them. "I will never forget that."

Keraf licked his lips, trying to imagine what rain would taste like. "Sometimes it is hard not to lose hope," he said.

Faruk lowered the revolver. "Hope is a powerful thing." He picked up the paper at his feet, carefully rolled it, and handed it back to Keraf. "Come."

Keraf followed Faruk up the embankment, leaving the others to dismantle the canopy. As he crested the top, Keraf stopped.

Below, in the dusty trough, a dozen dome-shaped dwellings ringed a small greenhouse. Through beads of water sparkling on the greenhouse glass, Keraf saw a pool of water nestled among green leaves. He drew an audible breath.

"Without hope, we are dust." Faruk said. "Before you leave, we will share water."

STORY NOTES
DREAMS IN DUST

I can easily point to the direct inspiration for "Dreams in Dust." In 2009, I stumbled across a regular column at the science fiction website *io9*: Concept Art Writing Prompt. It was a weekly feature (every Saturday) in which a visual prompt and an associated flash story inspired by the prompt was presented. Readers were encouraged to submit their own story in the comments.

The visual prompt was a picture from Pene Menn, an artist from Korea who made concept art, matte paintings and other very cool artwork. In the picture, a person with a rifle slung over his shoulder leads a camel through a desert. In the background the wreck of a submarine lies half buried in the sand. A ramshackle house has been built alongside the submarine.

It's not difficult to see where "Dreams in Dust" came from. The idea for Keraf and the waterless world immediately popped into my head. I knew he was on a quest, and I knew that quest needed to be about water, which gave rise to both the immediate narrative arc and the big-picture back story. From that, the rest of this story about hope quickly fell into place.

I wrote "Dreams in Dust" in a single sitting, revised it a week later, and a short time after that, I had it out the door to the world.

Still Life Through Water Droplets

First published in *Daily Science Fiction*, January 2012

BRANDON WANTED TO FIND A WOMAN he could put his arm around and have her shoulder slide into the nook of his armpit. Then he could smell her hair when he pulled her close.

Susan's hair had always smelled of coconut and jasmine. He still had a half-full bottle of her shampoo in the shower, waiting.

"My parents are from the Ukraine," Odette said over the top of her tea cup. "But I was born in Ohio." She didn't speak with a Midwesterner's flat vowels, but neither had Susan.

"I live in Chicago now," she said. "I'm in Boston on business, but I don't want to bore you."

Brandon wished she would stop talking. If he learned too much about her, he might not be able to go through with the personality transfer. He had spent months looking for the right woman.

His hand trembled as he set his cup down. If he failed now, he was afraid he could not go on.

Odette flashed a half-smile. "It's getting late ..."

After several heartbeats, Brandon realized she had left the sentence hanging. Had his clumsiness cost him? "Can I walk you to your hotel?"

Her eyes sparkled as she played with the string and little paper square that dangled out of the tea pot. "I was hoping you would offer."

Brandon's heart raced. He glanced at the other patrons in the coffee shop. Did they suspect the crime he was about to commit? It wasn't murder, he reminded himself. No, not murder. More like theft. He could live with theft.

Odette cleared her throat delicately. She stood with her coat buttoned.

Brandon fumbled his arms into his own jacket. Outside, an icy rain soaked them in seconds. Brandon wished he had remembered an umbrella.

Odette had a room on the twentieth floor of a mid-priced hotel. It looked east over the harbor. He shed his coat in the entry way as Odette danced into the bathroom.

She tossed him a towel before closing the door.

Brandon stared at it. He shivered despite the warmth of the room. He had planned every move in detail, but now he couldn't remember them.

Odette came out wrapped in only a towel. Dark hair, tussled and wet, framed her impish grin. She had muscular legs, not the match-sticks women seemed to value. They were like Susan's, but firmer and creamy white.

He backed into the wall as she came at him.

Her hands slipped around his neck and she pulled his face down to hers. She was the perfect height, Brandon thought, as her lips touched his. Then all thought of heights and legs vanished.

"Why don't you get out of those wet clothes while I fix us drinks?"

Drinks. That was what he was supposed to do. In his wallet, he had a packet of paralytic powder and neural activator to facilitate the transfer.

"Go, go," she said playfully as she pulled two small bottles of gin and a can of tonic water from the mini-bar. "I hope they have limes."

Still cursing himself, Brandon closed the bathroom door behind him. He could barely breathe as he propped himself against the vanity. What was he going to do now? He needed to make the next drinks, but that meant getting to "next drinks."

He turned on the tap to buy himself some time. You can do this, he told himself, for Susan. She had fought the cancer valiantly, even after it ate through her liver and into the heart of her bones. Even after the doctors told her there was no hope, Susan wanted to fight. In the end, after every medical procedure failed, they did not have enough money for a legal personality transfer and clone.

Brandon's fingers ached from gripping the edge of the vanity. After all the bills had been paid, he'd had just enough money to pay for a black market transfer. Now he needed a surrogate.

He pulled the wax-paper packet of paralytic from his wallet. Susan's transfer cache fell out onto the counter. Taped to the back of the credit-card sized device, was a wrinkled picture of Susan. He remembered the exact second he had snapped that picture. They had gone to the Japanese Tea Garden in Golden Gate Park. He remembered the sweet fragrance of the brown rice green tea, steeped perfectly, and the gentle cascade of water over stones into the Koi pond. Her hair had already fallen out from the radiation treatments, but even in the hat, she was so, so beautiful.

Why had she been afraid? The transfer agency had assured them any changes in her personality would be minor. She would still be Susan, mentally and physically.

If she had just surrendered earlier, they could have done a legitimate transfer. No need for Brandon to search for a surrogate. No need for him to dither in a hotel bathroom. The light playing through water droplets on the bathroom mirror distorted his face. He looked as haggard as he did the day Susan had finally, mercifully, died.

You can do this, he thought.

Brandon tucked the cache back into his wallet and stuffed it into the back pocket of his pants. He stripped and hung everything next to Odette's dress and bra and panties on the drying line strung in the shower.

Before heading out, he wrapped a towel around his waist and palmed the wax-paper packet.

Odette stood at the window, her face reflected in the black glass. Her eyes were closed, but tense lines pulled at their corners and tugged at the edges of her lips. She must have heard him because her eyes snapped opened. Seeing him, she forced a smile, but sadness clung to her like an oily sheen.

"A penny for your thoughts?" Brandon picked up the waiting gin and tonic, and at the same time, slipped the wax packet into the dish that held three tea bags.

"It's nothing," Odette said.

Panic gripped Brandon's gut. What if she had changed her mind and was going to ask him to leave? "No thinking," he said.

She gazed into her gin and tonic.

With a curled index finger, he raised her face up to his. He smiled, the one he had practiced so much that he knew it looked genuine. "To moving forward and not remembering what has passed." He clinked the edge of his glass lightly against hers and emptied it in one swallow. The drink burned pleasantly as it went down. "Corny. I know."

She smiled, more genuine this time, and finished her drink.

Brandon took the empty glass and turned toward the bar. She grabbed his elbow. Her grip was gentle, but firm. She rolled onto her toes to kiss him.

Reflexively he stepped back, realizing immediately—but still too late—that he shouldn't have.

Odette crumpled onto the edge of the bed. She buried her face in her hands. "Do you ever feel like your life is frozen?" she asked. "Like a painting?"

Brandon set the glasses down. He sat next to her on the bed. The warmth of her body radiated through her towel.

The last thing Susan had told him before she slipped into a coma was that life needed to move forward, with or without her. She would be disgusted by him, he realized. He felt certain of that now, and the thought made him numb.

"I've made a terrible mistake. I'm sorry, Odette." He started to rise, but she grabbed his arm.

"Don't leave."

He felt unsteady. His head spun with thoughts of Susan. The idea that she would despise him made him nauseous. "My wife …" It was difficult for him to find the words. His brain was muddled and confused. "I really need …"

He tried to stand but his legs were rubbery. He fell back onto the bed. "I don't feel well," he said. His jaw didn't work properly; the words came out slurred.

Odette leaned over him. She touched his cheek, but he couldn't feel her hand. "I'm sorry, Brandon." She fished a transfer cache from under the pillow. Unable to move or even blink, he watched her lower it to his forehead. "I miss him so much."

STORY NOTES
STILL LIFE THROUGH WATER DROPLETS

"Still Life through Water Droplets" started with a title that came to me after reading a review of an art show. That review contained a picture of a still life, whose actual title I can no longer remember, but it may have been something like "Still Life with Lobster." That's when I noticed that many still life paintings carry a title that's a variant of "Still Life with/through X" where X is either an unusual or everyday object. The title "Still Life Through Water Droplets" immediately jumped into my head and wouldn't leave.

For over a year I tried to find its story, writing and tossing several attempts in which the characters' lives literally stopped in time. Eventually I gave up, and worked on other things. After a while, I came back to the title. I realized a less literal approach might work better, and Brandon and Odette's tragic quests finally emerged.

Gift for the Cutter Man

First published in *Apex Magazine*, September 2021

THE BLADE OF LEGRUE'S SCALPEL flared in his headlamp's narrow beam, casting glints of light across the slender hand strapped to his cutting table.

"Deed done?" the woman asked, a warble in her voice.

Legrue adjusted his magnifiers. He had not eaten in over a day, and the emptiness in his gut gnawed at his focus and put a tremor in his fingers.

He had to finish before the woman lost confidence in him and he lost a scrip worth a hundred youn, more than he made most days. "Steady on," he said gently, as much to the woman as his hand.

He lowered the scalpel against the middle joint of her left pinky. The leather strap creaked as the woman's hand tightened.

"Easy, easy," Legrue urged. The tension would shift the underlying musculature and connective tissues, making his task harder, not to mention, more painful for her. "Steady, now."

The scars on her forearm made clear she was no stranger to a cutter's blade, albeit not his, but a finger was a next-level investment in the wet market. Blood would regenerate; her pinky would not, so it was only natural she flinched at the touch of his scalpel's edge to her skin.

Satisfied his blade was well-positioned, Legrue pressed firmly downward. Blood spilled onto the cutting table, flowing into the grooves that funneled it into a brass collection bowl for later tubing.

The woman had gone quiet, likely blacked out.

Legrue did not let it distract him. Through the joint now, he angled his blade so the final cut would create a flap of skin that he could use to cover the raw edge. He slid the severed pinky into a glass tube, capped it, and dropped it into the ice trough at his elbow.

He let the stump bleed for a five-count, then coated it with coag-gel and sutured the skin flap to cover the wound. He snapped on a pressure bandage.

Start to finish, less than a minute.

"Deed done." The woman stirred weakly as Legrue released the leather strap.

Slowly the hand scraped back into the shadows of Legrue's stall. He preferred the anonymity the darkness granted. Even so, he knew this woman's story. Desperate, hungry, likely even had mouths that depended on her, she had few choices but the wet market. Hers was everyone's story in the Under, and the service Legrue provided, barbaric as it was, helped people survive.

"Money me, cutter man."

Legrue bristled at the name. He was not a typical cutter; he took pride in his craft, even as it cost him youn—coag and sutures weren't cheap.

Legrue paid her the front money owed, and thankfully she left without another word. He set his magnifiers aside and slumped onto his stool. The woman's blood had cooled on his hands, but he did not have the energy to wipe it away. The youn he would make from the pinky and the tubes of blood would barely cover another cycle of Abigail's antipyretics, and with Livia's milk having dried up, they also needed cereal. And how much tighter could he pull his own belt?

His head down, Legrue did not immediately notice TwoTony enter until the rascal set a pocket lamp on the cutting table. TwoTony dragged on his atomizer and let the reddish steam trickle from his nose. "You tweaked?" TwoTony asked.

Legrue stifled a sigh. He wasn't ill; TwoTony was simply the last thing he wanted to see today. "I made my payment."

TwoTony tossed him the cloth from the wall hook. "Show respect."

Legrue wiped at his hands, but he would need a brush to dislodge the dried blood from the nail beds.

TwoTony poked at the tubes in the ice trough. "I need a cutter man, and you be him, Legrue."

The back of Legrue's neck tingled, but he held his tongue. Two weeks ago, Abigail had needed a stronger cycle of antipyretics to control the fever brought on by the wasting, and TwoTony had fronted the youn. Until he repaid the money, Legrue was indebted to the rascal, but that didn't place him in his servitude. Yet, he felt obligated to hear him out, especially if it might help him come even.

"A client needs twenty and five tubes. Not crusty, flowing clean like. You ken?"

Twenty-five tubes of uncongealed blood were a lot, but any cutter in the wet market could have provided them. And such a routine request, too, so why go through TwoTony instead of placing a scrip through a legit broker? There had to be—

"Special needs," TwoTony said, and Legrue's stomach dropped. "Must be sourced from a twobee."

He held up a finger. "One twobee."

Legrue felt like he was going to be sick. Twenty-five tubes would kill most adults; without doubt, it would kill a two-year-old. No wonder the buyer had gone to TwoTony. No legitimate broker would take a scrip like that for a twobee.

And what monster would request one?

"Find another cutter."

TwoTony grinned at him, but the flash of yellow teeth was an obvious threat. "Tomorrow," TwoTony said. "Tubes or youn, either way, skin come even."

#

The wet market smelled of fear and blood. Over the years, Legrue had grown accustomed to its stink, but as he pushed through the narrow, crowded alley, snaking through the tarp-and-wood cutter stalls, he felt nauseated. The market had always served a purpose, Legrue believed, even if he did not fully understand it. The Skylers, those that lived in the glittering domes high above the Under, used the blood and tissues from cutters like him as the raw materials for the vaccines and prophylactics that kept the plagues at bay, or at least beat them back when they came, which they inevitably did every few years.

Legrue had never met a Skyler; to his knowledge, no one in the Under had, not even brokers like ChimChim, but he had always thought of them as people like himself or Livia, only with plentiful lives. He used to begrudge that, but as he matured, he had too many worries of his own to waste energy hating people he would never meet.

Legrue pulled up suddenly as a tarp parted in front of him and a large man with a mane of shock-red hair and a body slung over his shoulder barged into the alley. The man turned and headed off, the lifeless torso dangling down his back, its gaunt and handless arms swinging back and forth, like pendulums of a macabre clock.

Legrue stood motionless in the alley, forcing the line of people to flow around him. Glass tubes clinked as he clutched his cloth sack tighter to his chest

It wasn't every day a whole-sale scrip was filled, but in his time, Legrue had seen many bodies carried out of cutter stalls and it never grew easy to watch. Early in his time as a cutter, Legrue had tried to fill a whole-sale scrip. Although the woman was old, and she had willingly made the decision to help her struggling daughters, Legrue had no stomach to drain her life into little glass tubes and sell the remains to the highest bidder.

No one had ever been carried out of his stall. He left that brutality to other cutter men.

Legrue's brow pinched. If he could not take that old woman's life, given willingly, how would he do what TwoTony wanted?

Legrue shook off his unease and continued on to the brokerage, hopeful his tubes would fetch a premium today, maybe even enough to buy his way out of TwoTony's debt. He exchanged all but one tube of blood for a dozen inadequate strips of youn that even folded over twice upon themselves barely raised a bump in his pocket.

He had struggled over the fate of the final tube of blood, eventually deciding to give it to Livia. Over the last month, she had turned increasingly to hemopyric therapies—blood burning—to treat the wasting consuming their daughter.

Legrue saw little value in the practice, promoted, in his opinion, by charlatans and embraced by those who mistakenly thought they could use blood just as the Skylers. Already, Livia had spent precious youn on a burning bowl and tubes of blood and had started a holistic round of treatments that included burnings for Abigail and herself. A waste, but Legrue could not doubt Livia's motives, and he shared her desperation. At least if he supplied the blood, it would be less of a financial drain.

#

Legrue's family lived in one room, but it was at the end of the tenement row, so it had a narrow window that overlooked the foundry. Due to the smoke and dust from the industrial yard, they never opened the window, but for an hour, the morning sunlight came through the hazy glass, and they did not have to waste their chem-lamps.

As Legrue entered, he found Livia on the floor crouched over her burning bowl, a cloth draped over her head to trap the smoke. She breathed deeply, coughed, and inhaled again a second time. In the middle of her treatment, she did not emerge to greet him. Legrue stood the tube of blood on the floor next to her.

Abigail let out a weak cry. Except for the rapid fluttering of her chest as she panted, she lay motionless in her bed, a basket tucked into one of the large floor-to-ceiling cubby-holes that covered the walls. Her skin, blotchy and red, was hot under Legrue's hand.

Until three months ago, Abigail had been a vibrant

child. She had started talking and had grown daringly rambunctious, climbing the cubby-hole shelves and knocking the pots onto the floor. Then, like too many children her age in the Under, she contracted the wasting, a contagion that consumed the young and for which no cure had come down from the Skylers. While the wasting claimed most of its victims, some children survived by outlasting the fevers.

With a cool, damp rag, Legrue sponged Abigail's forehead and down her chest, his fingers tracing the ridges of her ribs. Over the past month, her fevers had come more frequently and with greater ferocity, and despite their efforts, she had lost a third of her weight.

"We got no more," Livia said as Legrue filled the dropper with the last of the fever medication. "What comes tomorrow?"

The question made Legrue's heart ache. The painfully small lump of bills in his trouser pocket would not cover another cycle of antipyretic and food for them all, let alone what he owed TwoTony. It had been like this for several weeks now, and his and Livia's emergency reserves had vanished some time ago.

"Tomorrow won't matter if she burns down today," Legrue said.

Livia took the damp cloth from Legrue and edged him away from the basket.

The smoke from Livia's burning bowl snaked around him as he stepped over it and slumped onto the stool on the opposite side of the room. This was the third day in a row he had come home to find Livia crouched over that bowl and Abigail burning with fever.

"You're early," Livia said, an edge to her voice.

Did she think he was shirking his responsibilities? She had no idea what he had already done and would likely need to do, but he saw no value in sharing his burden. "Slow day," he said.

"Hmm."

Legrue could not decipher the meaning of her sound. A year ago, he was certain he could have, but a lot had happened, and in many ways, he felt he did not know his wife anymore. "I got you a tube."

Livia spared him a wan smile.

Legrue lowered his gaze to the dropper still in his hand. He might have enough youn to appease TwoTony, but then it would be two, maybe three, days before he saved enough money to buy another cycle, and he feared Abigail did not have that time. His stomach growled; there was that, too.

The stink of the smoke made it hard to breathe.

If Abigail had any chance, Legrue needed a rascal like TwoTony, and TwoTony knew it.

Legrue forced down the lump in his throat. He set the dropper on the shelf next to Abigail's basket and moved to kiss Livia on the neck, but she shrugged away from him.

"Where are you going?" she asked.

"To find a way."

#

After an hour of wandering the warrens of the Under, Legrue still saw no path forward. He had quickly dismissed giving TwoTony tubes of adult blood; he suspected whoever had made the scrip would detect such subterfuge, and the repercussion to Legrue and his family would be swift and brutal.

Even if Legrue had been willing to do TwoTony's cutting, the rascal had not even offered a client, something a legit broker would have done in such a specialized case. Just as well, because Legrue didn't know how he would have responded had TwoTony arrived with a child in tow. Finding a twobee presented significant challenges, however, and finding the right twobee even more so. Legrue thought that perhaps he could find a child with both feet firmly upon death's threshold, but he realized that he could never find such a child before tomorrow.

Lost in his thoughts, Legrue had not been tracking his progress through the crowded streets, and his focus returned only when he was bumped hard enough by a passerby that he nearly fell. It took Legrue a moment to shake off the impact, and in a sudden panic, he reached into his pocket. The money was gone, the pocket cut skillfully open by a razor. Frantically, Legrue scanned the crowded street, but distracted as he had been, he had not seen the thief's face.

He pushed his way through the crowd in the direction he thought the thief had gone. A rheumy-eyed woman cursed him as he bumped into her. Seeing nothing in that direction, Legrue turned back—maybe the thief had circled around. His panic rising, he rose up on his toes, scanning over the top of the crowd.

How could he have been so stupid?

Now, even if by some miracle he found a suitable client, he had no front money.

He suddenly found it hard to draw a breath. The crowded streets, the cramped buildings, and girders crisscrossing overhead blurred and spun as Legrue feared he was going to faint.

A hand on his arm steadied him.

It took Legrue a moment to recognize who was touching him. "ChimChim?"

ChimChim stepped back as if realizing Legrue might be ill. "You tweaked?"

"Just tired," Legrue said, looking to put ChimChim at ease. While several years had passed since the Under's last epidemic, memories still lingered.

ChimChim was a broker for the wet market, a legit one, not a poser like TwoTony. When Legrue had first started cutting, he had worked scrips for ChimChim because he lacked reputation and front money. Brokers came at a cost, however, demanding a high ratio, so when the conditions were right, Legrue had forged out solo. Understandably, ChimChim had been angry, but the years had cooled his ire, and now he occasionally brought Legrue scrips he felt uniquely suited to his skills. It had been years since Legrue had asked ChimChim for anything, but maybe the broker could help. "I've got a business prop."

ChimChim's left eyebrow rose under the brim of his cap.

"I need—" Legrue's mouth went dry, making it hard to form the words. "I—"

ChimChim shook his head. "No can help with that." He tapped his right fist against his chest, indicating his sympathy with Legrue's predicament. "Truth is, no legit broker would take that scrip, so they tap TwoTony."

Ashamed, Legrue looked away. ChimChim had ears everywhere in the wet market, so Legrue was not surprised ChimChim already knew what he was going to ask. Perhaps his fist tap had not been in sympathy, but pity.

"You and me, Legrue; we're solid. I want to help, you ken, but ..." ChimChim scanned the crowded street. Then, seemingly satisfied no one important was watching, he leaned closer. "Only place to fill that scrip is the Pit."

#

The Pit came into existence the year Legrue was born. Over the span of a week, a sinkhole that had first appeared next to a tenement north of the foundry had widened and deepened until the building itself had tumbled into it. Soon after, people migrated into the hole to escape the claustrophobic confines of the Under, and the Pit became a semi-autonomous warren where everything was overseen by a magistrate called the V.I.Per.

Legrue had been before the V.I.Per on one occasion, and the memories still troubled his conscience. He never spoke of the meeting to anyone, not even Livia, and as he spiraled down the narrow walkways into the depths, he fought against every attempt by his brain to dredge up the memories of that afternoon. The closer he got to the floor, the harder it became, and as the smell of the Pit engulfed him, he was overcome by the memory of the screams willed forth by Legrue's own hands and the glee of the V.I.Per's entourage at his impotence to stop it. He clung to a metal scaffolding for support, uncertain he could go on.

He thought of Abigail, innocent and frail. He and Livia had struggled for several years to bring her into the world and now to keep her there, a fight they were gradually losing. Legrue did not know if their sacrifices would matter, but he had survived in the Under by doing what needs required.

Legrue forced his left foot to rise, swing forward, and drop onto the metal ramp. He willed his body to roll forward, and for his right foot to follow his left. Two steps, three, each subsequent step lower into the Pit coming easier as his resolve solidified.

By the time he stood before the V.I.Per, he knew he would pay the price, no matter what it might be.

#

A smile slid across the V.I.Per's lips, sending a chill through Legrue. "I ken you. Cutter man all weepy over snip-snip of em drogy," he said, his Pit-slang thick and nearly impenetrable to Legrue. Arrayed behind his throne, the V.I.Per's entourage laughed and jeered, much to their boss's amusement.

The V.I.Per raised his fist and received silence. Leaning forward on the throne, he bared his teeth at Legrue. "Why come back, cutter man?" he asked, sliding effortlessly out of his Pit-slang.

Given the toll of the years, Legrue had not expected the V.I.Per to recognize him, but now that he had, he wondered how that might affect his ask. Legrue cleared his throat. "I have need."

The V.I.Per cocked his head in surprise. "Rim man slums low. Why should I help puss like you?"

Did the man want him to grovel? Legrue would if he thought it would help. It hadn't the last time, but then Legrue hadn't understood what he had gotten himself into when he came to the Pit to purchase a set of quality cutter tools. Young and ignorant, he had been unprepared to pay the V.I.Per's price, a mistake he did not intend to repeat today. "I can pay."

"Indeed," the V.I.Per said. He tapped his temple with his index finger. With a grin to his entourage, he said "Once, cutter man snip-snip good. All drogy bus eyes big and touch knee, slap skin 'n tribute. Respect." With the context, Legrue knew he was talking about the last time he had been there. Several in the V.I.Per's entourage nodded knowingly, and Legrue realized that at least some of them had also been present that day.

Legrue had always suspected the man he had dismembered in payment for his scalpel had been the leader of a rival faction to the V.I.Per. Legrue had skillfully amputated the man's feet and hands, keeping him alive for over an hour until the V.I.Per permitted him to mercifully end his suffering. The man's screams still rang in Legrue's head, but he most remembered the gleeful faces of the V.I.Per and his entourage as Legrue's actions effectively put an end to any challenge to the V.I.Per's power. That day, Legrue vowed to never let another human unduly suffer at his hand, a vow he feared would be challenged today.

"Speak your desire, cutter man."

Legrue licked dry lips. "A twobee."

"Mmmmm," the V.I.Per said as if savoring the sweetness of Legrue's request. "Twobee for cut? Dark, cutter man, dark." The V.I.Per lounged back in his throne, casually draping his left leg over the chair's arm. He picked at his teeth, some of which had been filed into points.

Legrue took a deep breath. He didn't think the V.I.Per understood his ask. "The twobee won't come home."

The V.I.Per showed no surprise, although some of

his entourage did. "Cutter man got jimmy for soul," he said, sounding impressed. "Why do you need this twobee?" he asked.

"Twenty-five tubes, skin to come even with a rascal."

With a speed that made Legrue jump, the V.I.Per leaned forward. As his left boot hit the floor, the sound rang through the small audience room. Amused by Legrue's startle, the V.I.Per smiled again. "That skin then comes to me, cutter man. You will owe me."

Legrue had no money, but then, he suspected the V.I.Per had little need for that. Legrue had skills more valuable than youn.

The V.I.Per's eyes narrowed as he watched Legrue fidget. "A deal," he said, but held up his index finger before Legrue could say anything. "You cut your two 'n five. For me, you dress down the morsel all pretty in tribute. You ken?"

The offer surprised Legrue. He could have sold the toddler's organs for enough to buy food and another cycle of Abigail's antipyretic, but giving the body back to the V.I.Per would be a small price to pay to free himself from TwoTony and any obligation to the V.I.Per.

Before Legrue could agree, the V.I.Per raised a second finger on his hand. He waited for the murmurs of the entourage to quiet. "When cutter man gets weepy and goes no-no, skin come skin; cutter man come to me."

Legrue's brow knitted. He wasn't sure he understood, but the flutter in his gut gave him a bad feeling.

The V.I.Per stood. In his heavy boots, he was two

hands taller than Legrue. "You no ken." The V.I.Per's amused tone drew snickers from the others. "I of mind you no got jimmy for soul, cutter man, and cutting that twobee will be too dark for you. If you don't deliver, then I own your weepy soul. You ken now?"

Legrue felt sick. If he did not deliver the remains of the child, the V.I.Per would own him.

It would not come to that, however.

"Deal."

#

The V.I.Per sent Legrue away with his promise to deliver a twobee to his stall in the morning.

The climb out of the miasma of the Pit did little for Legrue's spirits, and when he finally reached rimside, he clutched at the stitch in his side and could go no farther. The meeting with the V.I.Per replayed in his mind, each time Legrue's physical presence becoming smaller, the V.I.Per more imposing, and the deal to which he had agreed less palatable. As his regret grew, he became ill.

That night, sleep would not come, and Legrue sat at Abigail's side. Her closeness as he lay his head next to the basket allowed her ragged breathing to be heard over the noise from the foundry. Every so often, her rasping breaths would calm, growing so quiet Legrue wondered if she was finally free of her suffering. When it happened, he would close his eyes, and unable to see the red glow bleeding through the narrow window or Livia's form cocooned in a sheet on their futon on the floor, he felt weightless, as if floating in a void. The noise of the Under was lost beneath his whispering, light as a wind, as he counted off the seconds until Abigail's tiny lungs would rattle and gasp back into action, cutting into his heart more painfully than any knife.

Eventually, the dawn light shone through their narrow, dingy window, spotlighting the dust and haze that hung in the room. As the light crawled across the floor, it illuminated Livia's ritual bowl and glinted off the empty tubes, scattered about like pieces of a broken vessel.

In a way, they were, Legrue realized. Each tube had been cut from a person broken not just by the Under, but also by his own hand to patch others who were also broken. Yet, would cutting away the others ever fix Abigail or Livia or himself? He despaired at the futility of it all, but then, this was the Under, and what options did he have?

#

Legrue opened the shutter on the skylight of his stall, and the watery light fell across the packed dirt floor and the cutting table. He couldn't remember the last time he had done that, and he wasn't sure why he did it that morning. The darkness had masked how small and dingy his stall was. His cutting table filled nearly the entire space, and if he added all of the leaves to the table, it would leave only enough room at one end for him to squeeze around it.

Legrue stood three dozen tubes on the table, and next to them, he laid out a silk bundle. When he had returned from the Pit with his tools those years ago, Livia had cut the cloth from the hem of her nicest dress and given it to him. All these years holding such brutal instruments had left the silk tattered and stained, and he wondered how much longer before it came apart entirely.

The canvas flap rose slightly, and a woman peered in. Her grey shawl, pulled up to cover her head, obscured her face. Seeing Legrue, she stepped inside, leading a small child. Legrue could not tell if it was a girl or a boy; it wore only a cloth diaper and hid behind the dangling tails of the woman's shawl. What he could see, without doubt, was the child was healthy.

Legrue's words failed, as a sudden chill gripped him. He squeezed the edge of the cutting table to steady himself. Abigail was depending on him. He couldn't fail her and Livia.

The woman lowered her shawl. The smoothness of her skin suggested youth, but a dullness in her eyes spoke of desperation, and the dark skin of her chin and neck was crosshatched with pinkish scars from dozens upon dozens of cuttings. "You are Legrue?"

Unable to speak, Legrue motioned her toward the stool on the opposite side of the cutting table.

She sat, placing the toddler on her lap. The child buried its face into her breast. "Be brave, Che," the woman whispered into its curly hair. "Get 'em sweet when the cutter man done."

Legrue's brow pinched. There would be no sweets for the child after the cutter man. There would be no child, only tubes of blood and bags of fingers and toes, liver, heart, strips of muscles, and a pair of tiny, tiny eyes.

Bile rose in Legrue's throat. The V.I.Per had not told her. She was expecting Legrue to take a tube or two of blood from her child, like the other cutters; then some youn for them, and a sweet for her twobee to assuage her guilt. No, V.I.Per knew what he was doing, sending the mother with her healthy child when he could have had one of his entourage bring a sickly twobee from a desperate family. He sent this one because he wanted Legrue to fail. Because, as he had said, Legrue had "no jimmy for soul."

Legrue squeezed his eyes shut, but try as he might to envision Abigail's face, he saw nothing but darkness.

The toddler started wailing, healthy lungs throwing forth fear. "No, no," it shrieked.

Legrue thought he was going to vomit.

"Shh, Che. No hurt, no hurt. Shh."

Legrue opened his eyes. The woman had placed the squirming child on the cutting table. She struggled to fit its tiny arm into the restraint made for an adult. The child was already missing a pinky finger and several scars puckered its forearm and chest. Whoever had cut its tender skin had not been particularly skilled.

She finally managed to secure the wailing child's arm. "Sorry," she kept saying, and Legrue didn't know if the apology was meant for him or the twobee.

Legrue unfolded the tattered silk. The light shone dully on the nicked scalpel, the dull grey tines of the forceps, and the pitted curves of the clamp. In the hazy light, the tools looked efficiently brutal atop the tattered silk.

"Hurry," the woman pleaded, tears welling up in her eyes. She stroked the child's hair. "Shh, Che."

Legrue donned his magnifiers and adjusted the headlamp. He felt faint, but he dismissed it to his hunger.

He drew a deep breath; he could do this.

Legrue picked up the scalpel.

The child had stopped struggling and lay spread on the table crying despondently. Even so, it was a beautiful child—curly dark locks framing its round face. Legrue could see its mother in the color of its eyes.

He turned away, his hands shaking and his chest so tight now he could not draw a full breath. His mind raced with fantastical scenarios that would save him having to take this woman's child, but he knew he was out of time. Soon TwoTony would return and finding neither tubes nor youn, the rascal would shatter Legrue's hand, destroying his livelihood. Yet, Legrue might not even be there if the V.I.Per discharged someone to collect him before TwoTony arrived.

With him gone, what would happen to Abigail and Livia?

"One for three," he whispered—one healthy child for three lives. But they were broken lives, and Legrue did not know if they could ever be repaired. Yet, he knew if he did this, it would break him forever.

"I won't." He tugged at the strap, releasing the child's arm.

"But—"

Legrue swept his tools onto the floor and scattered the tubes across the stall. "Go!" He turned away again, ashamed of his outburst, but the woman left, and the wails of the twobee were swallowed by the noise of the waking market.

Spent, Legrue slumped onto the stool and buried his face into his hands. His whole body shook. What had he done?

He rushed out into the alley. Frantically, he craned his head above the crowd looking for the woman's grey shawl, but he could not find it. She was gone, and with her went any hope.

Back inside, Legrue gently dusted off the blue silk, retrieved his scalpel and forceps from under the cutting table, and carefully rewrapped the tools and what glass tubes he could find.

He contemplated waiting for fate to come to him, but as he stared at the small bundle of silk, he realized he had never been that type of man.

Maybe he could still find a way, perhaps luck would be with him, and a child that had died of the wasting will have been left in an alley. He had heard stories that this still happened, although he had not witnessed it since the last pandemic had swept through the Under.

He took his tools and headed out. For many hours, he searched the alleys behind the tenements. Finally, his feet hurting, he found himself before his own door.

#

The sun, long past its zenith, no longer came in through the window, leaving the apartment dark and smelling of burnt blood.

"Livia?"

Abigail coughed pitifully from her basket. Legrue placed his hand on her forehead. She burned with fever, hotter than Legrue had ever experienced, and the dropper was empty.

Where was Livia?

Legrue picked up his daughter. Her head rolled back and then forward onto his shoulder. She lay limply against him, her breath rattling in her chest. So light now, she felt almost like a newborn again. He cupped her head in his hand to hold it steady; her hair, fine and thin, felt like nothing against his palm.

Legrue's legs threatened to buckle, so he sat on the stool and hugged his daughter to his chest. He remembered his joy the day she had been born. "Shh," he whispered gently. The heat of her fever radiated through his shirt.

"Livia?" She hadn't left the apartment in weeks except to purchase the bowl and tubes of blood to burn. Could she have left Abigail to buy another tube? Over the past days, Livia had grown distant. He could not recall her comforting Abigail, and she had avoided his touch at night when he wanted—needed—her caress. A vacant stare had settled into her eyes, the same emptiness he saw on those who came to the wet market over and over, those who were ready to whole-sale themselves to bring it all to an end.

No, she couldn't be gone. Abigail still needed her. He still needed her.

"Livia?" he whispered into the room's lonely shadows.

The lingering smoke from the burning bowl stung his eyes. The tube Legrue had brought home yesterday lay empty on the floor next to it. False hope, all of it, Legrue thought. The blood, the burning, the cutting, all of it meant nothing.

He kicked the bowl and it clanged dully off the door.

In his arms, Abigail's frail form had gone still. Legrue did not move, but lowered his ear gently to her hair and started to count, waiting for her fragile lungs to rattle back to life, but they did not.

Like his daughter, the Under was quiet.

Legrue screamed, months of pain released in an anguished howl. He had failed her. That morning, if he had cut the twobee, he would not have wasted hours wandering alleys in his futile search. He could have sold any extra tubes of blood and some of the organs that surely the V.I.Per would not have missed and used the youn for another cycle of antipyretics. He could have come home, and Livia would still be there. Broken or not, they would have survived another day, and in the Under, that's what life was. Living had a price that came due every day—skin to come even—and today Legrue had failed to pay.

Drained, he slumped over the tiny, still body and wept.

"Legrue?"

He raised his head.

Livia stood in the doorway. Legrue blinked several times, not sure if he was hallucinating.

Her lip started to quiver as she noticed the body on Legrue's lap. A bottle dropped from her hand, shattering on the floor. "No," she said. "No." Her voice grew thinner as her throat tightened. She dropped on the floor next to Legrue and scooped Abigail into her arms.

Legrue stared at the broken bottle. She had gone for a cycle of fever medication, but how had she paid for it? He noticed then her disheveled hair, the top of her dress askew.

Legrue knew she would not speak of what she had given for her daughter, and he would not ask. That was the way in the Under. He slid onto the floor and pulled them both into his arms. She turned into him and cried into his shoulder.

Gently he stroked her hair. He should not have

doubted her.

A lump rose up in Legrue's throat. Soon his own debt would come due, but finally, he saw the path forward, and it was a path both he and Livia would need to follow together, as they had always done.

They could give nothing more to their daughter, but she could give them one final gift.

❦ Story Notes ❧
Gift for the Cutter Man

Of all the stories I've written, "Gift for the Cutter Man" is the one that creeps me out the most. It's dark, brutal, and unforgiving on every level, and it's one of the few stories that's made me look in the mirror and wonder: *Where the hell did that come from?*

So what inspired such a dark story? I'm a longtime member of an online critiquing group called Critters. This group does one thing (and does it well): gets writers to critique other writers.

One of the stories I critiqued involved the collection of body parts to fuel dark magic (written by the talented Lauren Banka). While I thought the story was strong, one of my critiques of it was that I didn't understand what would make the main character willing to sell off parts of her body.

The idea that someone would be desperate enough to sell body parts stuck in my brain, and I decided not to explore the motivation of the person doing the selling, but those of the person doing the buying. This became the foundation for "Gift for the Cutter Man."

This story may feel like a product of the pandemic, but its genesis came several months before COVID and wet markets even entered the public's lexicon. While a plague is omni-present, "Gift for the Cutter Man" is not a plague story. It's a study of a man who must decide how much of his humanity he is willing to risk to save those he loves.

All Things of Grace and Beauty

First published in *Allegory*, November 2023

THE FALLING ASH SETTLED on the yellowed leaves of the rowan tree like fragments of Logan's past life. How many days had it been since he'd last seen the sun? He'd stopped counting at a hundred and had lost track of the passing days since. A hundred and fifty? Two hundred?

However long, Logan feared Kayleigh's tree wouldn't last much longer.

Kayleigh had planted the rowan tree the year she and Logan had bought the off-grid cabin. She had been six months pregnant, but the baby, a girl who was to be called Rowan, was never born, and with her died Kayleigh's ability to have children.

Logan had been much younger then, both in years and wear.

Lightning flashed, followed by a rumble of thunder. Another storm brewed atop Rounder Peak and would soon roll down onto his homestead.

Logan ran his gloved hand down the trunk, the bark smooth from his frequent caresses. "Hang in there, Katy-kay."

Kayleigh had been away in Chicago giving the keynote address at a conference on green carbon when the asteroid had vaporized half of the Siberian taiga and triggered an impact winter. She might still be alive, but Logan had growing doubts. She spoke to him now through the tree she loved as much as him.

Logan adjusted his respirator mask and turned back to shoveling the ash blocking the intake of the smudge pot. He couldn't risk the pot failing to light if the night got too cold. The last time that had happened, the tree's smaller branches had frozen when the temperature dipped below minus forty.

The ash fall had eased in recent weeks, but before everything had gone silent, the newscasters had said it would be years before it all settled from the atmosphere. At the time, Logan hadn't appreciated such a timescale, but he quickly learned life didn't like perpetual cold and darkness. All the trees up Rounder Peak had died months ago, and the gnarled trunks of the Douglas firs and spruces stood like matchsticks in the strange afternoon twilight.

A gust of wind carried a faint sound, like a low groaning, not the usual clattering of the dead trees. Logan pushed aside his hood to better hear it. An animal? Maybe a person?

Logan retrieved his shotgun and worked his way cautiously upslope. The groans were coming from one of the many springs on the property where deer had once gathered in the evening. As he approached, lightning lit the scraggly twigs poking up through the gray drifts. If not for the lightning, Logan would have missed the body half-buried in the ash.

Was he too late?

Another flash of lightning illuminated a backpack next to the body. The pack clanked as Logan yanked it over to him. It likely carried something useful, but this wasn't the place to open it. He slipped a strap over his shoulder and backed away.

The body emitted a faint groan.

Logan froze, his shotgun raised. He realized now the body was a woman. Her ski goggles had come dislodged, and tawny strands of hair had fallen free of her hood. If not for her youth, she could have been Kayleigh's sister.

"Leave her be, Logan," he warned himself.

The asteroid had changed the world. Logan knew it was dangerous to look out for anyone but himself. Yet, Kayleigh would have never left anyone or anything that needed help. How could he?

"Hey, lady." Logan poked her hip with the tip of his shotgun. "Get up or you'll freeze to death."

She didn't move.

Lightning crackled, followed by a thunderous boom that startled Logan off his feet. He scrambled to his knees, his heart pounding. The storm was close; he couldn't stay any longer.

He grabbed the woman's hood and pulled. She slid across the ash with surprising ease, and he dragged her down to his cabin. Logan got her into the mudroom and then sat on the wooden bench, his lungs burning from his efforts.

The woman had not moved, but her shallow breathing showed she was still alive. Her skin was ice cold. If he could get her core temperature up, she might recover.

Logan stripped off his parka, dirty coveralls, and boots. He carried the woman to the couch near the cabin's potbelly stove. He pulled a blanket over her and put a kettle of water on the stove's top. When the kettle whistled, he filled a hot water bottle and placed it next to her feet.

Soon, she had started to shiver, which Logan took

as a good sign.

Having done all he could, Logan collapsed into the lounge chair opposite the couch. He stood the woman's backpack between his knees and unzipped the main compartment.

Inside was an empty canteen, two cans of green beans, a Swiss army knife, a silvery thermal blanket like those once used by mountain rescue teams, and a small stuffed unicorn with one of its glittery, pink wings missing. In a side pocket was a pistol. Logan removed the magazine and cleared the chamber. The magazine went into his shirt pocket—he'd return it when she left—and the pistol went back into the pack along with everything else.

#

An hour later, Logan realized the woman was only pretending to be asleep.

"I've got no interest in hurting you," he said, "and I hope you intend the same." The cool light of an electric lantern reflected off the shaft of the baseball bat laying across his lap.

Thunder cracked with enough force to rattle his bones. Pebbles and ash skittered off the windowpanes as the electrical storm raged outside.

Logan looked up at the ceiling. "Worse than usual."

Giving up the pretense, the woman opened her eyes.

"That's better now," Logan said. "Mind explaining why you're on my land?"

She licked cracked lips that were stained gray from the ash. Logan was amazed she was here at all, given she had no respirator and how far up Rounder Peak they were. "Passing through," she said, her voice raspy.

Her response implied a journey from one place to another, but what place was there to go anymore? In the hours following the impact, things had unraveled with a dizzying quickness. Rioting, looting, violence— human society had quickly come apart.

"I'll be on my way," she said.

"On your way to dead if you step out that door right now. But I'm not going to get in your way if that's your desired destination. You can stay until the storm settles. The water is free to use, but nothing else." Kayleigh had insisted on a well-provisioned pantry because access to Wodsford, the nearest town, could be cut off at any time by snow, tree falls, or washed-out river crossings. With grow lamps and a smudge pot, Logan had kept the greenhouse running, bringing in a rolling harvest of potatoes, carrots, and kale. But that didn't mean he could afford to give them away.

"I'm Logan," he said, deciding to try civility. Kayleigh would have wanted that.

"This your house?"

"For the past thirty-two years."

The woman nodded toward the backpack at Logan's feet. "That's mine."

"It is." With his foot, Logan pushed the pack closer to her.

"You went through it."

"I did."

The contents clattered as she dug through them. The horn of the unicorn poked out above the zipper.

"You'll get your bullets back when you leave; otherwise, everything is there," Logan said. "I don't recognize you." Wodsford may have been two-hours down old logging roads, but he knew everyone there.

"Just passing through," the woman said again.

Logan sighed. He could tell Kayleigh he had tried, but this woman wasn't interested in civility. Looking at her, he couldn't blame her, either. Yet, here she was on his couch, living and breathing, so she was tougher than he could ever be. That also made her dangerous.

"You come from the east? Do you know what happened to … to Chicago?" He almost didn't ask the question, afraid of the answer, but not knowing was worse.

The woman shrugged. "I'm going that way. My mom lives in Peoria."

Logan noted her choice of words—her mom *lives* in Peoria. The world didn't allow for that type of certainty anymore.

The woman dug out one of her cans of beans and pulled off the tab-top. She placed the can on the stove. While it warmed, she wandered around the cabin's living room looking at the paintings on the walls.

She stopped in front of one of them, an abstract portrait of Kayleigh. "Did you paint this?"

"I did." Throughout his career, Logan had had his share of gallery showings, but other than guests into his home, no one had ever seen that painting. To his dismay, Kayleigh loved that picture, even as Logan found it infinitely inadequate. He had tried to capture what he loved about Kayleigh, but he never found the right combination of hues and shapes that embodied the grace and beauty of her soul.

The woman said nothing and returned to her warmed beans. Using her flannel sleeve as an oven mitt, she moved the can to the breakfast counter separating the kitchen and the living room.

Logan followed her and leaned against the kitchen sink. "Peoria's a long ways away."

"What's it to you?"

Logan tired of the woman's rudeness. He could have let the storm finish what the cold and ash had started, so a little civility should have been in order.

The woman stopped eating. "I'm sorry," she said. "It's been a long time since I've had to make small talk, and I was never good at it to start with. Maybe we can start over?" The woman extended her hand. "It's nice to meet you, Logan. I'm Shannon."

Logan stared at the offered hand, wondering whether to take it. He felt guilty at his hesitation. What had the world come to that he did not automatically shake an offered hand? Kayleigh would have been disappointed.

"Good to meet you, Shannon," he said, taking her hand into his.

#

The room lit up and the crack of thunder that followed was so close Logan dropped to the floor, afraid the cabin had been hit.

Shannon screamed, and her can of beans landed on the floor next to Logan. Her wide-eyed face appeared over the counter. "Jesus H. Christ, that was close!"

Logan pulled himself up using the edge of the kitchen sink and squinted out the window. He could see nothing through the swirling ash. His heart thumped as he tried another window in the living room. "Oh, no!"

Logan rushed into the mudroom and pulled on his mask and parka. He didn't bother with his boots or gloves. A gust ripped the outer door from his grip as he opened it. He leaned into the wind, and forced himself out into the swirling ash and around the side of the cabin.

Logan reeled back in horror. The lightning had struck the rowan tree, splitting the trunk down the middle, exposing the heartwood. Half the tree lay on the ground, the splintered wood smoldering. The other half leaned against the side of the cabin.

"Kayleigh!" Logan fell to his knees. The world went dark as ash swirled around him, pelting the eye pieces of his mask. He hoped this was a nightmare, but when the swirl of ash shifted, the broken tree remained.

A roof shingle ripped free in the wind and flew toward him. Logan turned away, but the shingle hit him in the head, knocking him to the ground. When he touched his temple, a warm stickiness coated his fingers.

"Logan." A hand touched his shoulder.

"Kayleigh?"

Shannon held the electric lantern to his head. "You're injured. Can you walk?"

"Yes." Logan nearly fell as pins and needles shot through his feet.

Shannon caught his arm and steadied him.

"My feet are a little numb."

Shannon held his arm and helped him back to the mudroom where he collapsed onto the wooden bench. She wrestled the outer door closed, and the air in the room fell still.

Logan's head throbbed. He could barely feel his

hands and feet. Yet, none of that mattered because the lightning had split Kayleigh's tree and burned its core. Surely it was dead now.

When Shannon tried to check his wound, he slapped her hand away.

"Sit still," she chided.

Chagrined, Logan didn't move. "There's a first aid kit on the wall."

Shannon pulled on latex gloves. "I'm a trained responder, or I was before … well …" She searched through his thinning hair. "Looks like a superficial laceration. I'll need to flush it, but I don't think it needs stitches."

"Small miracles," Logan mumbled.

He let her wash the wound at the kitchen sink. He then sat in the lounge chair pressing a gauze pad against the cut.

Shannon rewarmed her can of beans and sat on the sofa to finish them. "Who's Kayleigh?" she asked.

Logan didn't like the sound of his wife's name on Shannon's lips. More importantly, that Shannon had to ask made it painfully clear that Kayleigh wasn't there, that Kayleigh was an unknown, a hypothetical. How dare she?

"Who's stuffy is that?" Logan asked, nodding toward the backpack at Shannon's feet. He watched with satisfaction as the color drained from her face.

"That's none of your business."

"Same to you."

"Asshole." Shannon snatched up her pack and sat on the floor in the kitchen where Logan could not see her.

He listened to the wind and rubbed at the ash ground into the creases of his palm. His anger burned like a terrible road rash, but after a time, its edge bled away, much like the strength of the storm.

Shannon's question about Kayleigh had been innocent, his response cruel. The stuffed animal must have belonged to her child, and the fact that she traveled alone told Logan everything.

No one still alive was untouched by loss. He had known this when he chose to strike out at Shannon. His intention had been to hurt her for showing him that Kayleigh wasn't there.

When he had first let Shannon into the cabin, he never intended to let her out of his sight. That seemed unimportant now. With the storm's passing, he had to get out.

Logan took the time to dress fully: coveralls, parka, respirator mask, boots and gloves. Once outside, he just stood, the ash fluttering down through the twilight like snow flurries.

He was afraid to go around the side of the cabin. By standing there, he could cling to that hope that his memory of the damage was wrong. The minutes passed, and the knot in his stomach drew tighter.

Slowly, he went around the side of the cabin, and even though he had prepared himself, he let out a gasp. Surely, the tree could not survive this. Perhaps, if this had happened a year ago, before the asteroid, it might have had the reserves to come back, but in the cold and dark, Kayleigh's tree had barely been hanging on. What the lightning had not killed, the falling ash would finish.

Logan's mask steamed up as his tears dripped into the bottom.

"It's just a tree," he said, trying to lie away the pain. But Kayleigh had planted this tree, watered it, and cared for it when it had been infested with gypsy moths. Like Logan, this tree was a product of her love.

And now, the world had taken them both from him.

Boots crunched on the ash behind him. "Looks like it was a beautiful tree," Shannon said.

Logan couldn't speak around the lump in his throat.

"Before I leave, I can help you cut it off the house." She started to remove her backpack.

Cut Kayleigh's tree? The half against the cabin was still attached to the roots. If the tree had any chance, it would come through that piece.

"No."

"It'll damage—"

"I said no." No one would lay a hand on Kayleigh's tree if it had any chance to recover. Perhaps he could give it more fertilizer and move the grow lights from the greenhouse.

"It's gone, Logan."

"She's not gone!"

Shannon stumbled backwards, tripping over a downed branch. She scrambled back to her feet and retreated away from him.

"Go!" Logan pointed away from the cabin.

"Give me back my bullets."

Logan dug the pistol magazine from his shirt pocket and slapped it into her outstretched hand. In her eyes, he saw the hardness of a survivor, someone capable of putting one of those bullets into his head. At that moment, Logan didn't care.

Shannon stared at the magazine. With a shake of her head, she pushed it into the pocket of her parka.

"Good luck, Logan." She backed away several steps before turning and fading into the falling ash.

#

The way Shannon had dissolved into the ash left Logan wondering if she had been a hallucination conjured to torment him. Surely, no one was left in the world to appear on his doorstep. Yet, he was certain she had been there, as certain as he was that Kayleigh had once been there, and would, one day return. He believed that, or what reason did he have to go on?

If there was a chance to save the tree, he had to try. He had some lumber in the shed and bolts left over from when he'd made a dozen planter boxes. With some old-fashioned elbow grease, he could pound together some supports to carry the tree's weight while it regained its strength.

He retrieved the keys to the shed from the mudroom, and as he came back around the cabin, he drew up short at the unmistakable sound of a bullet being chambered.

"Not a peep," the owner of the pistol said. The man stepped away from the wall of the cabin where his dark jacket had blended into the shadow. He wore a ski mask and goggles and had a bandanna tied around the lower half of his face, making him look like a two-bit, western outlaw.

Logan raised his hands. "Don't shoot me." He could barely say the words.

"Don't give me no reason, then. How many are here?"

Logan's mind raced. He could barely understand the man's question.

"How many?" the man asked again.

"Just me."

"If you lie to me, lots of people will get hurt." The man raised a walkie-talkie to his lips. It looked military grade to Logan, but then he was basing that on what he'd seen in the movies. "Come on up, Colm. He says he's alone."

The walkie-talkie crackled, but Logan could not make out the response.

A second man, Colm, appeared from the ash. He was shorter but stockier than the first. "You're sure no one else is here?" Colm asked, as he patted Logan down.

"Just me."

"This yours?" The man with the pistol held up a stuffed unicorn in his offhand. It was smudged with ash, but the single, glittery pink wing was unmistakable. It must have fallen out of Shannon's pack when she tripped over the fallen branch.

"Not mine," Logan said. "Where did you find it?"

Colm took the unicorn from his partner. "Did you see the woman?"

Logan's senses tingled. These two didn't just arrive by chance—they had been following Shannon. But why?

That didn't matter. If they were interested in catching up with her, they might leave him be if he told them which direction she had gone. Logan knew where she was going, assuming she had told him the truth. Yet, telling these two anything, didn't seem right. They hadn't followed Shannon through ash and storms to exchange pleasantries. They intended harm.

Logan swallowed hard. Shannon had caused him no trouble and had even left peacefully after he had treated her poorly. "What woman?"

Colm made a sucking sound behind his bandanna.

"She can't have got far," the first man said. "The stuffy wasn't even buried."

"It's taken us days to get this close. I don't want to go the wrong way." Colm stared menacingly into Logan's eyes. "How about we go inside, Sweens. Have a little chat with our friend."

Sweeney chuckled. "I could stand a sit beside the fire." He motioned with his pistol towards the front of the cabin.

Inside the mudroom, Logan paused to remove his parka and boots, but Sweeney nudged him forward. Logan didn't resist, but shed his gloves and respirator mask as he stepped inside.

"Daaaamn," Sweeney said as he followed Logan into the living room.

Colm pulled down his bandana and peeled off his ski mask. A mass of unruly red hair tumbled forth. He pushed it back out of his face.

Both men were twenty-or-more years younger than Logan and hardened by their very survival. Logan didn't like his chances if this came down to a fight.

"What's your name?" Colm asked.

"Logan."

"Sit down, Logan." Colm motioned him toward the stool at the breakfast counter. Colm shed his pack and removed a pair of handcuffs from a side pocket.

"Whoa," Logan said. "We're all friends, aren't we?"

"No, Logan. We ain't."

Sweeney steadied his pistol with his offhand. He had dead eyes, and the coldness of his gaze made Logan more afraid of him than of Colm and his handcuffs.

"See, friends help friends." Colm snapped one of the cuffs onto Logan's wrist and yanked his arm across the top of the counter, bending Logan's torso painfully across its surface. "We could still be friends, but that's up to you now. *Comprende, amigo?*"

Stretched across the countertop, Logan could not see either man. He feared that even if he told them what they wanted and they left, they'd want to come back after they finished their business with Shannon. If they did, things would be easier for them if Logan wasn't here.

Colm placed the stuffed unicorn on the counter where Logan could see it. "Now, anything you want to say about this?"

"Will you leave if I tell you what I know?"

"So, you saw her?" Sweeney asked from somewhere behind him.

Colm leaned into view. The skin around his mouth where his ski mask did not cover was stained gray from the ash. "We're going to leave either way. You see, that bitch cut one of our friends real bad. We have business to settle."

Logan didn't know Shannon well, but she didn't seem the type to bring violence for no reason. She could have harmed him—she had opportunity—but she didn't. Maybe, she still held old notions of gratitude. About Colm and Sweeney, he wasn't so positive.

"Sorry about your friend," Logan said.

"That's why we need to find her," Sweeney said. "Justice. Ya see?"

They spoke of justice, even as they had him handcuffed and were threatening him with violence.

Was this the justice they would extend to Shannon?

Colm's gaze narrowed as his patience ran thin. "She's getting farther away," he said.

If they wanted to scare him, it was working. "You're going to kill me." Logan's knees wobbled, but most of his weight was already spread atop the counter, so it didn't matter.

"Sweeney and I ain't killers," Colm said.

Yet, he spoke with the coolness of a killer. Logan could tell them everything he knew about Shannon, but he doubted it would save him. In that same moment, Logan also decided he would not give in to his fear. He would tell these two nothing.

Kayleigh would have been proud of him.

"Never seen that before," Logan said, struggling to keep his voice steady. "I thought I heard something outside a few hours ago. Maybe—"

Colm yanked hard on the handcuff, nearly dislocating Logan's shoulder. "Sweeney would love to put a bullet in your face."

Logan clenched his teeth against the pain. It had been so long since he had seen Kayleigh, that her face had begun to fade from his memory, as if the raining ash were washing her away. But this time, when he closed his eyes, her gentle blue eyes materialized from the blackness. She slowly blinked at him, the way she did when she had reached a calm resignation about something he intended to do, but to which she disagreed. And like always in those moments, that look of resignation was followed by a small, gentle rise of the corners of her mouth into a half-smile that told Logan she would see him when he got back from whatever adventure he was about to set out upon.

"We're wasting time." Sweeney sounded agitated.

"Maybe we can find her trail in the ash."

Logan prayed they'd just want to be gone, and that dealing with him would take more time than they wanted to commit.

"You're right, Sweens, time's wasting." Colm came around the counter and pulled Logan up by the back of his parka. He pushed him toward the mudroom.

"We're not taking him, are we?" Sweeney asked.

"Nope."

They didn't let Logan put on his mask or gloves; he wouldn't be needing them.

Colm opened the outer door letting in a swirl of ash that made Logan cough. "Out."

Logan stumbled out into the twilight, squinting to keep the ash out of his eyes. They were going to kill him if he did nothing.

Colm followed him out, still holding the handcuff. Behind him, Sweeney waited for his turn at the door.

As Colm stepped down, Logan dodged to the right and yanked hard on the handcuffs. Caught unaware, Colm slipped on the stairs. He let go of the handcuffs to catch himself on the doorframe.

Logan sprinted around the side of the cabin. The ash in his eyes obscured his vision, and he did not see the downed branch of the rowan tree. His ankle buckled as his boot landed on it, and he tumbled to the ground.

His lungs felt like they were going to explode, and as he tried to get up, coughs wracked his body. Sweeney pushed him back to the ground, and as Logan rolled onto his back, the man's boot pushed into his chest.

"Wait, Sweens," Colm said, coming up beside his partner. He held up Logan's shovel. "Don't waste the bullet."

Sweeney tucked the pistol into his parka pocket and took the shovel. "Last chance," he said.

Last chance for what? His fate would be no different if he told them which way Shannon had gone.

The burning in his lungs went away, and a calm settled over him. To his left, where the rowan tree should have been, Kayleigh nodded reassuringly. He was ready to hold her again. "Go to hell, Sweens."

#

"Have it your way." Sweeney raised the shovel.

"Don't!"

Logan could not see the owner of the new voice, but he recognized it immediately. "Gun," he yelled. He hugged Sweeney's boot to his chest and rolled as hard as he could to his left.

Sweeney cried out as his ankle popped. The shovel thunked into the ash next to Logan's head.

A pistol popped.

Logan curled into a ball and covered his head as Sweeney fell on top of him.

Another shot. Colm cursed. Feet scuffled in the ash. Before Logan could comprehend what was happening, the noise stopped.

Sweeney's dead weight rolled off him.

"You okay, Logan?" Shannon asked.

He wiped at his eyes but could not clear the ash. "Been better, to be honest." The burning in his lungs had returned, confirming he was still alive.

"Looks like you reopened that cut. Let's get you inside."

Face down in the ashes to his left, Sweeney lay

motionless. Shannon picked up his pistol from where it had fallen from his pocket and handed it to Logan. She collected Colm's pack, which lay nearby. "He ran off," she said about the pack's owner, "but I wounded him pretty bad. He won't last long out there."

With his adrenaline rushing, Logan hadn't noticed the cold. Now, he started to shiver.

"You need help getting inside?"

Logan coughed and pulled the collar of his shirt over his mouth. His fingers and ears burned painfully, but he couldn't go inside yet. He zig-zagged his way back toward the front of the cabin, his eyes scanning the ground.

Colm had been carrying the stuffed unicorn when Logan had broken free at the door. Surely, he had dropped—and there it was, half-buried in the ash near the corner of the cabin. "I think this is yours."

Shannon took the stuffed unicorn from him and carefully dusted the ash from it.

Logan knew Shannon had not come back for him. He realized now that she had also not come back simply for the unicorn. She had come back because she was not ready to give up on the world that used to be, the one where humans were decent and helped each other. She could have walked away or simply let Sweeney bash his brains out onto the ash. But she didn't want to live in a world where life was transactional, and everything came down to kill or be killed.

She wanted to live in Kayleigh's world.

So did Logan.

The old world may be gone, and Kayleigh with it, but that didn't mean a better world couldn't rise from the grief and ashes of the old.

Shannon had been right about the rowan tree. Logan realized pruning it back from the cabin would not be an affront to Kayleigh. She may have loved that tree, but she loved him more, and she would have wanted him to move on to a better place, a new beginning.

"Maybe we can start over," Logan said, extending his hand to Shannon. "I'm Logan, and it's so nice to meet you."

Story Notes
All Things of Grace and Beauty

Over the past decade, British Columbia (Canada) has experienced several difficult forest-fire years. Where I live, 2021 was a particularly bad fire season, with the ordinarily blue summer skies darkened by smoke and falling ash for months. I recall noon looking like twilight, and my nose and eyes stinging from the smoke. Friends posted pictures of ominous red skies, and it looked like the end-of-times had arrived.

The falling ash reminded me of a few days I spent in Rabaul (Papua New Guinea) in the late 1990s, soon after it had been buried by a volcanic eruption. A new cinder cone had appeared in the harbor, and ash was actively raining down. I recall walking down the street to meet some fellow biologists (we were departing on a coral reef survey cruise the next day) and seeing metal plates on the ground. It took me a while to realize those square metal sheets were the roofs of cars, buried in the ash. What was most remarkable, however, was the city was still inhabited. Somehow, the residents had found a way to move forward with their lives, even in the face of such remarkable hardship.

Humanity is incredibly resilient, and "All Things if Grace and Beauty" grew directly out of these experiences.

The Last Horse

First published in *Aoife's Kiss*, September 2012

FROM THE PERIMETER RAIL, OLIVIA watched her employer, Catherine Pestille, warily circle the carousel as if assessing its menagerie of horses for danger. Apparently satisfied, Catherine mounted the riding platform and walked the aisles between the rows of horses with her eyes closed and her finger tips barely caressing the animals' flanks and necks as she walked by them.

"You sure you don't want to ride it?" Jim Helmer asked Olivia. The elderly attendant, his knit cap pulled down snugly over his ears, had let them into the carousel house even though it was off-season. "It's a beaut when it's wound up."

Olivia knew Jim's assessment wasn't simply civic pride. The carousel, a 1913 Herschell-Spillman and one of the last of its kind, was hung with twenty exquisitely carved horses and six menagerie animals. Olivia had seen it once before, about six years ago while researching her book on the historic carousels of America. At that time, she had been impressed by the carousel's 1936 Wurlitzer organ. With the pride the folks of Story City, Iowa, lavished on their historic piece of Americana, she suspected it still had the same kick as when she last heard it.

"When I ride, my old bones get young again," Jim said. "This one's got magic in it. Then, don't they all?"

Olivia had believed that once, not long ago.

"Ms. Pestille never rides them," she said. Over the last three months, she and Catherine had zigzagged across the country five times, viewing over three dozen carousels. Not once had Catherine asked to ride.

Jim tsked. "Shame."

Olivia didn't pretend to understand it. Catherine paid her top dollar to act as tour guide, so it wasn't Olivia's place to question. But for someone prepared to spend a considerable sum of money on carousel horses for her private museum, Catherine seemed oddly disengaged.

Olivia's cell rang the special ring assigned to her mother. A cold knot twisted her stomach.

She dug her phone out of her purse and checked the number, hoping her ears had been wrong. With all her recent time-zone hopping, Olivia had lost track of the time in Boston. Had enough time passed for it to be good news?

"Excuse me, I need to take this." Without waiting for a response, she left Jim at the perimeter railing.

"Is Lizzy okay?" Olivia asked as soon as she put the phone to her ear.

"They just finished the treatment. Everything went well." Her mother sounded tired but relieved.

Olivia exhaled a cloud of frost.

"She's asking for you."

Olivia's chest tightened. She should be at her daughter's side, but Catherine had been insistent about this trip and had even dropped a not-so-subtle hint that if Olivia couldn't do the job, she would find someone who could. Olivia couldn't afford to lose this job. More importantly, Lizzy couldn't afford it.

"Mommy?" Her daughter's voice was small and frail, more than simply the threadiness of long distance. "Mommy, I want you."

"Sweetie, I'll be home soon."

"Mommy?"

"I'm here." Olivia slapped at the tears collecting in the corners of her eyes with the back of her hand.

"Did you find the magic flying horse?"

Olivia laughed. Three weeks ago, she had taken Lizzy to the Paragon Carousel south of Boston to take their minds off Lizzy's upcoming plasmapheresis and experimental auto-immune treatments. Olivia could not remember how many times they had ridden the carousel that afternoon, but Lizzy had ridden every horse at least once. For many rides, Lizzy had chosen a winged horse she had named Magic. Nearly every day since, Lizzy had asked Olivia to buy her a magic flying horse.

"No, sweetie, but I'm still looking." Olivia fought to hold her voice steady. "I'll buy you the first flying horse I find."

Thankfully her mother came on the line. "Will you be home this evening? She needs you."

"I know." Olivia winced at the sharpness of her voice. Since Lizzy's diagnosis with Bourbaki's Syndrome three months ago, her mother had been a godsend, dropping everything in her life to help.

"I'm sorry, Mom, it's just—" Olivia shook her head. "I'm on the 5:10 from Chicago."

"Will you be staying a while?"

"I don't know. Catherine hasn't said—"

"The nurse is coming—gotta go. See you tonight."

"Tell Lizzy I love—" But the connection had gone dead. Olivia squeezed the phone to her breast. Lizzy was in good hands, but they should have been *her* hands. She turned back to the carousel, wondering if Catherine had finished.

Catherine stepped off the platform and came toward Olivia shaking her head. "None of these are what I am looking for, Olivia. What else do you have for me?"

Olivia's shoulders slumped. "That's all, Ms. Pestille."

Catherine pursed her lips. Olivia had never been able to pin an age on her. Catherine could have been an ex-model anywhere from thirty-five to fifty years old with coal black hair and the angular features and knife-edge nose that on most people would have looked harsh, but on Catherine were sophisticated beauty. Olivia thought it was the way she carried herself, upright and confident, as if she knew she was beautiful but wasn't bragging, only presenting the evidence.

"We've seen six collections in four days." Olivia tried to hide the fatigue in her voice, but she couldn't tell if she succeeded. "I need to do more research, or I'll be wasting your time."

Catherine sighed heavily. "I suppose you're right." She thanked Jim Helmer for his time and headed for their rental car. Jim fell into her wake, like a seagull chasing a luxury yacht.

"I'll be there in a minute," Olivia said. She needed to use the restroom before the long ride back to the Des Moines airport.

After she had finished, she washed her hands and face. The icy water stung her fingers but felt good on her gritty eyes. A sour, ammonia stink, like something had died in the pipes, crinkled her nose. Olivia reached for a towel and noticed a man behind her in the mirror.

With cobra quickness his hand covered her mouth, catching her scream. His other arm wrapped around her neck. On the back of his hand, the tendons stood out like cables under his leathery skin. His fingers reeked of dead animal.

Olivia gagged.

"I can break your neck with one twist." His breath smelled of boiled beef and garlic. He spoke with an eastern European accent that Olivia could not place.

Olivia started to cry. He was going to kill her, especially when he learned she had left her purse in the car. Her knees buckled, but her attacker held her up by her neck.

"This woman you help. Stop or I will kill you."

Olivia's brow knitted. This was about Catherine?

"You stop helping her and you never see me again. You tell anyone about me... ." He pulled her chin to the side and made a sound like a walnut popping in a vice. "You hear?"

Olivia nodded her head vigorously—little nods, like the little breaths of a person hyperventilating.

He pushed her into a stall and pulled the door shut. "Stay and count to ten," he said. "Don't come out before then."

She started to count, each number bracketed by sobs. When she hit ten, she broke down and cried. "Everything's okay," she whispered, trying to focus her racing thoughts. He hadn't hurt her. She would see Lizzy again. "Everything will be okay."

The whole incident now seemed surreal, and she wasn't exactly sure what had happened. She didn't know what to do, but she couldn't stop working for

Catherine. Olivia's insurance through her previous job as a historian with the National Carousel Association had not covered Lizzy's experimental treatment. Thankfully, Catherine had offered her four times her NCA salary and a benefits package that covered everything.

Olivia washed her face with soap from the hand dispenser. She scrubbed until the paper towel disintegrated, but the stink of dead animal continued to sit in the back of her throat like a coating of rancid grease.

He had said tell no one, and she intended to do that. For now at least. Olivia took several deep breaths before leaving the bathroom.

Catherine waited near the rental car. She stubbed out a cigarette and, without a word, climbed into the driver's seat.

Olivia wanted nothing more than to hold Lizzy.

#

Olivia's flight out of Chicago was delayed for nearly two hours, so she didn't arrive home until after midnight.

She inched open the door to Lizzy's bedroom. Her daughter lay flat on her back, arms straight at her side. She never used to sleep like that. Olivia used to find her sprawled sideways across her mattress or with her feet on her pillow.

Olivia caressed her daughter's cheek. The skin was warm and dry, a side effect of the treatment.

Lizzy stirred, but did not open her eyes. "Mommy?"

"I'm here, sweetie."

"Don't go."

"I won't."

Olivia lay down and carefully wrapped her arms around Lizzy's spindly shoulders. Only four months ago, Lizzy had been a normal four-year old, singing nonsense songs and learning how to swing "all by herself" on the "big kid's swing."

Things like this weren't supposed to happen to little girls.

Lizzy shifted under the sheet and groaned.

The sound tore at Olivia's heart. The treatments were Lizzy's only hope, and Olivia would let nothing stop her from getting them.

#

Olivia awoke with a start and tumbled out of Lizzy's narrow bed. Her heart thumped in her chest. Long shadows splattered across the walls and furniture from Lizzy's pink Disney Princess nightlight. Her assailant from the bathroom could be hiding in any of them.

Olivia searched the room, but finding nothing did little to ease her mind. She checked the rest of the townhouse. Sometimes her mother forgot to latch the sliding door. Olivia found it locked. Still rattled, Olivia settled into a chair at the kitchen table.

She should call the police, but what could they do besides take her statement. She couldn't risk it. She would buy something to protect herself in the morning.

Olivia rubbed at the tight muscles in her neck.

The message light on the kitchen phone winked.

"Ms. Deshay, my name is Dr. Barrett Sanders." The voice was warm, not the clinical voice she had come to expect from doctors. "I'm with the Center for Disease Control in Atlanta. As part of your enrollment in the Bourbaki trials, your contact information was added to the CDC's malediction database. I'm using that information to do an epidemiological study of rare immunodeficiency disorders, and I was hoping to get additional information from you. I don't need an answer immediately, but please call me."

Olivia scribbled down the number. She didn't think Dr. Sanders would be able to help Lizzy, but she needed to try everything.

#

Olivia called Dr. Sanders that morning and learning that he lived in the Boston area, agreed to meet him at a nearby coffee shop during Lizzy's afternoon nap.

Dr. Sanders sat near the front window, an open laptop on the table. He wore a heavy parka-style jacket with a fur-edged hood. It hung open to reveal a dark sweater and jeans. When she approached, he jumped to his feet and extended a hand. "Ms. Deshay?"

"Please, call me Olivia."

"Certainly, Olivia."

She declined his offer of coffee and sat down. "How can I help you, Dr. Sanders?" she asked, hoping to push the meeting along. She wanted to be back before Lizzy awoke.

"I appreciate you meeting with me. I'd like to ask you a few questions for my study of several rare immunodeficiencies, including Bourbaki's Syndrome."

Olivia's throat used to tighten when someone

named her daughter's illness, but recently she just felt numb. "Are you trying to find a cure?" she asked.

His jaw tightened. "I'm sorry, but I won't be able to help your daughter that way."

"So what are you doing then?" Olivia grimaced. Her tone had been harder than she had meant it to be. "I'm sorry, I didn't mean—"

"It's okay," he said. "I can't say that I understand what you're going through, because I have no children, but I do understand the emotions. Let me explain what I am doing."

He rotated his computer so Olivia could see a satellite photo of the U.S. freckled with multicolored dots.

"I study the pattern of diseases to see if I can find environmental links. I do this by mapping all of the documented cases that are reported to the CDC using Geographic Information Systems, or GIS. I can then search for disease clusters which would suggest that the disease is not randomly affecting the population, but that something in those specific areas may be contributing to the disease."

Olivia found it difficult to focus on what Dr. Sanders was saying. She hadn't expected him to arrive on a white horse bearing the miracle she prayed for, but unconsciously... .

"Are you okay, Olivia?"

"I'm just tired. Maybe I will take that coffee."

"Sure, sure." He left her at the table and went to purchase a coffee from the barista.

The map with its hundreds of dots held her attention. If she understood him correctly, each dot represented a sick person. Olivia's chest tightened.

Her eyes were drawn toward Boston. The city was

covered with multi-colored dots, but so were most cities. That made sense, however. Cities had the highest population densities, so she expected they would also have the greatest number of cases. So what constituted these clusters that Dr. Sanders had mentioned?

He placed a cup in front of her.

"I'd like to collect a little personal information. It'll be anonymous, and I won't ask for any credit card numbers." He smiled mischievously. "Anything you don't want to answer is fine."

Olivia agreed and he began to ask questions. Where had she and her daughter lived? Where had they vacationed? Had they used certain types of products?

Olivia did her best to answer. None of the questions were difficult, but the answers brought up memories of better times.

He recorded her responses into a database on his computer.

"That's it," he said after about thirty questions.

Olivia stared blankly at the cup of coffee in her hands. "I really need to get back to my daughter." She rose, gathering her coat around her.

Dr. Sanders fumbled a card from his pocket. "I know you don't know me from Adam, but I know that people sometimes just need to talk. If there is anything I can do… ."

Olivia glanced at his card without really seeing it. She stuffed it into her coat pocket. With a wan smile, she turned and left.

#

The next day, Catherine emailed Olivia yet another

list of search criteria. This time, she had attached a photograph of a horse and written only a single sentence: "I'm looking for a horse like this (see picture), pale in color, with a bird motif."

The attached picture was a carousel horse caught mid-stride, its head raised and mane flaring. Olivia recognized it as a stargazer model, made famous by C. W. Parker in the early 1900's, but carved by several of the major carousel manufactures, including Dentzel and Herschell-Spillman. Stargazers had been popular on traveling carousels and were now among the most common models around.

Olivia groaned. Dozens of horses could match Catherine's parameters and she would want to see the animals as soon as possible. The thought of leaving Lizzy again was painful. Maybe she could convince Catherine to delay the next trip.

Olivia set to work. After several hours she had nine prospective horses that met Catherine's description. She compiled the list with the pictures she had for four of the animals and crafted a short email requesting that they visit the horses after Lizzy's next treatment.

Within a minute of sending the message, Olivia's phone rang.

"Book the flights for tomorrow," Catherine said, skipping any pleasantries. "I want to see them all."

#

They arrived in San Francisco early in the morning and drove up into the hills over Berkeley to the 1911 Herschell-Spillman carousel at Tilden Park. The caretaker, an elderly woman with a spry twinkle in her eye, met them at the entrance. Catherine studied the dun-colored stargazer with robin motifs on the saddle and bridle. After a minute, she shook her head. "This isn't it."

They flew into Denver, arriving in the late afternoon. Olivia was tired and ready to check into their hotel, but Catherine insisted they drive out to Lakeside Park to visit its 1908 C.W. Parker carousel. Olivia made arrangements to be let in by Joshua Fredrick, an old friend from the National Carousel Association.

"The NCA hasn't been the same without you." Joshua stood next her, bundled up from the Colorado chill.

His words felt good.

Catherine came around on her circuit and stopped suddenly. She backed up to a standing horse; three legs on the ground and the left front one raised as if in parade march. "What horse is this?"

"We call that one Treebeard," said Joshua. "That's not an official name, of course."

Catherine circled the animal, gingerly running her finger tips along its haunches. She cupped its head in her hands and gazed into its eyes. "Who carved it?"

Joshua arched a graying eyebrow.

The Lakeside carousel had always fascinated Olivia. While manufactured by C. W. Parker, several of the animals appeared to have been carved by a rival company, in this case Charles Looff. During the carousel heyday of the early 1900s, when demand often exceeded production, it wasn't unusual for a company to purchase animals from other manufacturers and sell them as their own. This made identifying a horse's carver difficult.

Olivia searched the animal for any indication of the

artist. "I'll be!" she said. "I think this is a Campollini."

"Are you certain?" Joshua squatted next to her.

Olivia pointed to a faint cross impressed into the wood near the joint where the front standing leg joined the body. "That's his mark. This must be one of his early horses." Olivia admired Campollini's carvings. His realistic rendering of musculature and eyes suggested he had studied horse anatomy. While this particular horse lacked definition in the body, it had the Campollini eyes.

"But Campollini left Parker to work for Herschell in 1905. That would predate this carousel."

"Maybe Parker found the animal in a closet," Olivia said. "He was obviously desperate."

"Find me more horses by this Campollini," Catherine said.

"That won't be easy," Olivia said. "Campollini signed some of his horses, but like most carvers, he often left no mark. With copy-cat carving—"

"Olivia." Catherine put a hand on her shoulder and turned her away from Joshua. "If anyone can do this, I know it's you. That is why I pay you a ridiculous amount of money." Catherine smiled, but there was little warmth in it. She stepped off the carousel platform and headed toward the car without looking back.

Olivia started to follow, but stopped when Joshua grabbed her elbow.

"Campollini's daughter is still alive," he said. "She used to be active in the carousel world. That was some time ago, but she might be able to help. I can make a few calls. Set something up?"

"That'd be helpful," Olivia said.

"I'll call you tonight."

#

Catherine decided to cancel the rest of their trip until Olivia could locate more of Campollini's horses. Olivia wasn't sure how she was going to do that. Her database didn't have that level of detail.

Joshua called her about an hour after she had settled into her room at the airport Marriott. Campollini's daughter, Beatrice, had agreed to meet with her. "Bea's excited about meeting you," Joshua said. "You're like a rock star." He gave her instructions on how to arrange a meeting.

True to Joshua's word, Beatrice was excited. She had admired the catalogue Olivia had written, calling it the "Carousel Bible." Beatrice lived in Tonawanda, New York, not far from the old Herschell-Spillman factory building. Olivia arranged to meet with her the next day; she could stop on the way back to Boston and still be home by dinner.

Exhausted, Olivia unwound in the room's Jacuzzi tub. The warm water and massaging jets put her to sleep.

She awoke feeling cold and disoriented. It took her a moment to realize where she was. Olivia felt helpless. Her life had been messy—a failed marriage, an unusual career choice—but the mess usually had been her own doing and something she could always rely on herself to clean up. But the last four months, her life felt like dirty dish water spiraling down the kitchen garbage disposal.

Shivering, Olivia pulled on the plush robe hanging behind the door and stepped out of the bathroom.

Her breath caught in her throat.

The man who had attacked her in Iowa sat in a chair between her and the door. "Sit. We will talk only."

A voice in her head screamed "Run!", but she had nowhere to go. The bathroom door wasn't strong enough to keep him out for long. Her phone was on the nightstand near the bed. The hand stunner she had bought two days ago was in her purse, but that sat on the floor next to the man's chair.

"I could have killed you while you slept. Sit."

The thought of him seeing her naked in the tub turned her stomach. She pulled her robe tighter around herself and sat in the chair on the opposite side of the room. "What do you want?" Her voice cracked.

"I realize my last way was not the best way. I am sorry. You are a strong woman, not easily scared by threats, but you do not know who you help."

Olivia's brow scrunched together.

"This woman you call Catherine Pestille is no woman. She is death. She is the plague. Everything she touches is doomed to rot. She uses you to find what she has lost. When she finds it, the world will end."

Olivia's laughter burst from her before she could stop it. Her hand shot to her mouth to stifle the sound.

The man didn't move, except for a pulsing vein in his right temple. "She brings death where she goes and hell follows her. She is one of the four that signal the apocalypse."

"The apocalypse? Like the four horsemen? That's cra—" Olivia snapped her lips shut.

"You are a smart woman. Have you talked to Mr. Lee recently?"

Olivia stiffened. Mr. Wen Lee managed six historic

carousels in the Endicott, New York area. Olivia had known him since she was a graduate student. She had last seen him three months ago, shortly after she had started working for Catherine. He had been his usual dynamo of health and energy.

"What did you do to him?"

The man's right eye twitched. "Me, nothing. You should talk to him soon." He unfolded his legs, like a spider rising. "When you are ready, find me." He dropped a ragged strip of paper on the floor and left.

Olivia ran across the room and slammed the bar lock in place. She fought to control her breathing as she listened at the door. No footsteps, no elevator doors closing, only silence. She peered through the peephole; the hallway was empty. Olivia sat with her back to the door and buried her face in her hands.

The ragged strip of paper sat near her toes. On it was written a phone number in jagged print. Olivia had no intention of calling the number, but she was afraid to throw it away.

#

Early the next morning, Olivia called Wen Lee's cell phone. He didn't answer, and, oddly, his voice mail was full. She called his wife, who picked up after several rings.

"Yi-Ling, this is Olivia Deshay. Is Wen there?"

Silence.

"Yi-ling?"

"Olivia." The calm in Yi-ling's voice sent a shiver through Olivia's body. "Wen died last night."

#

"It's a pleasure to meet you, Ms. Deshay."

Beatrice's smile was as warm as fresh baked cookies.

"Please, call me Olivia."

"And you call me Bea. I've never liked Beatrice." She pushed open the storm door. Warm air flooded out. "Do come in from the cold."

Olivia stepped into a living room filled with antique furniture. Miniature wind-up carousels, old black and white photos of carnival rides, and dozens of scale model horses sparkled in the grey light filtering through sheer drapes. Bea led her into the dining room where a pot of hot tea awaited.

With a shaky hand, Bea poured two cups. "Joshua explained what you needed." She slid a cloth-bound book across the table top. "My father's carving book. He catalogued every horse he ever carved, complete with descriptions and the carousel number it went on."

Olivia hesitantly touched the cover. The cloth was thin and smooth, like the back of an old man's hand. Slowly she lifted the cover. Her breath caught when the binding crackled.

"Go ahead," Bea said softly.

Each yellowed page was dedicated to a horse, complete with drawings and descriptions. The meticulous cursive script had faded but was still legible.

Olivia frowned. How was she going to transcribe all of this information in the short time she had?

Bea must have sensed her dilemma. "You can take it with you."

"Oh, no. I couldn't do that."

Bea patted Olivia's hand. "Don't worry, Joshua vouched for you. That's good enough for me."

Olivia slipped the book into her purse and

promised to return it as soon as she was done with it.

The two talked while they drank their tea and ate shortbread cookies. Before she realized it, Olivia was talking about Lizzy, her inadequacies as a mother, and her overwhelming fear that Lizzy wouldn't live to Christmas. Her words spilled out as if she were being bled of a toxin.

Bea handed her a tissue.

"I'm sorry. I shouldn't have …"

Bea's warm smile returned. "Let me show you something." She led Olivia out the back door. "I don't get out here much anymore," she said as she struggled down the back steps. Her cane clicked on the cracked concrete walk leading back to a weathered outbuilding at the fence edge. Bea pushed the door open and stepped aside.

Olivia gasped.

The grey afternoon light filtered through the dusty workshop windows illuminating dozens of carousel horses and carving benches littered with saws, chisels, and square-headed mallets. The room smelled of old wood and varnish.

"My father's personal work room," Bea said. "I never could bring myself to clean it out." She switched on the lights. Naked bulbs glared over the top of each workbench, but left the corners of the room in shadow. "He loved these horses as much as he loved me," she said without malice. "These were my brothers and sisters."

Olivia was drawn into the room as if led by an unseen hand. On one of the workbenches sat an unfinished horse head. The nostrils and one of the eyes had already been coaxed from the wood, but the ears were still rough-hewn triangles.

"After Papa died, I spent years locating some of my favorite horses. Many of them had been lost or destroyed, but I managed to find these." Bea named each horse as Olivia inspected it. Most were faded to drab specters of their former selves, a few were damaged, but all of them deserved a place in a museum.

Dozens of sepia colored prints covered the wall. Antonelli Campollini surrounded by his family, his horses, his friends, with tools in his hands, with his daughter on his lap.

"Papa in his element," Bea said. "He always smelled of wood."

After a time, Olivia had to leave if she was going to catch her flight back to Boston. As she reluctantly turned toward the door, a photo in the corner caught her eye. It sat perfectly positioned on the wall so it was illuminated by a polygon of light reflecting off the blade of a wood saw.

A coldness came over Olivia.

It was a photo of Campollini and another man standing next to a horse. The photo was a hundred years old, but there was no mistaking the other man. He was the same man who had been in her hotel room last night.

"Who is that with your father?" She could barely speak.

"That's Oskar Volshenkov," Bea said. "He painted horses for Papa for many years. My father said Oskar was the best. He could bring a horse alive, as if he were breathing the spirits of real animals into them."

"What happened to him?"

"I don't know. One day he just disappeared and

no one ever saw him again."

#

Olivia sat at the airport gate reviewing her planner. In the three months she had worked for Catherine, they had visited nearly forty carousels and museums and met with hundreds of people, many of whom Olivia considered friends.

A lump formed in her throat.

What if Oskar Volshenkov was right?

Olivia dialed the International Carousel Museum in Hood River, Oregon. It seemed to take forever for someone to answer.

"Is Fiona Jansen there?" she asked. Fiona had been the first person she and Catherine had visited.

"I'm sorry, Fiona's not here. Perhaps I can help you?"

"No, I'll call back tomorrow."

The voice on the other end hesitated.

Olivia got a hollow feeling.

"Fiona won't be in tomorrow either. She's on long-term medical leave."

Olivia hung up quickly and clutched the phone to her breast.

She set to calling everyone she and Catherine had visited in that first month. After five calls she stopped, unable to continue. Paul Penner, a jovial man who operated the Carousel at Lagoon, Utah had passed away from a rare blood disease two months ago. Larry Pendergrass, a restoration specialist at Running Horse Studios had succumbed to an aggressive form of leukemia five weeks ago. Gary Jones, Sandra Boterelli, Yuko Yoshikawa...all either dead or currently suffering from a rare terminal disease.

Olivia stared out at the tarmac, the slate tablet sky, and the coming darkness. She pulled her coat closer around her shoulders, but couldn't ward off a shiver.

She remembered the first time she had met Catherine in person. Unable to find a sitter, she had brought Lizzy along to the cafe. Catherine had been friendly, polite, but obviously disappointed when Olivia had turned her down. Catherine had tried a hard sell, but Olivia had held firm. With a chill, she remembered Catherine looking at her daughter. "What a lovely child," Catherine had said. "They're so alive at this age." Then she had reached out and touched Lizzy on the head.

Three weeks later Lizzy was diagnosed with Bourbaki's Syndrome and Olivia phoned Catherine to see if her offer was still good.

Olivia jumped when they announced boarding for her flight. From her coat pocket, she fetched the strip of paper that Oskar Volshenkov had dropped on her hotel room floor. Her hand shook so much she could barely see the number.

She had a few minutes before the plane door would close.

#

Olivia had intended to meet Oskar Volshenkov in public, but he had refused. "What I say is for you only."

She slipped her hand stunner from her purse into her coat pocket and stepped out into the drizzle. Her breath circled her like a wraith before fleeing into the night. Across the street, a neon sign flickered in the window of a shuttered liquor shop. The number on the abandoned building in front of her matched the one Volshenkov had given her.

Olivia's heart raced.

During their brief conversation, she had called him by name, and he had not denied it. Whatever Oskar Volshenkov was, he had the answers she needed.

The plywood over the front door had been pried back far enough for her to slip through. The inside of the building was as cold and still as a meat locker. The room reeked of sour urine and rotting meat.

Volshenkov stood in a doorway, his features flat in the darkness. The ember of a cigarette glowed as he pulled on it, faintly lighting his face. He dropped the stub to the floor and ground it out. "Now you understand."

Olivia fought the urge to flee. "No, I don't understand." Her voice quivered. "You're telling me Catherine Pestille is one of the horsemen of the apocalypse, and that we're on the edge of Armageddon?"

"The world has been close to Armageddon for a long time. People like me stop it from coming."

"What do you mean people like you?"

"That is not the right question, Olivia Deshay."

"What are you?"

His lighter flared as he lit another cigarette.

"What does she want?"

Volshenkov said nothing.

"Her horse?"

"I knew you were a smart woman. Without it, she is weak."

"Weak? She's killing people."

"Yes, killing people. But upon her horse, she will kill nations."

"So you're saying her horse is a carousel horse?"

Volshenkov's grin made the hairs on Olivia's arms stand up. "A hundred years ago, I was brought a horse. A pale horse with eyes green like the color of a corpse. It smelled of death, and where it walked, the grass shriveled and died. Any who stood in its presence were cursed to rot."

Olivia's eyes were drawn to Volshenkov's hands.

"Yes, I have been stained by it." Volshenkov exhaled a cloud of cigarette smoke. "That horse cannot be killed, because it does not live. So I trapped it in a prison of wood."

"One of Campollini's horses."

"Yes," he said, his voice sounding pleased.

"Why should I believe this?"

The vein in Volshenkov's right temple pulsed slowly. "Believe or not, but we want the same thing."

"How do we stop her?"

"Stop helping her."

"I can't do that. My daughter—"

"She is one casualty in a greater war."

Olivia's face flushed with anger. "She's my daughter!"

Volshenkov bared his teeth. "If she finds her horse, you will beg her to kill you and your daughter and let Hell take your souls. There is nothing you can do for your daughter."

The words hit like a hammer. "You don't know that."

"She is not of this world. She cannot die. All you can do is stop helping her."

"If Catherine is so close, why don't you move the horse somewhere else?"

Volshenkov's lip twitched.

"You don't know where it is either."

"No. Through the years, the animal has been lost. I was not concerned until recently, when she figured out it was imprisoned in a carousel horse."

Olivia removed Campollini's notebook. "Show me which one."

Volshenkov turned the book gently in his leathery hands, dragging his fingertips lightly over the cover. "Campollini was a man of great skill," he said. "I preserved the spirits of many powerful beasts in his creations." He opened the book and slowly paged through it. About a third of the way through, he stopped. "This one," he said, handing it back to Olivia.

"If I find it, can you move it so she will never get it?"

Volshenkov crushed his cigarette on the floor. "Find me the horse, Olivia Deshay, and I will do what I can."

#

Dr. Sanders had sounded surprised when Olivia asked to meet at the coffee shop. She arrived early and claimed a table near the back.

At the appointed time, he slid into the seat next to hers. "What can I do for you, Ms. Deshay?"

Olivia gripped her latte to stop her hands from shaking. "That map of yours, could you show it to me again?"

Dr. Sanders arched an eyebrow.

"I'm curious."

His eyes bore into her.

Olivia sighed and averted her eyes. "I find what you do interesting," she said. "Since my daughter has gotten sick, I have taken an interest in rare diseases. I guess it makes it easier knowing that there are others out there going through the same thing. That sounds lousy, doesn't it?"

"Yes, but it also sounds normal. If I show you the maps, will you tell me about your daughter?"

He opened his laptop and placed it on the table. While the machine booted, he asked about Lizzy. At first, Olivia's answers were brief, but gradually they grew longer. She found that she wanted to tell someone what a wonderful little girl Lizzy was. It was more than that, she realized. She needed to remember her daughter again as the funny, beautiful, energetic kid that she had been and would be again.

When his computer finished booting, Dr. Sanders showed her his research maps. "This is a classic epidemiological investigation—like John Snow's study that linked cholera to a Soho water pump handle in 1854, but with updated technology."

He displayed the distribution of cases of an endocrine disorder called Hashimoto's Syndrome on his map. "We know relatively little about Hashimoto's, but—" he manipulated his database and zoomed in on a cluster of ochre dots in the middle of West Virginia "—the incident rate in this area was three thousand times the national average. I've been able to show a strong correlation between Hashimoto's and a proximity to Clear Creek—a misnomer, I assure you. The CDC has now focused its efforts on the creek to determine if there is a causal relationship."

"Doesn't this show cause?" she asked.

"No. Correlation does not imply causation." He said the words like a mantra. "None of this proves that one thing is caused by another, but it allows us to focus our investigations and hopefully learn something new."

He reset the map view to the entire continental U.S.

"What's this," she asked, pointing to a dense cluster of multi-colored dots in South Dakota?

Dr. Sanders' brow pinched together. "That one's a mystery. Small town, but a lot of cases of rare disorders. Oddly, just looking at a single disease, there's nothing unusual, but it seems to be a node for rare disease in general."

"Where is that?"

"Madison, South Dakota," he said. "Just north of Sioux Falls."

Olivia knew the town. She had been there once before, to visit a 1900 steam powered Herschell-Spillman carousel.

"I'm still trying to figure that one out," said Dr. Sanders, rubbing his chin.

Olivia barely heard him. Her eyes narrowed on the cluster on the computer screen. "Got you," she whispered to herself.

#

Olivia squinted through the icy rain pelting the windshield of the rental car. Although it was morning, the thick clouds left the flat South Dakota landscape in gloom. She watched Volshenkov out of the corner of her eye. He stared without blinking at the glistening road sliding under the car.

The carousel was housed at Prairie Village, a restored historic farming town just north of Madison. A gate blocked access to the parking lot, so Olivia turned down the next cross street and pulled onto the shoulder.

"We have to walk from here." She wished she had brought an umbrella.

Volshenkov stepped out into the rain and leapt over a split-rail fence. He strode with purpose toward the admissions gate.

Olivia snapped up her jacket collar, but the slushy rain bit into her cheeks and nose.

Volshenkov kicked in the metal grill blocking the entrance. "Which way?"

Olivia shivered as much from the rain as from Volshenkov's voice.

The locked entrance to the carousel's roundhouse presented little problem for Volshenkov.

Even in the grey light bleeding through the skylight, the carousel was magical. An early model, it had two rows of what Olivia considered early-style Herschell-Spillman horses. Solid and square-bodied the animals lacked many of the realistic details she had come to expect from Campollini, but their simplicity suggested power. While this carousel predated Campollini's arrival at the company, few carousels these days had their original animals.

Volshenkov mounted the platform and began to circle between the horses.

Olivia walked around the perimeter. She ran her hand along cool polished wooden flanks. Her parents had taken her to the carousel on the Santa Cruz Boardwalk when she was four. The experience had been magical in a way only a child could appreciate, but it had stayed with her all her life.

Volshenkov stepped in front of her, making her jump. "It's not here," he said gruffly. "Are you sure this is the place?"

"Most carousels have reserve horses in storage. There's a museum around—"

Volshenkov leapt off the platform and hurried into the gloom.

Olivia followed him to a locked door on the other side of the roundhouse.

Volshenkov grabbed a nearby fire extinguisher from its cradle. "Step back," he said, and without waiting, he shattered the glass with the extinguisher's base.

The small museum had a few exhibit panels describing the history of the carousel and its restoration. Volshenkov examined the reserve horse on display. He shook his head.

Behind the gift shop counter, a door led to a back corridor and several small rooms. In one of the storerooms, a half dozen or more wooden horses mounted on stands were covered with white sheets. They began to pull the sheets aside.

"No," Volshenkov said curtly, with each animal revealed.

Olivia stopped at the final horse, tucked along the back wall. Its sheet was grey with dust.

She licked suddenly dry lips. This is hopeless, she thought. How could she have been wrong? She staggered back as her chest tightened and ached. She started to cough.

Volshenkov yanked the sheet aside. The buckskin-colored horse seemed to glow faintly in the darkness. Its lips were pulled back to reveal yellowed teeth. Its eyes sparkled with a sickly gleam.

A sudden pain knifed through Olivia's temples. She doubled over, gripping her head in her hands.

Drops of blood splattered onto the ground. Olivia wiped her nose. Blood smeared the back of her hand.

Volshenkov pushed her out of the room with enough force that she fell to the floor. "It is not safe for you to be close to it. Its cage has deteriorated."

The pain eased, but her head still throbbed. Blood spots speckled her blouse.

"You are done here. Go to your daughter."

Olivia staggered back into the carousel room. Her head ached and the room teetered beneath her feet. She stopped at the carousel and lay down between the horses. She focused on the two animals above her. Their lines were simple, the painting and trappings bold with detail. As she admired their beauty, she forgot about her pain. She forgot about the future and what it probably held for her. These animals truly were magical.

Olivia froze when she heard someone enter the roundhouse through the exterior door. Police? The museum might have had a silent alarm. She peered between the horse legs at a shadow that circled the carousel and stopped in front of the shattered museum door.

Olivia's breath caught.

Catherine's erect posture and slender physique were unmistakable. The glass pebbles ground under Catherine's designer shoes as she turned toward Olivia. "Did you think I wouldn't be watching your every move?" Catherine's smile slit the gloom open like a flaying knife. "I knew you could do it, Olivia. I always had faith in you. You just needed to be convinced."

"You put my daughter through hell."

"Go home, Olivia. Be with your precious

daughter." Catherine disappeared into the museum.

Olivia's pulse raced. Using the horses for support, she started toward the exit. She had done her part to help Volshenkov. Now she needed to go to her daughter.

As she thought of Lizzy, she stopped.

If Catherine freed her horse, she would bring an Armageddon of festering sores and rotting bodies. All Lizzy's suffering would be meaningless. Olivia could not allow that.

With trembling hands, Olivia turned and gripped the mounting poles. She pulled herself toward the museum door and slipped inside. From her coat pocket, she removed the stunner.

A loud crash from the back hallway startled her. Olivia peered around the door jamb.

Volshenkov had Catherine wrapped in his arms. She struggled to free herself, but Volshenkov gritted his teeth and held her. Catherine's eyes grew wide as Volshenkov shifted his weight and spun her into the wall. The plaster cracked as Catherine bounced off it and back toward Volshenkov. He stopped her with a blow to the base of her neck and she stumbled away clutching her throat. Grimacing, Volshenkov closed on her, his fists raised.

Catherine struck quickly. Her jab rattled Volshenkov's jaw and he retreated. She followed, delivering another blow to the side of his head. He dropped to his knees, blood oozing from a cut above his left eye.

Catherine straightened her tailored jacket with a sharp tug along the bottom edge. She grabbed Volshenkov by his shirt. His nose split as she struck him in the face with her fist. She hit him again and blood splattered in an arc across the wall. Volshenkov tumbled to the floor and lay groaning as blood pooled around his cheek.

Olivia looked down at the stunner in her hand. It sparked feebly.

Catherine turned her attention to a sheeted object on the floor. She peeled back the edge of the cloth. "At last," she cooed. Her hand trembled as she caressed the neck of the carousel horse. "Let's get you free of this so we can finish our work."

The wood began to smolder. The paint and varnish bubbled. The horse's front legs twitched.

Olivia's mouth went dry.

Volshenkov tried to rise, but slumped back to the floor.

Catherine pulled on the bridle and the horse's head lifted. "Come now; you can do it." The horse's eyes flared greenish.

Olivia's vision blurred as pain sliced through her head. She let out a startled scream.

Catherine looked up from the horse, but then returned her attention to what she was doing as if Olivia did not exist.

Olivia knew she could not defeat Catherine. Despair squeezed her chest as she thought of Lizzy. Her daughter would die one day, probably soon, but Olivia wanted every day she could get with her. Every day Lizzy lived, meant hope that she would live another. If Catherine succeeded, Lizzy would not get that. Lizzy deserved a chance to live a long time.

Gritting her teeth, Olivia charged down the corridor swinging the stunner.

Catherine slapped the weapon aside, and it flew from Olivia's hand. With a wave of her arm, she swept Olivia aside.

Olivia tumbled awkwardly on her right shoulder. Her arm went numb. The skin along her hand and neck where Catherine had touched her erupted with pustules. They burned like the jagged edge of a white hot knife scraping along her nerves. Waves of nausea rolled over her.

"Like war and famine and death itself, Olivia, I cannot be stopped by mortal men. You can only delay the inevitable for so long."

A dark shadow passed over Catherine's face and her eyes widened as they rose from Olivia's prone form.

Volshenkov put his entire weight behind his blow. His fist connected with Catherine's temple and her head snapped around so violently, Olivia thought Catherine's neck would break. Volshenkov knelt on Catherine's chest and cocked his fist back, ready to strike another blow.

"Get out of here," he said. "Go!"

Olivia crawled toward the door, leaving a trail of blood on the tile. Behind her, she heard the pounding of Volshenkov's fist.

Once in the museum she pulled herself to her feet using the counter. The pain in her head began to ebb, and with it the floor steadied. Feeling returned as pins and needles in her right elbow.

Outside the roundhouse, sirens and flashing blue lights approached down the main highway. Gritting her teeth, Olivia ran for the rental car. She pulled herself over the split rail fence, falling into the grass on the other side. Two police cars stopped at the gated parking lot as she fumbled to get the keys into the ignition. Olivia prayed they wouldn't hear her start the engine.

After fifteen minutes of watching the review mirror, Olivia was convinced they weren't following her. She pulled off the road and allowed herself to shake.

#

The pustules on Olivia's neck and hands had disappeared, but they had left her skin raw. Her blouse was bloodied. As she looked at herself in the mirror of the airport restroom, she was thankful her coat had covered her sufficiently to get through the security checkpoint.

The cold water felt good on her face.

She looked up when she smelled death in the room. She sighed heavily, too tired to do anything more.

"It's done," Volshenkov said. "I have moved the horse. It is safe for now."

"And Catherine?"

Volshenkov shook his head slowly. "She cannot be killed. You and your daughter should disappear."

"There's no place to go."

"The world has many places."

"Her only hope is in Boston." To Olivia's surprise, her voice did not crack.

Volshenkov's expression did not change.

Again she wondered what sort of creature he was and what she, a mortal human, meant to him and his kind. She suspected she meant nothing.

"Do not give up hope, Olivia."

Olivia propped herself up on the counter with elbow-locked arms. It took a great effort to even hold her head up anymore. With her future so uncertain, hope was a fragile thing.

She looked at the water going down the drain in the sink. When she looked up again, Volshenkov was gone.

#

"Mommy?" Lizzy looked up from the floor where she lay watching cartoons.

Olivia scooped her daughter into her arms and buried her face in Lizzy's hair. "I love you," she whispered over and over into Lizzy's ear.

"Why are you crying, Mommy?"

"I'm happy to see you; that's all."

Olivia's mother frowned at her from the sofa. Olivia had told her mother nothing about South Dakota, except that she was going and that she wasn't sure when she would be back. Her mother opened her mouth to ask a question that Olivia was sure she didn't want to answer.

"What's that?" Olivia asked, pointing to an envelope sitting on the coffee table.

Olivia's mother looked from the envelope to Olivia. After a moment she said, "I found it slipped under the door this morning."

The envelope had no stamp and nothing written on it but Olivia's name in jagged print. Inside was a faded Polaroid with a sticky note stuck atop it that read: "For Elizabeth's health. Benton, TX."

Olivia peeled off the note. The picture was of a carousel horse, frozen in mid-stride, its head tossed toward the sky, its mane flaring behind it, its silver wings spread. The rich details of the muscles identified it as a Campollini, and the sparkle in its eyes suggested something more magical than just wood lived within.

Unable to help herself, Olivia started to cry. It felt like her world had opened again. "Mommy's found your magic flying horse."

Story Notes
The Last Horse

All of my stories are special to me, but this one more so because it was inspired by my daughter. When she was three, we took a trip to visit family in the western part of New York state. While there, we visited the Herschell Carousel Factory Museum in Tonawanda, New York. In addition to fascinating exhibits on the carving of carousel horses, the museum had two historic carousels that my daughter rode over and over, grinning the whole time. She was smitten by them, and for the rest of the trip, we visited carousel after carousel—a half-dozen of them at least—across multiple states. I still have fond memories of picking out our horses together, climbing into the saddles, and going round and round to the calliope music.

I was so impressed by the beauty of these machines, I decided to write a fantasy story about carousels and magic. The craftsmanship that went into each horse inspired the idea that the only thing stopping them from galloping off the platform was that they lacked an actual spirit within them to bring them alive. The final piece of the story came together when I saw a Gideon's bible in our hotel room.

Upon returning home, I wrote the first draft, a sprawling 15,000-word manuscript that had way too much detail about carousels. A lot of cutting and focusing got me to the final story. I hope "The Last Horse" has allowed you to appreciate at these historic pieces of Americana in a different light.

Clownspace

First published in *10Flash Quarterly*, January 2012

RENE DE HUYGENS HAS ALWAYS appreciated a clowning challenge, but this time Peejay's efforts to increase gate sales have gone too far.

"It can't be done." Paolo's face is painted into a frown beneath a frizzy shock of purple hair.

Like Rene, Paolo is a clown. So are Johan and Mitchy and Angus and Beerface Betty, to name only six.

Forty-two clowns in all; one car much too small.

At least that's Paolo's assessment as he stares through the slit in the curtain at the garishly-painted, vintage VW beetle parked in the circus ring. "One hundred and seven cubic feet," he says, citing the volume of the car.

Rene knows the number like his own name.

"Three cubic feet per clown," Paolo continues. "That's what? Thirty-five clowns?"

"Thirty five and two-thirds," says Beerface. She's good with numbers, which has always impressed Rene.

Paolo throws up his hands.

Rene pinches the bridge of his nose. He thinks he has a sinus infection because when he blows his nose—his real nose, not the cherry red, prosthetic hippo penis currently stuck to his face—brown snot comes out. It should be clear, he thinks. Brown snot and a lot of pressure, like someone screwing down an invisible vice on his face.

"We canna do it," says Putty. His face paint says "happy clown," but in reality he's chronically depressed.

Peejay, the owner of P.J.'s Bigtop Circus and Extravaganza, announced this latest brain-fart publicity stunt last night on local cable access channel 995 without consulting Rene. When Rene told him it was physically impossible to put forty-two clowns in a VW, Peejay simply said, "Make it happen … or all you clowns can hit the road."

In addition to his sinuses, Rene's stomach is digesting itself. He's a clown, not a magician.

Paolo continues to rant. "Forty-two clowns. Since when is forty-two the answer to anything?"

"We need a tardis," says Bogie.

The clowns go quiet.

"You know, a tardis," repeats Bogie as if that's enough explanation. "It's dimensionally transcendental." He sighs. "It accesses alternate dimensions in Hilbert space—"

Beerface slaps him on the back of the head, opening a flood of clown jeers and guffaws.

Rene shakes his head and regrets the motion. His eyes rattle in their sockets. He wants a drink, or better yet a button of mescaline. He'd like to forget today, not to mention yesterday.

"Shit, he's calling us out," says Paolo, his voice up an octave.

"If we all exhale, we can get an extra one and a third in," says Beerface. "That's still only thirty-seven."

"—we need a tardis car—"

"—it canna be done—"

"What are you going to do about this?" Paolo shakes Rene by the shoulders.

Rene's brain bounces off the inside of his skull.

As the longest tenured clown, Rene is their *de facto* king. He used to take pride in that, at least until the limitations of three-dimensional space took an elephantine dump on his life.

He's tired of this reality and wishes he could go to another one where he isn't a clown but a cake decorator instead. Everybody loves a cake. But things like that don't happen.

And the show must go on.

"What the hell." Rene pushes past Paolo and tumbles out through the curtain into the spotlight.

The crowd roars like the gears of a mechanical T. rex.

Rene rolls to his feet, and with exaggerated motions, waves for the other clowns to follow. Then he gallops toward the car—no easy feat in shoes eight sizes too long and with spring loaded heels that are handy during the clown act's big finale. He circles the car, more to see if the other clowns are coming than for any other reason.

Paolo's white pancake face can't help but frown at him through the slit in the curtain.

Rene opens the car door. It's pitch black inside like the mouth of a hagfish. Maybe it's a tunnel to a new reality, Rene hopes. He frowns, knowing it's only a hundred-and-seven cubic feet of rigid space, too small for forty-two clowns no matter how they are packed.

He tries to be optimistic: maybe he will be crushed to death trying to do the impossible.

The curtain parts, and Beerface tumbles out into the spotlight followed by Ike and Frizzy Fred.

Rene tingles with adrenaline at the sight of cavorting clowns pouring into the ring. He dives into the car. The inside has been gutted—no seats, door or ceiling panels, no dashboard. He squirms to the front and lays panting in the darkness.

The crowd roars as Beerface tumbles in after him. She scrambles up next to Rene and presses against him until his back is against the bonnet lid. Her blue hair reeks of mothballs.

Frizzy Fred is next, but he moves to the rear of the beetle. Bogie and Angus follow. The crowd roars louder, but as more clowns squeeze into the car, Rene hears only frantic clown-chatter as they piece themselves together like a topographic puzzle.

Rene's head pounds. The air grows hot and smells like armpit. Someone farted, probably Mitchy—he's always doing stuff like that.

Beerface groans, and Rene gently squeezes her shoulder.

So much pressure pushing against him from everywhere.

Rene can't see anything anymore. The car must be nearly full with still seven or eight clowns outside. Someone whimpers in the darkness. Sweat stings Rene's eyes. Stink plugs his nostrils like fetid wads of cotton.

"Get your ass in there!" Paolo's voice cuts through the metal shell that squeezes Rene tighter and tighter, like an asylum straightjacket.

Rene grimaces. Something's got to give. He can't keep going on like this. Something's … got … to … give.

"More clowns," Rene yells.

The darkness tears; the pressure releases like air

from a man crushed beneath a falling piano.

Rene laughs in delight as forty-two clowns tumble into Hilbert space.

STORY NOTES
CLOWNSPACE

"Clownspace" is one of my *out there* stories. Interestingly, its inspiration is considerably more down-to-earth than the story itself. "Clownspace" grew out of my writing group, Hopefull Monsters. One of my critique comments on the story submitted by one of my fellow Monsters was that I thought the principal characters were cliché—a bunch of scientists discussing a variety of possible scientific theories for how a device worked. I saw no reason the characters needed to be scientists, so I threw out a crazy idea: what if they were all clowns—not in the figurative sense (scientist are already a bunch of clowns, ka-boom), but *literally* clowns.

The idea of writing a speculative fiction story with clowns as the main characters stewed for about a month, and then "Clownspace" was born, in all its fun, chaotic glory. I wrote this one in a single sitting and after some minor editing, it was complete.

Sinking Holes

First published in *Perihelion*, April 2015

THE WAIL OF THE BACK PRESSURE buzzer cut the thick air, pulling Truman's attention from the mud bubbling from the borehole at his feet.

"Shut it down!"

Veya threw her hands into her hair and searched frantically across the drilling rig's control board for the cutoff.

A column of mud geysered out of the borehole into the air. Truman twisted away, but the explosive force knocked him into the knee-deep mud pit and scattered the metal pipe casings across the ground.

"Run, run!" Truman yelled. He knew the bit and cable were next up the hole.

Veya stared at him, her eyes big. Then her shock broke like a pane of glass, and she bounded off through the bog's sickly grass and twisted shrubs.

Truman curled into a fetal position at the edge of the mud pit, protecting his head as black, sulfurous mud rained down. A two meter section of metal pipe, part of the casing, whoomped from the hole. It splashed into the nearby pond and sank beneath the oily surface.

A final burp of gas splashed the remaining mud from the borehole, and the blowout was over.

Truman pressed the cutoff switch—a big red button in the middle of the rig's control console. The rotary coughed and shut down.

"Too old for this shit," he mumbled, wiping the mud from around his eyes with leathery fingers. In his career, he had seen a lot of men killed in accidents just like this. How could Veya have not seen the cutoff switch? Big red button. Right in front of her damn fool face. She might be some sort of a genius, but she wasn't a roughneck.

"I—"

Truman held up his right hand while he pinched the bridge of his nose with his left. It wasn't her fault, he told himself. He should have insisted on another roughneck, but with the world ending, there weren't enough hands to do everything that needed doing.

"The cutoff," he said, pausing to draw a breath. The adrenaline bleeding from his system left him winded. The air reeked of sulfur and methane. "That big red button."

"I know," Veya said. "I panicked."

His anger now diffused, Truman could look at her. When he did, her eyes went elsewhere—the ground, the equally muddy sky. He didn't know how old she was. Maybe thirty? Everyone said she was whip smart, a doctor of genetics or something. Likely she was, but book smart didn't keep a drilling rig running or roughnecks alive.

"We hit a methane pocket. A small one," Truman said. "Lucky it didn't catch fire."

Veya's lips pressed into a line. Mud dripped from her chin as she surveyed the drill site.

Expelled mud ran down into the bog's black water. Silvery threads of reaping fluid that had been mixed in with the drilling mud squirmed across the oily surface, coalescing into longer chains. Several silver strands as long as Truman's arm now wriggled like severed lizard tails.

"We have to collect it; it's all we've got," Veya said.

Truman grabbed her arm to stop her from wading into the murk. "I wouldn't," he said.

On the opposite bank, fibrous disks the size of dinner plates pressed up together to form a carpet over everything. From the edge of each disk, stubby tentacles probed the air like leeches looking for something to bleed. Truman had been warned to avoid the tentacles because they contained a toxin that could drop a man in minutes. In the month since the creep had first appeared at dozens of locations on every continent, it had spread quickly to cover much of the Earth. Nothing had slowed its march.

Veya's shoes squelched as she stepped back from the pond's edge. She warily eyed the creep, as if sizing up her chances and concluding the risk wasn't worth it.

Truman pulled a hose out of the mud pit and laid the end of it at Veya's feet. He returned a second later with a section of casing and pushed the hose through it. "Start the pump."

Veya grinned. The hose circulated the drilling mud from the mud pit down into the borehole to facilitate drilling. Truman had the suction end, and he used the casing to push the hose out into the bog near the silvery threads.

Veya started the pump.

Long threads slurped into the hose, and seconds later, broken pieces sloshed into the mud pit where they began to coalesce again into long silvery threads. Truman swept the hose around collecting the rest of the reaping fluid.

"That looks like most of it," he said. "Looks like

we're still in business."

#

It was nearly dark by the time Truman had finished repairing the rig and re-stacking the casing sections. The bog should have been buzzing with mosquitoes, but the dusk was quiet. The whole world had grown quiet, Truman thought, eaten or smothered or whatever the hell the creep did to what it overgrew.

As night settled in under the cloud pack, the creep-covered land luminesced a sickly green. Truman spun a slow circle finding the creep glow everywhere except for a narrow spot to the east.

Veya worked by lantern light in their makeshift lab processing the salvaged reaping fluid. Her research group had developed the silvery liquid to collect genetic material from aquifers to test for microbial contamination. Not exactly *her* research group, Truman corrected himself, because that's what Veya always did. She was a postdoc, but Truman didn't understand the distinction.

What Truman did understand was the two of them were in this bog looking for genes from microbes that could survive without air or light. Even if they outlasted the creep, they had no idea what would be left, so the genes of creatures that could survive in extreme places—like deep in the sulfur-rich, waterlogged soil of the bog—would be the key to their survival. Or so the smart ones said, and who was Truman to argue.

Veya looked up from pipetting liquid into a line of small snap-top tubes. A strand of thick black hair dropped across her face. She tucked it behind her ear with an irritated thrust of her hand.

"I'm sorry I froze," she said. "You could have been killed."

"True enough." Drilling was dangerous work. More men died drilling wells than fighting fires or chasing criminals. Under that kind of stress, Truman knew anyone could freeze. Three years ago, his best friend froze when a natural gas well kicked. Three good men, including his friend, died in the blast. Today they'd been lucky; the gas pocket had been small and the kick hadn't seriously damaged the rig. More importantly, no one had been hurt.

Veya's brow crinkled, as if she had expected Truman to say something different. "I shouldn't be out here."

"No, you should be out here," Truman said. Another roughneck likely could have prevented today's accident, but there were only six experienced drillers, and each had been sent to a different location with a portable rig, reaping fluid, and someone like Veya. "I know how to drill. You know how to do what you do." He nodded at her array of vials. "Both of us need to be here." He turned away and headed for his tent.

"Truman."

He paused.

"Thank you."

"Don't stay up late." Truman didn't look back, but felt her smile, warm on his back.

Mud flaked off Truman's shirt as he pulled it over his head. He lay atop his bag unable to sleep. After a while he gave up and slipped out into the night. Veya was still working in the lab, so he went the other way, until the glow of the creep swallowed the lantern light.

Less than a week ago he and his drilling team had been above the Arctic Circle sinking exploratory wells for ICE Petroleum. With limited radio contact they had heard nothing about the creep until a long-range military helicopter found them and flew them south. He first saw the creep at the edge of the ice pack, stretching as far as he could see across the tundra.

"That's the creep, sir," the airman said in reply to his question. "That's the end of the world."

They flew Truman and his crew to a military base north of Weetonka, where he learned the creep had already overgrown most of the world's major cities, not to mention the majority of the world's arable land, crippling food production and whatever social order there had been.

"What about Boston?" Truman asked the admiral in charge.

"Gone."

"Anyone survive?"

"Unknown," the admiral said stiffly, but the pitying look in her eyes betrayed her true thoughts.

Truman's daughter lived in Boston, but he hadn't seen her since his wife had died three years ago. He and Sandra weren't on talking terms—she was still angry at him for being in Venezuela when her mother's cancer had finally killed her. Rightly so, Truman figured, but he'd always thought there'd be time to fix things with his daughter.

The dead grass rustled behind him.

He wiped his cheeks; he didn't want to talk to Veya right now, but ...

He turned and looked into the end of a pistol.

#

The handcuffs dug into Truman's wrist. Veya sat on the ground next to him, her hands in her lap. A teenage girl pointed a pistol at the two of them while an older man shoveled the remains of a fourth ration into his mouth. His pistol sat in easy reach on the bench top. The ration tin clattered onto the bench with the others, nearly knocking over a rack of open sample vials.

Veya flinched.

"Try the beef, Margie," the man said.

"Maybe later, Dad." The teen had eaten two rations already.

They were both muddy and scrawny, like they'd been living off worms for weeks. Dried grass and clods of dirt littered Margie's tangle of hair; mud caked the man's beard.

"More for later, then." The man picked at his teeth with the wooden sliver from the ration tin. After a moment he pointed the toothpick at Truman and Veya. "Where'd you get all this stuff?" he asked. "You government?"

Truman didn't know how to answer that. The government was gone, even if the military still seemed to exist. The creep had taken D.C. a week before the military chopper had found Truman and his team. "We're not government," Truman said, deciding the man looked like the type who would appreciate that answer.

"What're you doing here, then?"

"We're collecting genetic material," Veya said, surprising Truman. He hadn't expected her to say anything.

The man snorted. "You mean like dee-een-aye?"

"DNA, RNA, yes. Microbial genes from an

anaerobic environment for a genetic catalog."

The man picked up the pistol and carried it easily. Truman could tell he was comfortable holding it, and likely equally comfortable using it. "The world is ending, and you're collecting dee-een-aye?"

"Why?" Margie asked. The teenager's steady hands impressed Truman. Her pistol didn't waver.

Now she's done it, Truman thought. Only people with something to live for collected stuff.

"Why?" the teen asked again. She poked her gun at them to show she expected an answer.

"It's not a secret," Truman said. "We're getting out of here."

Veya's head whipped around, her mouth hanging open.

Truman ignored her. These two would shoot them if he didn't give them a reason not to.

"What do you mean getting out of here?" the man asked.

"Submarines. Big ones. Capable of spending years underwater. They've got three of them at a naval base near Weetonka. We're going to set to sea and wait the creep out in deep water. Once it's got nothing left to eat and dies back, we'll return and start over."

The man's eyes narrowed.

"There's room for you and your daughter." Could he tell Truman was lying? Not about the subs—those were real—but about the room. There wasn't enough room as it was to take everyone already at Weetonka.

"Dad?" The teenager's pistol dipped.

If he hadn't been handcuffed to the tarp pole, Truman might have made a move for the gun. If he had been thirty years younger, he might have tried even with the cuffs, but he had done a lot of stupid stuff when he was younger. Working rigs attracted a certain type of person. He liked to think he was still that man, just thirty-years-of-hard-living slower. But also wiser.

"Why should I believe you?" the man asked.

"What kind of idiots do you think we are?" Veya said. "Would we be sitting here with a couple days of food if someone wasn't coming back for us? And how do you think we got here with twenty-five hundred kilos of gear."

Truman was impressed by the disdainful edge to her voice. Surely that was enough to sell it.

The man looked around the makeshift lab, at the crates and drums of fuel, the propane freezers, the rumbling generator powering scopes and a computer.

"We're expecting a helicopter pick-up day after tomorrow," Truman said, "but if we're not standing out there waving at them, they won't land."

"Dad?" Margie asked in a wisp of a voice. "This is what we've been looking for, ain't it?"

Dirt flaked out of the man's beard as he scratched it, revealing gray hairs. "Yeah," he said, "this is what we're looking for, Margie."

To Truman's ear, the man didn't sound convinced. He sounded like a father trying not to shatter his daughter's hope. Truman knew that tone well.

The man stood over Truman and Veya. "I don't know you from Peter, and I don't trust you neither, but I don't see as we have much choice. I ain't stupid, though. You don't do us no wrong, and I don't shoot you. You right with that?"

"Right as rain," Truman said.

#

Truman slept cuffed to the pole, but the man, Henry Benford, allow Veya to use her tent. Margie slept in Truman's tent.

Before he curled up on the ground near the work bench, Henry said to Truman "I don't want to hurt anyone, but I will if you or your friend try anything."

Truman didn't doubt Henry would shoot him or Veya. Truman's goal was to get through the next thirty-six hours, until the chopper returned. Then he'd figure it out from there.

Henry snored loudly, but sleep wouldn't come for Truman. He remembered when his own daughter had been a teen. She'd been expelled from several schools and did a two week stint in rehab when she was seventeen. Truman's wife had blamed it on his long absences, but it wasn't uncommon for a roughneck during the boom years to spend nine months deployed in remote oil fields. Truman had once spent fifteen months sinking exploratory wells in Cameroon and managed to call home only three times during that span. At the time, it was what he needed to do, but now, thirty years later, he wished he had been there for his daughter, like Henry was for Margie.

#

The next morning, Veya convinced Henry to let them keep working. Surprisingly, it was Margie who convinced her father to uncuff Truman and allow him to operate the rig.

Henry watched from the side while Truman and Veya set to work.

Veya leaned in close, pretending to help Truman prime the mud pump. "What happens when the chopper shows up?" she asked.

"Everything will get sorted out," Truman mumbled back.

"You mean everything gets ugly."

Truman glared at her. "Just do your job," he said, his tone harsher than he meant it to be.

Truman sank the well to bedrock by noon. Throughout the drilling, the silver reaping fluid cycled through the borehole, presumably harvesting genetic material, although the stuff looked no different to Truman when it came out of the borehole than when it went down.

Veya recruited Margie to help her skim the silver threads from the surface of the mud pit and bring them to the lab so she could focus on extracting the DNA and RNA fragments from the fluid and preserve them in small sample vials for later sequencing. Henry had been hesitant at first, but eventually let Margie help.

"The reaping fluid lyses the cells and binds the fragmented genetic material," Veya explained as she continued to work through lunch. Margie hovered at the workbench, her beef stroganoff ration untouched on the countertop. "We have hundreds of primers back in the lab that can amplify, that is make more copies, of targeted DNA strands. Those strands should contain some useful genes that, depending on what we encounter, can be inserted into crop plants to improve their post-creep survival."

"That's cool," said Margie, wide-eyed.

Henry's face betrayed mixed emotions, and Truman knew the man was torn between seeing his daughter's enthusiasm with his fear that she was getting too close to Veya. Henry wanted the best for his daughter, that was apparent, and Truman could respect that, even as it tugged at his own conscience.

"Margie," Henry said softly as if he was unsure of himself. "Quit your yapping and eat. There's work to be done."

In the afternoon, they sank a second well closer to the edge of the pond. Since yesterday, the creep had advanced across the bottom of the pool. The water, once thick with life and mud was now clear to a bottom covered with fleshy disks, the creep having filtered everything from it.

Truman watched it as he worked—it was less aggravating than watching Henry sit guard. In the time it took to drill the second hole, the creep had advanced to two thirds across the bottom of the pond. By morning, it would be crawling up onto the shore. If the chopper didn't come, they'd have to abandon the site tomorrow afternoon.

The thought of running curdled Truman's stomach. He had never run away from a job. His crew had continued to drill during the Nigerian coup. When the militant KLF had started shooting foreign oil workers in Kazakhstan, his team had sunk what would become the most productive well in the Mangistau oil field.

No, Truman didn't like running, which made the times he did even more galling.

#

"Weetonka, Weetonka, can you hear me." Veya released the switch and static crackled through the lab. Disgusted, she lowered the radio's volume and put down the handset. She had been trying since dinner without success.

"Is this right?" Margie asked from the workbench.

Veya had left her to snap the lids onto the sample vials and drop them in the cylinder of liquid nitrogen. Veya came over to inspect the teen's work.

Truman could see Margie's admiration for Veya, and why not? Veya was intelligent and motivated, the very type of role model he would have wanted for his own daughter.

Margie beamed when Veya complimented her excellent work.

Henry sat on the other side of the field lab working a toothpick between his front teeth. His eyes never strayed far from Truman, who did his best to ignore them. Henry's posture made sure the handle of the pistol sticking up from the front of his jeans caught the light.

"There used to be nine of us," Margie said, continuing her story of how she and her father had escaped the creep. "We joined up with them on the road, figuring it was safer that way."

"Where are the others?" Veya asked.

Truman flinched. The world was ending; what did Veya think had happened to them? Either the creep got them, or hunger, or someone else.

Margie shrugged, her jaw trembling.

Veya must have realized her error. "I'm sorry," she said.

Margie shrugged her shoulders, trying to put on an air of nonchalance. "It's okay. We ran into some bad people, and lost a few of our group, but most of them just … I don't know … sort of wandered off, you know, lost hope, I guess. Probably just as well because we didn't have much food.

"There was one guy though. Jason. He was so cute. I was real sorry when he left. Maybe we'll see him at

Weetonka?"

Veya lowered her eyes. "Yeah, maybe, but I wouldn't get my hopes up."

Truman sat up straight. He thought Veya was smart enough not to say something stupid, but he was ready to interrupt if needed.

Henry interrupted for him, however. "You sure that chopper's coming?"

"It'll come," Truman said. "Just keep your cool."

Henry's jaw twitched.

"I've got to relieve myself. Would you mind?" Truman raised his cuffed wrist.

Henry eyed him warily. He tossed Truman the key. "Don't anyone do anything stupid."

The glow of the creep gave Truman enough light to see the hummocks of grass and scraggly shrubs. Henry followed, staying back enough so Truman couldn't jump him. Once he was out of sight of the tarped lab, Truman unzipped his fly.

When Truman and Veya had choppered in four days ago, the bog had been at the middle of two advancing patches of creep, like a finger caught in a tightening vise. The two creep fronts had joined to the west, but from the fainter glow to the east, there was still unspoiled land in that direction. For now.

Behind him, Henry's boots squished in the mud.

"That Jason guy. He didn't wander off, did he?"

A rustle of clothing, and Truman imagined Henry shrugging.

"I don't blame you," Truman said. He remembered how hungry the two had been last night. They probably hadn't eaten anything in a couple of days, and more people meant less to go around. "I would have done anything for my daughter, too. I get that." Truman's stomach felt hollow as he said the words. There was a lot more he could have done for his daughter, but hadn't.

"You have a daughter?"

"I don't know." Truman was surprised how little the words cut. He had to still be numb from everything that had happened. When that numbness went away, Truman wondered what would be left. "She lived in Boston."

"I met a family going the other way on the road who'd got out of Boston." The sound of the shrug again, punctuating the implication. "Sounds like everything is shit, and from what we've seen, it is."

"What's your excuse then?" Truman asked. He finished and zipped his fly. "Where you running to?"

Henry said nothing. His sweaty face glistened sickly in the creep-glow.

Margie's laugh carried lightly through the heavy night.

Truman's throat tightened. "That's why there's hope," he said, his voice barely a whisper. He squeezed his eyes shut as the tightness spread into his chest. As long as people had a reason to struggle on, they would. That was why Henry had been on the road, why he had done whatever he had done to Jason, and why he was here now. That was why humanity would find a way to survive.

Henry cleared his throat. "The creep's closing in on this place," he said. "By tomorrow night there ain't gonna be a way out of here."

"I'm not interested in running. The job's not done."

"That chopper's coming?"

Truman found it didn't matter to him if the

chopper came or not. No, that wasn't right. If it had been just him, it wouldn't have mattered, but Veya deserved a chance. So did Margie. Even Henry.

Truman's stomach clenched.

"To be honest, I don't know, but you could get to the coast in three days hard walking from here. I bet you could find a boat."

"But that choppers gonna take us all, right?"

Truman hoped Henry didn't notice his hesitation. "Every last one."

\#

Veya and Margie were huddled together whispering like schoolgirls when Truman returned to the lab. He sat down next to the tarp pole and snapped the cuffs back onto his wrist. He tossed the key to Henry, who threw it back to him.

"You keep it," Henry said. "We got to start trusting each other sometime, or none of us'll make it."

\#

Even free of the cuffs, Truman slept fitfully, haunted by dreams of tomorrow. In them the chopper would land and Truman had to tell Henry he couldn't get on. Sometimes it wasn't Henry when he turned around; it would be Margie or Veya. When he turned to find his daughter standing there, he awoke with a start.

Watery light filtered through the thick cloud pack. His watch told him it was an hour past sunrise. Henry lay slumped over the bench top snoring lightly, otherwise the bog was quiet.

Truman shook the dream from his thoughts. His

joints ached as he stood.

He couldn't have helped Sandra, he told himself, and even if he had been there, he didn't think his daughter would have accepted it. But Sandra had always been a resourceful girl. Maybe she had gotten out of Boston.

Truman cursed under his breath and went down to the rig. That line of thinking wasn't healthy.

Overnight the creep had spread across the bottom of the pool and its leading edge was now an arm's length from coming onto shore. Truman crouched, the steel toes of his boots in the water. He had never been so close to the creep. Gold flecks sparkled in the creature's mottled brown flesh, and the ring of tentacles along the scalloped edges waved in the water hypnotically. Inside an aquarium, it would have been beautiful.

No one seemed to know where it had come from. Outer space maybe—it looked alien enough—but some of the scientist types had suggested it might be a genetic experiment escaped into the environment. Truman never heard what the military folks thought, but then, Truman figured it didn't matter to them— the creep was simply another adversary to overcome, and they seemed confident they would prevail.

He checked the rotary and the drill bit. The oil and the fuel levels in the mud pump were okay. He siphoned more drilling mud from a metal drum into the mud pit.

"What are you doing?" Henry asked, wiping dirt and sleep from his eyes.

"Sinking another well," Truman said.

"But what about—"

"Job's done only when the helicopter gets here,"

Truman said.

"Don't you mean when the subs sail?"

Truman looked up from his final check of the rig. He hadn't been thinking that far out. "Either help me, or get out of the way."

Henry took a step back.

Truman started the pump to circulate the drilling mud, then activated the rotary. The bit ground into the moist soil. The grey drilling mud bubbled out of the deepening borehole, gradually growing darker as the bit hit black dirt. Truman retrieved the first section of casing and prepared to drive it into the hole.

"How can I help?" Henry asked.

#

They had just passed fifteen meters when Veya and Margie arrived.

Truman kept the drill running. "Get the reaping fluid," he said.

Veya scanned the clouds to the east. "They should have been here already."

Truman paused in checking the flow rate of the mud. The chopper wouldn't have left Weetonka until first light. Veya knew they wouldn't be here for several more hours.

"It's possible for you and your Dad to make it to the coast," she said.

Henry's eyes narrowed. "They were supposed to be here?"

Truman glared at Veya. He saw what she was doing. If it backfired, things would get ugly. "They're not late yet," Truman said turning back to the rig, trying to make it seem like everything was fine. He hammered another casing into position. "Veya, we're past fifteen meters. Quit talking and get the fluid."

Veya ignored him. "Margie, you and your dad have to get out of here. Just in case. When the chopper comes, we'll … we'll find you and pick you up."

"But you're not leaving," Margie said. "I want to stay and help."

Truman grabbed Veya by the arm, but she shrugged him off. "Let it be," he said.

"What's going on?" Henry asked. "Why are you trying so hard to get us to leave?"

"She's not," Truman said. His body tingled as adrenaline started to flood his system. "She's just scared."

"There isn't a lot of time left, Margie," Veya said. "You need to go."

"There is no chopper, is there?" Henry said. "No, there must be or you'd be getting out of here, too." Henry's voice trailed off; then his body stiffened. "You're not going to take us."

Truman's hands came up as if ready to deflect a blow.

"Is that true, Veya?" Margie asked.

Veya's jaw hung open. When she blinked, a tear rolled down her cheek. She stammered, but no words came out.

"Is it true?" Margie asked, her voice rising above the whirring of the rig.

Veya buried her face in her hands.

Margie leaped at Veya, her fists in tight balls. Veya turned, and Margie landed on her back. She punched Veya in the ear.

Out of the corner of his eye, Truman saw Henry reaching for his pistol tucked into the back of his jeans.

The pitch of the drilling rotary changed, rising in tone. A wail sliced the air.

"What the—" Henry's eyes grew wide.

Drilling mud bubbled out of the borehole.

Truman knew instantly the odor of methane. "Get down!" He dove at the two women knocking both of them away from the rig as the well kicked and methane exploded out of the hole, launching casings dozens of meters into the air. Sparks from the flying metal ignited the gas. A fireball whooped across the back of Truman's neck.

A pillar of fire crackled into the sky. Flaming chunks of mud splattered to the ground.

Truman pounded out the flames on the cuff of his pants. The heat from the fire blistered his arm nearest it. The mud pit on the other side of them had caught fire. Thick smoke swirled around, stirred by the heat of the flames.

Truman couldn't see. The roar of the fire filled his head. Veya and Margie lay in the mud under him. They weren't moving, but he could tell they were alive.

Truman coughed, barely able to draw a breath. He pulled the collar of his muddy shirt over his mouth and nose, and the wet fabric cooled the heated air and filtered the smoke.

"Move!" He pushed Veya in the direction he wanted her to go, but she resisted. "I'll get Margie."

The skin on the back of Veya's hand pimpled into blisters as she shielded her face from the growing heat. She crawled away from the fire.

Truman struggled to his feet and grabbed Margie's shirt. At first she didn't move, but he pulled at the fabric, and she started crawling across the ground.

Metal groaned. The rig tower bent as the intense heat softened the metal struts. With his last bit of strength, Truman yanked Margie out of the way and threw up his arms to protect himself from the falling tower. But the tower never hit him as Henry knocked him out of the way.

Henry screamed as the falling rig crushed his legs.

Truman wiped hot ash from his eyes.

Henry lay pinned in the mud, his jeans smoldering and smoking.

Margie struggled to her knees, smoke swirling around her, her shape rippling in the heat waves. She struggled to breathe.

Truman grabbed a section of casing and wedged it under the fallen rig, but the ground was too soft to provide the leverage he needed to lift the tower.

Henry grabbed Truman's ankle. "Save Margie," he said into the roar of the flames. The strands of his beard curled back in the heat.

Truman kicked Henry's hand off his ankle and put his weight onto the length of casing. The casing bent suddenly and Truman fell into the mud next to Henry.

Margie collapsed to the ground, coughing violently. The thick smoke swirled, obscuring her from view. A wave of heat knocked Truman over, singeing his denim shirt.

Another blast like that and they would all be dead.

Henry grabbed Truman's sleeve. Hurt filled his eyes, more than just the pain from his broken body. "Please."

Truman squeezed Henry's shoulder and nodded at him because he didn't know what to say.

He grabbed Margie's arm and wrapped it around his neck. His legs strained as he pulled her to her feet. "Run with me," he said into her ear, and Truman pulled her through the flames without looking back.

\#

Truman didn't know when the fire would go out. That depended on the size of the methane pocket.

Margie wanted to go back for her father, but Truman stopped her.

"No one could survive that," he said, hugging her to him.

She wept into his shoulder, like other loved ones whose husbands and sons and wives had died on a rig.

"He wanted you to live," Truman said. "You owe it to him to do that."

Truman's stomach wrenched. The creep was everywhere, relentless as the tide, and the only thing that would stop it would be its own success.

Veya took Margie from him. She didn't say anything; for that Truman was thankful.

"You did right," he said to Veya. "Now don't let go of her."

Veya held Margie as they sat on the ground next to the cylinders holding the genetic samples.

Quietly he shouldered a backpack and edged away from the crackling flames. On the horizon the chopper was a speck of black against the low hanging gray clouds. He had decided a while ago that once the job was done, he would find a quiet place to sit—just sit—because he was tired and not ready to face a new world alone. His daughter was gone, but it wasn't the creep that had killed her. He had let her die a long time ago.

The backpack hurt his shoulder where the fire had burned him. The back of his hand was raw and painful, but that meant he was still alive. Being alive meant he still cared.

He looked back to where Veya and Margie sat in the scraggly grass, unaware of the approaching chopper. Margie wasn't his daughter; he owed her and her father no allegiance, but she deserved a chance. Truman couldn't control if Margie got onto the sub, but unlike his own daughter, he could be there for her, doing everything possible to make it happen.

The first faint thumps of the chopper blades reached him, and Veya and Margie turned in his direction. He had been wrong about the job being done when the helicopter returned, and he realized he couldn't abandon Veya and Margie. The two women rose and joined him as the helicopter circled them once before settling onto the grass.

"Let's get out of here," Truman said. "We've still got a lot of work to do."

Sometimes I don't know what inspired a particular story—it's like I simply channeled the story out of the void—but usually I can trace the germ of a story to a particular thing, be it something I saw or heard or read. "Sinking Holes" is no exception, except for this story, I can trace it to *two* different things.

"Sinking Holes" traces its origin back to 2013 and a contest run through the Codex writing group called "Setting the Stage." For that writing contest, I was sent a couple of paragraphs describing a setting, and from that, I was to write a story. I received a few paragraphs that included this description:

Silver threads snake through the murky water, some separate, some entangled with each other but still managing some form of movement as a group, and some wound around and through the wilting dull green and pale beige reeds that cluster in forlorn clumps along the mucky bank, chaining the reeds to each other but also to themselves, at once jailer and jailed. There should be clouds of insects buzzing about, but there are not.

There was more, but this is really the part that caught my eye, and with a little modification, it gave me the bog setting for "Sinking Holes."

With the setting in hand, the next piece of inspiration actually came from my day job at the time, which for me is unusual. As part of my job, I had spent some time on Palmyra Atoll, a remote and uninhabited Pacific Island. Part of the reason I was there was to help develop a treatment method for an invasive animal that was overgrowing and killing Palmyra's coral reefs. That animal was something called a corallimorph, which looks like a fleshy donut with a ring of stinging tentacles. This invasive species inspired the mysterious "creep."

Thief of Futures

First published in *Lightspeed Magazine*, September 2011

MR. NAAJY PADWAL, Mumbai business magnate and collector of eclectic futures, slides a rectangle of paper across the counter. He doesn't remove his hand, the back of which is covered with coarse black hairs.

The smell of spiced tea and charcoal smoke hangs heavy in the humid air of Subang Jaya's market.

Not certain anymore why I agreed to meet him, I start to turn from the chai wallah's cart.

Mr. Padwal puts a hand on my arm.

"I'm retired," I say.

"Retirement is a state of mind, not an incurable malady." His accent betrays his Oxford education. When he speaks again, he lowers his voice, even though the portable privacy shield protects our meeting from prying ears and eyes. "I need you to obtain a future for me."

Out of habit I look to see who is watching. Outside the privacy screen, Mr. Padwal's two Sikh guards funnel the crowd away from our chai cart, no small feat in a city of sixteen million.

I settle back against the counter. "Why not Bautista?"

"Interpol has him at a black site somewhere in Africa."

The news surprises me, but it doesn't upset me. The world is a better place without him. "What about that new girl?"

"Jessica Cavendish? She's not what I'm looking for."

"What are you looking for?"

"Someone special. You." He drains his cup of chai in a single swallow. "I know your circumstances, Mr. Kingston. How long can you survive scrubbing walls in a Trenchtown brothel? For a man who has stolen so many futures, you seem to have no future yourself." He lets this painfully accurate assessment seize hold; then he says matter-of-factly, "Is this what you want for your daughter?"

"Leave her out of this."

Mr. Padwal raises his hands in mock surrender. "I am sorry. I did not mean to offend."

He lies. Years in business have made him a man of supreme calculation. Even knowing this, I find it hard to collect my thoughts because I know what he says is true. Kimbelle deserves better.

"With what I'm offering, a man could do anything." Mr. Padwal shifts his weight. Over his left shoulder, the ISF launch facility glistens in the distance along the Puchang ridgeline like the spinal plates of a dragon. An orbital shuttle stands ready to launch that afternoon, taking lucky colonists to an orbiting ship bound for Echelon colony.

He pushes the paper closer to me and withdraws his hand. It's an old-style cashier's cheque with a very big number.

My mouth goes dry. At the height of my career, even a high-end job wouldn't have fetched half the sum Mr. Padwal is offering. For a fee like this, he wants something exceptional. Given his reputation, that means something *really* exceptional.

He grins at me, and my spine tingles. Like any

successful businessman, Mr. Padwal knows he has me where he wants me. He produces a finger cache. "The details," he says, putting the thumbnail-sized data unit on the counter. "Like my offer, that advance is good for twenty-four hours."

He snaps the shield generator closed. The market crashes in on us like the Red Sea. Flanked by his guards, Mr. Padwal vanishes into the flood of flesh and sweat and noise.

I stare at the finger cache, trying to decide if I should walk away, but a tightness in my throat tells me what I already know. I can never walk away, not as long as I am Earthside.

#

Trenchtown sits at the bottom of the Klang Valley in a haze of smoke and dampness thick enough to turn the sunlight the color of cockroach wings. Levees to the south hold back the steadily rising sea but can't stop the water from seeping up through the ground. Even on a good day, the streets are a pig wallow of trash and shit.

Two million people squat in Trenchtown. Like me, they have come to Kuala Lumpur hoping to win a lucky seat on one of the ISF's monthly colony ships. For those without money, the only ticket comes through the indenture-service lottery, but a hundred seats a flight means the odds are long.

I rent two rooms on the ground floor of a decaying two-floor walkup. I step over the sandbags and slip inside. Kimbelle and Shayana, the Tamil girl from upstairs, are in the other room singing a nonsense song in Bahasa, the only language they share.

Where the mildew from the water line hasn't
obscured them, the walls are covered with Kimbelle's
stick figures and smiley face suns. She's a five-year old
master, and her dancing girls, butterflies, and trees
give life to this otherwise dreary box. One day, I hope
she will be an artist, but I'll take anything, as long as
she has a future.

I pull the cashier's cheque from my pocket. Fifty
million rupees are enough to get Kimbelle out of this
place, but the money isn't free, and I'm not sure I can
pay the price. My chest tightens. As a father, I should
be willing to do anything for my daughter, but it's
hard when I've already lost one person I love.

From under the futon, I remove a watertight box.
My hands tremble as I fumble with the lock and clasp.

You would think a future has no value, except to
the person who owns it. All our futures, however, are
intertwined. My future is as much Kimbelle's as it is
mine. Stealing one future has far reaching
repercussions.

The lock clicks open, but I don't lift the lid. I don't
know why I torture myself. I should throw the box
away, but I can't.

Bao thought I worked as an acquisitions manager
for a transnational aerospace firm, acquiring electrical
components for off-world shipment. It was the only
secret I ever kept from her because I'm sure she
would have left me had she ever found out.

I think it would have been better if she had known.

I take a deep breath and open the box.

Inside is a picture of Bao. She sits in the arcade
near the Bethesda fountain in New York's Central
Park. I remember that day like it is today. I had
snapped the picture quickly, catching her glowing face

before she had a chance to mar the perfect moment with a plastic, picture smile. She had just told me she was finally pregnant after years of trying.

Under the crinkled photograph, the pieces of a blown-glass globe are smoky and dark, covered with a dull black film that seems to absorb the light.

They're all I have left of Bao.

#

I snap Mr. Padwal's finger cache into the BIOSlot at the base of my palm. It hums as it draws power from my flowing blood. In my hand appears a holographic dossier of a woman named Sulee Hendricks, a widowed American of Chinese descent, who rents a flat in Subang Jaya, the once affluent suburb of Kuala Lumpur that now sits just above Trenchtown. While she waits for her lucky number to be drawn, she earns enough to survive by chopping cows at an industrial slaughter-factory.

When I come to a series of holographic portraits, I am struck breathless. While Sulee wears her hair pulled back into a tight bun firmly cemented to the back of her head, she shares the same round face and delicate nose as Bao. I spend many minutes staring at the images before a queasiness grips me.

For men like Naajy Padwal, collecting futures is like stealing priceless art to hang for their own edification in an underground gallery. Some collectors believe that possessing a future of great promise will exert a positive force on their own futures, but that reeks too much of Chinese mysticism for me. Others simply admire them for their physical beauty, and I must admit, an exceptional future glowing pink or electric blue in its blown-glass sphere is spellbinding.

But a future is not a painting. A person without a future is nothing more than a body unable to move forward in time. It simply exists in a comatose-like state, as long as food and water are provided. If the future is returned, the body will recover; otherwise, it slowly dies.

It's for this reason I have never worked for a collector. Instead I ransomed stolen futures back to loved ones. A dirty business, true, but my conscience could reconcile it.

I sit quietly on the futon, my mind a jumble. I take several deep breaths and continue to read. It isn't until I get near the end of the dossier that I realize Mr. Padwal doesn't covet Sulee's future, but rather her five-year old son's.

The dossier shakes in my hand, and if it hadn't been a hologram, I would have dropped it. I remove the finger cache and drop it on the table. My pulse races painfully in my neck.

I have never stolen a child's future, not even to ransom. The thought makes my stomach twist into knots. I can't do this.

The singing in the back room stops. The door swings open and Kimbelle and Shayana rush in. They skid to a stop when they see me on the futon.

"Mista?" Shayana says, surprised. It's the only English word I've ever heard her say. She's a good kid, and I know she's safe. For a handful of coins, she watches Kimbelle anytime I need her.

Kimbelle's long black hair hangs in a braid over her right shoulder. Between her delicate eyebrows is a smudged crimson bindi.

She looks so much like Bao it hurts.

"Daddy!" She leaps into my arms, and I hug her

until she struggles to get away. I will do anything to make her safe.

#

I cash Mr. Padwal's advance and set to work. Every night Sulee travels by a circuitous route past curry carts shrouded in films of ghee and grease, and tarp-covered stalls from which women with missing teeth hawk meager piles of rice or fish or bananas. At dawn she stumbles home and is barely able to turn the key in the lock. During the day she stays shuttered inside. I never see the boy. The only evidence he exists is the presence of an old Malay woman who arrives minutes before Sulee leaves and departs soon after she returns.

After a week, I am left wondering if I can even do this job. Stealing a future is not like pinching a purse—not just any rascal with fast feet and a set of *cojones* can do it. Only a handful people have the innate talent, and of these, few have the necessary moral flexibility.

Before I can take a future, I must sufficiently attune myself to my target's spatial-temporal trajectory. This means getting close, literally and figuratively. Only then can I take the threads that are their future life. I need to spend time with the boy—lots of it—and the only way to do that is to get close to Sulee.

I finally get my opportunity when she digs into her bag to pay for a bundle of rambutan and a head scarf drops unnoticed to the ground. I retrieve it and push through the crowd calling to her in Bahasa. She does not hear me over the market din, so I grab her elbow.

She spins and sweeps my legs from under me with

her foot. I land with a crack. The air explodes from my lungs.

"What do you want?" she says in Bahasa. Her foot presses painfully against my windpipe.

I can't say anything, so I wave her scarf in surrender.

The pressure on my neck eases. She takes the scarf. "I'm sorry," she says, kneeling next to me. Up close, she resembles Bao more than I expected. Although Sulee's eyes are a lighter shade of brown, they have that same depth and complexity of color.

I rub my neck. "It fell out of your bag."

Sulee studies the ground. "These are dangerous times. You shouldn't grab people." After a moment of awkward silence, she says, "Can I repay you with a chai?"

#

By the time we wend our way through the market, Sulee is late for work. She offers to buy me a chai anyway.

"Maybe tomorrow?"

She smiles demurely. "Tomorrow then, Mister ..."

"Eshram."

She turns into the crowd and before she is swept away, I pray she will look back. She doesn't, and I feel like I have been robbed.

The chai wallah grins at me and motions hopefully to his pot of steaming tea. I wave him off and head back toward Trenchtown.

I remind myself that she isn't Bao, but that doesn't fill the hole.

I turn onto the road down the hillside. Even at this hour bicycles weave through throngs of sari-clad women armed with bamboo switches to fend off the gangs of sticky-fingered children. The night air is thick, and I labor to force it into my lungs. It is like breathing water.

Near the toe of the hill, I get an odd sensation that I am being watched. In the shadows ahead, a dark silhouette sits on the side of the road. As I approach, it unfolds spindly legs, like those of a spider, and pushes its torso up effortlessly to an incredible height. The man is easily over two meters tall.

Mr. Oduya. It can be no one else.

We have history. He works for Interpol, hunting people like me.

He draws up on my right and matches my pace. His skin is as dark as the night, so his white cotton shirt seems to float in the blackness. For a full minute the Kenyan says nothing to me.

Finally, as we near the archway that marks the edge of Trenchtown, he says, "I hear you've come out of retirement."

"That's none of your business."

"It is if it's true."

"Are you bored with Bautista already?"

Mr. Oduya's grin floats like the Cheshire cat's.

I wonder how long he has been shadowing me in Kuala Lumpur. I would think by now that he would have given up and gone after someone else, like the new girl, Cavendish. I suspect he doesn't know about her yet.

"I like you, Eshram," he says. "You have scruples, unlike the others, which is why I find it odd you'd work for Naajy Padwal." I feel his eyes on me, watching for a reaction that will give something away.

As we reach the archway, Mr. Oduya stops me

with a hand on my elbow. "Padwal is not a man to mess with. If you were to help us …"

I pull my arm away and leave him, riding the flow of people into Trenchtown.

#

I fill Shayana's hand with coins totaling just over a ringgit. She leaves with a wide grin, and I latch the door bar behind her. I check on Kimbelle. Her room is filled with acrid smoke from a smoldering mosquito coil. She sprawls across her bed in a position only a five-year old could find comfortable—arms akimbo and body twisted awkwardly at the waist.

Only after seeing her do I relax.

Other than the bed and a few toys purchased a year ago, the room is empty. With the upfront from Mr. Padwal, we could afford to move to the top of the hill, but we will need every rupee if we're going to buy passage off-world. So the scattering of toddler toys will need to amuse her a little longer.

When I kiss her sweat-damp forehead, her eyes flutter, but never quite open. "Mommy?"

"No," I say gently, unable to say more. I stroke her hair until she fades back into sleep. Reluctantly I close her door behind me.

The apartment is sweltering. Before I lay down, I sponge my face and chest with a damp rag. The water is precious—hand carried in a twenty liter bottle from a public fountain—but the heat is oppressive.

Outside a gunshot cracks the night. I don't even flinch at the sound.

I lay on the futon, crushed by the weight of the darkness. When I close my eyes I see Bao's face, not as it was when she eventually died, but as it was when we shared a future. My chest aches. I don't know who took her future. I paid the ransom, nearly all of the money I had, but all I got back were broken pieces of glass and a shattered future of my own.

It hurts to admit, but that's not what troubles me most. To steal her future, someone had to get close to Bao, and it eats at me to think that someone could get that close without me knowing it. If they could get Bao, they can get Kimbelle. The only way to protect her is to get as far away as possible from people like me.

#

I meet Sulee the next night. Instead of wearing her hair pulled back into a bun, she wears it down, softly framing her brown eyes. I can barely take my eyes off her. Twenty minutes later she rises. Her dress clings to her body. She has barely touched her chai because our conversation seldom broke long enough.

"Can we do this again?" My spirits drop when she frowns. She is going to say no.

"I have a son," she says, haltingly. "If you're not okay with that, I understand."

I pause for a minute, pretending to contemplate her revelation. "That doesn't scare me."

The tension drains from her body. As it does, my spirits rise.

She shoulders her bag. "Tomorrow."

As I watch her leave, I notice Mr. Oduya's head poking above the crowd. He leans against the post of a fruit stall sucking at a mango pit. He nods at me.

I see Sulee regularly after that. We meet almost nightly in the market. At first for only twenty-minutes, but as we increasingly find the time too short, she comes earlier and earlier. Tea becomes dinners of nasi goreng or spiced beef.

I tell her my fabricated history. Like any good lie, I have assembled it from bits of truth, to make it seamless and easy to remember. I find it difficult to lie to her. Gradually she reciprocates with stories about her childhood, her dead husband, and most importantly her son.

Every night after I kiss Kimbelle's forehead, I meticulously transcribe our conversations into a paper notebook. The act of writing reinforces even the smallest details.

Some nights I see Mr. Oduya's head rising above the market crowd. I try to ignore him, but my eyes are drawn to him, and I am afraid Sulee will notice. I don't want uncomfortable questions. Even when I don't see him, I sense him nearby, like an unspoken threat.

Any day now, I fear she will invite me in to meet her son. I become irritable and contemplate ending it. How can I take her child from her? I wonder, but then I look at Kimbelle, thin and fragile, lost in the slums of Trenchtown, and I think, how can I not?

#

The next time I see her, Sulee suggests I come to her apartment the following night. I can barely accept the invitation around the lump in my throat. Before she leaves, she whispers in my ear, "I hope you will stay." She pecks me on the cheek and disappears into the crowd before I can answer.

I wander in a daze to the end of the market and sit on a low, stone wall trying to breathe. Mr. Oduya comes up to me, his hands thrust into his pockets.

"Do you think this is his dance of destruction or reincarnation?" he asks, his gaze over the top of my head.

Behind me is a statue of Shiva, his four arms waving gracefully and his right foot raised in dance.

"Aren't they the same?"

Mr. Oduya shrugs. "I am not Hindu."

In no mood for his games, I walk away, but with his long strides, he catches me easily. "You have gotten close with this Sulee woman, yet you do not take her future. I am confused."

"I'm not going to take her future."

"I've already figured that out. What would Naajy Padwal want with her? She is … unremarkable."

The word stings me. Sulee is no less special than Bao, and someone took her future. "Do you have something to say?"

"If it is not Sulee," he says, as if musing to himself, "then it must be someone close to her." A confused look slides across Mr. Oduya's face. After a second of contemplation, his eyes widen. "The boy?"

My stride breaks. I try to recover quickly, but Mr. Oduya notices.

"You're after the boy. But you don't steal from children, unless you've changed."

My face flushes. I walk on, refusing to look at Mr. Oduya. People change.

He follows a step behind. "Help me catch him," he says.

"Why should I do that?"

"Because it's the right thing to do."

I walk faster, but Mr. Oduya comes up along my side. I refuse to acknowledge his presence.

"Padwal does not have a reputation for collecting

young futures," he says. "They are risky, too much possibility for them to lose their luster."

He falls quiet and waits to see if I will let something slip. I wish he would go to hell.

"Padwal has the reputation for working the long game. He is very patient."

Mr. Oduya's comment causes me to pause. What is this new game he's playing? I learn nothing from the Kenyan's blank expression.

"Piss off." I storm on, tired of being talked at.

Mr. Oduya doesn't follow, but he yells at me as I walk away, "Do what is right, Eshram. Think about your daughter."

I bite back a retort. He plays me again, trying to goad me into saying something stupid.

As I walk down into Trenchtown, I can't shake the surprise on Mr. Oduya's face when he figured out Sulee's son was the target. I had never stopped to question Mr. Padwal's motivation, but Mr. Oduya is right. As a collector's item, a child's future is a boom or bust proposition. Initially it may look special, but any number of things could cause it to lose its luster as it matures. No collector would pay big money for a child's future unless he was certain.

Something isn't right, but I haven't time to sort it out. I know someone who can, but his services aren't cheap. With a curse I turn away from Trenchtown. I have no choice but to visit Hiruku.

#

I pay a hefty fee for a secure connection at a reputable VR conferencing facility in Petaling Jaya, a bustling business district north of Subang Jaya. When I transfer another one million yen to gain access to

Hiruku's location, I try not to do the math in my head. The implications are too painful.

With the attendant's help, I don the VR neural net and lay down in the coffin-like module. She closes the lid and the equipment hums as it powers up. I close my eyes ...

... and open them to birdsong and the clean smell of pine trees. Crouched in the mist ahead is a squat Japanese cottage with a clay-tile roof pulled like taffy into long overhanging eaves.

Inside Hiruku sits cross-legged on a cushion, eyes closed in meditation. He wears a black *haori* and the pleated *hakamas* of a fifteenth century samurai.

Without a word I sit on a cushion opposite him.

Eventually he opens his eyes.

Hiruku is a Yogen-sha, a seer capable of foretelling the quality of a person's future. While he smiles at me from across the table, I don't think he's human. I think he may be an artificial intelligence that examines probabilities to extrapolate a likely future from a person's past actions. However he does it, whatever he is, I've never found him to be wrong.

I hand him the finger cache. "I need to know about the boy."

"A child? Children are difficult and uncertain, usually not worth the fee." Hiruku's lips press into a thin line. After a moment, he exhales loudly and takes the finger cache. "This is not your child," he says. "What is your interest?"

Even if I wanted to tell him, I'm not sure my mouth would form the words. "I paid for no questions asked."

Hiruku sets the finger cache back on the table, and I return it to my pocket. "Are you sure you wouldn't rather have a reading more worthy of your fee? Yours perhaps?"

I don't want to know my future, because the only one I wanted is gone.

"A shame. I see special things."

"I bet you say that to everyone."

Hiruku shrugs non-committally. "All gold does not glitter. The boy, however, he is like any other. Special? Not at this time."

I want to ask if he is sure, but I know it is a useless question. I can only assume Mr. Padwal has access to someone as good as Hiruku. "Could someone less skilled see anything different?"

"Only if he were incompetent."

#

I have been lazy. Unlike my usual approach to work, this time I gathered none of the information on Sulee myself. It gave me a sense of distance, as if by doing so, the taint of it all would somehow be less. As I review the dossier again, I see how superficial it is. It points me toward an obvious plan of action. Exactly the one I took.

I stop at a pay terminal and access the datasphere. I begin with a search on Sulee's name. Nothing. A search of the birth records in her hometown also comes up empty. I curse my stupidity. I can't trust anything that Mr. Padwal has given me because Sulee is a carefully crafted invention.

Creating an alternate identity is difficult, especially one that must withstand the scrutiny of a close relationship. I know from experience—it's the stock of my trade. Questions always arise that need details, and the easiest way to create details at a moment's notice is to draw from something known. The best lies are built on the truth. Somewhere out there is a real person from which Sulee has been constructed. I need to find her.

I recall the many details of our conversations and pluck out the ones that could not be easily scripted ahead of time: the name of her college roommate, names of friends, her first job, places visited on vacation, and dozens of others. From this information I assemble my own profile of Sulee.

I then begin to search for this person. I haven't done this type of research in over a year, but after a few failed attempts, I hit my stride. I delve into university records, search employment databases, visit genealogy websites, newsfeed archives, and advertising databases. After several hours, I find Sulee, except her name is not so exotic: Jennifer Costa, mother of three and owner of a NGO that specializes in building homes for the impoverished in the southeastern United States. She has all the pieces that come together to make Sulee's life.

On an Atlanta newsfeed, I find a picture of Jennifer wielding over-sized scissors at a ribbon cutting for a new low-income housing project. She's not Sulee—I never expected her to be—but she has the same eyes.

I dig for information on Ms. Costa. Her maiden name—Cavendish—puts a cold lump in my belly. "Can't be," I say, but my fingers shake as I run the lead to ground. A few minutes later, I have it.

I locate a picture of Jennifer with her mother, Jaiying, and her sister, Jessica. Her hair is different, but from her eyes I have no doubt that Jessica and Sulee are the same person.

"Shit." Jessica Cavendish, the new girl who backfilled the void created by my retirement.

The boy isn't Mr. Padwal's target.

I am.

#

I stand outside Sulee's apartment trying to decide if I should leave. I want to believe it could be that easy, but I know it isn't. Mr. Padwal plays the long game, and I suspect I have been in his sights for at least a year. I know people are often poor judges of their own future—maybe my future holds more than I can see—but I can't imagine why he would want to add it to his collection. Yet he does, and he won't give up.

I take a deep breath; I'm surprised at the way my nerves vibrate.

When Sulee opens the door her smile looks genuine. I wonder if any of what we have shared was real. She is a professional, so I suspect everything has been an act—just as it has been for me, right?

Her expression changes quickly when I remove the blown-glass sphere from my pocket. Caught unaware, she turns to flee back into the apartment, but stumbles and falls. I sense her future coiled around her like the coarse fibers of a hemp rope, anchored to her in the here-and-now, but extending off into the what-could-be.

As I reach toward her, she looks up at me. In her eyes—brown and deep and so much like Bao's—I see fear, white-rimmed and stark.

I wonder if Bao knew what was happening as her thief unspooled her future, and if she, like Sulee does now, looked up at her attacker and whispered, "Please …"

My fingers hesitate. I know that I am taking more than Sulee's future. I am taking the future of anyone who loves her. My hands grow weak. The strands scrape across the pads of my fingers, slipping away, fiber by fiber. I can't do it. Yet I know I must, for Kimbelle.

Sulee can do nothing except watch as I wrap my fingers around the threads of her existence and yank violently, snapping them free. I slide to the side to avoid getting entangled in the loose ends that swirl around me, but as they brush close, the hairs on my arm stand up. Carefully I begin to feed the hours and days and years of her future into the glass ball. With each sweep of my hand, my throat constricts, and by the time I tuck the last threads into the sphere, I can barely breathe.

Sulee's head lulls back against the floor. Her eyes, now shrouded and dull, stare out into nothing.

#

Mr. Padwal tries hard to hide his surprise when I place the glass ball on the counter. It starts to roll toward the edge. For a moment I think it's going to drop, but then he stops it a hand's-breadth from falling.

He forces a smile that is unpleasant to look at. He peers into the sphere's smoky interior. It is gray and thick, almost oily. Nothing about it is remarkable. Certainly he already knows that. As he lowers the sphere, he looks nauseated. "The rest of the payment—"

"No need. I did it for Bao."

In that split second, his expression confirms my suspicions. He removed Bao, because with her around, he would never have gotten anyone close enough to me to take my future. In the process, he cleverly took everything I had, leaving me desperate and rudderless. Taking my future should have been easy.

Surprisingly, I don't feel anger. I feel an oppressive weight lift away.

"I—" Mr. Padwal's face hardens. He has decided not to lie to me because he believes I cannot take his future.

"You are special, Mr. Kingston," he says. "Resilient. A man that will overcome anything for those he loves. For one like you, the world is open. I should have known you wouldn't end wallowing in Trenchtown shit." His teeth bare in a predatory grin. Although he does not say it, he doesn't consider this over.

But it is.

I step through the privacy screen, into the din and bustle of the market. A few strides into the crowd and I turn to watch as Mr. Oduya's men descend on the chai wallah's cart so quickly the Sikh guards don't react. Mr. Padwal does not have the wherewithal to dispose of the sphere. The agents force him onto his belly.

Mr. Oduya falls in at my side, and I wonder if he is going to arrest me, regardless of our deal. He may be on the wrong side of the law, but he is still honorable.

I begin to walk toward Trenchtown and Kimbelle. I need to hold her.

"The boy is safe," Mr. Oduya says. "We're looking for his family."

The news is welcome, but I say nothing.

Mr. Oduya keeps pace at my side. "Tell me

something, Eshram," he says. "Would you have taken the boy's future?"

His question is one I don't want to answer, but I must. If I don't, it will devour me.

"That's not a future I could live with," I say. As I speak the words, I can taste bile in the back of my throat. Have I just traded Kimbelle for someone else's child?

Mr. Oduya nods, as if satisfied with my answer. "Did you know there is a reward for information leading to the conviction of Naajy Padwal? If the charges stick, I'll see you get it."

I stop walking and Mr. Oduya's momentum carries him several steps farther. "Why would you do that?"

He shrugs. "I like you, Eshram; didn't you know that? You have scruples. The reward is enough to retire anywhere." He arches a knowing eyebrow.

"Who says I ever came out of retirement?" I leave Mr. Oduya standing with his hands in his pockets. His smile tickles my spine.

The Subang Jaya market fades into the night as I careen down through the crowd into Trenchtown. I don't stop to pay Shayana, but go straight into Kimbelle's room and scoop her into my arms.

A rectangle of light streaming through the open door illuminates her innocent face. My racing heart slows to match her gentle breathing.

Mr. Padwal was right. My future is remarkable and it lies before me. We will not end down in the wallows of Trenchtown; our journey upward is just beginning.

Kimbelle stirs. Her eyes flutter open. "Daddy?"

I kiss her forehead. "I'm here," I whisper. "I will always be here."

Story Notes
Thief of Futures

The central idea for "Thief of Futures" came out of a brainstorming session with my writing group, Hopefull Monsters. We were brainstorming things that could be stolen in a speculative-fiction story. As is typical with brainstorming, the "ordinary" ideas came out first, but soon more interesting ones surfaced. The idea that a thief could literally steal someone's future was one of those ideas.

From there, Eshram, his daughter, Mr. Padwal, and Mr. Oduya quickly emerged. The setting came with a major rewrite and was inspired by my travels through Indonesia, even though the setting of the story is actually Kuala Lumpur. The rest, to be cliché, is history.

While "Thief of Futures" was not my first professional *sale*—"Observations on a Clock" holds that distinction—it was my first story to *appear* in a professional market.

Wheat King

First published in *Every Day Fiction*, March 2014

UNDER THE CHAPEL OF SKY, the wheat whispered to John McIntosh. It spoke of the rain, the sun, the rich, rich earth, of his father and grandfather who had worked these fields before him, and of Daniel, who would work them after he was gone.

Daniel watched the wheat bow as his father passed through the south field. Even after a decade, Daniel still struggled against the stalks.

John stopped, planted his hands on his waist. His body ached and not just from the pains of work and age. Arching his back, he breathed deeply. The new wheat smelled dry, and with no rain in the forecast, the field would need water tomorrow.

Hesitantly, Daniel put his hand on his father's elbow. Something was wrong, but his father had always spoken to the wheat better than his family.

The wind had tangled his boy's straw-colored hair. His blue eyes were deep as infinity. Daniel was still small and skinny, like he had been at fourteen, but John knew the muscle would come.

The wheat would see to that.

The thought cut like a threshing blade.

"Went to the doctor," John said, struggling to keep his voice flat. "Been having fierce pain in my back …" He was dithering when he knew to-the-point was needed. The wheat caressed the legs of his jeans, giving John courage. "This will be my last harvest."

#

Through the winter, the wheat slept.

John mourned in silence, like he'd done when his wife had died. But seasons pass, and minute by minute, the days lengthened and warmed, and the wheat came alive again. As the harvest neared, John took Daniel into the south field, where the wheat heads hung heavy and golden. John scraped kernels into his hand and handed them to his son. He drew sharply a breath.

As the wheat had grown taller, his father had grown frailer. Daniel had urged him to rest, but his father only worried about the wheat. Daniel knew the drugs no longer masked the pain, but his father had declined stronger pills because they would cloud his mind, making him incapable of bringing in the harvest.

"Is it time?" John asked.

Daniel rubbed the kernels between his hands then opened his palm. The breeze swirled the chaff away. The kernels popped between his teeth and grew softer as he chewed. His father watched him, eyes wide, pain momentarily forgotten. Daniel wanted to be right in his assessment … the kernels should be soft, but not gluey. Soon, he thought; then looking at his father, too soon.

"I think it's ready," he said after he knew he could delay no longer.

John rubbed a wheat head between his own leathery palms. The chaff, like earthly skin, flew into the wind. The kernels weren't ready yet.

Three days, the wheat whispered.

John eyed the grey clouds on the western horizon. A hard rain now would ruin the crop.

Daniel looked at his dusty boots. Like his father's face, the wheat seemed to droop. Some men had an ear for the wheat. Those were farmers who could will their lives from the land.

The wheat closed in around John like arms holding him up. For the first time in his life, he didn't want the harvest to end, but they had already cut the east field. The northwest field would be ready tomorrow. Soon the season would be over. Too soon.

"The east field is fallow next season." John said. The stalks bent closer to hear his words, and if necessary to whisper to him what needed to be said. Like his father, John never seemed to know what to say.

"I know," Daniel said, irritated. He wanted his father to talk to him.

All John's life the wheat had demanded his labor, his attention, his blood. When he died, he hoped his soul came back as a stalk of hard red winter wheat.

The wheat sighed and bent close once again, whispering assurances. The wheat would watch over his boy as it had watched over him.

Daniel felt the heat of the sun reflect off the golden shafts. He strained to hear anything, but he heard nothing, no matter how he tried. To lie hurt, but the truth would hurt his father even more.

"Look around you, son," his father said. "This isn't wheat. It's the sweat of my grandfather, when this was nothing but dust. It's the tears of my father, when the rains were late. It's the blood of my life, when the banks tried to bleed me dry."

But all Daniel saw was wheat. All he heard, wind.

#

As they worked to bring in the northwest field, John McIntosh collapsed. Daniel found him, a ring of wheat bent over him in prayer.

Glassy eyes, reflecting gold, stared up at the vault of heaven. "Bring the harvest home, son," John whispered, his voice barely a rustle, and then he went quietly, like the fields into fallow.

Daniel left his father there, in the arms of the wheat. The harvest had to come in. Unlike Daniel, the wheat was ready.

#

On the morning he cremated his father, Daniel went into the south field alone. In his hands he carried a simple box. Inside, the ashes of a simple man.

Although Daniel tried not to, he cried.

The earth drank his tears.

Around him, the wheat sighed and bowed. It caressed him until his sadness flowed away. As Daniel stared across the golden wheat, heads heavy beneath the infinite blue sky, he heard his father's voice in the rustle of the stalks.

"I am ready," he said.

STORY NOTES
WHEAT KING

I wrote "Wheat King" a long time ago, and it found its way almost immediately into the trunk. It simply didn't work, and at the time, I wasn't a good enough writer to diagnose why. Slide forward about fifteen years or more, and I found a hard copy of this one stuffed in my writing folder. I thought it had some good stuff in it, so I tore it down and rebuilt it, focusing on the fears and dreams of farmer John McIntosh and his son and their mystical connection to the crop that was their life. (A little piece of writing trivia: "Wheat King" is the only story I've ever written in the third person omniscient point of view.)

I still remember very clearly what inspired this story. I'm a huge fan of the band The Tragically Hip, and one of their songs is called "Wheat Kings," which tells the story of David Milgaard, who was wrongly convicted of a horrendous crime and served 23 years in prison before gaining his freedom. My story has no connection to the song's narrative; it was the song's title that inspired my story of the McIntosh family and their connection to the wheat they grow. From there, a few strong images drove my story—the prairie sky being like the dome of a great chapel, the wheat bent as if in prayer, and the way the stalks whisper when the wind moves through them.

The Schrödinger War

First published in *Lightspeed Magazine*, September 2013

YOU'D THINK AFTER SEVEN TRIES, I could get the living part right, or at least be a pro at dying, but both are still messy and painful. At least dying doesn't scare me anymore.

I yank Olshevski back into our wrinkle of black basalt before the Eatees mist his head.

"Keep it down," I say, my voice tinny in the helium tri-mix of my armor's helmet. As if it matters; if the Eatees don't get him, something else will.

To either side of me, prone soldiers in combat armor bead the lava, like dewdrops on a burn victim. Overhead, sunlight reflects off an arch of orbiting debris, which in another fifty million years will coalesce into the Earth's moon, the same moon under which I will lie as a kid, fantasizing about fighting space aliens.

A streak of fire scratches the sky.

"A shooting star," Olshevski says. His chuckle crackles through the radio-link. "Make a wish."

He's a first incar, fresh down the well from 2075 or some such. Like most firsts, he's gung-ho and stupid and won't live through the day. I'd like to think I wasn't as stupid as Olshevski, but I suspect I was. Then I died. And died again. And again.

Voices buzz through the radio-link. The Eatees are forming up across the no-man's land for an assault on the prize: a steaming pool of long-chain proteins,

RNA, and protobionts that may one day evolve into Earth's higher carbon-based life, provided we stop the Eatees.

"Cut the chatter," Tanner says. He mutes the squad's mics. The sudden silence presses on my ears.

I've known Tanner since we were first incars. He was a good soldier then; he's a good leader now.

Olshevski pops up again. Before I can pull him down, an Eatee sonic shears the top half of his body clean off, the atoms of his suit and every living cell vibrated apart by the high energy noise. The pink mist floats away on the methane wind, and Olshevski's legs tumble over like felled trees.

If he's lucky, his genetic algorithm never finished transmitting to H-Station, and he can find peace in the Big Dark.

The Big Dark sounds good. It doesn't matter if Christina is there or not anymore, either. I hope she is, but—

Fuck it.

I scramble over the basalt lip and charge the cluster of black lumps in the distance. If I hadn't known what I was looking at, I never would have recognized them as alive—featureless lumps of metalloborane, no head, no eyes, only a hole that periodically gapes open, presumably to breathe when it isn't emitting blasts of high frequency noise.

"Sam, what are you doing?" Tanner asks.

Behind me, soldiers scramble from the trench into the glassy no-man's land.

The Eatees rotate toward us. Their orifices open. A sonic blast glances off my armor hard enough to knock me down.

I struggle to my knees and launch an O_2 cluster

bomb. The skittering pellets explode, washing the Eatees in reactive oxygen. Their bodies fizz and glow, catch fire and burst.

Eatee sonics shimmer across the battlefield. The whine grates my eardrums.

My right arm vibrates, all the molecules shaking like ping pong balls in an earthquake. I'm lifted off the ground, spun around, and I lose all track of up and down. Then the glassy basalt crashes into my helmet plate and my feet flop over my head as I fold in half.

Red mist covers the right side of my visor. I struggle to recall who had been next to me.

Warnings flash across my HUD. Suit breach, and I realize my arm is gone. Whatever hasn't spray-painted my helmet has been splattered into the wind. But I'm still alive.

Dammit, I'm still alive.

I lie on my back, laughing at my misfortune through the haze of pain blockers.

Overhead, meteors etch fiery lines across the sky, like tiger claws opening up skin. They trace graceful arcs that anytime else would have been beautiful. I remember the time Christina and I made love in a Nebraska wheat field beneath the Perseids. They were beautiful. She more so.

Through the narcotic haze, I sense something wrong, but it takes me a full minute to realize what. One of the lines is shortening and growing brighter. Pressure sensors scream as the hammer of air pushed in front of the dropping meteor crushes—

#

—I sit up, clutching my right arm and gulping bites

of air.

"It's okay, Sam, we made a full recovery." Kim's hand is soft and smooth and warm.

H-Station's recovery room is a morgue: antiseptic and harshly lit. Odd, because H-Station is a mathematical construct cycling through nano-cores lodged in Hilbert space. You'd think they could create something more friendly to wake up in.

Algorithms or not, the cold metal beneath me burns against my balls.

At the foot of the table are a folded flannel shirt and familiar denim jeans broken in by hard use.

Kim rips a sensor patch from my neck.

I grab her wrist, a lightning quick reflex that makes her gasp.

Kim's face is different again. Her narrow eyes have grown rounder, the sharpness of her nose has dulled, and her hair, once black and thick, has lightened to a sun-bleached tan. Today her hair is pulled back into a ponytail, revealing a morning-clean face with freckles splashed like the Milky Way over her cheeks and nose. The same as—

I release her and pull the shirt over my shoulders; focus on pushing buttons through their holes.

Kim rubs her wrist.

"I'm sorry," I say.

"I should have warned you." She turns away as I pull on the jeans.

When I look up, a desk and chair have appeared, and the morgue table is gone. The lights have softened to the gold of a Nebraska sunset. As a new recruit, I had found H-Station's sudden shifts disconcerting, like the architects had gone to great lengths to create the illusion of a real world, but had never finished the programming. Like living in a movie—the unimportant stuff had been cut away, leaving only the scenes necessary to move the story forward to its inexorable climax.

I've never taken a shit on H-Station.

The chair squeaks as I sit. The leather cools my back.

A window behind Kim opens onto a field of wheat and a curtain of blue sky. Sometimes that window has familiar Colorado mountains or a slice of Caribbean beach or a hillside of golden poppies. Tanner thinks we have subconscious control over what we see on H-Station, and that Kim uses this information in her work.

"Can you tell me what happened?"

"A meteor," I say. It isn't what she wants, but if I give her what she wants too quickly, I would have to leave.

Kim taps a yellow pencil against her cheek.

After every recovery, Kim is here. I sit in the same chair and answer the same questions. The only thing different is the view out the window. And the way Kim looks.

"I got hit by an Eatee."

Out the window, the wheat bends over in an afternoon breeze. I expect to see Christina in her jeans and floppy hat checking its ripeness by the angle of the heads.

The lump in my throat hurts.

"And how did that happen? You getting hit."

Each visit, I find it harder to concentrate on the interview. I get distracted by what lies beyond the window or by the changes to Kim's face or the clothes I'm wearing. I see ghosts of my past everywhere, but I know they're not here, except in my head. No matter how I try, I can't seem to get rid of them.

Every death seems to chip away a flake of my sanity. Eighths and ninths talk about not being whole anymore. As a third, I thought it would never happen to me. When I was a sixth, I fought it. Now I'm a ninth ...

"I sighted the enemy, and I charged." I feel oddly disconnected from the room and the moment. When I blink, I see Olshevski's legs tumble over on the back of my eyelids. Something that horrible should have crippled me, but it didn't faze me at all. "How many were recovered?" I ask.

"There was no order to advance. What were you thinking when you made the decision to charge?"

"I don't get paid to think."

"You don't get paid at all." A half-grin slides across her face, her lips parted to reveal perfect teeth.

Christina had perfect teeth.

My knuckles pop as I crack them. The noise surprises me, and I look down at my hands. The scars I remember having are gone, because they are not part of my genetic algorithm. The physical ones, that is.

"Why did you charge?"

I forget sometimes that Kim knows everything that happens on the battlefield. These post-recovery sessions allow her to learn why. Kim has been tasked with optimizing our fighting force.

H-Station sits in Hilbert Space, just up-well of a white hole that opens into the solar system four and a half billion years in my past. H-Station is a haven of sorts, safe from the Eatees, but disconnected from space-time as we humans know it. It's also the critical junction point for down-well travel, because you can't send matter down-well, only information, in this case a soldier's genetic algorithm, a multidimensional information array that captures a person's genetic code and a neural map of the brain. The problem is, H-Station can hold only a limited amount of information, so Kim is searching for the optimal soldiers to fight this war. So we fight and die and learn and change, each time spawning new incars that Kim tosses back into her battlefield experiment. At some point, one of our incars will reach the zenith of our martial skill, and Kim will delete the rest of us.

"Why did you charge?" Kim asks again.

"I saw an opportunity."

Kim doesn't say anything.

Does she know I'm lying?

Kim resumes tapping her pencil against her cheek. "How do you feel otherwise?"

"Like hell. I just died, for the eighth time."

"Fair enough." Kim's pencil scritches against the pad. With her head down, I see her scalp in the wide part of her hair. The skin is pale and smooth.

The familiarity unsettles me. "Is that all?" I ask, wanting to get away.

She doesn't look up from her writing. "Are you ready to go back?"

"No, but it's what I signed up for."

#

H-Station is a maze of memories half-remembered. Maybe it's the shared human condition, distilled by algorithms into surroundings that are both numbingly generic and achingly familiar. Like the wheat field outside Kim's window.

When I first came down-well, nothing about H-Station was familiar. Yet each time I come back, I see more places that remind me of my past. I suspect it has something to do with Kim's work.

This time, the processing room is a smoky bar with a low ceiling and barely enough space to breathe. It reminds me of the beaten honky-tonk on the outskirts of Omaha, where a fresh-faced girl from the wheat fields snookered me of forty bucks at eight ball. She was nice enough to share her garlic fries with me, confident enough to kiss me afterward, and stupid enough to spend the rest of her life with me.

Why do I remember this? There's no pool table here, and the air smells of anticipation, not garlic.

I recognize few faces; most are firsts and seconds I don't want to know.

Against the wall with his arms crossed, Tanner raises his chin to catch my eye. I slide through the crevices between conversations, but before I can reach him, a woman grabs my collar and kisses me on the lips. "Hey, lover," she breathes across my cheek.

From the patch on her uniform, I see she's a fourth, but I've never met her before. "You've mistaken me for someone else," I say.

She frowns. "You don't recognize me, Sammy?"

Then she sees the patch on my shoulder and looses an expletive. "Sorry," she says, straightening my collar. "I knew a third—"

I raise my hand. She knows an earlier incar of me, a third, but not my third. I don't know how many different incars of Samuel Hohlman exist, but each one is spawning branches in the probability function that is me. Kim is betting that one of us is an optimal soldier.

Before I can say anything, the woman turns her back to me and pretends I don't exist.

I continue through the crowd until I get to Tanner. He shoves a glass tumbler in my hand. Vodka on the rocks.

I see from his patch that he's a sixth.

Tanner arches an eyebrow when he sees my own patch. "Lava?" he asks.

I've served with many of Tanner's incars, so there's always a good chance we can find common ground. Tanner and I decided long ago not to associate if we had more than a four-incar difference—too much personal misery to overcome.

"Methane explosion?" he asks.

I nod, recognizing how I died as sixth. This incar knew me two or three lives ago.

The lines pinched into Tanner's forehead relax. "So a ninth," he says. "Still no command?"

My patch has the crossed swords of a G. I. grunt. "I'm not leadership material, but it looks like you are."

Tanner flushes. As a sixth, this is his first command.

"Who's the fourth?" he asks, motioning with his glass. "She's hot."

I shrug. "Never met her, but that doesn't mean I didn't …"

Tanner makes a noncommittal sound. He's died enough to understand.

As a second and third, I screwed everything and anything willing. There are probably three dozen incars making it in the bar's backroom right now. Dying is still scary to them, and they don't fully appreciate that they'll be back again and again. To cope with the fear, they seek solace in the most base and carnal of human actions. It's a way to forget, at least for a little while.

Tanner searches the bottom of his glass and asks, "Is it still worth it?"

He knows he isn't supposed to ask questions like that; it violates our agreement. Even so, I find myself answering. "I don't know," I say softly.

Tanner frowns. I've said too much. I remember being a sixth, when I started to realize the senselessness of the dying.

"But we're still here, so we must win." The uncertainty in his eyes is gut-wrenching.

That isn't how it works. Our lives are an arrow, always moving forward, and we can never know the future until we get there. The future has no bearing on my past. If we fail to save humanity, I won't simply poof out of existence. I'm fighting the Eatees for some other humanity. I'm not fighting for Christina, because she's lost three years in my past, and while one day there may be another Christina, she will not be *my* Christina.

That thought drains the noise from the room, and all I hear is the roar of silence in my ears.

My drink tumbles from my shaking hand and shatters on the floor.

What the hell am I doing here?

The conversations crash in around me, like a cave collapsing. I can't make out any voices or words. It's all just noise.

I leave Tanner standing alone, staring into his glass.

The noise dies around me as new deployment

orders flash across my visual cortex.

It's time to die again.

#

I inch to the top of the trench and peer through the heat-ripples distorting the no-man's land. I can't be certain that I've been here before, but I get an unsettling sense of déjà vu.

I've heard ninths and tenths talk about rejoining battles they've already died in and sometimes even meeting earlier incars of themselves. It's never happened to me before, but if it did, I think I would tell myself to find a way to put an end to the circle, to join the Big Dark.

My HUD picks up movement and zeroes in on a line of Eatees half a kilometer away. Like a train of charcoal briquettes, they move in formation across the jumbled basalt, venting trails of pinkish gas from their orifices.

I slide down the trench wall and check my weapon. Working on military muscle-memory, I chamber an O_2 grenade without thinking.

By now, others have seen the Eatees. Chatter pollutes the comms.

"Keep it down," Tanner says.

The second incar on my left stares at me with saucer-big eyes. For a moment I see Christina's face through the helmet shield. Not her face as the cancers ate her body, but her face on our wedding day. Even though her hair had already fallen out, she never looked more beautiful.

I squeeze my eyes shut. I have done everything I can to forget her and make the pain go away, but she never seems to leave me.

The recruit with big eyes touches my shoulder. "You okay?" she asks through the private touch-link.

I recognize her now. I know her, or at least who she will be. Her sixth saved my life, back when I was a fourth, and paid for it with her own. I died a few seconds later, but I've never forgotten her. A few more deaths, and she'll be a good soldier.

I brush her hand away.

I'm not okay. I came down-well to get away from everything that reminded me of what I have lost. I needed to kill something, to become less human, so I could stop feeling. What Christina and I had is too strong, however, and now it eats at me like her cancer ate her bones.

My only way out is the Big Dark, but I can't have that.

My teeth vibrate painfully as Eatee sonics discharge nearby. The chatter in my helmet ends as Tanner kills the comms so his orders can be heard. We're to lay down a wall of O_2, and make sure the Eatees don't flank us. It all strikes me as pointless.

"Get down, Sam!"

Tanner's words jar me, and I realize I'm standing and firing my weapon over and over. My HUD tells me I've launched a half-dozen O_2 grenades as a seventh whumps from my launcher.

Across the smoldering cinder, an Eatee swivels. Its orifice opens and the world ripples. I close my eyes and see Christina.

My heart starts to vibrate and come apart.

#

"You're safe, Sam."

It takes a moment to put a name to the voice …

not Christina … Kim.

"It hurts," I say. It's not supposed to hurt—because I am no longer that person—but it does.

"It'll pass. Your brain is still reconciling what happened."

The cold metal gurney presses against me. Shivers wrack my flesh.

"Try to calm down," she says.

I raise my head from where it's tucked against my chest. This time, her eyes are amber, flecked with gold. They aren't Kim's eyes; that isn't Kim's face.

"We made a full recovery," she says.

"No," I say.

Her brows pinch together. I know she is checking H-Station's data-core, confirming a full recovery of Samuel Holman, tenth incar.

But I'm no longer complete, no matter what the genetic algorithm says.

Kim helps me to a sitting position, and I pull on the clothes at the foot of the table. When I look up, Kim is sitting at her desk. Outside the window, aspens quiver at the edge of a lake, glassy smooth and filled with clouds. I recognize the place immediately: the Montana cabin where Christina and I spent a week every summer, and where—

"Tell me about this place," Kim says.

I am surprised for a moment by the change in script. "No."

I expect her to pry, but she doesn't.

Backlit, Kim's ponytail is pulled so tight she looks bald.

The silence picks at my resolve. I exhale, and my body deflates like a punctured bladder.

"Every summer, we'd come to this place."

"This is a special place then."

"I hate this place." The lump in my stomach threatens to come up my throat. "Christina died here, the day after we were married." I have never talked about Christina with Kim. I'm sure she knows about her; she knows everything about me.

Kim's pencil stops, frozen mid-tap. Everything seems to stop—the shimmering trees, the clouds on the surface of the lake—like the program that is H-Station has crashed.

"She had been diagnosed with an inoperable brain tumor. They tried chemo and radiation, but it didn't work. The cancer spread into her lungs and bones. When the doctors gave her a week to live, she asked me to bring her to the cabin. We were supposed to have a life together."

Christina is motionless behind the desk, the pencil frozen near her perfect lips. It's not her, I tell myself.

"I want to forget because it hurts."

I hear a pounding sound that starts in time with my heartbeat, but slowly slides out of synchronization. When I blink, Kim's pencil is tapping again.

"Is that why you volunteered?"

There are as many reasons for joining up as there are soldiers. What does it matter if I came here to lose my past? It's not like I volunteered as a way to commit suicide.

My fingernails are square and perfect, not chewed to the quick like when I enlisted. Every time I'm recovered, the scars of living are polished from my surface.

"Everything back there reminded me of Christina. The way the wheat bent was her smile. The smell of sunshine was the fragrance of her hair. Now, everywhere I look here.... . I don't want to go on."

Kim studies me quietly. After a moment, she says, "That's not up to you."

"You have nine incars of me, and probably dozens more I don't know about. Why can't I retire?"

"There is no retirement here, Sam." Kim's lips continue to move, but I don't hear her through the pounding of blood in my ears and the rasps of breath through my lungs. Those are the sounds of life, but I'm not alive anymore, so how can I make them?

Kim scribbles on her pad with her pencil; then she looks up at me. "I need you to go back."

The words stab me like a cruelly curved knife. I can't go back there. Why can't Kim see that? "I'm finding it hard to be a good soldier," I say. "I don't know what I'm fighting for anymore."

"Maybe you didn't come here to forget. Maybe you came here to remember."

It sounds like something Christina would have said when I was belly-aching about something ridiculous.

"You need to go back one more time, Sam."

My HUD flashes to life with new deployment orders. I squeeze my eyes shut, but I still see them on the inside of my eyelids.

It's time to die again.

#

The basalt crunches like broken glass as I step off the drop-ship. More ships streak in low across the crimson sky, their engines sun-flaring as they pivot and drop. The clouds glow as the orbital battle continues; each flash is one of our ships bursting and burning.

A concussion wave from a distant explosion vibrates my faceplate. Even though the surface battle is a kilometer away, first and second incars dive into a laser cut trench at the edge of the drop circle. Their chatter is loud and fast in the comms.

A ship booms overhead and skims the battlefield, stirring up dust and sulfur steam. From its bottom, cluster bombs whiz toward the ground. They explode, killing Eatees and humans alike.

My third incar died from friendly fire. It had been painless—a bright flash, intense heat, like I had been dropped into the middle of a supernova—and then I awoke on H-Station with baby-new skin and another hole in my psyche.

My visor lightens as the flash fades and the glowing battlefield cools from white-hot to red to glassy black basalt.

Tanner taps my helmet, opening a touch-link. "Orbital's picked up an Eatee incoming; we got ten minutes 'til this place gets hot." He dashes off toward the rally point.

The last drop-ship lifts into the red sky, vanishing slowly into the methane clouds, like a fleck of copper sinking into blood. For the moment, the world is quiet.

The edge of the landing zone drops off into a steaming pool of scummy organics and proto-life. In a hundred million years, this pool will be teaming with the first anaerobic lifeforms, which will produce oxygen as a waste product of their metabolism. It's that oxygen that will make this world uninhabitable to the Eatees, and will make it my—

No, it will never be my home.

I close my eyes and see Christina's face, beautiful

and smiling. Every minute I had with her is something to cherish, not forget. Maybe Kim is right.

Damn her.

Movement to my right catches my attention. A third has stepped up to the edge and is looking down into the steaming pool. Maybe he's thinking about throwing himself in. It's hard to say with a third; they're a critical transition incar, from the wide-eyed newbie to either a well-adjusted soldier or to someone who will eventually be like me.

I'm not sure why, but I place my hand on his shoulder, opening a touch-link. "It's not high enough to even damage the suit," I say.

When he turns toward me, I stumble back. He grabs my elbow and saves me from tumbling over the edge.

His face has the same lines as my own, only fresher, and the same eyes, only more alive. He shows no recognition of who I am, even though he looks into his own face, half a dozen deaths later. I am no longer the same person, but am I so damaged he does not recognize himself?

But he is also not the same person I was as a third. He has been shaped by different experiences and today he will likely die a different death, which will make him a different fourth, and a different fifth, and so on. Yet, in his eyes is the shadow of our common bond, and I know this grief will force him down a path parallel to my own.

His eyes narrow, but they do not yet glimmer with recognition. "You okay?"

Afraid he will release my arm, I seize his wrist to keep the touch-link open. "I've learned something recently," I say softly. "Our past makes us who we are today. If we forget what happened before we came down-well, then our past is only this: war, dying, and more dying. How can that be any good for anyone?"

"I—" His eyes widen then, and he sees what could be his future, but I also know he's smart enough to realize the future holds infinite possibilities, and that I am not necessarily his fate.

It's too late for me—my scars are all below this perfect skin—but I am only one possible future for Samuel Hohlman. How many of my thirds are out there, forging new futures and trying to get it right? Maybe, because of me, this is the one that will get it right.

"Wait—"

I release his wrist, breaking the touch-link. I move toward the rally point. He follows me at a short distance, but stops when our HUDs come alive. The Eatees are here.

Time for me to die.

"The Schrödinger War" was a hard story to write—probably one of the hardest I've ever written. It took me a year to get this one right. Not all at once, either; I would periodically pick the story up and put it down again after failing. I struggled with the speculative element a little, but mostly I struggled with Sam's internal conflict. I failed a lot with this one.

"The Schrödinger War" came out of a call for an anthology about extreme planets back in 2012. The topic intrigued me, so I started brainstorming ideas for a badass placed to set a story. Mind you, I had no story to go with that location; at this point it was all about the setting. I worked through the usual places most people would think of, discarding them as quickly as I thought of them. I then came upon the idea of a proto-planet—a planet in the early stages of its formation—and this captured my attention, even more so after I decided that planet would be primitive Earth (called Hadean Earth).

The plot elements fell together quickly: a seemingly futile war, a man who's lost himself as he fights over and over, the speculative element of *incars* and the physics of wave functions. What was missing, however, was Sam's true reason for being here and any sort of cohesive character arc for him. The story was missing that human element, and when I couldn't find it, the story went on the shelf.

Every few weeks, I'd pull "The Schrödinger War"

down and re-read it, hoping to find the missing piece before the anthology call closed. I tinkered with it, gradually adding bits of Sam's past: his wife and the shifting landscapes of H-station. The anthology deadline passed. I continued to work on the story. "The Schrödinger War" finally came together when I figured out how it needed to end for Sam, and I re-wrote his last meeting with Kim and the final scene of the story in a single sitting. I spent a hard week cutting it into final shape. I got enthusiastic responses from my critiquing group, and sent it to John Joseph Adams at *Lightspeed Magazine* who accepted it in about six hours—the fastest I have ever gotten an acceptance.

I'm particularly proud of this one.

~ THANK YOU ~

for reading my collection of short stories. I hope you enjoyed them.

Gaining exposure as an independent author relies mostly on word-of-mouth, so if you have the time and inclination, please consider leaving a short review wherever you can.

Meet the Author

D. Thomas Minton lives on the shores of a mountain lake in British Columbia, but still pines for the tropical waters of the Pacific Ocean. When not writing, he works as an aquatic biologist and helps communities conserve important fish habitat (and the occasional coral reef).

He has published four books in the Calypto Cycle, and his short stories have appeared in some of speculative fiction's top magazines and anthologies. His fiction has been translated into numerous languages, and his stories frequently appear on annual recommended reading lists.

He can be found online at dthomasminton.com.